David Alex Jones

SPIRITS

The Survivor Trilogy: Book Three

Cover Art by Lianne Viau Photography

Published by:
Apparently Normal Publishing
Waterloo, Ontario, Canada

ISBN (Paperback Edition) 978-0-9951963-3-9
Version 2023.01.01

LAND ACKNOWLEDGEMENT

This book was written in Southwestern Ontario, Canada, on land located within the Haldimand Tract, land that was granted to the Haudenosaunee of the Six Nations of the Grand River, and is within the shared traditional territory of the Neutral, Anishinaabe, and Haudenosaunee peoples

TABLE OF CONTENTS

FOREWORD

I joined the Air National Guard in 1996 at the age of 24. At the onset of my career, I was raped by my recruiter at his house. I was invited to a new recruit party, drugged, and raped. I never told anyone because I was too ashamed. I had PTSD before I even left for basic training ...

Anonymous

PART SEVEN: CONSPIRACY

CHAPTER 1

DARKNESS settled over the streets of Las Vegas as the sun disappeared behind the Spring Mountain Range. Lights twinkled peacefully and a surreal spectacle of flashing neon and glowing hotel towers emerged from the desert landscape. Suddenly, the squealing of tires shattered the silence. A white delivery van careened around a corner onto West Cheyenne Avenue. Its engine roared as the vehicle accelerated away from the intersection on the six-lane road, weaving and swerving around vehicles that impeded its progress.

The driver, clad in black, leaned hard as his vehicle careened around another corner. Another black-clad man sitting in the passenger seat gripped an automatic weapon on his lap with one hand, while tightly gripping the handhold above him on his right. A brown-haired woman, clad in the brown uniform of a UPS delivery person, tried in vain to sit on the floor of the vehicle's cargo compartment, but her body slammed hard against the side of the van as it took another corner.

"Fuck!" Helen screamed.

She glared down at Fran, lying on the cargo floor beside her, with blood oozing from a wound in her right shoulder. The hatred in her eyes burned into the other woman like lasers.

"Capellini, you bitch! Don't you ever get tired of fucking me over? This time you're going to pay. Nobody fucks with Lady Helen and gets away with it!"

Francesca Capellini wrinkled her forehead and stared back at her captor. *We've met before?*

Francesca quickly averted her eyes from Helen, turning her gaze to the blood oozing from her wound. She winced from pain, then she looked up at her captor again.

Helen's eyes shifted from Francesca's wound to her swollen belly. At the same time, the look in Helen's eyes suddenly softened, signaling a one-hundred-eighty-degree shift in her mood. For an instant, Fran almost thought she saw compassion in the other woman. Then, just as quickly, Helen's eyes became distant while she was deep in thought.

"How far are we from the garage?" she shouted abruptly to the driver.

"Almost there! Just a few minutes."

"Well, hurry it up! We're going to need to improvise. We need a doctor. This woman's been shot and the bleeding won't stop."

Time felt like it was standing still for Fran. An uneasy feeling spread through her as she stared back into Helen's eyes. Hazy images from long ago flashed through her mind, trying to intrude into her consciousness … a rear view of a nude woman, passionately kissing an unidentified man in a hot tub.

Fran's mind felt cloudy … confused.

Is it the same woman? Was I in that tub too?

She couldn't be sure. She almost felt as if she was floating over the hot tub scene, looking downward. She saw another woman with short black hair, also nude, sitting beside an older, grey-haired man. His hands wandered over the woman's body. A shiver surged through Fran's body and jolted her back into reality.

The seconds ticked as Fran strained to make a conscious connection to the distant memories. Nothing came. Suddenly, she became aware that Helen was still staring at her. A grin spread slowly across Helen's face and she started to laugh.

"You know what, Capellini? This could just work out alright after all."

Helen's smile turned wicked. "You may turn out to be a blessing in disguise as a hostage."

Helen's words brought Fran crashing back to reality: only a few short weeks after she had been freed from Indio Prison, she was a prisoner yet again! The realization swept over her like a tsunami. Hopeless and dejected, she looked down at her wound, then at the blood on the cargo bay floor. She curled up in fetal position, clutching at her stomach. She felt like she was going to vomit. All Fran heard was the roar of the van's engine.

"Slow down!" Helen screamed to the driver, above the roar. "Last thing we need is an effin' speeding ticket!"

The van's engine instantly lost its urgency as the driver backed off the accelerator. The ride in the cargo department stabilized, allowing Helen to reach into her pocket. She pulled out a cell phone and quickly dialed a number. She waited impatiently while the number rang: … once … twice … three times … and then a fourth … finally there was a click on the line.

INSIDE the gates of the lavish Las Vegas estate, Las Vegas PD squad cars littered the driveway and long strands of yellow tape marked the area as an active crime scene. CSI technicians in protective clothing combed the area like a colony of ants. A black SUV passed through the gates and crept slowly up the driveway, receiving directions for where to park from a uniformed police officer.

An overweight middle-aged man, wearing a poorly-fitting black suit, climbed awkwardly from the driver's side of the vehicle. He removed his sunglasses to survey the scene. FBI Agent Gabe Martinelli's eyes were as keen and sharp as his wardrobe clearly was not. A younger woman who was shorter, muscular and fit from competitive running, slipped easily from the passenger side of the vehicle. Unlike her male counterpart, Agent Lindell Simpson was stylishly dressed in expensive navy slacks and a jacket. They walked up to the officer who had directed them to their parking spot.

"You in charge here?" Simpson asked.

"No, ma'am. Over there," the officer said, pointing to another young man in a suit who was interviewing a group of people. The younger man looked up, saw the two new arrivals, and began walking towards them.

"Hi. Detective Ryan Lewis, LVPD. I'm in charge here." He exchanged handshakes with the two newcomers. "My partner and I were nearby, so we were first to arrive when the call came in."

Lewis nodded towards his partner, another male officer, who was now taking statements from the same group of people whom Lewis had been interviewing.

"They sure didn't waste any time calling you guys in when we told them about the abduction."

Simpson's skilled eyes quickly took in the scene: she glanced at the group gathered outside the front door of the estate, and then brought her gaze back to two other men, one Caucasian and the other African-American, standing a few feet in front of her. The Caucasian man was clearly distressed and agitated. While she scanned the scene, Martinelli took control of the situation.

"Hi, Detective. I'm FBI Agent Martinelli. This is Agent Simpson."

"Good to meet you," Lewis said.

"Who are those two men in front of us?" Simpson said.

"The white guy is the homeowner. The black guy is a friend … appears to have a background in the military and private security."

Simpson glanced at Martinelli, then back at Detective Lewis. "Guess we may as well start with them, if it's okay with you."

"Go ahead. It's your case now," Lewis replied.

Simpson and Martinelli wandered over to where the homeowner and his friend were standing.

"I'm FBI Agent Martinelli; this is Agent Simpson. And you are?"

"Whitney … Dr. Dan Whitney … my girlfriend … the woman who was abducted … this is our new home.

Martinelli and Simpson glanced at each other and raised their eyebrows after hearing Dan's name. Simpson pulled a note pad from a pocket in her suit and scribbled a note to herself.

"And you sir?" Martinelli asked, turning to the African-American man.

"Holloway … Richard. I'm a friend of Dr. Whitney an' Fran. My wife an' I were here fer th'party," he drawled. His voice had a distinct Texas accent.

"Party?" Simpson replied. "What were you celebrating, Dr. Whitney?"

"Our housewarming. We'd just moved here from Palm Springs, so we invited some friends to celebrate with us," Dan answered.

"So, what happened?" Martinelli asked.

"I'm not exactly sure," Dan answered. "My girlfriend … Fran … Francesca Capellini … She went to answer the doorbell. Somebody said there was a delivery for Angela, one of our guests. They were shouting for her to go to the front door. The next thing I knew, we heard shots and screams."

"Shots? How many?" Martinelli interjected.

"I don't know … a lot," Dan replied. He looked to Richard for help with the question. "What do you think, Richard? How many?"

"One, initially," Richard answered. "Then I ran t'the front door with two o' my colleagues. We're all former military an' we do security work. Once th'intruders saw we were armed, they gave a barrage of coverin' fire - lots of it - t'allow the delivery person t'pull back'n escape. One o' my colleagues caught a glimpse from th'upstairs window. Looks like there were three o'them - two with automatic weapons. The smaller o'the three - th'one that took Fran - looked t'have a handgun."

Simpson looked to Detective Lewis for help.

"Did anybody get a good look at the delivery person?" She looked at her notes. "Have you talked to this … Angela … yet?"

"Yeah, we talked to her. Her name is Angela Baranyi. She only caught a quick glimpse. Apparently, Capellini pushed her out of harm's way … Must have seen the gun or something … Angela thinks the perp was a woman … Only about five feet tall, short brown hair … Looked like she was a UPS delivery agent … Brown ball cap pulled down over her eyes … That's about it," Lewis reported.

Martinelli turned to Richard Holloway. "What about your colleague upstairs? Did she see anything?"

"Not much more'n Angela. She only got quick peeks cuz she was under fire. But it pretty much confirms what Angela said … Short female, shoulder-length brown hair, brown UPS uniform, ball cap, an'a handgun," he answered.

"Any idea why they took your girlfriend, Dr. Whitney? Simpson interjected.

"Not a clue. Fran would never hurt anybody … For some crazy reason, everybody seems to be out to get her … I don't get it," Dan replied.

Martinelli and Simpson exchanged glances and raised their eyebrows again. Simpson paused for a moment, thinking.

"You said Palm Springs, Dr. Whitney? And your girlfriend's name is …?"

Simpson took a quick look at her notes.

"… Capellini? Have I heard your names recently?"

Dan hung his head and sighed, suddenly feeling extremely weary.

"Is this necessary?" Richard asked. "Dan an' Francesca have been through a lot lately. They both lost their spouses …"

Martinelli's eyes suddenly went wide as he made the mental connection. He turned to Dan.

"I remember now. Weren't you the two who were involved in that kinky shooting a few months ago in Palm Desert?" he asked.

Dan managed to raise his head enough to flash Martinelli a look of resentment. Seeing Dan's response, Simpson shot Martinelli a glance that said, "*Lay off.*"

"We're sorry for your recent losses, Dr. Whitney," Simpson interjected. "You stated earlier that everybody seems to be out to get your girlfriend. Do either of you have any enemies we should know about?"

"I already told you," Dan huffed, his frustration surfacing again. "I don't know. If they were after me, I'd understand."

"Why you?" Simpson retorted.

"If you'd really been watching the news closely, maybe you'd already know about the recent attempts on my life by Soren Kristiansen and a woman who calls herself Helen. And you'd know they're still at large," Dan replied sarcastically.

Simpson and Martinelli exchanged glances and raised their eyebrows again. Simpson turned to Richard.

"Anything else you'd like to add, Mr. Holloway?" Simpson asked.

"Not right now," Richard answered. "It all happened so damned fast."

Simpson scribbled a few more lines in her notepad and then looked at Martinelli to see if he had anything else to ask. He shook his head from side to side. Simpson turned to Dan.

"Thanks for your patience, Dr. Whitney. I'm sorry to bother you with all these questions, since you've obviously been through a lot. I think that's all we have for now, but I'm sure we'll have more questions once CSI finishes with the scene."

She pulled a business card from the pocket of her suit jacket and handed it to Dan.

"If either of you think of anything else, you can reach me at that number … Any time of day," she added.

Richard put his arm protectively around Dan's shoulder to help calm him.

"Thanks, ma'am. We'll be sure t'do just that if we think of anythin' else," Richard replied.

Dan and Richard shook hands with the two agents. Simpson and Martinelli turned their backs and began walking back towards their SUV. Martinelli paused to light a cigarette. Simpson stopped and shook her head disapprovingly.

"I thought you'd given those things up," she said.

"Yeah, me too," Martinelli answered. He took a drag, then exhaled slowly while he gathered his thoughts.

"So, if what they say is true, and Whitney's girlfriend was kidnapped, do you think it has anything to do with Kristiansen? Or maybe his mysterious lady friend?" he asked.

"Who knows," Simpson replied. "There's gotta be more to this than meets the eye, but it gives us a place to start. People don't just dress up in UPS uniforms or black camo, arm themselves with automatic weapons, and take innocent people in broad daylight for no apparent reason."

"No, they surely do not," Martinelli replied. He exhaled one last cloud of smoke, then threw the cigarette to the driveway and ground the butt into the pavement with his foot.

COLONEL Bryce Williamson smiled salaciously while two of his subordinate male officers, both partially dressed, struggled to subdue a young female officer.

"Stop! … Please stop!" the woman cried. "I beg you!"

Her pleas were met by a sharp slap to the face from one of male officers.

"Shut up," he ordered. He turned to his male counterpart and grinned. "She's a real fighter, isn't she? Makes it even sweeter when she finally gets tired and gives up."

"Never, you pricks!" the young woman screamed.

"Shut her up!" Williamson snapped. "You want somebody calling the cops?"

The two men joined forces to lift their victim off the floor and slam her onto the bed. One of the men ripped off one of his socks and stuffed it into the woman's mouth when she opened it to scream.

"There, that'll fix you. That's just a taste of what's comin', bitch!"

Suddenly, Williamson's cell phone buzzed in his pocket. Clearly annoyed, he retrieved it and looked at his call display.

"What do you want?" he said gruffly.

"It's Helen. Listen up. There's been some trouble and I need your help, right now!"

"What do you want me to do about it? I'm busy," he replied impatiently. The sound of muffled screams and breaking glass filled the room as the thrashing woman sent a bedside lamp crashing to the floor.

"I hear what's keeping you busy. I'm not *asking* for help, this is an order! Is that clear?" Helen shouted.

Williamson snapped instinctively to attention. "Yes ma'am. Perfectly clear. What do you need me to do?"

"That's better," Helen answered. "I'm going to need someplace very safe and very remote … far off the beaten track. And I need a medic and medical supplies to treat a gunshot wound … right now!"

"Are you crazy?" Williamson replied. "I can't make that happen right away. What happened? Are you hurt?"

He watched and grinned as the two men in the background climbed on top of the female officer. One of them tore off her blouse and bra, then he leaned over her and took one of her nipples into his mouth. The other man pushed up her skirt and ripped off her pantyhose and panties. His penis had tented under his boxer shorts. Still struggling, the woman fought hard as the man with the tent tried to spread her legs for his partner. Helen's voice jerked Williamson's concentration away from the assault and back to the conversation.

"I'm fine!" Helen barked. "I was taking care of some unfinished business. I just had some unforeseen complications, so I need your help, right fuckin' now!"

"I'll need a day or two …" Williamson began.

"Do I need to remind you what happens to *all* of us, if my cover is broken, Colonel?" Helen shouted.

"Yes, ma'am. I understand completely, but …"

"I'll call you at eighteen hundred hours with the address," Helen ordered. "You'd better have a medic and a place for us to stay by then! No excuses, Colonel, or I'll be most displeased with you. And you know what that means, don't you?"

"Yes, ma'am. I understand. I'll find a medic, supplies, and some temporary shelter," Williamson replied meekly.

"Good, you'll hear from me at eighteen hundred," Helen barked, ending the call.

Williamson shoved his phone back into his pocket, annoyed by the conversation.

"Let her go!" Williamson shouted to the two male officers. "We'll finish this with her another time."

The two officers stopped and stared blankly at their commanding officer.

"Let her go?" asked the man who was grasping the woman's struggling legs. "What do you mean? We ain't finished with her yet."

"I said let her go!" Williamson bellowed. "That's an order. That was Helen on the phone. Something urgent's just come up."

At the mention of Helen's name, the two officers immediately stopped what they were doing.

"We shoulda just drugged her an' fucked her brains out. It woulda saved us a lotta trouble," the first man grumbled, letting go of the woman's breast.

"You know Helen won't let us do things that way," Williamson continued. "The lieutenant here has to learn that everything will go a lot better for her when she learns to submit willingly to us … and to Helen's will. Now, let her go and let's get out of here," he ordered.

As Williamson watched, the men released the woman, dressed themselves, straightened out their uniforms, then saluted their commanding officer and left the room. Williamson walked casually over to the bed and sat beside the weeping, gagging woman, who had yanked the sock from her mouth once her hands were free. He picked up her clothing and threw it at her.

"Cover yourself up," Williamson ordered. "I'm sure I don't need to tell you that it would be most unwise of you to mention this event to anybody. This is part of your initiation, as it has been for many excellent officers before you. It's intended to make you strong."

He got up and walked towards the motel room's exit, then he stopped and turned to the woman.

"You wouldn't want anybody to think you were a weakling, would you? Besides, any complaints will inevitably come across my desk. Understand?"

The woman's tears stopped. Her eyes grew wide with a mixture of anger, fear, and helplessness as she fully understood her situation and her predicament. Slowly and silently, her head nodded up and down.

"Very well," Williamson said. "Get yourself dressed and report back to base. I'll expect to see your usual, professional demeanor. That will be all."

Colonel Williamson continued to the door, let himself out, and left the nearly naked woman alone in the empty motel room. Stunned and numbed by what had just happened to her, she froze. Finally, after a few moments, she began the process of putting on her panties and smoothing out her skirt with robot-like movements. She examined her pantyhose and dropped the ripped garment to the floor. As if on autopilot, she picked up her bra, fastened it around her waist, then rotated it and slid the cups up over her breasts. After adjusting her straps, she picked up her blouse, put her arms through the sleeves, and began fastening the buttons. She paused briefly, noticing that one was missing. She buttoned up the rest as though nothing had happened and tucked the blouse into her skirt.

Now as fully dressed as she could manage, she picked up her purse from the desk and went into the bathroom. She reapplied her makeup and did her best to cover the redness on her face and straighten her hair. Finally, she found a place, somewhere in her mind, where she stuffed the memory and all the emotions attached to it. She imagined herself slamming the door and throwing away the key. Reassuring herself that she was strong, she marched through the motel room's door and closed it firmly behind her.

CHAPTER 2

SOMEWHERE in a remote area of Nellis Air Force Base, a camouflaged Air Force cargo truck bounced through the dark, moonless desert night, along a dusty gravel road filled with potholes. Lying on a stretcher in the back of the truck, Fran opened her eyes and waited for them to adjust to the darkness. Her vision was blurred as she scanned the back of the truck, attempting to get her bearings. Her right arm was bandaged, but it still throbbed and still oozed some blood. Eventually her eyes found Helen, still dressed in her UPS uniform, staring down at her. The truck bounced around one last turn, rocked its passengers, and then lurched to a stop in front of a large camouflaged tent. A cloud of dust followed them into the back of the truck, causing the occupants to start coughing. The truck's uniformed driver jumped from the cab and rushed around to the rear of the truck, where he clambered up, lifted the rear tarp, and lowered the tailgate. A second man rushed from the tent and climbed into the back of the truck, making a quick survey of its occupants.

"I'm the medic, ma'am," he said to Helen. "Is this our patient?"

"Yes, she's lost a lot of blood and she's pregnant. Get her into the tent!" Helen shouted.

"Shit," the medic muttered. "Would have been nice to know *that.*"

Together, the medic and driver slid Fran's stretcher out of the truck and rushed her into the tent. Helen jogged along beside them, watching over her hostage with a look of concern etched deeply into her face. Once inside the tent, the medic transferred Fran to a cot, opened a case of medical supplies, and set out some surgical instruments as he created a hasty makeshift field hospital. Working quickly and efficiently, he wrapped a blood pressure cuff around Fran's arm and inflated it. Not happy with the reading, he unwrapped the bloody bandage from around Fran's wound. She winced and gasped in pain, and the bleeding resumed immediately.

"Sorry ma'am. Your bandage was clotted and stuck to your skin. You're going to feel a few pokes from a needle while I freeze the area around the wound. Are you okay?" He looked at Fran's baby bump, then looked her in the eyes.

"Don't worry, ma'am. Nothing bad is going to happen to your baby. We're lucky we got you here in time. Ready?" he asked.

Fran's eyes opened wide with fear. She sucked in a deep breath and nodded to the medic. He began giving the anesthetic injections while Fran exhaled slowly, trying to send her mind someplace else. The pain was almost unbearable. She sucked in more deep breaths as he worked, exhaling slowly after each one. When he finally finished the last painful injection, he set aside his syringe and prepared a scalpel. After about five minutes, he purposely poked the area surrounding the wound and looked at Fran.

"Do you feel that?" he asked.

Fran shook her head. Satisfied that the freezing had taken, the medic turned to Helen.

"I'll need your help. Put on a pair of those gloves and grab a handful of gauze while I get an IV going. Use it to soak up any bleeding while I work. Got it?"

"Don't worry about me, Captain," Helen snapped. "I did lots of this during Desert Storm."

"Okay, so this should be a walk in the park for you," he answered. Then he turned to Fran. "You're going to feel some pressure while I open up the wound - maybe even some pain. I don't know if I can get it totally numb in there."

The medic began by making a careful incision, exploring slowly and stopping occasionally for Helen to soak up excess blood.

"It's deep. The slug looks like it's lodged right beside the bone," he said to Fran. "Might even have nicked the brachial artery … another fraction of an inch and you wouldn't have been so lucky."

The medic looked Fran in the eyes. "You ready?"

Fran nodded affirmatively, swallowed, and took another deep breath. The medic set to work with his scalpel. As he explored further, Fran gasped and moaned a couple of times. Finally, the medic reached for some surgical tweezers, carefully guiding them into position while he held the wound open with instruments in his other hand. He attempted to grasp the shell.

"Shit," he muttered. "Damn thing's slippery. Let's try it again …"

The medic shifted his instruments and Fran gasped again. "Sorry ma'am. It's right next to the artery and the nerve … Alright! There's our culprit!"

He held the projectile up, illuminating it with his headlamp so both Fran and Helen could see it.

"You did great ma'am," he said to Fran. He turned to Helen. "Okay, I need you to keep it clean so I can see what I'm doing while I close off that artery. Then snip off each suture when I'm done. Scissors are right next to you."

He worked swiftly, putting in a total of four sutures and pulling each one tight. Helen snipped each one as he finished it.

"There you go," he said to Fran. "Good as new. You lost a fair amount of blood, so I need you to drink plenty of fluids over the next few days and get lots of rest. Any allergies to penicillin or other antibiotics?"

Fran shook her head silently from side to side, then she looked the medic in the eyes.

"Thank you," she said. Her voice was weak and tired.

"No problem, ma'am. That's what I do," he answered. He smiled and patted Fran's hand to reassure her. He turned away and began cleaning up his supplies and instruments, quickly and efficiently bagging the waste in special bags. He closed his instrument case, then he rose and took Helen aside. Fran tried to let on that she wasn't listening to their conversation.

"She'll be fine once she gets some rest. Here's some antibiotics to prevent infection. Make sure she takes them till they're gone," he said.

"Understood," Helen replied. She grabbed his arm and drew him closer. "You understand … not a word to *anybody* about this!"

"Don't worry, Major," he said under his breath. "The Commander's instructions were perfectly clear in that regard. He told me to tell you that this area is off limits, so nobody will be flying overhead and bothering you."

"Thank you, Captain. You're dismissed."

The medic, assisted by his driver, packed up the case of supplies along with the plastic bags of waste and dirty instruments, and carried them out of the tent. Fran heard the truck's tailgate slam as they finished loading the truck. Seconds later, the driver and passenger doors slammed and the engine rumbled to life. The sound of tires crunching on gravel signaled their departure. In a matter of moments, the sounds disappeared into the darkness.

Fran and Helen remained in a total, eerie silence in the midst of the desert night. After pausing for a moment, Helen rose. Fran watched as her captor began searching through container after container of supplies that were piled in the tent. Finally, Helen found a satellite phone that was apparently the object of her search. As Fran watched, Helen checked the battery. Satisfied that it was fully charged, she turned her back to Fran and walked to the far end of the tent.

"Soren?" she said quietly. "It's me. We've arrived safely at the rendezvous. You'll get a phone call from Pit Boss with instructions for where and when you can pick up the truck … I'll explain everything when you get here … I miss you too … safe travels … see you tomorrow, my love.

CHAPTER 3

FRAN'S EYES flickered open. She was disoriented, trying to make sense of where she was. Gradually, the reality of her situation hit home. She was amazed that she had somehow managed to fall asleep at some point, given that her mind had been racing well into the night. Despite her few hours of precious rest, she still felt exhausted.

The inside of the tent was bathed in a golden glow of early morning sunshine that permeated the shelter's camouflage skin. The temperature inside the tent was already beginning to climb. Fran became aware of a dull throbbing sensation in her upper right arm. She brought her gaze back towards the area that was throbbing, and she saw a row of neat sutures, encircled by a large blue and green bruise. Images of the gentle medic performing surgery on her arm flashed into Fran's consciousness. The snapshots triggered a flood of other terrifying images, sounds, and emotions from last night's chaos.

Fran struggled to push the flashbacks aside, gradually managing to bring her mind back into the present. Her eyes slowly and deliberately scanned the inside of the tent, helping to ground herself to the present. Containers of supplies, all bearing the letters *USAF,* were stacked neatly along one wall. The cot on which she was lying was placed against the tent's opposite wall, across from the row of containers. Two other cots were arranged neatly between Fran's cot and the supplies, parallel to the containers and at right angles to her cot. A blanket laid askew on the far cot, while a neatly folded, untouched blanket laid on the cot closest to hers.

The sound of swishing and dripping water suddenly captured Fran's attention.

At the far end of the tent, two tables stretched across most of that wall. A portable propane camp stove, some cookware and utensils, and a partly emptied container of supplies occupied one table. Fran recognized the woman from last evening's nightmarish events, leaning over a plastic basin on one of the tables. The woman was now dressed only in black panties and bra. Water swished and then dripped back into the basin as the woman soaked a facecloth and then scrubbed her face and the back of her neck. Fran watched silently as the woman continued scrubbing her underarms, torso, and legs, unaware that her hostage was awake and watching her.

Fran's captor was short, probably no more than five feet tall, she guessed. Her hair was short and straight, coming just past her ears and not quite to her shoulder. Despite the woman's short stature, her figure was perfectly proportioned and her muscles were firm and well-toned. Fran shuddered involuntarily. Something about the figure in front of her was vaguely disturbing, but the feeling passed quickly.

Fran's captor turned around for a towel and her eyes caught a glimpse of Fran's open eyes. Suddenly afraid and self-conscious, Fran instinctively closed her eyes, but it was too late.

"So, how is our patient feeling this morning?" the woman asked. "Can I get you something to eat?"

Fran opened her eyes again and tried to sit up, but her left leg was slow to respond. As she tried to move it, Fran heard a metallic jingling sound. Her eyes darted to her left ankle, where she saw a long chain attached to a shackle on her ankle. With some effort, she lifted a length of the chain and swung it and her leg over the side of the cot. The blanket that had previously covered her fell into her lap. She suddenly realized that she was wearing only white panties and a bra herself. Embarrassed, she quickly pulled the blanket up to cover herself.

"Where am I?" Fran asked. "Who are you?"

"So many questions," the woman answered. "It doesn't matter who I am.

The other woman paused to think.

"For now, you can call me … Helen … that will do for now."

"What am I doing here? What do you want with me?"

Helen tossed her head back and laughed. "What I really want, Francesca, is for you to get out of my life! But for some reason, you keep showing up to make things miserable for me."

Fran stared at Helen and frowned. It felt as if she had met her captor sometime in the past. But, as hard as she tried, Fran failed to make even the faintest mental connection.

"So, now we both need to make the best of a bad situation," Helen continued. "If you help me, I'll help you."

"Help you?" Fran answered, pausing a moment to think. "I'll do anything you want. In return, can you take this chain off my leg?"

Helen threw her head back again. This time her laughter was raucous, hearty, and dripping with sarcasm. "I wish it were that simple, dear. May I call you Fran?"

Fran shrugged ambivalently.

"You know I can't let you run around freely. I'm afraid I need to keep you inside this tent for now. Nobody can know you're here," Helen continued.

"I need to pee," Fran answered. "Can you at least take it off long enough for me to do that?"

"There's a portable toilet under an awning, just outside the tent. The chain should reach far enough for you to use it."

Fran's eyes narrowed and her forehead wrinkled, conveying her frustration. "What do you need me to do? I'll do it right now."

"All in good time, Francesca. I haven't got that worked out yet. Others are involved and we need time to think things through. In the meantime, think of yourself as my guest."

"You mean prisoner," Fran replied.

"Let's not quibble over words," Helen answered. "Rest … regain your strength … take care of that baby you're carrying."

Reminded of her baby, Fran looked down at her bump and caressed it with both hands. Helen turned her attention to the containers of supplies and began rooting around in one of them. Finding a pair of Air Force-issue camouflage pants with a drawstring waist, along with a roomy t-shirt, she dropped the clothing on the cot beside Fran.

"Here's some clean clothes. I'll take off the chain while you change and go for a pee. But I warn you, you're in the middle of the desert. There's nowhere to run. You and your baby wouldn't last a day wandering around in the heat out there," Helen cautioned.

Helen bent down and opened the lock, temporarily freeing the chain from the shackle on Fran's ankle. Fran massaged the irritated area, then she stood and turned her back, knowing that Helen was still watching vigilantly.

"What would you like to eat?" Helen asked. "I'm afraid there isn't much choice. I've got some fresh eggs, bacon, and field rations at the moment. That's pretty much it, apart from tea and coffee, until we can get some groceries."

Fran finished pulling up the camouflage pants, tied the drawstring, and sighed in resignation. She turned and walked towards the tent's entrance. She noticed the outdoor toilet sitting just outside the doorway, sheltered from the sun and any stray aircraft that might pass overhead. When she was finished, Fran shuffled back to her cot where Helen stood waiting. She was now wearing the same style of camouflage fatigues and t-shirt as Fran. Helen reattached the chain and shackle to Fran's ankle.

"So, what can I get you?" Helen asked again.

"It doesn't matter," Fran replied, resigning herself to her current situation. "Whatever is easiest. I'm not very hungry."

"Okay, then. Scrambled eggs and bacon it is. Nothing but the best for your baby," Helen answered. She walked back to the makeshift kitchen area and removed the eggs and bacon from a cooler. She lit the camp stove and arranged some bacon strips in the frying pan, then she proceeded to crack some eggs into a bowl.

While Helen focused on cooking breakfast, Fran sat on the edge of her cot. Her mind began sorting through the bits of information she had gathered about her surroundings and her situation since she had woken up. After a moment, she looked up at Helen.

"I am sure I have seen you somewhere before," Fran said.

Helen stopped what she was doing. She turned to Fran and began laughing, this time almost hysterically. As Helen laughed, her eyes seemed vacant and distant to Fran. She felt a shiver of fear surge through her body.

"Maybe you have …" Helen exclaimed between bursts of laughter. "And maybe you haven't …"

The hairs stood up on the back of Fran's neck. A distinct change had just occurred in Helen's mood. There was a cockiness and a disturbing sense of anger and domination in her voice.

I can't let my guard down around this woman. There is something about her that is not right.

Fran was so absorbed in thought that she barely registered the distant sound of a sonic boom, followed by the faint sound of a jet aircraft in the distance.

THE DAYLIGHT in Helen's desert hideaway gradually transformed into a golden orange hue, growing dimmer as the sun sank lower in the western sky. Fran had noticed the mountains in that direction when she went outside to pee and to get some fresh air. The intense heat inside the tent was oppressive during the day, making the temperature outside the tent seem almost refreshing in comparison. Fran gulped down another tin cup full of water and wiped more sweat from her forehead. Under her t-shirt and camo pants, she felt sweaty, sticky, and grungy. She tugged at the t-shirt to keep it from clinging to her body.

Fran's mind began to wander again. From what she had seen of her surroundings, both inside and outside the tent, her best guess was that they were somewhere near the huge Air Force base that she remembered was north of Las Vegas.

What IS the name of that base? The name was on the tip of her tongue, but still eluded her. She paused and sighed. *Oh well ... it will come to me.*

Fran noticed Helen pacing back and forth impatiently. She noticed patches of sweat on Helen's t-shirt, areas where the shirt was sticking to her body too. Helen wiped her forehead and went for another cup of water.

"Fuck, it's hot in here," Helen said to nobody in particular.

Fran's ears perked up. She sat upright on her cot, not trusting her senses.

Is that a vehicle? ... Is it coming this way?

She sat up, her ears attuned to the sound. As she listened, it grew louder. It was definitely coming closer. Helen stopped halfway through a gulp of water. Her body went as rigid as a statue.

She's heard it too, Fran thought.

As the sound grew nearer, Helen ran from the tent, leaving Fran alone. Before long, Fran heard the distinct sound of rubber crunching on gravel. The vehicle was drawing closer with each passing second. The crunching sound became more distinct and the pitch of the tires began to decrease as the vehicle decelerated. Finally, it stopped completely, just outside the tent. Fran heard a door open and then the sound of feet hitting the gravel. There was a long pause, then two sets of feet crunching on gravel.

"I missed you so much," she heard Helen say.

"I missed you too," a male voice answered. "It's so good to finally be with you."

Fran strained to hear the conversation from her cot, deep inside the tent.

"How was your trip?" Helen asked. "Any problems getting back from Denmark?"

"None at all," the man answered. "I did exactly as you suggested - I drove to Zurich to get out of the EU as fast as possible. After I sold the car, I flew to Moscow and connected to Hanoi. Tranh put me up in his home until he could get me onto a cargo ship to the States. Let me tell you, it was a bit eerie spending eight hours alone in a dark container, but it was worth it. There's no record of me reentering the country. Everything went like clockwork."

Fran waited for somebody to say something, but there was a pregnant pause. Finally, Helen broke the silence.

"We've got a problem … A big one."

"Why? What happened?" the man asked, concern registering in his voice.

"Whitney's wife, Capellini, sensed something was wrong when she answered the door. She pushed Angela out of the way and tackled me. My gun discharged and Capellini was injured. Somebody in the house was armed and we came under fire. We had to pull back and get the hell out of there," she said sullenly.

"Shit!" the man cursed, followed by a pause. "How could you let that happen?"

There was another short pause, then Fran heard Helen's voice.

"Don't you *dare* raise your voice at me! Remember who you're talking to!" Helen roared.

For the second time today, Fran felt a chill of fear surge through her.

"I'm sorry," the man said contritely. There was an abrupt one-hundred-and-eighty-degree reversal in both Helen's and the unseen man's demeanors. "I didn't mean it … So, what happened to Capellini? Was she killed?"

"Of course not," Helen snapped. "I dragged the bitch back to the van. I had to take her with us."

Fran waited through another pause before the man answered.

"She's here? In the tent?" he asked incredulously.

"Of course. What else was I going to do with her?"

"I don't know!" the man said. "You were supposed to kill the Baranyi bitch. You weren't supposed to take hostages!"

"Will you shut up for a moment and think!" Helen bellowed. "This isn't a catastrophe. We've still got the upper hand. We can use her as a hostage to get what we really want."

Fran went rigid as she sat on her cot. She got up slowly, picking up her chain from the ground. The conversation beckoned her nearer and she was helpless to resist. She crept slowly and quietly towards the tent entrance, being careful not to rattle her chains.

"How are we going to use Capellini to get Baranyi? Nobody in their right mind would trade one woman for another," the man asked.

"Maybe. But we've got an ace in the hole," Helen replied. "Capellini's pregnant."

"No way!" the man exclaimed, his voice full of surprise. "Really? … Shit, I leave the country for a few weeks and I lose touch with everything."

Fran noticed another distinct change in Helen's demeanor. She even thought she heard a chuckle.

"Yeah, but it gets even better. Dan Whitney is the father!" Helen exclaimed.

The man paused to digest this new piece of information. "So, they'll do anything to get a pregnant woman back alive."

"Exactly," Helen answered. Fran waited for the man to reply.

"Okay," he said finally. "But here's another thought. This could be the best thing that ever happened to us. We were finally supposed to be a family … you, me, and Jonah … after I took Jonah from Anika, right?"

"Yeah," Helen answered tentatively.

"And Baranyi fucked that up so we lost Jonah. But just think about it, Teri … We've got what we really want right in front of us! Capellini's going to have a baby. All we need to do is find someplace to keep her until she gives birth, and then we take the baby and send her back home," he said triumphantly.

Fran gasped. She waited, expecting Helen to reply. Instead, there was a long pause. *Is she sniffling? … crying? … Who is Teri?*

"You know I can't do that," Helen answered, her voice slow and deliberate. "I had to give up a child once … I can't do that to another woman."

Helen's bravado had disappeared completely, now replaced by an almost childlike tone. A long period of silence followed.

Then, without warning, the bravado came flying out of Helen's mouth again. "You can't make me do it!" she snapped. "If we do, then that bitch Angela wins! She must pay for what she did to us. We'd be together with Jonah now if it wasn't for her!"

Fran waited through another pause, wondering which version of Helen she was going to hear next.

"There might just be another way to get Baranyi to give herself up to us," Helen said, seemingly regaining control of her demeanor.

"How do you figure that?" the man asked.

"She already sacrificed herself once to keep herself and her children safe when she was in New York, didn't she?" Helen asked.

"Yes, but …"

"We could do something to scare her … make her think that we're still coming after her … and her family," Helen announced.

"Such as?" the man asked.

"Let's just say I know people who have a talent for scaring people," Helen replied. "What if we rigged Baranyi's parents' home to blow up while they're not home? Nobody gets hurt, but we scare the shit out of all of them!"

"I don't like it," the man replied immediately. "Keeping Capellini's baby would be so much easier."

"Are you *daring* to defy me!" Helen shouted.

She's like Jekyll and Hyde! Fran said to herself. *Her moods change with almost everything she says.*

"Okay … Okay, you're right," the man relented. Fran noted that he seemed to be well acquainted with Helen's mercurial moods, and with how to manage them. "Let's do it your way. Let me know how to contact your people and I'll arrange it."

Fran heard the crunching of gravel. They were walking towards the tent. Afraid they might catch her listening, she quickly picked up an armful of chain and hurried back to her cot. She carefully set the chain on the dusty gravel floor of the tent only seconds before Helen and the man appeared.

She looked up with anticipation. Although she suspected the identity of the new arrival, she was still mentally unprepared when he finally walked into the tent and stood in front of her.

"So, you must be the infamous Francesca Capellini," he said sarcastically. "I finally get to meet the woman who's caused us so much trouble! I'm Soren … Soren Kristiansen."

CHAPTER 4

FREELANCE reporter Ricki Marshall waited at her table in the coffee shop, her left leg bouncing up and down nervously, watching every person who entered. She felt self-conscious in the café, feeling as if her stocky frame stuck out like a lumberjack at a ballet in the shop's petite-sized tables and chairs and chic decor. The surroundings were a stark contrast to Ricki's tall frame, her heavyset features, her short blonde hair, and the cargo pants and tank top she was wearing. She heard the word *dyke* coming from a table behind her. The hair on the back of her neck bristled and anger started to simmer.

Ricki was about to turn around to educate the asshole behind her, when she spied a middle-aged African-American woman entering the café. The woman stopped, appearing nervous as she scoured the small room. In contrast to Ricki, she was slender, average height, and neatly dressed in a stylish skirt and blouse. Her hair and makeup were both flawless. Ricki jumped to her feet, raising her hand to attract the woman's attention. The woman's eyes stopped when they got to Ricki, who motioned for the woman to join her at her small table.

"I'm Ricki Marshall. You must be Kiara Wilson."

"Yes, I am," the woman answered.

"Thanks so much for meeting with me," Ricki continued.

"The pleasure is mine," Kiara replied.

"I appreciate you taking the time to talk to me about this. I know it must be difficult for you," Ricki said.

"After I read your article about military sexual abuse, I finally realized that I'm not the only MSA victim out there," Kiara replied.

"I'm retired from the service now, but I feel like I have a duty to speak up for the women who are still being abused."

"You're very brave," Ricki answered.

"This is still confidential, right?" Kiara asked nervously.

"Absolutely. I'll never reveal you as my source. You can count on that. But, do you mind if I record our conversation so I don't miss anything?"

Kiara stiffened in her seat and Ricki saw fear in her eyes.

"No way!" she whispered emphatically. "I can't take that chance."

She made a move to get up from her seat, but Ricki reached out and put her hand gently on Kiara's.

"It's okay, Kiara. I get it. I can just take notes. I won't put your name on them. Will that be okay?" she said, her eyes imploring the frightened woman to trust her.

Kiara hesitated while she thought things over. The fear in her eyes seemed to subside slowly. Finally, the tension left her facial muscles and shoulders as her body began to relax." I promise," Ricki repeated. "Can I get you something to drink?"

"Sure. I'll just have a latte."

"Alright," Ricki answered. "I'll be back in a minute."

Ricki rose from her chair and headed for the counter. As she passed the table behind her, she glared at the couple who were seated there. In particular, she gave the evil eye to an overweight young businessman, who had glaring patches of perspiration on his forehead and under the armpits of his white dress shirt. She decided it wasn't worth the effort to make a scene, so she kept moving and stepped up to the counter.

"One latte and a cappuccino," she said to the young man at the counter.

"That'll be four twenty-five. Here's your receipt, they'll call your number over there," he said, pointing to the far end of the counter where a barista worked swiftly and efficiently, working her magic on several variations of coffee and tea-based drinks. Ricki returned to the table and flipped open her notepad, leafing through it quickly to find a blank page.

"The drinks will be a couple of minutes," Ricki said. "Mind if I start?"

Kiara nodded silently. She was still fidgety and nervous, and she had difficulty maintaining eye contact with Ricki.

"So, when did the abuse start for you?" Ricki asked.

"Almost as soon as I joined the Navy," Kiara replied.

"The sexual abuse?" Ricki inquired.

"No, it wasn't sexual at first. You know … first it was the typical condescending remarks about being black … and being a woman. Even though the military is trying to show that they're gender and racially inclusive, it's still an old white boys' club."

"Must have been tough," Ricki answered. "How did you deal with *that*? Did you report it?"

"Are you kidding?" Kiara replied. Her nostrils flared and Ricki saw anger in the intensity of the other woman's non-verbal communication. "The minute you do that, you're screwed. Nobody has any respect for a crybaby. I did what women and blacks have done for centuries to survive. I sucked it up … pushed it deep down inside and smiled. I worked myself harder than any other recruit. I tried to fool myself into believing that if I worked hard enough, I'd finally earn their respect."

"But that didn't work, did it," Ricki answered.

"Of course not. When they couldn't get to me, they had to find another way. It wasn't long before their remarks were more sexually suggestive and demeaning. Always making comments about my breasts or my ass … about wanting to fuck me. I tried to laugh it off, but they just kept up the pressure."

"Who did it? The other cadets or the officers?" Ricki asked.

"Mostly my peers at first," Kiara replied. "It was like good cop, bad cop. Most of them were real jerks. But there was this one lieutenant who seemed like a real gentleman. He made it seem like he understood … telling me to forget about them … that they weren't worth worrying about. He gained my confidence, and I started to trust him."

"And …?"

"He was the first one who raped me," Kiara answered quietly, swallowing with difficulty. Ricki sensed Kiara digging deep for the energy to keep talking. "We'd get together and go out for drinks sometimes. Just the two of us. He managed to isolate me from the others … both the male cadets and the few other women … I started depending on him emotionally. And then one night, out of the blue, he came onto me in his car and wouldn't take no for an answer. He was a big strong guy … I tried … I couldn't fight him off … I should have been stronger …"

Kiara reached her breaking point. She broke into tears and reached into her purse for a tissue, sobbing quietly so as not to attract attention from people around them. The barista called Ricki's number, so she got up and went to the counter to pick up their drinks, leaving Kiara alone with her painful memories for a moment. When she returned to the table, she put the drinks down, took her seat, and then reached across the table to take Kiara's hand in hers.

"I'm sorry, Kiara," Ricki said, feeling a lump in the back of her own throat. "I can't imagine how terrible that must have been for you."

Kiara sniffled and raised her head. As she made eye contact with Ricki, she took a deep breath, seemingly gathering more strength to continue.

"Surprisingly, the rape wasn't the worse part for me," she said. "After that, I was totally isolated. I had nobody I could talk to. I was so ashamed that I never mentioned it, even to my closest friends or family."

"Did you ever think of quitting?" Ricki asked.

"All the time. But every time I thought about it, it just made me feel weak and more ashamed. So, I put on a face. I convinced myself that I was a strong … a warrior. That's when I decided to report the rape. I wasn't going to let him get away with it."

"Who did you report it to?" Ricki inquired.

"My CO," Kiara answered. "I was so naive. I followed the chain of command, figuring he'd report it to the higher-ups."

"And did he?" Ricki asked rhetorically, already knowing how Kiara was going to answer.

"Oh yeah. He reported it to the base commander, and I was called in for a meeting. He called it an 'unfortunate incident', but said it fell outside his jurisdiction because it happened while we were off duty. He said I should have reported it to the police."

"So, he swept it under the carpet and that was the end of it," Ricki muttered, shaking her head.

"Not by a long shot," Kiara countered. "After that, it was like everybody knew. The harassment started coming from the other officers. They made it crystal clear that my career could either take off or stall. The decision was up to me."

Ricki continued to scribble in her notepad, struggling to keep up with the sheer volume of revelations Kiara was sharing.

"The bastards," she cursed. "They had you trapped. What could you do?"

"The only thing I could to survive," Kiara continued. "I started sleeping around with the officers. I tried to fool myself into thinking that I was using *them* to fast-forward *my* career."

"And …?" Ricki asked, raising her eyes to contact Kiara's.

"I started to feel like I was two people," Kiara explained. "One part of me was proud of how I climbed the ranks. But another part of me felt dirty and more ashamed as time went on. I felt like a slut. I was conflicted and depressed, and it got harder to live with myself. Eventually, taking a bunch of pills just seemed like the logical way to escape."

Ricki lifted her eyes from her notepad again and the two women's eyes connected completely for the first time. Ricki felt Kiara's pain and she was thankful that Kiara felt a connection with her - that she trusted that Ricki truly understood her pain, as well as the unfairness and injustice of it all. Even though Ricki hadn't told Kiara her own story, Ricki sensed that Kiara understood they had something in common. They both knew what it was like to be victims, and they both understood the unfairness and injustice of their shared experience.

"Thank God you survived," Ricki said, once again feeling a lump in her throat. She fought to hold back tears for Kiara. "I'm so sorry you had to endure that."

Once again, Ricki reached out, this time touching Kiara's arm.

"So, when did it end for you?" Ricki asked.

"It got worse before it got better," Kiara continued. "The one-on-one sex eventually turned into orgies involving groups of officers and cadets. Before I knew it, I was an officer and I was taking part in the abuse. I heard stories that I couldn't believe … stories about high-ranking officers in all branches of the military …"

"Did you hear names?" Ricki asked excitedly.

"No. No names," Kiara answered. Ricki's shoulders slumped with disappointment. "But one of the stories that kept surfacing involved big brass - especially a particular major. I distinctly remember one night when one officer said it was too bad 'The Major' couldn't be here to sample this 'prime piece of ass'."

"The Major?" Ricki asked. "Any idea who he was?"

"Not at all," Kiara continued. "But that's when I finally realized how far it all went. It's a conspiracy that reaches into every corner of military culture. I'm sure of it. And there's absolutely no recourse for victims, nor any accountability for abusers. It's all supposedly handled within the chain of command. But in reality, it's just a big, closely guarded, dirty secret. Once I realized that, I couldn't go on. I resigned my commission last year. I see a therapist every week and I finally found a good job. I even met a good man. I'm having a hard time learning to trust … but so far, it's working.

"I'm glad things are gradually working out for you," Ricki replied.

"Yeah, but I'm one of the lucky ones," Kiara answered. "I know there's many more women - and men too - who haven't been so lucky. It's destroyed their lives. That's why I'm doing this. I hope I can stop it from happening to anybody else."

Ricki's eyes made contact with Kiara's again. The connection felt warm and good, full of mutual understanding.

"I know. Thank you for being so candid. It's only when brave people like you speak up that the secrets get exposed. It's the only way anything will ever change."

Kiara glanced at her watch, then she tipped back her cappuccino and drained the last few drops.

"I really need to be going now," Kiara said. "I need to get back to work. If you think of any other questions, please don't hesitate to call me. You've still got my number?"

"Absolutely," Ricki answered. "You've still got mine?"

"Yes," Kiara replied. She stood and extended her hand to Ricki, who rose to her feet as well. "Best of luck with your next article. I can't wait to read it."

"You'll be the first to know when it's coming out," Ricki said with a smile. "I promise."

Kiara smiled, then she turned and walked away. Ricki sat down and reached for her notepad.

"A major," she said to herself, her mind jumping into action. "How am I going to follow up on this?"

CHAPTER 5

DAN'S BODY knifed through the last few meters of his swim, his arms straining against the lactic burn, digging deep for a last ounce of energy. Then, his fingertips touched the end wall of the pool. His muscles let go and relaxed at the same instant. He pushed backward off the wall, allowing himself to float on his back, inhaling and exhaling in a long, slow, rhythm while his body recovered from his final sprint. He looked up at the blue Nevada sky and let his mind go blank as he drifted aimlessly on his back.

After his breathing gradually returned to normal, Dan rolled over onto his stomach. His arms stroked casually to the side and pulled his toned, naked body from the pool. He had just picked up his towel and started drying himself when he heard the doorbell ring. Quickly, he pulled on a pair of track pants and a t-shirt and rushed to the front door. The doorbell sounded again just before he reached the door.

"I'm coming, I'm coming," he said, half to himself and half out loud as he reached for the door handle. As the door opened, he gave a start, recognizing FBI agents Simpson and Martinelli standing in the doorway.

"Dr. Whitney. Sorry to impose on you," Martinelli volunteered. "Do you mind if we come in? We have a few more questions for you."

"Uh … of course. But you've caught me a bit off guard. I just finished my morning swim. I hope you don't mind my appearance," Dan replied.

"We understand," Simpson added. "It won't take long."

"Come on in," Dan said. "And please, just call me Dan. Can I get you a cup of coffee? It just finished brewing."

"Don't mind if I do," Martinelli answered. "I'll take mine black."

"None for me, thanks," Simpson added.

"I'll get the coffee!" a woman's voice called from the top of the stairs. Martinelli's and Simpson's heads gazed upward to see the person behind the voice. An elderly woman walked down the staircase towards them. She extended her hand to the FBI agents as she reached the last step.

"I'm Susan Keaner. I'm an old friend of Fran's." She shook each of the agents' hands. "Why don't you all have a seat in the great room, Dan, and I'll bring the coffee out."

"Thanks, Susan," Dan answered. He gestured towards the great room. "Come on in and have a seat."

As Susan disappeared into the kitchen, Martinelli and Simpson's eyes started scanning the room, looking back towards the main entrance from where Fran was abducted.

"Susan's an old friend?" Martinelli asked.

"Yes, she was very much like a mentor to Fran when she was growing up in Italy," Dan replied. "She was here to celebrate Fran's release from Indio on the night of the party. She's still in a state of shock, like the rest of us."

At that moment, Susan emerged from the kitchen carrying cups of coffee for Dan and Martinelli.

"Thanks, Susan. Is there anything more you wanted to tell the agents about the night of the party?" Dan asked.

"That won't be necessary," Simpson answered. "But you're welcome to stay, Ms. Keaner. We just dropped by to bring Dan up to date, and to ask him a couple of questions."

"If it's all the same to you, I think I'll make myself some breakfast," Susan replied. "Nice meeting you both."

Susan ambled off toward the kitchen, leaving Dan alone with the two agents.

"So, how can I help you?" Dan asked. "Have you got any new leads yet?"

"I'm sorry," Simpson responded. "Nothing yet. But we had a good chat with Detective Jameson in Palm Desert yesterday. We're very sorry about what happened to your late wife."

"Thanks," Dan answered. He paused and looked out over the pool, taking a moment to remember the events surrounding Michelle Whitney's death.

"Do you think there's any connection between Chelly's death and Fran's kidnapping?" Dan asked.

"What do *you* think?" Simpson asked. "Jameson was clear that there wasn't ever enough evidence to charge Fran. She thinks there could have been somebody putting pressure on D.A. Mulholland. It's possible that whoever was pressuring Fran might still have a grudge against her."

"Or you," Martinelli added.

"Any ideas who that could be?" Simpson asked again.

"If you know about Palm Desert, you must also know about the Jonah Kristiansen abduction … and the attempts to kill Anika Kristiansen, Angela Baranyi, and me," Dan answered.

"We do," Simpson replied. "Do *you* think there's any connection between all those events and Fran's abduction?"

"I do," Dan responded. "I don't believe in coincidences. I think it may have been another attempt on Angela's life … or maybe even Anika's or mine. But what I can't figure out is why! Isn't that *your* job?" Dan asked sarcastically.

Dan's face tensed and he grew more irritable as his frustration deepened. Wisely, Martinelli took a step back to defuse the situation. He walked back towards the home's main entrance.

"So, this is where it happened? In the front entrance?" Martinelli asked.

"Yes," Dan said, his tone one of exasperation. "I've already told you I was at the back of the room with friends. We were looking at that large portrait on the wall. It's one of Fran's best.

There was a lot of noise in the room. Next thing we knew, we heard the gunshot coming from the front door and everybody hit the floor."

"Where was Ms. Baranyi when this happened?" Simpson asked.

"She was talking with us, but somebody called her to the front door," Dan answered. "She only caught a glimpse of the delivery person before Fran apparently pushed her out of the way. She was lying on the floor … over here … when the gun went off."

"And Mr. Holloway and his associates?" Martinelli interjected. "They were out on the patio?"

"That's right," Dan confirmed. "The party had spilled out into the pool area. They were talking with some other friends from Orange County."

Martinelli and Simpson walked around the room, each making a mental picture of where everybody had been at the time of the chaotic event. They each stopped to look at Fran's portrait, then stepped out onto the pool area for a brief look. After a quick look outside, they returned to the great room.

"Who's that in the portrait?" Simpson asked.

"It's Angela," Dan replied. "It's a long story, believe me."

"Maybe some other time," Martinelli interjected. He turned his attention away from the portrait and back to Dan. "Have you heard anything from the kidnappers yet? Any ransom notes or phone calls?"

Dan frowned. "Nothing. Is that a bad sign?"

"No, not necessarily," Simpson answered. "We don't want to alarm you. Like you, we tend to think this delivery person was looking to either abduct or kill Ms. Baranyi. Your wife … er girlfriend … seems to have caused the whole thing to fall apart. It's likely that her kidnappers are trying to figure out what to do with her right now."

"We'd like your permission to tap your phones in case they do call you," Martinelli added. "If you get a ransom note, contact us right away."

"Sure, no problem," Dan replied. "So, what have you found out so far? Have you found the van? Any idea who owned it or who was driving?"

"To be honest, we don't have much yet, apart from the shell casings from outside," Simpson responded. "The blood definitely belonged to your wife. But plain white delivery vans are a dime a dozen, and we don't have a plate number. We don't even have any similar vans that have been reported stolen or abandoned."

With that bad news, Dan's demeanor changed suddenly. His face turned red and his facial muscles tightened. His frustration boiled to the surface.

"You're the FBI, for fuck sake!" he blurted. "It's been two days and you don't have *anything* yet?"

"We're doing the best we can, Dan," Simpson answered, remaining calm. "I know it's difficult, but you need to be patient. Something will turn up … it always does. It's just a matter of time."

Her reply did nothing to calm Dan. The muscles in his neck began to bulge and his face turned crimson.

"Patient?" he shouted. "That's my girlfriend out there! She's been shot and she's pregnant with our child. And you want me to be patient?"

"I understand how frustrated you are," Simpson empathized. "I get it. I'd be frustrated too if I was in your situation. But we've learned to be patient. Perps always make at least one mistake. We'll find it eventually. You're just going to need to trust us, okay?"

Simpson's empathy finally managed to have a calming effect on Dan. He paused, then took a long, deep breath, followed by a long sigh.

"Thanks," he replied. "Sorry for the outburst. It's not like me. I know you guys are doing the best you can. Anything else I can do to help?"

"Not right now," Martinelli answered. "We just wanted to look over the crime scene again and to see if there'd been any ransom demands."

"We'll take over once you hear from the kidnappers," Simpson added. "All you need to do is answer the phone, or contact us if you get a note." She looked at Martinelli and gave him a quick nod to let him know she was finished. "We'll stop bothering you and be on our way now."

The agents made their way to the main entrance. As they made their way out the front door, Simpson turned to Dan.

"Don't worry, Dan. We'll call you as soon as we have any developments."

The two agents turned and closed the door behind them. Susan emerged from the kitchen. She stood beside Dan and put her hand on his shoulder. They stood together in silence, feeling each other's grief. Finally, a tear escaped from Dan's eye and began trickling slowly down his cheek.

CHAPTER 6

FRAN WIPED the sweat from her forehead for what seemed like the hundredth time today. The daytime desert heat had been stifling and almost intolerable. Even now, with the sun sinking low over the mountains, the heat in the tent was still oppressive. She was totally bored and had lost track of time. It seemed like an eternity since she had shed her t-shirt sometime during the mid-morning, leaving only her bra to cover her breasts. The t-shirt's cotton fabric was little more than a sponge, not allowing her perspiration to evaporate and cool her. Fran gulped more water from a plastic cup as Soren returned to the tent carrying a large box of groceries and supplies. He went back to the vehicle and returned to the tent with two duffel bags. Fran watched as he dropped the bags, wiped his brow and then turned to Helen.

"Fuck! Could it get any hotter in here?" he exclaimed.

"Quit your bitching," Helen answered. "Beggars can't be choosers. There's only so much our connections could do for us on short notice. How'd it go?"

"It's all arranged. Your friends leave for Cleveland right away. As soon as the house is empty, they'll go in and rig the furnace. They can trigger it with a cell phone," he answered.

"Excellent," Helen said. Fran saw a smile form on her face. "Make sure they don't kill anybody. Just scare the shit out of Baranyi to show her that we mean business!"

Soren fell silent, pausing before he answered. Fran sensed him trying to get up his nerve to say something.

"I still don't like this explosion plan," Soren replied. It's one extra step where something could go wrong."

Helen moved closer to Soren and rested her hand on his head. She ran her fingers slowly through his hair, then leaned close and whispered in his ear, just loud enough so Fran could make out her words.

"You worry too much, my dear. Let Lady Helen get rid of those worries for you," she said softly.

"Here? Now?" Soren asked.

Helen seemed to stiffen with Soren's hesitation.

"Is something wrong? There's some reason why you don't want me?" she bristled.

"She's watching us!" Soren countered. "You want her to see everything?"

"Since when has doing it in front of other people been a problem for you?" Helen scoffed. "Who knows? Maybe it will turn her on and she'll want to join us next time."

"That's disgusting," Soren answered. "She's pregnant. And I have a problem with it since you committed a felony and kidnapped her! She's a witness. She can bring us all down."

Fran watched as Helen's anger went from a simmer to a low boil. "You weren't worried about felonies when you choked the life out of that blonde bitch in Little Rock!"

"You're right! I had to get rid of the evidence so Beth couldn't bring us down," he shouted. "Is that what you're planning to do with Capellini? Get rid of her too?"

A sudden wave of fear caused Fran to shiver. She curled up on her cot, unconsciously trying to make herself less visible.

"That's enough!" Helen screamed. "I don't want to hear any more of your insubordination. Get your collar … now!"

Fran watched with increasing fascination from her cot as Soren suddenly cowered, then walked over to one of the duffel bags he'd just unloaded. He looked like a puppy who knew he'd just disappointed his master. He rummaged through the bag until he found a studded leather collar with a short chain attached. He slunk back to Helen, whose chest was inflated and shoulders were thrown back. She almost appeared to Fran to have grown six inches as she watched Soren follow her commands.

Fran's eyes opened wide as Soren began to strip naked in front of her. When he had finished, he reached for the collar and buckled it in place around his neck.

"Down on your knees. Cower like a dog!" Helen shouted.

Without a word, Soren fell to his knees in front of her, his head to the ground and his arms and hands extended in front of him. Helen smiled her approval as he submitted completely to her will. She turned and walked deliberately back to the duffel bag and pulled out a shoulder-length platinum blonde wig, a pair of high black leather boots, a black corset, and a cane. She dropped the boots on the ground beside Soren and then walked towards Fran, cane in hand.

Fran felt herself shrink back into the cot. Her eyes looked away, focusing on the ground instead of her approaching captor. She felt her heart pounding. Her chest was tight and she struggled to catch her breath. Her entire body shivered as she felt Helen's presence beside her. Then she felt the tip of the cane under her chin, gently but firmly lifting it upward. As her eyes met Helen's, the scene in front of her seemed to recede into the distance, becoming hazy and then disappearing from Fran's consciousness. Instead, even hazier images from the distant past forced their way into her mind.

The same images that had flashed through Fran's mind two nights before, now drifted through the edges of her consciousness again. She saw the same view of a naked woman from behind, passionately kissing the unidentified man in the hot tub. Then, suddenly, that scene was replaced by another. Fran gasped. This time, the image of the woman was from the front but her identity was concealed by a black mask. She was dressed provocatively as a dominatrix, and she was taking the hand of Philippe Morel, Fran's recently deceased husband. The woman smiled knowingly at Phillipe, who smiled in return.

Before Fran could adjust to the shock of seeing this image, the scene was blocked by another new image - this time of an older man dressed in the attire of a French Army general, standing in front of her. The man wore a lecherous grin on his face. He extended his hand to Fran. In the distance, she felt part of her mind protesting - wanting to run. But her feet felt like lead. She stood still and found her hand taking the general's extended hand. She felt a hidden force pushing her body. She felt herself being compelled to go with the general, and to follow Philippe and the mysterious dominatrix …

Another tap of Helen's cane under Fran's chin brought her abruptly back into reality. The cane began to wander, tracing a path down Fran's neck, over her chest, and down into the space between the cups of her bra. Helen's eyes followed the cane, gazing lasciviously at Fran's bosom.

Without warning, Helen stood stiffly and withdrew the cane. She stared down at Fran, her brown eyes commanding Fran to obey.

"Watch and learn, Francesca," she said firmly.

Helen turned, walking away from Fran and back towards Soren. Fran's heart continued to pound. Her breathing was ragged. She watched Helen turn her back and begin shedding her military fatigues and undergarments until she was completely naked. Then, Helen stepped into the corset and pulled it up over her torso, expertly reaching behind her to fasten the zipper of the skin-tight garment. She carefully tucked up her own short brown hair before covering it with the blonde wig. Her feet still bare, Helen picked up her cane, then she turned and stepped confidently back to where Soren was still lying prostrate on the ground.

Fran felt herself feeling confused again. Part of her still felt that she should be very afraid of the woman before her. Yet another part of her was in awe of the other woman's overpowering natural beauty, sexuality, and confidence. Fran's eyes were drawn to the woman's corset, which pushed up Helen's breasts and barely covered her nipples, leaving little to the imagination. The corset was cut high on the sides, revealing perfectly proportioned, muscular legs and thighs. Between her legs, the corset was made of lace and had a slit that had only one possible use. Through the slit, Fran saw a patch of short, carefully manicured dark pubic hair.

"Stand up!" Helen commanded as she stared down at Soren. Then she broke into a sadistic laugh that sent another shiver through Fran's body.

"You're going to pay for your taste of pussy tonight, my dear," Helen hissed. She kicked the leather boots so they landed beside Soren's head.

"Lick them clean!" she ordered.

FRAN FELT surreal and detached from her body, as if floating and looking down at herself and Dan.

She saw them seated side by side on chairs, in what looked at first glance like a barn. The room was constructed from heavy wooden beams and the walls were covered by rough pine planks. Ropes and chains were suspended from the rafters, running over pulleys. A variety of leather or steel cuffs, shackles, floggers, and other sex toys hung on the walls. Straw covered the concrete floor. But unlike a real barn, the straw was fresh. There was no odor of urine or animal waste. Instead the room smelled of freshly hewn wood, leather, straw, and human sweat. As Fran looked down on the scene, she became aware of a naked woman kneeling on the floor in front of her and Dan. A man stood over the woman, dressed in black leather from head to toe.

Suddenly, the scene seemed to shift. Fran no longer felt as if she was floating over the scene. Instead, she was now part of it, sitting beside Dan and in front of the naked woman. She looked at herself and Dan and realized that they weren't wearing clothes anymore. The woman in front of them had disheveled, shoulder-length blonde hair. Her bare skin was covered in perspiration. A metal spreader bar was fastened to leather cuffs on each of her ankles. Her hands were cuffed behind her back, leaving her completely helpless and vulnerable. The leather-clad man held a leather flogger. The blonde woman raised her head and stared at Fran. A chill surged down Fran's spine. The woman was Chelly Whitney, Dan's wife, and her eyes were filled with hatred.

"This is all *your* fault, you bitch!" she spat. "You welcomed me into your home and now you're stealing my husband?"

The image blurred. Fran saw flashes of the leather-clad man flogging and caning the woman, who was now blindfolded and had a rubber gag stuffed into her mouth. The image blurred again. This time, Chelly was lying by the edge of swimming pool in a growing puddle of blood, her eyes gazing up into Fran's eyes.

"You'll … pay … for … this …," Chelly rasped. She mustered her energy for one more breath. "I'll … get … you …"

Chelly's eyes rolled upward. As the muscles in her body let go of life, her center of gravity shifted and she slid into the water with a final swish and a gentle splash …

FRAN'S EYES popped open. Her pupils were dilated and her breathing was shallow and ragged. Totally disoriented, her eyes darted around the tent, desperately looking for something - anything - that would connect her back to reality.

The sound of splashing water coming from the end of the tent caused her to freeze in fear. Fran felt her lungs seize up and her breathing come to an abrupt stop as the images of Chelly Whitney from last night's dream flashed through her consciousness yet again. She closed her eyes to escape the images. Once again, she heard the swish of water at the end of the tent. Cautiously, she opened one eye. Steam rose from a basin of hot water. Helen leaned her toned, naked body over the steam, soaking a cloth in the steaming water before she used it to scrub her face. Fran heard Helen sigh as the hot water seemingly washed away her captor's tension. Fran's lungs finally began to relax. A sigh of relief slowly escaped from her lungs as she realized that the splashing water came from Helen's ritual morning sponge bath. Fran's captor removed the steaming cloth from her face and began humming, unaware that Fran was watching her.

Without warning, Fran felt gas rising from her unsettled stomach. It escaped as an audible belch before she could control it. Helen wheeled around to look at the source of the sound. In an instant, her relaxed demeanor changed to embarrassment. She covered her bare breasts with one arm and grabbed for her nearby t-shirt with the other, when she realized that Fran was watching her bathe. She turned away and quickly pulled the shirt over her head, letting it fall so that it covered her breasts and genitals. Once covered, she turned back to face Fran.

"Did you sleep well?" Helen asked, blushing and trying to shift attention away from her embarrassment.

Fran shrugged and shook her head. "Bad dreams. Besides, how could I sleep with all that commotion going on?" She looked to Soren's cot but noticed it was empty. "Where is he?"

"Soren?" Helen asked. "He had business to take care of." Helen's eyes narrowed and her forehead wrinkled. Fran noticed a look of confusion written on Helen's face.

"What do you mean … commotion?" Helen asked.

"You know … you and Soren … carrying on," Fran answered.

Helen's confusion seemed to deepen. Then, just as quickly, a smile began to spread over her face. She broke out in a hearty laugh.

"Making love? You're kidding, right?" Helen said, still laughing. "You think I'd make love to Soren in front of you? What kind of girl do you think I am?"

This time it was Fran's turn to feel confused.

Did I dream that too? I'm sure I remember her humiliating and disciplining Soren before they made love.

Fran's thoughts were interrupted as her baby kicked inside her. She placed one hand over her rounded abdomen.

"I don't know … I guess I must have been dreaming," she replied.

Helen gazed at Fran. Seemingly out of nowhere, a look of compassion replaced the look of distrust and disbelief that had been on Helen's face a moment before.

"Where are my manners. You must want to bathe too. I'll refill the basin for you," Helen said. She took the basin to the tent's entrance and threw out her own wash water. She returned and poured hot water from a pot on the camp stove into the basin. She added some cold water and tested the temperature. Satisfied that it wasn't too hot, she walked over to Fran's cot.

"Do you mind? … May I feel the baby?" Helen asked timidly.

Fran was still confused. Helen's voice was suddenly meek and almost childlike. It was a total contrast to the controlling, domineering woman who flaunted her sexuality in front of Fran the night before. Fran hesitated. Finally, she reached out and pulled Helen towards her until her captor was sitting on the cot beside her. She placed Helen's hand on her abdomen over the baby. Helen smiled and stared at Fran's stomach, her countenance full of wonder, much like a child who feels an unborn baby for the first time.

"Oh, my God," Helen squealed with youthful glee. "I feel it kicking!" She turned her gaze from Fran's belly to her captive's eyes. However, the twinkle gradually left Helen's eyes and was slowly replaced by a distant sadness. Unable to keep up with the shifts in Helen's emotions, Fran felt even more confused. She gazed into Helen's eyes and squeezed her hand, trying to make eye contact and bring Helen back into the moment.

"Are you okay?" Fran asked.

Helen's eyes blinked and she gave her head a quick shake. She stared at Fran, taking a few seconds to gather herself.

"Uh … I'm okay," Helen answered. She straightened herself and seemed to get her bearings again. She removed her hand from Fran's abdomen. "I'll undo your chain so you can undress and have some privacy before Soren comes back," she continued."

Helen knelt and removed the shackle and chain from Fran's ankle. Fran made her way to the table with the basin of hot water. She turned, shyly, to look at Helen. Then she turned her back and pulled her t-shirt over her head before removing her bra and finally stepping out of her panties and camouflage pants. She heard Helen walking towards the tent entrance and watched out of the corner of her eye as Helen left the tent.

The second Helen was gone, Fran stopped bathing and began to frantically survey the tent, searching - knowing she only had a few moments to find what she was looking for. Finally, she spotted it on the ground near Helen's cot - a pencil. On the ground beside it, she also noticed a discarded white envelope. She moved her naked body quickly across the tent, grateful to be temporarily free from her shackle and chain. She quickly retrieved the two items and deftly stuffed them into the pillowcase beneath her pillow. She scurried back to the table and commenced bathing as quickly as possible. Only a moment later, Helen poked her head into the tent.

"Everything okay," she asked.

"Yes, thank you," Fran answered. "This feels wonderful. I'll just be a few more minutes."

"Take your time," Helen replied. "When you're finished, I'll cook something to eat … Then we'll talk about sending a message to your boyfriend."

CHAPTER 7

ANIKA KRISTIANSEN heard the phone ringing upstairs but disregarded the distant sound. After all, this was her sister Trudy's home in Calgary, where she and Jonah were now living temporarily. The decision to sell her pediatric medical practice in Victoria, and to move to Calgary to be nearer to her ailing father and the rest of her family, had not been easy. Jonah had adjusted much better than she expected. There were too many memories in Victoria of the family they had once been - and too many memories of his father, Soren. Much to Anika's relief, living with his cousins in Calgary seemed to be filling Jonah's need to be with family, and to feel safe.

"Come on, Jonah!" Anika shouted. "You have to be at school in twenty minutes. Nicholas, Julia, and your cousins are all waiting outside for you."

"I'm coming," he shouted. "Have you seen my other shoe?"

Anika sighed. "Have you tried looking under the clothes on the floor?" She heard her name drifting down from upstairs.

"Anika, can you hear me?" Trudy shouted. Her voice was full of concern.

"Yes. What's up?" Anika called back.

"Get Angela right away. It's her father on the phone ... He's upset ... Something terrible has happened!"

Anika hurried to the basement suite's bathroom, ready to knock on the door to pass along the message to Angela.

"Angela ..." she began, but the door flew open. Angela's face was etched with concern, having already heard Trudy's call from upstairs. Anika followed Angela as she ran upstairs. She watched as Trudy handed the phone to Angela.

"Papa! What's happening? Are you and Mamma alright? … Explosion? … *Our* house? … Oh, my God! … CNN? … Right now? … Just a second." Angela turned and saw Anika. "Turn on CNN right now!" she shouted.

Anika ran to the TV and grabbed the remote. The screen came to life and Anika scoured the on-screen guide, finally finding CNN. She looked back to the hallway and nodded to Angela, confirming that she'd found the channel. Tears streamed from both of their eyes as they watched the newscast in a state of shock. The images on the screen showed Angela's childhood Cleveland home in ruins, the result of a massive explosion. Pieces of lumber and debris littered the street and adjacent yards. Anika went to her new lover and wrapped both arms around her.

"Papa, where are you?" Angela asked. "What are you going to do? … I see … Okay … I'll see what I can do … I'll need to make some calls, but I'll call you back … I love you Papa. Take good care of Mamma."

Angela hung up the phone and broke down, weeping inconsolably. Anika wrapped Angela in her arms to comfort her.

"What happened? Are they okay?" Anika asked.

Angela sniffled, taking a moment to compose herself. Her eyes were ringed with red from crying.

"Everything was going fine … no signs of danger. They went out to get groceries, as usual. When they came out of the grocery store, they saw a cloud of smoke in the distance and heard sirens everywhere. When they got home …"

Angela's voice trailed off. She wiped her eyes and blew her nose before continuing.

"The police think it might have been a gas explosion … They're both fine, but they're scared out of their minds now. They don't know where they're going to go," she continued.

Anika's face turned red and her nose flared. Her pupils were dilated. Her face filled with rage.

"It's Soren!" she shouted. "That bastard is behind this! I just know it! We need to do something. They're not safe ... *We're not safe! ...* Until he's caught!"

Suddenly, Anika caught a glimpse of somebody in her peripheral vision. She turned and saw Jonah standing in the doorway.

He heard me accusing his father! He knows we're not safe! Shit!

As Anika noticed him, Jonah turned and ran out the front door to join the other children.

"Jonah!" she shouted. "Wait!" She ran to the door to catch him, but he was already halfway down the street with Angela's children and his cousins. Torn between Jonah and Angela, she stood in the doorway, her mind racing. She was jolted back into reality by Angela's voice.

"Anika ... What are we going to do?"

Anika gave herself some time to think.

"First, we need to call Dan and FBI. If this has anything to do with Fran's kidnapping ... or with the attempts on our lives in Darwin or Hanoi ... then we need to find some protection for your parents, right away!" Anika turned to Trudy.

"Is there room at Mom and Dad's place for Angela's parents? Just until we can find another place for them?" she asked.

"You know Dad's still recovering from his surgery," Trudy answered. "And would we be putting ourselves in even more danger?"

"Maybe," Anika replied. "You know how much I appreciate you taking Angela and the kids into your home Trudy. I can't ask you to do any more. But I know Mom and Dad. They won't be able to stand by if they know Angela's parents are in need. We have to do something, Trudy. They're in danger!"

"Okay, we'll talk to them later. You need to call Dan first," Trudy answered.

"Thanks, Trudy." Anika gave her sister a hug. Then she turned to Angela and wrapped her arms around her again. She kissed her distraught lover on the lips and ran her fingers through her hair. She whispered in Angela's ear.

"Don't worry, baby. We'll make sure they're safe. We'll figure something out."

THE DAYS dragged on. Fran sat on the edge of her cot, the relentless afternoon heat taking its toll again. Sweat ran from her forehead and down into her right eye, stinging and causing tears to form. Having shed her t-shirt once again, her chest only covered by her bra, she felt drops of sweat trickling down her chest and into her cleavage. She reached for her cup of water and drained it in a few eager gulps.

How many days have I been here? Has it been a week yet? ... Or even more? I need to find a way out of here!

Helen's and Soren's angry voices wafted into the tent, interrupting Fran's thoughts. Their intended private discussion about what to do with Fran had quickly escalated into another argument.

Fran had other concerns. She hurried to her pillow and reached for the pencil and envelope. She scribbled a note while the argument carried on in the background. Helen's mild-mannered personality had vanished, once again replaced by her aggressive, domineering persona.

"It's done," Soren shouted. "They left the house to go grocery shopping. Thirty minutes later, it was nothing more than a pile of matchsticks. Are you happy now?"

"Happy? You bet I am! She'll be shitting herself now. Not just for herself, but for those kids and her parents. Now we can make our ransom demands to Whitney … Angela for Francesca," Helen boasted loudly.

"I still don't like it," Soren bellowed. "No matter how careful your people were, the FBI will figure out that they're military. And the feds definitely aren't going to let a swap happen. We'll be walking right into a trap, and you know it!"

Fran noticed Helen's bravado and anger escalating.

"Are you defying me again?" she screamed. "Maybe you didn't learn your lesson last night. Do you need Lady Helen to punish you again?"

Hearing Helen losing control of her emotions once more, Fran put her pencil to the envelope and started scribbling another note to herself. *Jekyll and Hyde - psychopath or kind, caring person?*

"You know I'm always in your service, my lady. I'd gladly receive your punishment again, if you wish," Soren replied. His voice was suddenly full of contrition.

"That's more like it! Did you get the video camera?" Helen asked, unexpectedly changing topics.

"As you ordered," Soren answered. "But the batteries will need to be charged before we use them. The solar panels I picked up should have them charged by tonight."

Soren appeared to be having some success at defusing Helen's temper. Fran stopped writing and focused her concentration on her captor's conversation.

"Perfect. I think it's time that we had a little talk with Francesca about her film debut tomorrow."

Fran hurried to hide the pencil and envelope inside her pillowcase, finishing only seconds before Soren and Helen entered the tent. She lay down on her cot and closed her eyes, pretending to be napping. Helen walked over to her cot and sat on the edge, only inches from Fran's covert notes. With one hand, Helen jiggled Fran's shoulder to waken her.

"Francesca … wake up," she said.

Fran pretended to be groggy and disoriented.

"What?" she moaned.

"We need to talk," Helen continued. "You want to go home, don't you?"

"Home? When?" Fran feigned.

"Not so fast, my dear," Helen countered. "First you need to do something for us. We need you to convince your boyfriend to cooperate with us. If he helps us get what we want, then he gets you back. It's that simple."

"What can you possibly want from Dan?" Fran asked. This time she was genuinely puzzled. "I don't understand."

"It's not your job to understand, Francesca. It's just your job to convince him. I'll write a script for you, and then you and I will deliver our message to Dan. Soren will record us on video. All you need to do is read exactly what I tell you to read. You leave the rest to me. Understand?"

Fran nodded silently. Her eyes connected with Helen's to confirm.

"And don't get any ideas about being a hero," Helen added. "You saw what happened to Soren when he disobeyed me last night. I'm sure you don't want that to happen to you."

"No ma'am. I'll do just as you say," Fran replied.

"Good. I knew we could count on you," Helen said. She rested her hand on Fran's shoulder. "You can rest again if you like."

Helen placed her other hand on the cot, only an inch from Fran's ear and the end of her pillow. Fran felt her heart pounding in her chest, hoping that Helen would leave. She felt the perspiration beading on her forehead and on her chest again. She felt a drop of salty liquid trickle slowly from her cleavage onto her left breast. Fran's eyes stared at Helen's hand, begging her silently not to move it closer to the pillow. Time seemed to stand still for Fran as she waited breathlessly for Helen to leave.

Finally, Helen patted Fran on the shoulder again. She stood up from the cot.

"Okay, Soren," Helen said. "I need to write the script for our young star, while we still have some daylight.

Helen went to an open container on the other side of the tent and began searching for something. She turned over objects inside the container, lifted other containers, and searched the ground in vain. In desperation, she got down on her hands and knees, looking under the cots. When she got to Fran's cot, her head was only inches from the open end of Fran's pillow. Fran held her breath again, trying to avoid contact with Helen's eyes.

"Fuck!" Helen cursed. "I had a pencil here somewhere. Where the fuck did it go? I'll tear this tent apart until I find it."

"Relax. I've got a pen you can use," Soren said. "We'll find it later. It's got to be here somewhere."

Fran held her breath, waiting to see whether Soren could calm Helen one more time. She wiped her brow yet again.

"Okay, fine," Helen huffed. "Find me a piece of paper and let's get to work."

Finally realizing that she'd been holding her breath, Fran exhaled silently and gradually while Soren and Helen sat down in their folding camp chairs. Soren found a piece of paper to go with his pen. He handed it to Helen, along with a magazine for her to write on. While they were occupied with getting themselves settled, Fran unobtrusively pushed her pencil and scrap of paper further into their pillow hideaway.

"So, what do I want to tell Whitney in our ransom video?" Helen asked aloud.

Fran lay back on her cot and closed her eyes. But while her eyes might have been closed, but her ears were fully awake.

Her life - and the life of her unborn child - depended on it.

CHAPTER 8

FRAN SAT on the edge of her cot, staring into the lens of a tripod-mounted compact video camera. Haggard from worry and lack of sleep, her eyes were bloodshot with dark bags sagging below them. She turned her right shoulder towards the camera, allowing Soren to zoom in on her healing wound.

Soren leaned over the camera, watching the tiny screen as Fran's wound filled the screen. After a moment, he zoomed out again until the screen showed Fran's image from the chest up. Beside Soren, Helen held a page of paper with the script for her ransom demands. Fran took the script, faced the camera, and cleared her voice.

"Go," Helen ordered.

"Hello, Dan. I want you to know that I am being treated well. Although I suffered a minor injury in the confusion last week, I have received medical attention and I am in excellent health. My captor's demands are simple. Their argument is with Angela Baranyi, not with you or me. They wish to exchange me for Angela, since she has a large debt to repay. We will be contacting you again with instructions for where and when we will do the exchange. If you do not follow those instructions to the word, I am instructed to tell you that you will never see me alive again."

Fran's eyes began to water. She looked down and took a moment to compose herself. She lifted her head and stared into the camera again, this time with a look of resolve.

"Dan, you probably think that the person who abducted me is a psychopath, but I am asking you not to judge a book by its cover. She is really a kind, caring person like the rest of us. Please try to overlook her anger and see her good side. Do as she asks … for the sake of our baby. I love you."

By the time Fran finished, rage had filled Helen's eyes. Her jaw was clenched and the muscles in her neck stood out like thick ropes.

"Stop the fucking camera!" she screamed. She lunged at Fran, grabbing her by the collar of her camouflage t-shirt, jerking her to her feet. "You cunt! I told you to read the script … nothing more, nothing less! Was that too hard to understand? Do you want to live long enough to have your baby and see your boyfriend again? What the fuck is wrong with you!"

Helen continued to shake Fran back and forth violently. Finally, she pulled Fran so close that the two women were nose to nose. Soren leapt to Fran's aid, using his strength to pull Helen away.

"Teri! Stop it! Don't hurt her!" he yelled.

Helen's eyes turned to Soren, exploding with rage.

"Who do you think you're talking to? Who the fuck is Teri?" she screamed. "This is Lady Helen you're talking to, remember? Now, get back behind that camera before I use it to show the world what a weakling you really are. Get away from me!"

Soren's body wilted under Helen's rage. Without a word, he took his place meekly behind the camera again. Helen turned her glare back to Fran.

Fran tried to speak, but only managed to emit a weak croak. She swallowed as she tried to gather her thoughts.

"I was just trying to help," she finally whispered. "I don't think you are evil. You just want your debt repaid. I see that. I just wanted Dan to know that you're a human being, not a monster."

Helen's angry eyes bored into Fran's like lasers for a few seconds. Then her anger started to soften. The rage in her eyes was gradually replaced by a glazed, distant look as her personality transformed. Fran held her breath while Helen's softer, mild-mannered side slowly re-emerged. Finally, Fran felt the grip loosen on her t-shirt. Relieved, she let out a long, slow breath.

"You're right, of course," Helen whispered. "I'm not a monster. Nobody really understands me … that's all I've really wanted … for people to understand …"

FRAN LEANED forward awkwardly, picked up the chain attached to her ankle, and moved it from her cot to the floor. Then, she stood up, put her hands on her lower back, and arched her spine backwards to stretch her aching back muscles. She picked up a length of chain and paced back and forth the best she could, trying to take some high steps to stretch out her legs. She felt beads of sweat trickling slowly down her chest between her breasts, then she tugged at the back of her t-shirt to peel it from her sticky back. She felt as though the oppressive afternoon desert heat, combined with the suffocating boredom of captivity, were slowly sucking the life from her.

Soren sat in front of her in a foldout chair with his laptop computer in his lap. He let out a long, drawn-out sigh as the laptop spat a DVD from its disc drive. He slipped the disc into a white envelope, allowing a triumphant smile to cross his face as he slammed the laptop closed.

"It's finished," he shouted to Helen. "Do you want me to drive into the city? If I send it this afternoon, Whitney should get it in the morning."

"It's all right," Helen answered. "I've been away from work too long already and people will be starting to ask questions. I'll deliver it to UPS on my way back."

"No, it's too risky," Soren said. "What if they track the package back and find you on a security video? I'll do it for you."

"Don't be stupid," Helen countered. "Every police department on the planet is looking for you right now. But so far, nobody knows *I'm* involved."

"And that's the way we want to keep it," Soren argued. "Let me do it."

Helen spun around, glared at Soren, and took a menacing step towards him. Fascinated, Fran watched as Helen once again went into her Jekyll and Hyde transformation, unleashing her anger on Soren.

"I said I'd do it!" Helen screamed. "What don't you understand? Why aren't you listening to me!"

Fascinated by Helen's sudden transformation, Fran watched Soren cower again, his shoulders slumping and his eyes looking down at the ground.

"Okay, Ter … Helen … I hear you. You're right. Just make sure nobody recognizes you. When are you leaving?" he asked.

"Right away," Helen snapped. "I have some business to tend to in Vegas over the weekend, but I'll be back at my desk in D.C. on Monday morning. As far as they know at work, my poor father in Nevada is still clinging to life. I've told them I may need to fly out here again on short notice. They're so accommodating," she added, laughing sarcastically. Then she glanced in Fran's direction.

Seeing her pregnant captive had an almost immediate calming effect on Helen. The reason for the transformation did not go unnoticed by Fran. Helen walked over to her and placed her hand on her shoulder.

"Dan should get our ransom demands sometime tomorrow," Helen said softly. "Don't worry, dear. He's a smart man. He'll do the right thing." She patted Fran on the back and the two women locked eyes. Fran saw a hint of empathy - the seeds of an unspoken bond that seemed to be forming between them. And in that moment, Fran felt a faint glimmer of hope beginning to emerge for the first time since this latest, unexpected, nightmare began.

DAN FINISHED toweling himself and slipped into his training suit and flip flops. He continued drying his hair as he walked from the pool deck towards the house. He opened the sliding glass door and entered the kitchen. As he continued to dry his hair, the early morning silence was disturbed by the sound of the doorbell.

"Again?" Dan said aloud to himself. "Why does everybody pick this time of morning to ring the doorbell?"

He dropped his towel on a chair and hurried to the front door. As he opened the door, he was startled by the sight of a woman dressed in a brown UPS uniform. Flashbacks of chaotic images, along with the sounds of screaming and gunfire, raced through Dan's mind as he unconsciously began reliving the events of Fran's abduction.

"Good morning," the agent said. "Are you alright, sir?"

The UPS agent's words startled Dan back into the present.

"Uh … yeah, I'm okay," he answered.

"Is there a Dan Whitney here?" the agent asked.

"Yeah, that's me," Dan continued.

"Sign here, please," the woman said, handing Dan an electronic pad. He scribbled his electronic signature on the pad and returned it to the agent. In return, she handed him a small padded envelope.

"Thanks. Have a good day," the woman said cheerily. She turned and hurried back to her brown delivery van. Dan examined the envelope, closed the door behind him, and ripped open the package as he hurried back to the kitchen. He pulled a white envelope containing a DVD from the package as he entered the room. Agent Simpson's warning about not handling a ransom note was the furthest thing from his mind at that moment. He flipped up the screen, waking up his laptop on kitchen table. He popped the DVD into the machine's disc drive and waited impatiently for the disc to start playing. After a few seconds, an image appeared on the screen, displaying the head and shoulders of a figure clad entirely in black, except for the eyes.

The person in the video started talking. The voice was altered electronically to disguise its identity, but Dan was captivated by the person's eyes as he listened to the eerie electronic voice.

"Hello Dr. Whitney," the voice began. "We have your girlfriend, Francesca. If you ever want to see her again and see your baby alive, listen carefully …"

The voice droned on in the background, but Dan wasn't listening. He was transfixed by the eyes of the mysterious person in the video.

"It's her again!" he whispered to himself. "Who the hell *is* she?"

AGENTS Simpson and Martinelli sat around the kitchen table with Dan, Angela, and Susan Keaner, watching as the ransom video ended. When it was over, they all sat in eerie silence until Martinelli finally cleared his throat and made eye contact with his partner. Simpson nodded, giving him the floor.

"So, it looks like we need to get ready for a hostage exchange," Martinelli announced.

"We can't do that!" Dan interrupted. "You heard what she said about Fran and the baby. She specifically said not to involve the police. We can't take that risk!"

"Why are you so sure it's a woman, Dan?" Simpson responded.

"You heard Fran," Dan said, clearly frustrated. "She referred to her captor as a woman. And it's in the eyes. I've seen those eyes before in Darwin and Hanoi! I'm sure of it! I'm sure she was behind the plane crash and the bombing. That means Soren Kristiansen is mixed up in this too. I already told you that. What have you guys done about it!"

"We're doing our best, Dan," Simpson answered. "Kristiansen's disappeared. He could be anywhere on the planet right now."

Angela let out an exasperated huff and rolled her eyes. "Well, your best just isn't good enough. Can't you see how frail Fran is in the video? You haven't even got any leads on that white van yet, have you? Not to mention the destruction of my parents' home!" she shouted in frustration.

"We already told you," Simpson countered. "There's a million of those white vans out there. Be patient, something will turn up."

"Listen," Dan sighed. "We've suffered enough losses. I can't afford to lose Fran and the baby. Angela doesn't want to see anybody in her family get hurt. You'll need to pardon us if our patience is wearing a bit thin."

"Okay, okay," Martinelli replied. "Let's assume it is your mystery woman in the video. We still need to prepare for an exchange. If the captor contacts you directly, tell her you're willing to go along with her. We need to stall for some time … Tell her there's no way that Angela is going to willingly put herself in danger … that you're going to need time to convince her to cooperate. Can you do that?"

"Yeah, I guess," Dan answered reluctantly.

"You can tell them it'll take me a couple of days to travel here," Angela added.

"By the way, Angela," Simpson said. "We were shocked to hear about the explosion at your parents' home. How are they doing?"

"Thanks for asking," Angela replied. "I've been doing my best to make sure they're safe since the explosion. Now that they're okay, I'm determined to stay here in Las Vegas until we find Fran and catch Soren."

Dan found himself distracted while Angela and Simpson talked. His reverie was interrupted by the sound of Agent Simpson's voice.

"What's up, Dan?" she asked.

"I was just thinking," he answered. "Don't you think the last part of the ransom video was funny? Why would she allow Fran to tell us about her?"

"Because she wrote the script for that video, Dan," Martinelli responded. "She's trying to make you believe she cares about getting you and Fran back together. Don't believe it for a minute."

"I agree," Simpson added. "She's trying to get into your head. Stay positive … maybe we'll get lucky and she'll contact you by phone next time."

Having sat silently, listening to everybody else, Susan finally cleared her throat and stood up from the table.

"Well, I hope we get lucky soon," she replied. "I don't know how much more of this waiting all of us can take."

65

PART EIGHT: DAYS OF DARKNESS

CHAPTER 9

FOR THE first time in his young life, nine-year-old Soren Kristiansen felt a sense of pride inside, and he felt excited to go home from school. He carefully folded his arithmetic test, with its ninety-four-percent score and Miss Stone's glowing remarks: 'A+ … Well done, Soren! I knew you could do it!' printed at the top of the page in red pencil. He tucked it into his tattered old book bag. He slung the bag over his shoulder and left the classroom, walking as quickly as he could, his eyes darting around nervously in case a teacher accused him of running in the hallway. He had mastered the art of not drawing attention to himself.

He burst out of the school, still feeling a confusing mixture of emotions - excited to show his father how well he had done at school, but wary of everybody he passed on the street. After all, he had learned father's message well: 'You can't trust anybody. You'll learn in time, son - they're all out to get us.' He kept his head down, compulsively making sure to avoid stepping on cracks and avoiding eye contact with anybody along the way. He stepped off the sidewalk at an intersection and the screech of tires caused his head to snap to attention. An angry driver shouted at Soren through an open passenger window.

"Jesus Christ, kid!" the man shouted. "You trying to get yourself killed? Watch where you're going!"

His body still trembling from the encounter, Soren walked tentatively across the street, keeping an eye out for other cars. He broke into a careful jog as he reached the sidewalk on the other side, still making sure to avoid the cracks. By the time he had covered the last two blocks to the apartment building where he lived with his father, mother, and older brother, William, sweat dripped from his forehead and his shirt clung to his skin. The mid-June stretch of hot, hazy, and humid weather was the first heat wave of the year for Chicago, portending hotter than usual Great Lake weather for the rest of the summer.

Soren entered the decaying building. The air was stale, the residue of years of cigarette smoke, sweat, urine, and hidden mold, all fused into a single stench that reeked of poverty. Afraid of encountering another person in the building's decrepit elevator, he trudged up the stairs to their fourth-floor apartment. Remembering the good news inside his book bag, his step lightened as he reached the fourth-floor landing. The dark hallway was sparsely illuminated by an occasional wall sconce whose forty-watt bulb had not yet burnt out, so Soren ran the remaining distance along the creepy hallway to their apartment. His hand shook as he fumbled with his key, finally inserting it into the lock and pushing the grimy door inwards. He closed the door behind him and heaved a brief sigh of relief at making it safely into the apartment. Then, instinctively, his eyes darted around the dwelling to see if his father was home.

The first thing he saw was his mother, sitting at the kitchen table with a plume of cigarette smoke emanating from the cigarette in her hand. Dorothy Kristiansen's eyes stared blankly into space. Not wasting any time, Soren's eyes moved quickly towards the hallway and his ears perked up, listening for telltale signs of his father.

"Is Dad home?" Soren said to his mother. Her eyes blinked and it took a moment before it registered that Soren was standing beside her.

"Watching TV. Best not to disturb him," she answered, without any hint of emotion in her voice.

Soren weighed her words carefully against the good news he carried in his book bag. His newfound sense of pride and excitement won out. He tugged at the bag's zipper, which had become stuck on a frayed thread from the decaying bag. Finally, he managed to wrestle the zipper free so he could open it. He pulled out his arithmetic test and carefully unfolded it. He gazed at Miss Stone's message one more time, just to make sure it was real, and then he trod slowly down a short, narrow hallway, careful not to make any sound, and emerged into the apartment's cramped living room. His father, Torben Kristiansen, his massive frame sunk into a sagging armchair, had his eyes glued to an oversized, second-hand color TV that he had rescued from the curb on garbage night many months before. A cigarette burned in his right hand and a bottle of Miller High Life rested in his left as he watched *The People's Court*. He wore a cotton wife-beater that was once white, but was now a grimy grey, along with a pair of light blue boxers. A pair of worn blue jeans, reeking of grease and sweat, laid on the floor beside the chair. His feet were bare.

"Fuckin' asshole!" Father blurted. "He shouldn't owe that bitch a cent! Shouldn't even be in that fuckin' courtroom."

He turned his gaze toward Soren and stared. "What's the matter? Cat gotcher tongue, ya' stupid little fucker?"

Soren paused for a moment, second-guessing his decision to show the arithmetic test to his father.

"What's that?" Torben said suddenly.

"Nothin'" Soren answered. He started to turn around to leave the room.

"Come back here, ya' little prick. Show me whatcha got!" the menacing voice hollered.

Soren felt as if his legs were tree trunks, rooted firmly into the floor.

"Come here, I said!" Father bellowed.

Pushed forward by fear, Soren inched his way towards the armchair, his hand holding out the test paper. As soon he was close enough, the older Kristiansen ripped the paper from Soren's grasp.

"What's this?" Torben commanded.

"My arithmetic test," Soren answered in a timid voice. He tried to muster some of his newfound pride. "Miss Stone gave me an A+."

Torben took a drag on his cigarette and then exhaled. He slammed his bottle of beer on the arm of the chair and then pushed his massive frame out of the chair so that he towered over Soren.

"Who the fuck cares?" Torben hollered. "You only got ninety-four percent! What about the other six percent, ya' good-fer-nothin' little bastard?"

He crumpled the test in his fist and threw it back in Soren's face.

"Don't fuckin' bother me again till ya get it perfect! Now get the fuck outta here. Cantcha see I'm watchin' TV!"

Soren bent over and picked up the ball of paper, then he turned a scampered quickly from the room. He stopped in the hallway, tempted to show the test to his mother. She was still staring at the wall in the kitchen. The glowing ash on the end of her cigarette was seriously long, threatening to fall to the filthy linoleum floor at any second. Instead, he picked up his book bag and headed down the hallway to the bedroom he shared with William, hoping his older brother wasn't home yet. He just wanted to be alone.

Once inside the room, Soren felt an inner rage begin to boil. He felt as if his guts were tying themselves in knots. The anger was a part of him that he knew he should never show inside their home. But before he knew it, his fist slammed into the hard plaster wall. The pain in his knuckles was immediate. With it, he felt the anger subside slightly. Then his other fist slammed into the plaster. Once again, he felt a surge of pain in the other hand, followed by a wave of relief from his anger. He allowed his mind to dissociate from the rest of his body, enabling him to watch himself as he pounded the walls again and again. Gradually, his anger subsided and he felt himself regaining some semblance of control over his small world. Too late, he allowed his mind to merge with his body again. Torben Kristiansen's heavy footsteps were pounding down the hallway towards the bedroom. Instantly, panic and terror pushed Soren's remaining anger aside, taking control of the young boy's mind and body. He looked for a way to escape, but he knew he was trapped. There would be no escaping his father's wrath.

BLOODY, beaten, and naked, Soren slunk out of his bedroom and down the hallway to the bathroom. His eyes and ears were hypervigilant to any sights or sounds of his father. The sound of Torben Kristiansen's muttering and cursing drifted down the hallway from the living room. Inside the bathroom, Soren heard the sound of water coming from the shower. He knocked timidly on the door. There was no reply. He tried the doorknob and found it unlocked. Quietly, he crept into the bathroom, lifted the toilet seat and sat himself down. No matter how hard he tried, he could no longer push away his pain and his tears. He sobbed quietly, the sound of his whimpering overshadowed by the sound of the shower. Suddenly, the water stopped. For a moment, the sounds of dripping water and Soren's sobbing were the only noises in the room.

"Soren, is that you?" His mother's voice came from the other side of the shower curtain. A hand reached out from behind the curtain and grabbed a bath towel. A moment later, a hand pulled the shower curtain aside, revealing his mother's emaciated body, wrapped in the bath towel.

His mother knelt beside him. "What's wrong?"

Soren didn't answer. Then Dorothy Kristiansen noticed the fresh bruises on her son's ribcage and thighs. She managed to gather whatever maternal instinct she could muster and put her arms around him, helping him stand. "You need a nice warm shower," she said.

When Soren was on his feet, his mother glanced downward and noticed blood in the toilet.

"What did you do?" she asked. "Why did you make him angry again?"

Through his fear and his pain, Soren felt his old friend, anger, starting to churn in his gut again.

"I'm going to tell Miss Stone," Soren said suddenly. "I don't give a fuck what he does to me."

Fear filled Dorothy Kristiansen's eyes.

"No, Soren!" she begged. "You mustn't! We need him to take care of us."

"He doesn't give a shit about us," Soren cursed. "He doesn't give a shit about anybody but himself!"

"You don't know him like I do," his mother answered. "That's how he shows his love to us. He wants you boys to grow up tough."

"I don't care," Soren muttered. "I ain't gonna keep his secrets."

Dorothy Kristiansen grabbed Soren by the shoulders and locked her terrified eyes with his. "You can't tell anybody. You can't trust them. They wouldn't understand. They'd make him leave and we wouldn't have anybody to take care of us!" Tears spilled from her eyes.

"You know I can't work," she continued. "I'm legally blind. I beg you not to tell anybody. How would we live? How would we eat? It would all be your fault! Is that what you want?"

She reached for the shower and turned on the water.

"Now wash away that blood and those tears," his mother said firmly. "This never happened. You're never to mention it. If you do, your father and I will deny it. You're just an angry, lying little troublemaker anyway. Nobody will ever believe you."

With those words, Dorothy Kristiansen turned and walked out of the bathroom, closing the door behind her and leaving Soren to care for himself.

SOREN HAD just finished drying himself when the bathroom door opened. William, his eleven-year-old brother, poked his head in the door.

"Get the fuck outta here!" Soren shouted. William tumbled into the bathroom. Soren's eyes grew wide as his father squeezed his massive body into the small room with his two sons. In his right hand, he held a small carrying cage. Soren was confused. Their pet rabbit, Bugs, quivered anxiously inside the confines of the cage.

"Why do you have Bugs?" Soren asked.

"Sit down," Torben ordered. "Both of you!"

William sat on top of the toilet seat while Soren sat on the edge of the bathtub. His father set the rabbit cage on the floor and then started running water into the bathtub. Once the water was flowing, he plugged the drain with a rubber stopper. As the tub began filling with water, he turned his gaze to his two sons.

"There's things you boys gotta learn 'bout life," he said. He reached for the cage and set it in the bathtub. As the water rose, the cage began to float. Torben grabbed Soren's hand and pressed it down on the cage. His eyes bored into Soren, full of anger. "You keep pressin' on that cage an' make sure it don't float. You let go o' that cage an' you'll get more of whatcha got from me earlier. Understand?"

The water rose in the tub and the cage began filling with water. Soren's eyes filled with fear as Bugs started to panic inside his prison.

"He's going to drown!" Soren shouted. As the last word left his mouth, Torben's hand slammed into the side of his son's head. Soren lost his balance. His hand abandoned the top of the cage and landed in the water, just in time to keep him from falling into the tub. Torben grabbed Soren's other arm and yanked violently on the limb. Pain tore through Soren's shoulder.

Torben pushed down on the cage and water rushed into the cage again. It was now up to the unfortunate rabbit's neck and the animal emitted squeals terror. Its paws thrashed around violently inside the cage. Torben grabbed Soren's hand and pressed it back down on the cage.

"Don't you dare let go again," he threatened.

Soren shook with fear. Waves of guilt and anger mixed with his growing terror. It was more than his young brain could manage. He sent his mind floating out of his body, allowing him to take in the grotesque scene from a surreal distance. Soren's body went completely numb. By now, the cage was full of water. The unfortunate animal continued to struggle until finally, the thrashing slowed. Bugs lost control of his bladder and bowels, and yellow liquid flowed out of the cage and into the bath water. The rabbit's body went limp.

Torben calmly stopped the flow of water into the tub, then he turned to his two sons.

"It's a hard fuckin' world out there, boys. What just happened to Bugs could happen ta you, any time, any place, if ya know what I mean."

Deep in Soren's brain, part of him knew exactly what his father was implying. That part of his psyche was terrified by his father's words. The numb part of him, still floating above the scene, felt nothing.

"Ya can't trust no one out there," Soren continued. "Everybody's out t'get us. They're all out t'get *you*! The only people in this world ya can trust are me an' yer mama. Understand?"

Soren's head nodded robotically. But the only thing his brain registered in that moment was the dull, lifeless stare of his beloved pet rabbit's eyes. Separated from the rest of his body, Soren's mind continued to float over the scene. It was the only thing that kept him from connecting to the rage that boiled somewhere in a distant, dissociated corner of his mind.

CHAPTER 10

SOREN SAT quietly in his chair, one of three teenagers and their parents who were gathered in a circle. His father, Torben, sat on his left. Across the circle, a middle-aged, grey-haired man's mouth moved. Soren didn't hear a single word the psychologist was saying. Instead, his thirteen-year-old mind was wandering, preoccupied with the enticing young red-haired woman to his right, his case worker Sarah Gilman. He was in the midst of fantasizing about fondling her large firm breasts when he noticed himself growing hard. Suddenly, he felt self-conscious. He forced himself to focus on the man's words.

"What about you, Jane?" the grey-haired man asked. "Do you think it's okay to be angry at your dad?"

"Fuckin' right," Jane answered. "Wouldn't you, Dr. Milner?"

"It's not about me," Milner answered quietly, undeterred by Jane's vulgarity. "Go on. Tell us more about why you're angry."

"It wasn't right. It *isn't* right. No kid deserves to be treated that way," Jane continued.

"Do you agree, Mrs. Bachman?" Dr. Milner asked. He turned to Jane's mother, who sat beside her daughter.

"It wasn't right, and she has every right to be angry at her dad … and at me," the woman said. She took a tissue from her purse and began wiping tears from her eyes. "I feel so guilty for not leaving sooner … for Jane's sake. But I didn't know how I'd survive financially if I left."

"What does everybody else think?" Dr. Milner continued. "Does Jane have a right to be angry? How about you, Soren? What do you say?"

Suddenly the center of attention, Soren felt his body going rigid with fear. His right leg bounced up and down involuntarily in an unconscious attempt to calm himself. His penis deflated rapidly.

"I dunno," he muttered. He felt Sarah's eyes staring at him. The room was silent. Finally, Sarah rescued him by breaking the silence.

"That's okay, Soren," she said. "Anybody else have an opinion? Shawn?"

"I still feel like my abuse was my fault," answered a boy with curly black hair. "Every time I think about my dad, I hear his words: 'You're fuckin' useless. Nobody's ever going to want you.' I believed him. I hated myself for being so useless."

"So, do you still believe him?" Dr. Milner asked. "Are you still angry at yourself?"

"Fuck, yeah," Shawn continued. "I think that every day, dude. It's fuckin' hard to stop believin' it!"

"What about you, Jane? Do *you* still believe it?" Sarah asked, redirecting the same question to the young girl.

"Not anymore … at least not most of the time," Jane answered.

"So how did you manage to stop believing it was your fault?" Dr. Milner asked.

"I couldn't stand keeping the secret. My dad's abuse … the beatings … feeling his hands on me … he made me believe we had to keep it a secret … that nobody would believe me if I told them. But keeping the secret was tearing me apart. So, one night when I couldn't stand it anymore, I finally phoned the cops. I told them everything when they showed up. Now I know the abuse is over. I'm starting to believe that I shouldn't be angry at myself anymore."

"That must have been so difficult," Sarah said. "You were very brave."

Soren felt as if everybody's eyes were on him, even though they were all watching Jane at that moment. All the talk about family secrets made him feel confused, anxious, and angry. The tempo of vibrations in his right leg increased as his anxiety intensified. He looked at his father and saw his eyes narrow, daring Soren to say anything. When he couldn't stand Torben's intense gaze, and the fear it induced, any longer, he glanced to Sarah on his right. Her look was friendly and reassuring, but it also made him feel anxious at the same time.

"You've been awfully quiet, Soren," Dr. Milner said. "Jane felt angry about having to keep the secret of her father's abuse. Shawn feels angry at himself. Can you tell us what makes you feel so angry?"

"I'm not angry," Soren muttered.

"Then I guess I'm a bit confused about why you're here at reform school," Dr. Milner replied. "Doesn't beating up your classmates and defying your teachers seem like angry behavior to you?"

"It wasn't his fault," Torben snapped. "They were all out to get him."

"Perhaps we can let Soren answer that question for himself," Dr. Milner said calmly. Then the counsellor turned his attention back to Soren. It made Soren feel even more uncomfortable. He sensed that Dr. Milner knew he and his father were both lying. Part of him felt like standing up and screaming their family secret to everybody in the room. Then he glanced at his father and saw the menacing, threatening glare in his eyes. In desperation, Soren directed his eyes at Sarah Gilman. Once again, the young woman's eyes were friendly and reassuring, but they left him feeling even more confused.

"My dad's right," Soren replied, barely raising his voice. "Everybody at school was out to get me. It wasn't my fault. I don't wanna talk about it."

"That's alright," Sarah said, coming to Soren's rescue again. "You're new to the group. We know it takes a while to feel comfortable … to feel like you can trust us."

Dr. Milner looked disapprovingly at Sarah, then he looked at his watch. "It looks like we're running out of time and we need to wind things up. Does anybody else have anything they'd like to add?"

He looked around the room at each participant, but there were no further comments.

"Then I'd like to thank Mrs. Bachman and Mr. Kristiansen for joining us today. And thanks to Sarah for sitting in with us too. Remember, you're all welcome to join our family group every week at the same time. I hope I'll see you all again," Dr. Milner concluded.

As people vacated the room, Torben Kristiansen lingered behind with his son, planting himself menacingly between Soren and the door.

"You done good, kid," Torben whispered under his breath. "We're family. We gotta stick together."

"Yeah, right," Soren mumbled. "Family."

SOREN LAID awake in the darkness of his bedroom. He glanced at the clock on his bedside table. It was just after midnight. He wondered why the other kids hated being here at reform school so much. He laughed to himself. It was the devious, cunning side of himself that was laughing. It was a part of him that had eventually learned to use his anger to protect himself. After all, as long as he was here, he wasn't at home and he was safe from his father.

Suddenly, Soren heard his bedroom door creak open. Light from the hallway leaked into the room and he saw a dark shape silhouetted briefly against the bright background. Then the door closed and he heard the sound of rustling fabric as the mysterious visitor walked towards his bed and stopped to undress. He heard the sound of garments dropping to the floor. Seconds later, a warm, sweet smelling body slid under the covers next to him.

Soren's body stiffened. A warm hand touched him on the chest and began stroking him tenderly. He felt a pair of loving lips gently brushing his. On one hand, the passionate caresses made him feel wanted and loved. It was the one thing he had always wanted. But on the other, the sensations terrified him. His breathing quickened and he felt his heart thumping in his chest. No matter how many times she came to him, he still couldn't get used to feeling her warm, gentle touch.

"You did well in group today," she whispered.

Soren didn't reply. He didn't know how to tell Sarah about the confusing mixture of feelings he'd had earlier that day.

"Is something wrong?" she asked. "I'm here now. You can tell me anything, remember?"

He felt the warmth of her body pressing against his skin. Instinctively, he knew it should feel good when she touched him and when he touched her. He knew she was different from his father. But a huge part of him still felt dirty as Sarah's hand crept slowly downwards towards his penis. That was the confusing part … if it was so dirty, why did he get hard so quickly when she touched him?

"I didn't like talking about secrets today," he whispered.

"It's okay," Sarah said softly. "Your secret is safe with me. I won't tell anybody."

Soren paused to think, but was immediately distracted as Sarah wrapped her hand around his erection and squeezed.

"Ahhhh …," he groaned.

"Shhhh," she whispered. "Not so loud."

"Are you sure it's okay? About my secret, I mean?" Soren whispered. "Aren't you supposed to report what I've told you about my family? Aren't we keeping our own secret? Isn't this just as bad?"

"No, absolutely not," Sarah whispered defensively. "There's a big difference. If a person, let's say it's me or Dr. Milner, thinks that reporting your secret would put you in danger, or cause you psychological harm, we can decide whether or not to report it."

Soren went silent while he digested Sarah's information.

"Are you sure?" he whispered.

"Of course," she said softly. "Remember, what we're doing here is healthy. Think of it as part of your therapy. I'm helping you get over your father's abuse … trying to teach you how beautiful it is to make love with a woman who cares for you."

"So, if it's so healthy, why do we need to keep it a secret?" Soren asked.

"It's complicated," Sarah whispered. She resumed stroking his engorged penis. "Most people wouldn't understand. Just don't worry and leave things to me."

She reached for Soren's hand with her free hand, bringing it between her legs. Soren felt the moisture seeping from between her labia.

"Doesn't that feel good?" she asked. She pulled his hand up from beneath the covers, holding it between their faces for them both to smell. Then she raised Soren's fingers to his lips.

"How do I taste?" she asked. The rich, cheesy, salty taste of her womanhood was more than Soren could resist.

"So good," Soren mumbled. Sarah pressed her lips against Soren's. His hands reached for her breasts, groping them desperately. As he did, Sarah rolled on top of him. He felt her grab the tip of his swollen cock and his body went rigid.

"Shhh … relax," Sarah whispered. "It's where it belongs. It's soft and warm inside me … not like those things your dad did to you. Just let it slide in … there … how does that feel?"

A flood of mixed emotions washed through Soren's brain. His breathing quickened and his heart pounded in his chest.

"Just breathe," Sarah whispered. "Breathe slowly … don't move … don't do anything else … just let yourself relax and enjoy the feeling … that's it, Soren … you're doing great.

Soren focused on his breathing, like Sarah had taught him. It took a minute or so, but he gradually got his breathing under control. Then he felt Sarah start to move slowly. Almost immediately, his body tensed and his fight or flight response kicked in again.

"What's wrong?" Sarah whispered.

"I don't like you moving," he answered quietly. "It feels like he's in me. I'm sorry."

"Ahhh, I see," she replied softly. "Let's roll over so you're on top of me. You can move inside me."

"No!" Soren said quickly. "Then I'm just like him."

"Shhh," Sarah whispered again. "No, you're not. You're just becoming a man. This is the way it's supposed to be. And it feels so good for me when you move inside me. Trust me."

Soren felt the different parts of his brain fighting against each other again. Part of him felt dirty. Another part of him felt angry at his father for making him feel that way. He felt guilty for keeping this secret with Sarah. But the instinctive feelings in his body - the throbbing of his hard manhood inside Sarah's soft, moist vagina - trumped his conflicted emotions. He let himself go and began moving inside the woman beneath him. For the first time in his life, he felt like a grown man instead of a powerless child. And he loved what he was feeling.

"I'M PLEASED to see that Mrs. Bachman and Mr. Kristiansen have joined us again today. And I see that Mrs. Kristiansen has joined us as well. Welcome," Dr. Milner said. He nodded to acknowledge all of his guests. "And once again, I'd like to thank our case worker, Sarah, for being with us today."

Soren's eyes made a furtive glance in Sarah's direction, but he couldn't force himself to maintain eye contact with her. His right foot pumped up and down rapidly, barely helping him contain his anxiety.

"Last week, we were talking about anger," Dr. Milner said. "Jane Bachman let us know that she felt it was okay for her to be angry about what was happening to her when she was younger, but she knows her abuse is over now. She's been able to let go of her anger. Is that right Jane?"

"Damn straight," Jane agreed.

"Does anybody else have anything else to add to last week's discussion?" the psychologist added.

Soren cleared his throat. His leg continued to vibrate. He glanced at his father, whose threatening eyes once again bored into him like red hot lasers. Finally, Soren couldn't stand the anxiety any longer. He accessed the devious, cunning part of himself and made a split-second decision. Without warning, he unleashed his anger, leaping to his feet and turning his livid eyes on his father. Although there was still a hint of fear in Soren's eyes, that emotion had now taken a back seat to his rage.

"I'm fuckin' mad as hell too," he shouted. He raised his fist in the air, threatening to bring it down on his father.

Dr. Milner jumped to his feet, his normally calm demeanor giving way to alarm.

"That's enough, Soren," the man said nervously. "Why don't you sit down and tell us all why you're so angry."

Sarah was on her feet now too, wearing a look of alarm on her face. Her eyes pleaded silently with Soren to breathe and to calm down. Soren took one quick glance at her, but his anger wouldn't be denied. He ignored both Sarah and Dr. Milner. He took a threatening step towards his father, who was momentarily stunned by his son's sudden outburst. His mother's face was white with shock. Soren pointed his finger at his father, holding it just inches from the stunned man's face.

"You're a fuckin' pervert!" Soren screamed. "You've been fuckin' me in the ass and in my face for as long as I can remember!"

Soren turned his glare and his anger towards his mother.

"And you never stopped him!" Soren continued. Tears filled his eyes as a flood of emotions swept over him. "You're just as fuckin' guilty and filthy as he is!"

Sarah and Dr. Milner stood in stunned silence. Torben Kristiansen's face turned red and his eyes filled with rage. He rose to his feet and raised his fist defiantly in the air. But before he knew it, Soren grabbed his wrist and twisted the older, slower man's arm violently, resulting in a sickening cracking sound. His father yelped in pain and dropped to his knees.

"You ever touch me again, I'm gonna fuckin' kill you!" Soren screamed. He launched himself at his father and landed on top of the bigger man. He wrapped his hands around his father's throat. Unable to defend himself, Torben's eyes opened wide with fear. He tried to scream, but only muffled gasps emerged.

"Sarah, call security!" Dr. Milner yelled.

She had already grasped Soren's shoulders in a futile attempt to drag him off his father. "Let go, Soren! He can't breathe!"

"I'm grown up now. I'm going to fuckin' kill him!" Soren roared.

Sarah released her grip on Soren's shoulders and ran from the room while Soren continued to squeeze the life from his struggling father.

Moments later, three security officers, two men and a woman, burst into the room. The two men grabbed Soren while the woman went to the aid of Torben, who laid writhing on the floor, gasping desperately for air. Sarah ran back into the room behind them. She watched helplessly as Soren thrashed his arms and legs, trying to break free from the two men's grasp. His efforts frustrated, he turned his rage towards his mother.

"I never want to see either one of you again!" he screeched hysterically.

With the situation now more or less under control, Dr. Milner looked at Sarah.

"I need you to call 911 right now," he said calmly. "Tell them we need the police and an ambulance right away. Then phone Family and Children's Services and tell them we need somebody here as soon as possible."

Soren's head turned towards Sarah. For a moment, the angry fire in his eyes subsided and he seemed to calm himself. His eyes met Sarah's and he nodded to her, almost imperceptibly, to let her know that their secret was safe with him. After a moment, she responded with the same non-verbal message. Then she turned and ran out of the room.

At that moment, Soren knew his life would never be the same again. On one hand, he felt empowered and liberated. But on the other, he felt a pang of sadness. He wondered if he'd ever see Sarah again.

CHAPTER 11

FIVE-YEAR-OLD Teri Taylor felt the familiar pangs of fear in the pit of her stomach again.

"Mama, where are you going?"

"I'm just going into Elk Ridge for groceries. I won't be gone long."

Teri's mama stood at the tattered screen door, ready to leave the dilapidated old clapboard house. The midsummer heat was oppressive. A persistent housefly kept trying to land on Teri's face. She gave a half-hearted swat at the insect, but her mind was elsewhere. Instinctively, Teri went into defensive mode.

"Take me with you. Pleaaase!" she begged.

"Nonsense, girl. There's no sense taking ya with me when your daddy's here t'look after ya."

"Pleaaase, Mama. I promise I won't be any trouble. All the other kids get to go with *their* mamas."

"I said no, child," Mama said firmly. "I'll be back soon."

"You always say that, Mama. But you're always gone most of the day."

"Can I help it if old Mrs. Johnson needs help with her shopping an' chores? It's what good Christians do, Teri."

"I could help!" Teri countered, searching desperately for a way out of the house.

"That's enough!" a male voice boomed from behind Teri. "Yer' mama said no, an' that's final!"

Teri felt the stomach pangs stab her insides. She felt as if she was going to throw up.

"Dontcha wanna stay home with me?" Teri's dad asked in his thick Southern accent. "I'm just gonna be workin' on this Sunday's sermon." His eyes glared at Teri, letting her know what her answer should be.

"Yes, sir," she answered dejectedly.

"I'll be back in time for dinner," Mama said. "You an' your daddy have a good time."

The screen door slammed, letting in another half dozen flies. It wasn't as if the door, with all of its tattered holes, was any real impediment to the pesky creatures.

Teri knew she didn't have much time. She started running for the screen door. But before she'd taken more than two steps, a pair of strong hands grabbed her from behind.

"Just where d'ya think yer goin'?" Daddy boomed.

"I'm gonna ride my bike over to Anna Mae's" Teri answered. "She got a new Barbie for her birthday."

"You are not!" Daddy shouted. "Those dolls are the devil's work. No daughter'a mine is goin' t'be dressin' naked dolls."

"They're just dolls, Daddy," Teri pleaded. "Barbie doesn't even have real boobies. And Ken doesn't even have a dink"

"Bite yer tongue, young lady. I don't care. It just ain't natural. The Good Lord don't mean fer ya t'see naked bodies."

Teri immediately felt confused.

"If God don't mean us to see naked bodies, how come you've seen me?"

"That's different, girl. We're family," Daddy answered. "Come 'ere. Come an' sit in daddy's lap."

Teri's feet felt as if they were nailed to the floor. She felt the sick feeling rising in her stomach again and her face felt like it was on fire. She knew what was coming.

"Mama an' I seen yer bare bottom from the day you was born. Come here," he insisted. He grabbed Teri firmly by her wrist and pulled her into the sitting room. She dragged her feet, but it was to no avail. When they got to Daddy's tattered old armchair, he lifted her off the floor and into his arms, then he plopped himself down on the chair, with Teri in his lap. He started running his fingers through her hair.

It felt creepy. The sick feeling in Teri's stomach grew more intense. She felt Daddy wiggle in his chair beneath her bum, then she felt a lump underneath her.

"I don't wanna do this," Teri whimpered, tears starting to form in her red eyes. Suddenly she was stunned by a slap to the side of her head.

"If I say we're gonna do this, we're gonna do this!" Daddy bellowed. "I'm the head of this family, an' what I say goes! The Lord said 'Children, obey yer parents in the Lord, for this is right.' Ya don't wanna be disobeyin' the Lord, do ya?"

"No, Daddy," Teri sobbed. She couldn't look him in the eye. No matter what the Lord said, whenever she was alone with Daddy, it never felt right.

"It mus' be just about time fer our little siesta," Daddy said. He looked at the old watch on his wrist. Teri felt a cold chill creeping up her spine. She shuddered. Daddy lifted her from his lap, stood up, and grabbed her firmly by the wrist. He led her out of the sitting room and up the rickety staircase to the second floor. When they reached the landing, Daddy's grip loosened. She tried to tear her wrist from his grasp, but his hand tightened. An unexpected slap to her head temporarily stunned Teri and disoriented her. Daddy dragged her down the hall to her bedroom.

"Daddy's disappointed in ya, Teri. Looks like I'm gonna havta punish ya in the Lord's name. Take off yer dress!"

Teri froze. This time she saw his arm rise over his head, so she covered her head with her hands. But instead, she felt a stinging, burning sensation on her butt, a split second before she heard the sharp smack of his hand. Teri yelped in surprise.

"I said, take yer dress off!" Daddy boomed.

Teri's entire body shook with fear. Slowly, her fingers fumbled with her buttons until they were all unfastened. Before she could loosen the bow that was tied in the back, Daddy pulled it loose and whipped off the dress, throwing it on the floor. He whipped down her panties, leaving her standing in front of him, naked and humiliated.

"Head down on yer bed, girl. Bum in the air!"

She did as she was told. She heard him unfasten his belt and knew what was coming. Her tiny body shuddered with fear as she lay face down on her bed. She heard, and then felt, a rush of air just before she felt the searing heat of the leather strap slashing at her skin. Tears filled her eyes, but she dared not cry. As she had done many times before, she sent her mind soaring into the sky, as if it was a bird. Through that bird's eyes, she looked down and watched the grown man's furious, crimson face as his arm propelled the belt towards a poor little girl's swollen red bum.

When the beating was over, she looked down and watched as the little girl curled up on the bed facing the wall. The man pulled off his pants and crawled onto the bed, pulling her naked butt up against him. She watched without emotion as the man rubbed his body against the girl's backside and fondled her flat chest with his rough hands. She lost track of time. Finally, the man tensed and then his entire body relaxed. She felt as though the little girl beneath her could finally relax too.

She watched until she was sure the man was asleep. Only then did she know it was safe to fly down out of the sky and merge back into the little girl's body.

THE DUST-COVERED, seventies-model Oldsmobile screeched to a stop in front of the tiny church. A cloud of dust caught up to the car, laying down yet another fine layer of grime on the vehicle's exterior. The church's wood siding, peeling from years of neglect and the searing southern Utah sun, bore the same tired appearance as the aging Olds. The passenger door flew open and sixteen-year-old Teri Taylor jumped out. She slammed the door and began stomping away, wearing a determined pout on her youthful face.

The driver's door swung open. Teri's father, wearing his black suit and white pastor's collar, stood up and gave an exasperated huff.

"Stop right now, young lady," he shouted. "I'm talkin' t'you!" He began chasing after her.

"You're not talking, you're preaching!" Teri screamed back over her shoulder. "You treat me like I'm a possession instead of your daughter. Did you ever think to ask what I want or what I think? Just once!"

"It has nothin' to do with what *you* want," her father huffed as he ran after her. "It's 'bout what the Lord wants! And He don't wantcha bein' a cheerleader. D'ya think I don't know what those girls do with the boys on that football team? Those boys only want one thing!"

Despite his age, Pastor Taylor was still bigger, faster, and stronger than Teri. He gradually closed the gap between them as she ran towards the rear of the church.

"So, they aren't any different than you, you fuckin' pervert!" she shouted again, stumbling as she looked over her shoulder at him. As she did, she felt her father's strong hand grab her flailing wrist. A jolt of pain shot through her shoulder as he gave her arm a violent jerk. Her body whipped around and she felt the burn of his hand as he slapped her across the side of her face.

Pastor Taylor looked around quickly, making sure nobody in the tiny village had witnessed the attack. He turned his attention back to his stunned daughter and dragged her by the wrist until they were in the shade behind the church, out of sight from any possible passersby on the dusty street.

"Don't you ever talk like that to me again, you little slut!" he hissed.

"Well, it's true!" Teri hissed back. She spat in his face. "That's not how normal fathers love their daughters! They protect their daughters. They listen to what they want. They don't sneak into their rooms at night!"

Pastor Taylor slapped her viciously again. Teri put up her arms to protect herself, but she was no match for him. This time he punched her in the stomach, and then in the ribs. The air rushed out of Teri's lungs and she gasped for breath. Her head was fuzzy and distant. Through the fog, somewhere in the distance, she felt the front of her dress tearing. A sweaty hand found her breast, then her nipple. It squeezed and twisted it violently. Teri started to scream, but another sweaty hand clamped over her mouth.

"You're hurting me!" she mumbled.

"It's nothin' compared to what the devil's goin' t'do with ya in hell!" he cursed. "So, you listen to me. You're goin' t'join the Air Cadets so you can learn some discipline. An' if you ever say one word t'anybody about me, I'll beat the shit outta you an' putcha out on the street where you belong! Nobody'll believe you. It's yer word against mine … their pastor. Understand?"

He slapped Teri viciously one more time, knocking her to the ground. She cowered as he reached for her again, grabbing her by the wrists and yanking her back to her feet. He pushed her up against the building and she felt the peeling paint scratching her upper back. Pain seared through her shoulder again and she whimpered in pain. He pressed his face up against hers and she felt the heat of his fury in his sour breath.

"I said, d'ya understand?" he hissed.

Teri slowly moved her head up and down.

"Now, do up yer dress. Git in there an' clean yerself up!" he ordered. His voice gradually becoming more controlled. "An' don't say nothin' t'yer mom, you hear?"

He turned and walked away. Teri's body slid down the side of the church, oblivious to the tiny slivers of wood and paint that lodged in her skin, until she finally sat on the ground. She leaned back against the building, her legs fully extended in front of her. Tears full of fear, sadness, helplessness, and rage filled her eyes.

She sucked in some breath and focused on her rage and the energy it generated. Using that energy, she forced the other painful emotions - the sadness, fear, and helplessness - far away behind high, impenetrable walls. She imagined she was Helen of Troy, hidden safely behind the fortified walls of the ancient city - a woman with so much power over men that they went to war to possess her. Imagining herself as Helen made her feel invincible and strong. And it kept the weak, disgusting Teri Taylor hidden safely away.

CHAPTER 12

SOREN FELT the man's fist slam into the side of his head. He reeled across the room, completely off balance, falling and slamming into a glass coffee table. The table shattered and a woman screamed.

"Stop it, both of you! Please stop!" the woman screamed.

The fifteen-year-old teen's rage had taken control, once again called upon to protect Soren from danger.

"You're no better than my old man!" Soren screamed. "You might as well fuck me in the ass like he did, you fuckin' moron!"

"You little bastard," the man bellowed, towering over Soren. "It's no fuckin' wonder nobody wants you! You don't listen to anybody. The only person you care about is yourself! I'll teach you how to listen. I'll teach you some discipline!"

The man dived, trying to grab Soren by the neck, but Soren was too quick and rolled away. As he did, he grabbed a long, jagged piece of broken glass. The man lunged again and Soren lashed out, slashing the man's triceps muscle. Soren's adversary howled and his wife screamed. She ran into the kitchen and grabbed the phone, her terrified fingers shaking as she dialed 911.

"It's Joyce Wilson at 7928 West Cortland! It's our foster son. He's trying to kill my husband! Please help us!" the woman screamed.

"I'm going to kill you, ya little fucker!" the man shouted, oblivious to the pain and bleeding in his arm.

"Not if I snuff you first!" Soren roared back. He held the jagged glass menacingly in front of him, like a knife. He lashed out, trying to keep the older man at a distance. When he looked at the man, all Soren could see was his father. All he could feel was fear and rage churning inside his stomach. As his raging emotions overwhelmed his brain, he felt himself leaving his body, floating over the scene of destruction below.

From overhead, Soren saw himself lash out continually at the older man, keeping him at bay. He saw the man's wife and vaguely heard her screams. He saw himself back the man into a corner, trying to keep him at arm's length with the giant shard of glass. The man tried to lunge at him, but he lashed out and slashed him again, this time in the forearm. The woman started throwing ceramic ornaments and he saw some of them strike his own head and his back, but he felt nothing. Beyond the woman's screams, he heard a siren. The woman ran from the room.

After a moment, he saw two police officers enter the room with arms extended and guns in their hands. They appeared to be shouting at him. He saw the shard of glass fall from his hand to the floor, then he saw himself raise his arms over his head. Almost immediately, one of the officers forced him to his knees. Things started to go fuzzy. The last thing Soren remembered, he saw a paramedic go to the aid of the man whose arms were bleeding. Soren's world went dark and the woman's wailing floated away as a distant memory …

"THE CHARGES against you are most serious, young man. If you were eighteen, you realize you would be facing felony charges?"

Judge Clarence Abernathy peered over his reading glasses at Soren.

"Yes, sir," Soren answered.

"Do you have anything to say for yourself?" Judge Abernathy asked.

Soren turned and looked over his shoulder at Sarah. Part of him didn't give a shit if the judge sent him to juvenile detention for six months. But another part felt guilty about letting Sarah down.

She was the only person who ever really cared about him. Apart from another middle-aged lady in the row behind her, Sarah was the only person who had showed up in the courtroom for Soren's case. He turned back to face the judge.

"Yes, sir. I'm truly sorry for what I've done. I'd like to be sent back to the residential school instead of another foster home. I do better there."

Judge Abernathy looked over the papers on his desk. "Ms. Gilman, would you come forward please."

Sarah left her seat and walked confidently up to the bench. She was wearing a short skirt, well above her knees, that revealed her shapely legs. She wore a plain white blouse, with enough buttons undone for Soren to want to see more. He laughed to himself. Although he'd felt her legs and her breasts in bed, in the dark, he'd never seen her body in the light.

The judge looked up over his reading glasses again, unable to avoid seeing the young woman's legs and bosom himself. He cleared his throat and purposely redirected his attention to Sarah's eyes.

"Dr. Milner's report states that Soren … Mr. Kristiansen … seems to do better in the residential school setting than in foster homes, is that correct?"

"Yes, your honor," Sarah answered. "We feel that it's his best chance for being able to change his behavior and reintegrate into society."

The judge paused to consider Sarah's comments. Then he looked up over his bifocals again at the other woman in the courtroom.

"Ms. Jenkins, would you please approach the bench," Judge Abernathy said.

A tall, shapely blonde woman in a cream-colored suit, expensive olive and cream-colored high heels, and matching silk scarf, approached the bench. Whereas Sarah had walked assertively up to the bench, Rebecca Jenkins was the model of self-assurance. Soren had never seen anything like her in the neighborhood where he'd grown up.

"You appear to have a difference of opinion to that of Dr. Milner. Can you elaborate?"

"Yes, your honor," Rebecca replied. "Soren Kristiansen was raised in the most dysfunctional, disgusting family background and foster homes one can imagine. He has virtually no communication or social skills and little ability to feel love or empathy. A residential school setting is a poor environment for teaching those skills. It does little more than institutionalize this boy, rather than socialize him. He needs a functional, loving family environment if he is to overcome his developmental delays. The foster system has often failed to provide the type of loving family environment I'm talking about. As you know, I represent the League of Christian Foster Homes, which provides functional, loving Christian family homes for children like Soren. Not only do we think that our network will give him the best chance to turn his life around, I personally would like to take on the responsibility of welcoming Soren into our home."

Soren stared at Rebecca Jenkins. *Which planet did you come from, bitch?*

Judge Abernathy peered at the woman over his glasses, then paused for a moment to reflect.

"I tend to agree with you, Ms. Jenkins," Abernathy concluded. He turned to Sarah.

"I thank you and Dr. Milner for your submission, but I think this young man needs to try something different, very soon, or he may be institutionalized and lost to society. I'm granting Ms. Jenkin's request to be Soren Kristiansen's custodial parent."

"I understand, your honor," Sarah answered, trying her best to hide the disappointment she felt. Soren saw her turn around to look at him. He thought he saw tears forming in her eyes, but he couldn't be sure. He had mixed emotions as she gave him a small wave, turned, and then walked from the courtroom and out of his life.

OUT OF HABIT, Soren's mind detached, allowing him to look down from above the Jenkins family's Sunday dinner. He had never sat in a formal dining room before. The modern white china, shiny silverware, crystal glasses, and linen napkins contrasted with the threadbare blue jeans and hoody he wore. It seemed to Soren that he and his opulent surroundings belonged in completely different universes. Dr. Isaac Jenkins, orthopedic surgeon, sat at the head if the table. His full head of silver hair, formerly carrot red, was immaculately groomed. As usual, he was impeccably dressed in expensive dress slacks, a blue pinstriped dress shirt, and a perfectly matched blue and white patterned silk tie. Isaac's wife, Rebecca, sat at the far end of the table, nearest the kitchen. She was still dressed in the same designer dress that she had worn to church that morning, with its palette of autumn colors.

The Jenkins' daughter, sixteen-year-old Cristina, sat on the side of the table opposite Soren. Soren had difficulty tearing his eyes away from his new foster sister's creamy white complexion, blonde hair, and warm smile. Even after four months with his new family, he still felt awkward and uncomfortable in Cristina's presence, and he still had difficulty making contact with her deep green eyes. Her older brother, eighteen-year-old Matthew, sat on Soren's right. He was home for the weekend from Lincoln Christian University. The tall redhead's smiling, freckled face exuded an overabundance of confidence that irritated Soren to no end. Come to think of it, Soren couldn't ever remember being around people who smiled so much. It was so foreign to him that he still couldn't trust that their happy, friendly smiles were genuine.

"Happy sixteenth birthday, Soren!" Rebecca said, holding her glass of red wine aloft.

"Happy birthday, Soren!" the remaining family members chanted, raising their glasses in salute.

Soren felt himself blush. Being the center of attention was the most uncomfortable thing he could ever feel. It stemmed from the message that father had hammered into him. 'Everybody's out to get you. They're all plotting to take you away from us. You can't take your eyes off anybody!' Looking down on the family dinner from above was the only way he could distance himself from the intense social anxiety he felt at that moment. He shifted his attention away from himself. Instead, he gazed down at the huge custom-made birthday cake in the middle of the table. *Happy 16th Birthday Soren* was written in white icing against a chocolate icing background, while multicolored fall leaves, carefully crafted from fondant, completed the custom design. He saw Mrs. Jenkins pointing to his untouched glass of wine and heard her voice seeping into his conscious mind.

"Have some wine, Soren. It's a special occasion - nobody's going to know," his foster mother said, smiling.

Soren felt himself descending slowly from above the scene, his mind gradually allowing itself to merge with his body. He reached out and felt his hand grasp his glass of wine. He raised it to his lips and took a sizeable gulp of his first ever taste of wine. Expecting the red liquid to taste like grape juice, the dry, astringent bite of tannins brought a sour look to his face. He felt himself blush instinctively, expecting everybody at the table to laugh. Instead, Cristina smiled knowingly.

"It doesn't taste at all like it looks, does it?" she admitted. "I still haven't got used to the taste."

Cristina put down her glass and gave her mother an excited smile. Rebecca smiled back at her daughter.

"Excuse me for a second," Cristina said. As she left the room, Dr. Jenkins cleared his voice.

"So, Rebecca tells me that you've settled into Jefferson quite well after the first week. Any more problems with that Vucovic kid?"

Soren's head hung low and his mind raced to find words.

"No, sir," he mumbled.

"I'm the last person to advocate violence, but it was about time somebody put him in his place," the doctor said candidly. "I assume we won't hear any further reports of that kind of behavior."

"No, sir," Soren replied.

Seeing Soren's discomfort, Rebecca jumped into the conversation.

"We had a meeting last week with Mr. Martinez, the guidance counsellor, didn't we Soren?" Rebecca announced. "He told me that Soren is getting A's in every one of his classes so far. He said Soren should be very proud of his progress."

"Is that right?" Dr. Jenkins answered, nodding his head in approval. "Have you joined any extra-curriculars yet? Any sports you enjoy? Basketball?"

"No, sir," Soren answered quietly, finally daring to look up at Dr. Jenkins.

"Not everybody likes sports, Isaac," Rebecca said. "Maybe Soren's more interested in something else … like debating … the student radio station …"

At that moment, Cristina returned to the dining room. She carried two giftwrapped boxes and wore a broad smile on her face.

"Or maybe even the Student Christian Association, like Cristina," Rebecca added.

"Time to open your presents, birthday boy!" Cristina announced. "I wrapped them myself." Rebecca moved Soren's dinner plate and wine glass to the side and Cristina set the two gifts on the table in front of him.

Soren felt himself blush and felt his anxiety building again. Cristina placed her warm hand gently on his shoulder and a flood of other confusing emotions swept over him. Images of his father and Sarah Gilman flashed through his brain at the same time, and his body flinched instinctively. In contrast, the warmth of Cristina's hand was strangely soothing. He glanced quickly at his foster sister and saw something he had rarely seen in a person's eyes before, apart from Sarah Gilman's - empathy and tears. It sent a strange feeling of warmth through his body.

Soren allowed himself to pull back his veil of distrust just a crack. He turned his attention to the carefully wrapped gifts in front of him. Nobody had ever taken the time to wrap a gift so beautifully for him.

"Go ahead," Rebecca urged.

He looked at Cristina and saw the look of excited anticipation in her eyes. Then he reached out and took the first box. He started by loosening flaps of wrapping paper, one piece of tape at a time, not wanting to ruin Cristina's work of art.

"For Pete's sake, just tear into it," Matthew said impatiently.

Soren looked at Cristina. She smiled and laughed.

"It's okay," she said. "You won't hurt my feelings."

Soren let himself go and ripped the paper from the box, which appeared to be from an expensive retail store. Then he opened the lid. He pulled a pair of stylish denims from the box and held them up. Looking down at his own threadbare jeans, he felt both embarrassed and grateful to his new family at the same time. He tried to speak, but the words caught in his throat.

"Thank you," he muttered, his voice thick with emotion. He looked at Rebecca, then at Cristina, seeing the immense pleasure they were feeling from his reaction to their gift.

"Open the next one," Cristina said excitedly.

This time, Soren reached for the second box and ripped the paper from it without delay, revealing another box from a different trendy store. He lifted the lid and removed a stylish teal-colored Merino wool sweater. He'd never handled a sweater that felt so soft. In fact, he couldn't remember ever wearing a real sweater. His wardrobe had always consisted of jeans, t-shirts, and hoodies.

"Do you like them?" Rebecca asked.

"Yes, thank you," Soren answered quietly. He still felt overwhelmed by emotion and was trying not to let it show.

"We thought you could use some new clothes for school," Dr. Jenkins added.

"Thank you, sir," Soren replied.

He turned his attention to Cristina, who was still grinning from ear to ear. Her eyes sparkled

"Look in the box again," she said.

Soren looked back into the box and flipped up the tissue paper that had covered the sweater. He saw a gift card from a shoe store lying in the box.

"We thought you could use a new pair of Nikes," Matthew said.

Soren had to work hard to choke back the flood of strange new emotions that were overwhelming him. He tried to summon words to convey them, but couldn't. Instead, he looked at Rebecca and Cristina and said it with his eyes.

Rebecca saved him from having to speak.

"Let's join our hands and give thanks to God for our new family member."

CHAPTER 13

"WE'RE HOME," Cristina shouted. She and Soren dropped their book bags and hung their coats in the hall closet of the Jenkins home. Cristina made her way into the kitchen to look for her mother. She turned to Soren, who was trailing behind her.

"She must still be at work. Want something to eat before we do homework?" Cristina asked. She grabbed a banana and started peeling it.

"Sure," Soren answered. "You got anything more than a banana? Any pizza leftover from last night?"

"Sheesh," Cristina replied. "Are guys always hungry? You act like nobody ever feeds you."

Soren shrugged and blushed. "I can't help it. I'm still growing."

Cristina opened the fridge and found a large plate of leftover pizza. She put two pieces on a plate, put them in the microwave, and then she poured two glasses of milk while the pizza was reheating.

"I'm glad you joined the Christian Students Association," she said. "The group really seems to like you."

"I'm glad I joined too," Soren admitted. The microwave beeped and he removed his plate of pizza. "I'll say the blessing."

Soren took Cristina's hand, feeling her warmth and her slender fingers in his hand.

"Thank you, Lord, for your many blessings and for sending me to the Jenkins family. Thank you for showing me your way and for showing your love through my new friend, Cristina, and the other Christian Student members. Amen."

"Amen," Cristina added. "That was sweet."

"I meant it," Soren said. "Who knows where I'd be now."

Cristina paused for a moment.

"Why were you in reform school?" she asked. She paused again. "Why were you so angry?"

Cristina's question caught Soren by surprise. Just hearing the words *reform school* triggered a rush of flashbacks, emotions, and sensations - not just of the school and Sarah Gilman, but also of his mother and father. A wave of conflicting emotions surged through him - anger, guilt, betrayal, helplessness, and sadness. He felt hot and the room seemed like it was closing in on him. His heart raced and he started hyperventilating.

"What's wrong?" Cristina cried. She tried to take him in her arms, but he pushed her away.

"Don't touch me!" he gasped. He felt himself leaving his body, as if he was floating over the kitchen. Now safely separated from his emotions, his body went numb. From above, he saw Cristina's fear and the tears of sadness filling her eyes. Then he felt a strange sensation threatening to creep into his own psyche. Was he feeling Cristina's fear and sadness? The thought of feeling her emotions, as well as his own, terrified him. He saw her trying to take him in her arms again. Somewhere in the distance, he felt the warmth of her hands. At the same time, he felt a sensation deep inside that he had always craved - somebody wanting to take care of him. He fought the growing feelings of terror and vulnerability.

"Soren! Talk to me!" Cristina begged, tears streaming from her eyes. "You're scaring me!" She kissed him on his forehead, desperate to comfort him.

Cristina's words and the warmth of her lips and hands slowly drew him downwards and back into his body. He still felt the overwhelming flood of emotions in his body. But the warmth of Cristina's lips, hands, and body comforted him and helped him tolerate his emotions. Cristina's face slowly came back into focus. At the same time, Soren struggled instinctively to slow his breathing, gaining control over his panic and gradually bringing himself back into the present.

"I'm okay," he whispered.

He felt Cristina squeeze him tightly. Then her lips were on his. They were tentative at first, until Soren's body responded instinctively, just as Sarah Gilman had taught him. He was hungry for more of Cristina as her lips and tongue responded. Then, just as suddenly, Cristina pulled her lips away. She blushed, ashamed that her body's primal urges had begun to betray her.

"I'm sorry," she whispered. She briefly glanced upwards towards the heavens, then back at Soren. "I was just scared for you. I shouldn't have asked you about reform school. Mom said I should never ask."

Soren felt another fear. He didn't want Cristina to let go of him. He wanted her to care. But at the same time, he was terrified of talking about his past. His mind raced until he finally managed to find a solution to his dilemma. He felt as if he was putting up a big wall of opaque glass somewhere in his mind. Somehow, he managed to separate his reform school memories from the earlier memories of his home life, forcing the childhood memories behind the glass wall. He was aware that they were there, but he felt nothing. The memories of Sarah and reform school remained accessible in his memory.

"What do you want to know?" he whispered.

Cristina stood up and took Soren by the hand. "Let's go upstairs in case Mom comes home."

She led him out of the kitchen. They picked up their books and climbed the spiral staircase to the second floor. They paused outside Soren's room, but Cristina took his hand and led him to her room at the end of the hallway. They dropped their bags on the floor and she sat Soren on the edge of her bed.

"Let's put on some music," she said. "This house is creepy when there's nobody else home."

She went to her desk and picked up an iPod. Soren heard the music player click repeatedly while Cristina found what she wanted. The sounds of *Reliant K* suddenly reverberated from a small boom-box connected to the iPod. Cristina turned the volume down, so they could still talk comfortably, then she sat on the bed beside Soren. She reached for one of his hands and intertwined her fingers with his.

"Tell me what happened," she said. Her eyes gazed into his, silently inviting him to share his traumatic story.

Soren swallowed and he took a deep breath. He sifted through the foggy images behind the opaque barrier in his mind, and then he chose his words carefully.

"My father was always angry at everybody," he said slowly.

"Did he beat you?" Cristina asked, her eyes moist.

The foggy images of his father's atrocities lurked ominously behind the glass barrier, but Soren managed to keep them at bay.

"Yes," he whispered, refusing to allow Cristina to know the true extent of the abuse he had endured. "So, I became angry too. I acted out at school. I picked fights with any kids that tried to bully or tease me … or any other kids, for that matter. I beat them up just for stupid things, like brushing against me in the hallway. If anybody asked me to do something, I did the exact opposite, just to piss them off. I guess the school couldn't figure out what to do with me, so they shipped me off to reform school."

Soren felt Cristina clutching his trembling hand in both of hers. Her warmth and compassion helped to calm him.

"Mom said that reform school helped you in some ways," Cristina said. "How did it help?"

Soren felt his face growing hot, aware that he was starting to blush. He swallowed again.

"If I tell you, you can't ever tell anybody. Do you promise?" Soren pleaded.

"I promise," Cristina answered. She put one hand over her heart and looked upwards. "God is my witness."

Soren took a long breath while he pondered where to start and what to say. He felt both of Cristina's hands holding his again. The warmth radiating from her hands finally gave him the courage to begin.

"There was this one really nice worker," he said. "Her name was Sarah …"

REBECCA JENKINS inched her sleek white Mercedes C-Class into its spot in the triple-car garage and turned off the ignition. She reached for the leather attaché case in the passenger seat and hurriedly exited the vehicle. As she entered the house, she pressed a button on the garage wall and heard the garage door creaking and closing behind her. Out of habit, she removed her shoes in the back hallway and hung up her leather jacket. After closing the closet door, she scurried through the kitchen to the front entrance in her stocking feet. The entrance was unusually clean, with no signs of teenage clothing or book bags littering the area.

"Nobody's home yet," she whispered to herself. "The Christian Students must have gone late today. Better get out of this suit and start working on dinner."

Rebecca made her way to the spiral staircase and began jogging upstairs, her stocking feet moving nimbly and silently over the plush carpet. As she ascended, she noticed the sound of rock music coming from Cristina's room. As she reached the hallway she paused, deciding to look in on Cristina first. She moved noiselessly down the hallway and the music grew louder. Just as she reached the doorway and opened her mouth to announce herself, she heard a male voice. It stopped her in her tracks. Anger began to simmer inside.

She has Soren in her bedroom? She knows we don't allow that!

Part of Rebecca wanted to burst into the room to catch her daughter in the act of disobeying her. But her curiosity took over, causing her entire body to freeze. She leaned closer to the door, which was still open a crack, to hear what the two teens were saying.

"… Sarah saw how scared and angry I became when anybody touched me … she told me she understood … she didn't ask questions … she just understood," Soren said.

"Did her parents beat her too?" Cristina asked.

"She never said anything about her own past," Soren continued. "But I knew … bad things must have happened to her too … we didn't need to use words … we saw it in each other's eyes."

"She helped you get over your fear?" Cristina asked.

"Yeah," Soren replied. "She tried, anyway. She asked me if I trusted her … I didn't really, but I couldn't say no … so she asked me if I could trust her enough to hold her hand … just like you're holding mine now."

"Did you let her?" Cristina asked again.

"Yeah," Soren continued. "Eventually … it felt surreal at first … part of me wanted to scream and run away … but part of me didn't want her to let go … it felt so good."

Rebecca remained frozen in the hallway. Her ears strained to hear the details of Soren's story, wanting to hear every word.

"What happened next?" Cristina asked.

"Sarah told me we'd need to practice if I was going to learn not to freak out when people touch me."

"Practice?" Cristina inquired. "What do you mean?"

"I had to take turns. After she held my hand, she made me hold hers. Then she asked if she could touch my arms … then my shoulders … then my back," he continued.

"And you had to touch her too?"

Soren nodded. "It was the hardest thing I ever did, but it gradually got easier. The worst was when she asked if she could hug me … I started to panic … but she was so gentle … she just wrapped her arms around me and held me close until I calmed down … it felt so good … until …"

"Until what?" Cristina asked.

Rebecca continued to stand in the hallway, transfixed by Soren's story. She felt as if she was going to cry. Her empathy for the young guest in their home was overwhelming. She could almost feel herself cradling the young man in her own arms.

Soren cleared his throat and mumbled something undistinguishable. Then she heard Cristina's voice.

"What did you say?"

"Until I got a boner," Soren snapped. "I felt like a fuckin' pervert! I tried to push her away, but she wouldn't let go … she said it was natural … nothing to be ashamed of … I'm sorry, I shouldn't be talking to you like this … you're not dirty like me …"

"You're not dirty," Cristina answered. "I've heard words like *boner* and *fuck* before. I don't care. What did she do then?"

"She said I had to get used to touching women if I was ever going to have a girlfriend. She asked if I wanted to touch her … everywhere …"

"Did you …" Cristina asked.

Rebecca realized she was holding her breath. Not only that, she was shocked to feel tingling sensations deep inside her belly and between her legs. She couldn't believe what was happening to her. Her body was betraying her.

This is sinful … I am sinful!

Soren was turning into a young man and he wasn't even an adult yet. Nevertheless, she found his story both captivating and erotic. She found herself blushing, briefly wondering what God was thinking about her at that moment. But no matter how shocked she was at her sinful response, she couldn't tear herself away from her daughter's bedroom door.

"Sarah taught me how to do everything," Soren answered.

Rebecca heard Cristina gasp in surprise. She was ready to burst into the room to protect her daughter, but her feet remained glued to the floor.

"You went all the way with her?" Cristina asked.

Soren didn't answer, but Rebecca knew what his non-verbal response was. The house went silent while the song on Cristina's iPod ended, and while Rebecca waited for one of the two teens to talk. She didn't know why, but she couldn't stop herself from needing to hear all the morbid details. She was both shocked by what the social worker had done with a minor, and yet intrigued to hear the intimate details. The tingling in her belly was growing stronger. She felt the blood flowing into her groin, feeling the heat and her lubrication growing in intensity. A new *Reliant K* song, this time a soft ballad, started playing in the background. Finally, Rebecca heard her daughter's voice.

"Do you like me?" Cristina asked.

"Yeah, I like you," Soren muttered.

"Do you want to kiss me? Do you want to touch me too?"

Cristina's room went silent except for the almost imperceptible sound of the young couple's lips and their breathing. Rebecca felt torn. As a mother, she felt the urge to barge into the room and break the couple apart. That part of her was protective and full of rage. But another part of her was shocked and embarrassed by her body's response to Soren's story. She felt her hand move slowly up the inside of her thigh, sliding under her skirt until she felt her own juices seeping from around the edge of her panties. Finally, she heard her daughter's voice.

"Here …" she said. "Put your hand under my bra … feel my nipple … tell me what it feels like …"

Rebecca found herself pushing her panties aside. It had been a long time since she'd felt this aroused. Her mind flashed back to the first time she and Isaac had sex at his parents' summer cottage - how delicious and hot the forbidden sex had been. Her fingers slipped into the moist cleft between her labia, finally settling on her clitoris. She caught herself just before she gasped out loud. The events behind Cristina's bedroom door suddenly seemed distant and unimportant. She wheeled around and scurried across the hallway into her own bedroom, quietly closing the door behind her.

She leaned back against the door, sliding two fingers into her vagina, then back out over her swollen clit. Her fingers moved in and out more quickly. She felt the tension growing steadily inside her belly, the muscles tightening inside her vagina. For a brief moment, she felt ashamed of what she was doing. But in the next moment, she found herself wondering what Eve must have felt in the Garden of Eden at the time of the original sin. Then she wondered what Soren's cock would feel like inside her. She found herself laughing to herself. She leaned back against the door, hiked her skirt up over her hips and urged her fingers onward. She let herself go, free from guilt, allowing her climax to build. When she finally peaked, she had to suppress her urge to scream. Instead, she emitted an exhausted whimper, blissfully unaware of the teenage voices whispering in the bedroom across the hall.

"You've got a boner …"

"Have you ever seen one?" Soren asked.

"No, but I want to," Cristina answered.

Apart from the mellow sound of *Reliant K* in the background, the room went silent.

"Oh …," Cristina gasped. "It's big … bigger than I expected … can I touch it?"

CHAPTER 14

TERI FELT Tommie Jo's mouth pressing hard against her lips, bruising and insistent. In the darkness and privacy of the back seat of his father's car, his hand groped and squeezed her breast through the crisp white blouse of her cadet uniform. Then his hand moved to the top button of her blouse and popped it free. She pulled her lips away.

"No," she whispered. "Slow down. Let's just kiss … it's nice."

"C'mon, Teri," he begged. "I just wanna feel em."

"No," she repeated. "It's not right."

Tommie Jo pulled back and huffed in frustration. "You afraid yer daddy's gonna find out an' send yer soul t'the devil? Ya don't really believe that shit, do ya?"

"It's not that. I'm just not ready for that yet," Teri answered.

"Well, I am," Tommie Jo replied. He grabbed Teri's hand and held it over his obvious erection. "See whatcha do t'me, Teri. It ain't right to lead a guy on this way."

"I'm not leadin' you on," Teri replied. "I'm just askin' you to slow down, that's all."

"I been goin' slow fer weeks. It's time t'put out or get out, Teri!"

He put both hands on her shoulders and pushed. She fell back against the car door, hitting the back of her head on the armrest.

"No, stop it! You're hurtin' me," she begged.

"Shut up, you little cock teaser," Tommie Jo ordered. "You know you want me."

Teri didn't see his hand coming out of the darkness. It landed hard against the side of her nose, under her eye. She felt something in her nose pop, then she tasted the sweet, salty taste of her own blood trickling down the back or her throat and into her mouth. Things started to go hazy, distant and black. She only felt like half of her was there in the car. The rest of her was somewhere in the distance. She vaguely felt her blouse ripping. One breast, then the other felt the distant sensation of something wet, sucking and biting on her nipples. Then she felt the sensation of her skirt being pushed up around her hips. She tried to fight back, but her muscles were numb and wouldn't respond, as if she'd lost control of them. The weight of his body pinned her against the seat.

Without warning, she felt something hard probing and pushing between her legs, followed seconds later by a sharp pain.

"You feel that?" Tommie Jo muttered. "Y'all feel my finger in yer pussy? It feels mighty fine t'me. Y'all like that?"

Tommie Jo pulled his finger out of Teri's vagina. He worked quickly to undo his belt. Finally, he unzipped the fly on his cadet uniform, yanked down on his shorts, and freed his engorged penis.

Teri's brain became aware of the full weight of Tommie Jo's body on hers, and she felt something bigger and harder probing and pushing between her legs. Her body went on autopilot. Her limbs came alive. She thrashed and struggled, desperately trying to push his body away. She never saw his fist coming out of the darkness again until it was too late and her world went black.

TERI LIFTED the bottle of Jack Daniels to her lips and tipped back her head, taking some of the harsh smoky liquid into her mouth. She tilted her head back, making it look like she was gulping far more than she really was.

The sound of gunfire and dramatic music blared in the background. The flickering light of a TV made like a random strobe light, illuminating the basement family room of Tommie Jo's home as if it was a strip joint. Bruce Willis's voice boomed through the room.

Welcome to the party, pal!

"Your turn, honey," Teri said, her voice seductive and sweet. She placed her lips on Tommie Jo's, letting him get a tantalizing taste of bourbon mixed with strawberry-flavored lipstick. He was bleary-eyed and blissfully unaware of what was happening in *Die Hard*. Teri handed him the bottle and watched him take a huge gulp. He cringed and closed his eyes momentarily as the liquid burned its way down his esophagus and into his stomach.

"Ahhh …" Tommie Jo sighed.

He opened his eyes and passed the bottle to the other teenage boy at the far end of the worn out, sagging couch.

"Am I ever getting hammered," Tommie Jo muttered.

The other boy, still engrossed in the rented movie until now, took the bottle from his friend.

"Have some more, Bobby."

Teri took Tommie Jo in her arms and locked lips with him, twining her legs together with Tommie Jo's while Bobby took a huge gulp of whiskey. She felt his hands slip under her shirt and start sliding over her smooth stomach. She let his hand slip under her bra to massage her breast and knead her nipple. Her hand found the hard mound of his erection beneath his jeans. She looked out of the corner of her eye and saw Bobby staring at them as they made out.

"Oh, darlin, you make me so hot," Tommie Jo moaned in Teri's ear.

"Not as hot as you make me," Teri whispered. "My panties are wet already. Maybe you should take my shirt off to cool me down."

Bobby continued to stare.

"Bobby's goin' t'see your titties," Tommie moaned. "You wanna turn him on too?"

Teri caught a quick look at Bobby, who was now massaging a growing crotch bulge.

"I get hot just seein' both you guys gettin' turned on," Teri whispered in Tommie Jo's ear. "Go ahead."

A lascivious smile formed on Tommie Jo's face as he lifted the t-shirt over Teri's head. He grinned. "You know what I'd really like, darlin'?" he said. His voice was louder and bolder now.

"What, babe?" Teri asked.

"I'd really like to watch you fuck Bobby. Would you do that fer me?" he asked. Teri smiled at Tommie Jo, then looked at Bobby and smiled.

"Would you like that, Bobby? Would you like to fuck me while Tommie Jo watches?

Bobby couldn't believe his good luck. He nodded slowly. "Sure would. You're the hottest babe I know."

"Share and share alike, I always say," Teri answered. "Hand me the bottle, Bobby."

Teri threw her head back and faked taking another large swig. She handed the bottle back to Tommie Jo.

"Let's party!" she shouted. "Drink up, boys!"

Teri reached behind her back and undid her bra, freeing her breasts as Tommie Jo took another large hit of the burning liquid.

"Ahhh …" he sighed again, handing the bottle back to Bobby again. He buried his head in Teri's breasts, taking one of her nipples in his mouth.

Teri looked at Bobby and smiled. "You know what would turn me on even more, and make me wet for both of you?"

"What, babe?" Tommie Jo asked.

"I'm dying to see you boys suck each other off," she said, her voice sweet as honey. "You know … doin' sixty-nine on each other while I watch. I'd be so wet, I'd want to fuck both of you at once. What do you say, boys?"

"Me an' Bobby? With each other? You kiddin' me? The guys would think we're fags if they found out!" Tommie Jo shouted.

"You want to turn me on, or not?" Teri whimpered. "I do things to make you happy. Won't you even do somethin' for me?"

"You know I'd do anythin' fer you, Teri. But this?"

"How hard can it be, Tommie? Us girls do it all the time." She looked at Bobby and smiled. "What do you say, Bobby?"

Slowly and deliberately, Teri undid the button on her jeans and unzipped the fly. She stood up in front of both boys and wiggled her way seductively out of the garment, finally letting the jeans fall to the floor. She closed her eyes, slid her hand down the front of her panties and licked her lip. She sighed as she began massaging herself.

"What do you say, boys?" she asked. "Have yourselves another couple of hits of Jack, relax, and get each other all hot 'n bothered for me. Sounds like a win-win for everybody."

Tommie Jo staggered to his feet and took Teri in his arms, fondling a breast while she kissed him seductively on the lips. He tried to slip his hand into her panties, but she took his hand before he could make any progress. She touched a finger to his lips.

"Tch, tch," she said. "You need to earn your reward. Come here, Bobby."

Teri made a *come here* motion with her finger, inviting Bobby to join her and Tommie Jo. When he was close enough, she took his hand and drew him towards her, placing his hand on her other breast. She kissed him softly on the lips and he responded quickly, wanting more of a taste. Just as quickly, she pulled back her lips and began unbuttoning Bobby's shirt. She cast a look at Tommie Jo.

"What are you waitin' for, Tommie? The sooner you boys get naked, the sooner we all get to have some fun."

Teri turned to Tommie and got him started on removing his shirt. Not needing any encouragement, Bobby already had his shirt and his jeans off, showing off an impressive tent inside his whiteys. She bent down and picked up the bottle of Jack from the floor. She passed it to Bobby, who took another generous swig, leaving just enough in the bottle for Tommie Jo. Teri passed it to Tommie, who quickly threw it back and made it disappear.

Slowly, methodically, Teri pulled Bobby's whiteys to the floor. She turned to Tommie and did the same thing. She fondled each boy's cock gently at the same time, then released them both. She dropped to her knees in front of Tommie and took him into her mouth, teasing his head and rim briefly before she slid down the shaft and took him deep into her the back of her throat. Tommie moaned.

"Come on down on the floor with me, guys. Entertain me and turn me on."

She guided the boys together with a hand on each other's back.

"That's it. Give each other a kiss … That's not so hard, is it?"

Teri sat back and slid her hand into her panties as Tommie Jo and Bobby started exploring each other. She felt the blood surging into her clit and felt a pleasant tickle growing inside. But even better than her growing sexual arousal, was the feeling of power she had over these two boys - and the power she now realized that she had over men.

It's simple, Helen, she said silently to herself. *Give them a little and they'll give you anything you want in return!*

A smile spread across her face, but her eyes were distant. Teri had disappeared. She had transformed into Helen, who was now lost in an imaginary world where she was strong and totally in control - a world where nothing would ever make her feel weak again.

CHAPTER 15

"GET A MOVE on, Cristina!" Rebecca shouted up the staircase. "You're going to be late for school and you still haven't had anything to eat! You too, Soren!"

"I'll be down in a minute," Cristina shouted. Her voice echoed into the Jenkins home's main hallway from her bedroom upstairs.

Rebecca pulled her housecoat together and refastened the sash, then she hurried back into the kitchen to put the finishing touches to lunches for Cristina and Soren. Moments later, she heard footsteps coming downstairs and Cristina sauntered casually into the kitchen. She dropped her book bag on the floor.

"Where's Soren?" Rebecca asked.

"Still in bed," Cristina replied. "It's Tuesday. He's got a first period spare … remember?"

Rebecca stopped to think. "He does? … It is? … Sorry, I guess I've got too much going on this morning."

Cristina rolled her eyes. "Do you ever listen to anything we tell you?"

"No, never," Rebecca responded sarcastically. "Do you need a ride?"

Cristina glared at her mother's housecoat and flashed her a look of disdain. "Really? You're going to leave the house looking like that?"

Suddenly remembering her partial state of undress, Rebecca pulled her housecoat closed because it was coming apart again.

"Don't worry about driving," Cristina continued. "Julie has her mom's car today. She'll be here any minute."

"Do you guys have a Christian Students meeting tonight?" Rebecca asked.

"Yup. It's Tuesday … remember?" Cristina answered, returning her mother's sarcasm. She rolled her eyes again and shook her head as a car horn sounded from the front of their home. "That's Julie. Gotta go."

Rebecca picked up a paper bag as Cristina picked up her books and ran to the front hall closet for her coat. Rebecca ran after her daughter with the paper bag. "What about breakfast? Don't forget your lunch!"

Cristina quickly pulled on her coat, swung her bag over her shoulder, snatched the lunch bag from her mother, and hurried out the door.

"See you for dinner!" Rebecca shouted, but there was no reply. She latched the front door and sighed.

They grow up so soon, she said to herself. Her thoughts drifted to the events of the previous evening. She felt herself blush. It was hard to think of Cristina and Soren being sexually active.

What were you thinking last night? Rebecca thought silently. *You should have marched right in there and put a stop to their lustful behavior. What kind of mother are you?* She felt her face growing hotter as she remembered her own carnal actions. At the same time, she also felt a familiar stirring between her legs and a sensation like fluttering butterflies deep in her belly.

"Stop it!" she muttered aloud, ashamed of her inability to control her libido. She looked upward to the sky. "I'm sorry, Lord. Forgive my lustful thoughts."

She pulled her housecoat together again and ascended the spiral staircase, wondering what she was going to wear. She headed down the hallway towards the master bedroom. As she passed Soren's bedroom, she wondered briefly if she should wake him up, but decided against it. Since he'd lived with them, he'd proven himself to be responsible. She entered her luxurious bedroom suite, untied her sash and let her housecoat slide from her shoulders to the floor. She entered the marble ensuite bathroom, stopping to gaze at her forty-year-old body in the mirror. Her eyes scanned downwards, skipping over the grey hairs that now mingled with her shoulder-length blonde strands. She looked approvingly at her maturing bust, noting that middle age had some advantages. Despite an added cup size, she hadn't drooped appreciably … yet. Her hands followed the smooth curves of her waist to her butt and then her firm thighs. And hardly any cellulite, considering her age. Her fingers traced a path to the inside of her thighs, then over the freshly trimmed landing strip of natural blonde hair to her plump, luscious vulva. She chuckled to herself.

A young guy like Soren wouldn't know what to do with a body like this after feeling up Cristina's little white boobs!

She smiled and then walked over to the giant glass shower enclosure, with its three-hundred-sixty-degree showerheads, turning on the water and carefully finding just the right temperature before climbing in. She allowed the hot water to stream luxuriously over her skin for a few moments before reaching for her shampoo. But where her shampoo always stood on the shelf, her hands found nothing but air.

"Damn!" Rebecca cursed uncharacteristically. Frustrated, she turned off the shower and opened the shower door. Her body still glistening with beads of water, she scurried back into the bedroom suite and quickly threw her housecoat on over her shoulders. Impatiently, she dispensed with tying the robe's sash, instead holding the garment loosely together with one hand while she ran down the hallway to the bathroom shared by the other family members.

"How will I ever get that girl to stop using my shampoo?" Rebecca muttered to herself as she reached the other bathroom. Without thinking, she reached for the handle and barged into the room, her head looking instinctively to the shower on her right. By the time she saw Soren standing in front of her, completely naked with a healthy teenage morning erection, she was halfway to the shower. Shocked, she gasped and her hands went to cover her mouth. In the process, she let go of her housecoat which flew open, revealing her still-damp nude body.

Both Soren and Rebecca stood frozen in a state of shock. Their minds both scrambled to find words.

"I'm so sorry," Rebecca gasped. "I didn't know …"

"It's my fault, Mrs. J," Soren mumbled. "I should have locked the door." He reached for a towel to cover his erection, but he couldn't take his eyes off the erotic sight in front of him. Either unashamed or unaware, Rebecca no longer held her housecoat closed, giving Soren a full view of the front of her naked body.

"No, don't cover yourself," Rebecca answered impulsively. She reached out, took the towel from the youth, and dropped it to the floor. "That's a beautiful erection. You should be proud of it."

She let her housecoat slide from her shoulders and drop to the floor at her feet.

"Do you like how I look? Do I look as good as Sarah? … or Cristina?" A sly smile spread across her face.

Soren's face turned red and his erection began to soften when he realized Rebecca knew about him and Cristina. He froze, unsure what to do or say next. But, without warning, her hand reached out and took his drooping organ in her hand. She started fondling and stroking the velvety warm skin. He responded instantly. As blood began pulsing back into his phallus, it started throbbing and rising again. As it grew, Rebecca's eyes opened.

"Oh, Cristina was right. It *is* big."

"You heard us?" Soren asked.

"Of course, I did," she answered, as she continued to stroke the throbbing hard-on. "Do you think I don't know what's going on in my own house?"

Soren remained silent, lost for words.

"Do you want me?" Rebecca asked. "Do you want to fuck me?"

Soren swallowed and nodded silently.

"Then touch me," she said, reaching for Soren's hand. She placed one of his hands on a breast and placed the other over her closely shaved pubis. She leaned close. She placed her lips over his, planting soft kisses on them while her tongue teased his lips and his tongue with quick flicks. Her stroking motions on his penis stopped. Without warning, her hand squeezed the organ. He groaned with ecstasy. She removed her hand and caressed his chest and nipples before her hands began wandering down his back, over his firm butt, and back to his still stiffening cock again. She pressed her body close to his erection.

Feeling bolder, Soren moved around behind Rebecca, pressing the front of his organ firmly against her until it worked its way into the warm valley between her butt cheeks, while one hand encircled her and fondled a breast and the other stroked the inside of one thigh.

Suddenly, he froze. He pushed Rebecca away from him and covered his throbbing cock with both hands, his face red with shame.

"What's wrong?" Rebecca asked. "Don't you want me?"

"Not like that - not from behind. It's disgusting!" Soren muttered, unable to make eye contact.

Suddenly, Rebecca understood.

"I'm so sorry," she whispered. "I should have known. I didn't mean for you to do *that* to me. It just felt good to have you rub against me there. Did it feel good for you too? … I mean … before you started to remember those awful things that happened to you?"

Soren paused. Rebecca gently lifted his hands away from his drooping penis and took his organ in her hand again. She stepped forward, took him in her arms, and held him close. She felt tears of empathy in her eyes for what he must have endured as a child. After a moment, he responded. She felt his warm body relax and melt against hers. He wrapped his arms around her.

Rebecca tipped his chin up with her other hand until their eyes made contact.

"Caress my ass, Soren," she whispered. "Feel my curves. See how smooth my skin feels? I'm not your father."

She felt his hands move, tentatively at first, then with more purpose, until they began gliding slowly over her buttocks. As his hands explored, she began stroking his erection, which was growing again and was now pulsing against her genitals.

"Let's try it again," Rebecca whispered softly into Soren's ear. "I'll turn around. Just press yourself against me and let it rub. Just let yourself enjoy how it feels."

Rebecca turned around and gently nuzzled her butt against Soren's erection. She took his arm and wrapped it around her, so that his hand laid over the soft skin of her stomach, tempting him with the touch of her warm flesh. Before long, he couldn't resist the urge to move downward and explore her landing strip and the moist cleft between her labia. He started rubbing her clitoris excitedly.

"Slow down," she whispered. "Don't rush. It feels better if you go slow."

Rebecca leaned back and turned her head so her lips could meet his. His lips and tongue responded eagerly while one hand fondled her breast and teased her nipple. His other hand continued to explore, this time teasing and exploring her clit more slowly. She felt her breaths growing shorter and faster while the tension started to build inside her vagina.

After a few minutes, Soren slipped his middle finger inside her pussy. She emitted a long sigh and they kissed, long and deep. She felt Soren's breathing quicken. She turned to face him, then looked down and stared at his engorged cock - not just its impressive length, but its gorgeous girth as well. She needed him inside her.

"Aren't you afraid somebody's going to come home and find us, Mrs. J?" Soren whispered.

"Afraid?" she answered, laughing out loud. "Are you kidding? It isn't just seeing that gorgeous cock that's turning me on. It's the danger - the fear of somebody finding us fucking - that's giving me this adrenaline rush. I've never done anything this bad in my life before … it's absolutely intoxicating. I've never felt such a feeling of freedom. I've never felt so turned on. Fuck me, Soren. I want that beautiful cock inside me!"

She took him in her hand and guided him into her wet, aching womanhood. She lifted one leg and wrapped it around him, pulling his body tightly against hers. Her body responded immediately to his fullness. She wanted more of him. She ground the front of her vagina back and forth over his rim, sliding herself up and down his shaft. She watched him, enjoying the expression on his face as he reveled in the sensations of his rim rubbing back and forth over the most sensitive area of her pussy.

"Sarah told me about her G-spot," Soren whispered. "Is that what I'm feeling now?"

"Oh, yes," Rebecca muttered breathlessly. "Don't stop! Keep rubbing that spot!"

She felt him respond enthusiastically, pressing her body against the wall, thrusting and grinding his cock into her womanhood. In turn, she clamped her pussy muscles around his cock, savoring the relentless rhythm of his hardness. As the tension continued to mount inside her and her breathing came shorter and faster, she also felt a sense of urgency in Soren's thrusts and his breathing. She knew it wouldn't be long before he came. She pressed her clit against his pubis and gripped his cock against her G-spot at the same time. Suddenly, he tensed and tried to keep from exploding inside her.

"Oh, fuck. Not now!" Rebecca shouted. "Don't stop!"

Rebecca clenched her muscles harder and slipped her finger onto her clit as she pumped herself more urgently up and down and around his cock. Unable to hold himself back any longer, Soren spewed jet after jet of semen into her. Her rhythm and her tension continued to build as she continued to pump up and down his shaft. Finally, her pussy tensed, and then it shuddered and gripped his hypersensitive cock, sending waves of ecstasy through both of their hungry bodies as her vaginal muscles convulsed around him. Her fingers dug deep into the flesh of his butt cheeks. Moans of euphoria escaped from Mrs. J's mouth.

Finally, exhausted and panting from the fulfillment of their animal urges, they rested their heads on each other's shoulders. After a few moments, when their breathing had slowed, Rebecca lifted her head from Soren's shoulder.

"That was the best fuck I've had in a long, long time. How was it for you?"

"Oh, yeah," Soren sighed.

Her eyes locked onto his. She sensed that the intimacy of their afterglow was uncomfortable for Soren. He tried to look away, but her eyes narrowed, demanding his attention.

"If you liked that, I can teach you how to make it even better. Would you like *that*?"

Soren's eyes lit up at Rebecca's offer. He nodded his head.

"Then I only have one thing to ask of you in return," she said. Her mood changed abruptly. The warmth in her eyes was instantly replaced by an icy, calculating glare. "You're mine now. Whenever I want you, you can have me. But in return, you're going to promise that you'll never touch Cristina this way again."

Before he could answer, Rebecca reached down and cupped his testicles in one hand. Then she squeezed. Soren squirmed with discomfort.

"If I ever catch you two like I did last night, I'll blow the whistle on you and that little slut, Sarah, at the reform school. You know what will happen to her if anybody finds out? She'll never work again. And I promise I'll kick you out of this house. You're going to be eighteen in a few months. No more reform school after that. No more Jenkins family to take care of you. You'll either be out on the street or you can crawl back home to live with dear old daddy! How would you like that?"

Soren shuddered with fear.

"Mrs. J, you wouldn't!" Soren replied, his eyes blazing in defiance. Rebecca's hand squeezed his balls tighter. Soren gasped in pain.

"No! Please!" Soren croaked. "I'll do whatever you say!"

"That's better," Rebecca whispered. "I knew you'd see it my way."

She stepped back and let Soren's flaccid organ slip from inside her.

"Now that we understand each other, I think we're going to get along famously. I actually fantasized about doing this last night. I thought I'd feel guilty doing you in my husband's house. But, you know what? I was wrong. Fucking you here today was the best sex I've had for at least ten years. It's been exhilarating.

"But, what if somebody finds out?" Soren asked, his eyes still filled with fear.

"I guess we'll both need to wear a mask and pretend so that doesn't happen, won't we?" she replied. "And if we do it well, which I'm certain you will do, nobody will be the wiser."

"What will I tell Cristina? She'll think I don't want to touch her anymore?"

"Tell her you want to save yourself for marriage, or you prayed to God for guidance. Tell her whatever the fuck you want. But don't ever let me catch you touching her again!"

Rebecca Jenkins patted Soren on the cheek, released her grip on his balls and bent down to pick up her housecoat. As she put first one arm and then the other into its sleeves and pulled the garment over her shoulders, she reached into the shower and grabbed the bottle of shampoo that Cristina had liberated from the master bedroom's shower. She turned and opened the bathroom door. As she left, she smiled at Soren.

"Time to get ready for school. We wouldn't want Cristina asking why you're late, would we?"

MAY SUNSHINE warmed Soren's face as he walked home from school by himself. White and pink blossoms covered trees along the way. He had just turned eighteen and Senior Prom was right around the corner. He wondered what Rebecca would say when he and Cristina told her they were going to the Prom together. Only a few short months ago, the fear of being cast out of the Jenkins home for disobeying Mrs. J had paralyzed him. Cristina accepted his excuse about wanting to become a pastor and wanting to save himself for marriage. But Soren knew the time was nearing when had to leave the Jenkins home. More importantly, he knew he had to escape from Mrs. J's domineering ways. He didn't yet know where he was going to go or what he was going to do, but he knew he had to decide soon.

He turned the corner, still deep in thought about his future, and he didn't notice the black limo parked in front of the Jenkins home. He casually wondered who Rebecca was entertaining as he walked up the front walk and opened the front door.

As he entered the house and closed the door behind him, he saw a man in a navy suit seated on the sofa with a cup of coffee. Rebecca sat demurely, but clearly upset, in an antique colonial-style chair. She rose to her feet as Soren set his backpack on the floor and removed his shoes.

"This is Mr. Jeffries, Soren. He's a lawyer and he needs to talk with you."

Soren nodded to Jeffries as the man rose to his feet and came forward to shake Soren's hand.

"Glad to meet you, sir," Soren said.

"Pleased to meet you too, Soren," Jeffries replied.

"Come in and sit down with us," Mrs. J said. Soren noticed that she was wearing her mask as a polite, refined Chicago socialite. It was a definite contrast to the crude, carnal, domineering bitch she became when they were together alone. If only people really knew the real Rebecca Jenkins behind that mask.

"Mr. Jeffries, will you please tell Soren what you've told me?" Mrs. J said.

Jeffries cleared his throat and reached into his briefcase, withdrawing a sheaf of papers.

"I'm sorry we need to meet under these circumstances, Mr. Kristiansen," the man said. "I represent the estate of your late mother, Dorothy Kristiansen."

Soren was stunned. His face remained expressionless as he heard the man's words.

"She died? … When?" he asked.

"Two weeks ago," Jeffries replied. "It was a motor vehicle accident with a tractor trailer unit. She never had a chance. She survived your father by just over a year. You knew that he was stabbed in a federal prison?"

"I didn't," Soren answered, his voice still flat. "But I don't give a shit. He got what he deserved. And he can rot in hell as far as I'm concerned."

"Soren!" Mrs. J exclaimed. "He was your father, that's no way to talk."

Normally passive and cautious around her, Soren glared uncharacteristically at Rebecca Jenkins.

"You didn't know him. If you did, you'd think the same." He turned back to Jeffries. "So why are you here?"

"Because you're the sole heir," Jeffries answered.

"What about William, my brother?" Soren asked, a look of confusion crossing his face.

"I'm sorry," Jeffries said. "He was driving the car. They both died instantly."

The news about William hit Soren hard. He felt tears rising in his eyes, but he refused to let them get the best of him. Instinctively, the walls went up in his mind, pushing the frightening sadness far away. He blinked, then glanced at Mrs. J with a blank look. He blinked again and turned his attention back to the lawyer.

"I still don't get it. They didn't have anything. There's nothing to inherit … except maybe a lot of unpaid bills. We never had any money."

"Apparently, that's where you're wrong," the other man said. "Your mother had a nest egg … three of them, actually."

"Nest egg?" Soren said, puzzled.

"She inherited the survivor's share of your dad's pension. It wasn't much, but she used it to pay for your father's funeral, with some left over," Jeffries answered.

"So, there's not much of that left …"

"Listen to him, Soren," Mrs. J interjected. "There's more."

"It seems she got lucky in the State Lottery. It wasn't the grand prize, but she won over three hundred and forty thousand dollars a few weeks after your father died."

Soren's eyes went wide. Jeffries' words didn't register for a moment. He blinked and then addressed the lawyer again.

"You said there were three nest eggs. That's only two."

"That's right," the man replied. "It seems that she also had a secret life insurance policy for a number of years. It paid another hundred and seventy-five thousand. Your mother was worth over half a million dollars when she died."

Soren stared at Jeffries, then at Mrs. J. "I don't get it. How did she ever afford a life insurance policy?"

"Our accountants think she must have managed all your father's money," Jeffries replied.

"The bitch," Soren answered.

"Soren! That's no way to talk about your mother," Mrs. J admonished.

Soren stood up, glaring and pointing his finger at Rebecca Jenkins.

"You don't know anything! We were dirt poor. She often didn't have enough food for William and me. She watched that bastard beat us … and worse … and she never did a thing to protect us. And you want me to be grateful because she used the grocery money to buy life insurance? I don't want her money. She can rot in hell with him, for all I care. So, don't tell me how I'm supposed to talk about my mother!" Soren shouted.

"I'm sorry," Mrs. J said. "I didn't know."

At that moment, the front door opened and Cristina walked in on the meeting. A look of confusion crossed her face. She looked to her mother for an explanation.

"What's going on?" Cristina asked.

"Mr. Jeffries is a lawyer. Soren's mother has died and left him an inheritance. He's having a hard time taking everything in."

Tears filled Cristina's eyes within seconds. She walked up to Soren and took his hand before wrapping her arms around him and giving him a long, empathic hug. The hug seemed to have a calming effect on Soren. When Cristina released him, he turned back to Jeffries.

"So, what do you need me to do?" he asked emotionlessly.

"I just need your signatures on these documents," Jeffries explained. "After that, we can release the bulk of the money within a few weeks."

"Let's get it over with," Soren replied.

Soren sat beside the lawyer and signed each document while Mrs. J witnessed them. When the signing was complete, Jeffries turned to Soren.

"I'm sorry to be here under these circumstances. Any idea what you're going to do with the money?"

Soren looked at Cristina, then at Mrs. J.

"I've always wanted to go to Bible college … maybe become a pastor," he answered. "I just never thought I'd be able to afford it."

"Then I guess something good will come out of this," Jeffries answered. "I wish you all the best in your future, son."

After shaking hands with Soren, Jeffries packed the documents in his briefcase and stood up.

"I'll see you out," Rebecca Jenkins said, rising to her feet. She walked the lawyer to the front door, accompanied by Soren, who had Cristina's arm wrapped around his waist. Soren noticed Rebecca glaring at them.

"Thank you for your hospitality," Jeffries said, then he turned and let himself out of the Jenkins home. Rebecca closed the door behind him.

When she'd turned to look at Soren, he saw a mix of emotions in Mrs. J's eyes. There was some anger at seeing Cristina's arm around his waist. But there was also sadness and a hint of fear. Soren felt a similar mixture of emotions threatening to break through the defensive barriers in his mind. His relationship with Rebecca Jenkins was a complicated one - love mixed with lust, dominance mixed with submission, resentment mixed with thanks. But both he and Mrs. J knew their relationship had to end someday soon, and that Soren had to find his own place in the world.

CHAPTER 16

TERI TAYLOR gyrated to the blaring music, with its pounding rhythm of live bass and drums. A mass of writhing teenage bodies packed the darkened gymnasium and the air was heavy with the aroma of sweat and cannabis.

"How'd you get yer daddy to let you come?" Tommie Jo shouted over the caterwauling scream of the band's lead vocalist, the relentless pounding rhythm, and the painful squealing of an inexperienced lead guitar.

"I told him the cadets were having a dance. I had to tell him it was chaperoned before he'd let me go," Teri hollered in return.

"You wanna get outta here for a while?" Tommie Jo bellowed. "I gotta bottle out in the truck."

"Okay," Teri shouted, nodding at the same time. "This is fuckin' boring."

Teri grabbed Tommie's hand and led him out of the gym. They ran down a hallway to the rear of the school and burst through the exit into the parking lot. Tommie's decrepit, rusted F150 was only about fifty feet away. They climbed into the cab and Tommie retrieved a brown paper bag with a bottle of Jack Daniels from under the front seat. He twisted the cap open and then tipped it back for a swallow. He handed it to Teri who did the same. Tommie pulled Teri close and pressed his lips against hers.

"Not here!" she scolded. "Somebody might see us and tell Daddy. The football field, under the bleachers."

Tommie needed no convincing. They jumped from the truck, slamming the doors behind them, then ran, tripped, and stumbled down an uneven hill from the parking lot, eventually rolling their way to the bottom. Picking themselves up, they laughed and giggled while they skipped and danced their way to the shelter of the bleachers. Once under cover, Tommie grabbed Teri and pressed his lips against hers. She responded with a light kiss, trying to get him to slow down and tease her with his tongue, instead of trying to force it down her throat. His hands were already under her tank top, making their way beneath her bra. Her nipples were hard and she sighed with a mixture of pleasure and pain as Tommie pinched one of the brown buds. Then, one of his hands was under her skirt, fondling her mound, urged on by the moisture he felt in her panties.

"Well, well. What'a we got here?" boomed a deep male voice with a southern accent. A silhouette appeared in front of Teri, backlit by light from the full September moon.

"Who's that?" Tommie Jo asked. There was panic in his voice. "Is that you, Bobby? Stop fuckin' with us!"

"Ain't no Bobby here," the voice answered. Teri heard a match strike. A black face appeared in the flickering yellow light.

"What do you want, Jerome?" Teri said stoically.

"Just a li'l bit o' what Tommie Jo's after, that's all," Jerome answered. He waved the match and disappeared into darkness. Teri heard shuffling sounds from behind Jerome. Her body tensed, but she refused to let herself feel any fear.

"This is between me an' Tommie," Teri said boldly. "Where's Neveah?"

"She an' her sisters got some gossip t'catch up on," Jerome answered.

"I hear she's real hot for you," Teri countered. "Wants to wrap those long brown legs of hers around your hips and take that black cock all the way inside. From what I heard, sounds like you're gonna get lucky tonight.

"Yeah, lucky!" Tommie Jo echoed.

Suddenly, Teri heard the silent swishing of fabric moving all around her, just before a number of strong arms grabbed both her and Tommie and immobilized both of the young lovers.

"Leggo o' me!" Tommie Jo shouted.

"Shut up!" Jerome bellowed. Teri heard a punch land beside her and heard Tommie grunt. He collapsed in a heap at her feet. By the time she heard the swishing of fabric again, it was too late. She felt at least four strong arms wrap around her, pinning her arms. She tried lashing out and kicking with her legs, but more arms grabbed her legs, rendering her completely helpless.

"You jealous of Neveah gettin' this big black cock, white trash? Well, maybe you're the one's gettin' lucky tonight, eh boys?"

"Yeah," shouted a chorus of voices. Teri's body trembled as she realized how many of Jerome's friends had joined him - probably every one of his black team mates on the varsity football team. She didn't even want to do the math.

"Down on yer knees, bitch!" Jerome shouted.

Resistance was futile. Her legs were kicked out from under her and at least three sets of strong arms pushed her down onto her knees. She heard herself breathing - short, rapid pants that gave away her fear. Without warning, she felt a warm, hard object push at her lips.

"Suck it, cunt!" Jerome threatened. "Nice an' slow. You even think o' hurtin' me, these boys'll beatcha till yer black 'n blue. Y'alll hear me?"

"Yeah …," Teri gulped, almost choking on her own words.

"I didn't hear nothin'! Y'all hear me, bitch?"

"Yes," Teri shouted. Before she could say another word, Jerome forced her mouth open with his erection, driving it against the back of her throat. She gagged and felt like vomiting.

"Suck it, slut," Jerome said sarcastically. "Enjoy this black beauty. He grabbed her by the hair and began yanking and pushing her head slowly up and down his shaft. He was huge and it was all she could do to keep from choking. He gripped her hair tightly and drove her head up and down more rapidly. She tasted salty pre-cum at the back of her throat.

Teri tried to send herself outside her body, trying to view herself from above. But the pounding of Jerome's throbbing organ kept forcing her back to reality. He seemed to last for an eternity, driving her head faster and pulling her hair more violently until her scalp screamed with pain. Finally, she felt his body tense. He drove her head down and pushed his throbbing cock as far up her throat as he could. A hot jet of salty fluid exploded into the back of her throat. Before she could swallow, he thrust again and another hot explosion clogged her throat. He shot at least five or six wads of cum into her throat before his orgasm finally ebbed. His cock continued to throb and twitch in her throat, but the attack finally relented. She managed to swallow the remainder of the thick, salty liquid, and then tried to take a deep breath, relieved that it was finally over. She felt anger rising from deep inside her gut, already thinking of how she could exact revenge on Jerome.

"Not bad for a white hoe," Jerome said, sarcastically.

Then Teri's world fell apart.

"She's all yours, boys," Jerome said calmly. "Lemme' know what that tight l'il cunt is like. Maybe by th' time you got 'er all greased up, I'll be back fer a second round."

By the time they had her on her back, tore off her panties, and spread her legs, Teri had already transformed into Helen. She soared magically, high over the bleachers, climbing upwards towards the brilliant full moon. Up here, she felt no fear or pain. She felt no anger. She used every ounce of energy from those distant emotions to soar, where she felt strong, powerful, and free. The only sounds she heard were the distant, muffled screams from somebody she vaguely knew from another time and another place … somebody named Teri.

TERI RESTED stoically in the recovery room. Showing absolutely no emotion, she stared into the face of the masked nurse standing beside her.

"It's for the better, dear," the nurse said, trying to console the young girl. "This is no time or place for a teenage mom to raise a mixed-race baby … We had to take it from you … You'd have died if we didn't … You'll get over it in time … You'll see …"

"I'll be able to have another one, won't I?" Teri asked, her eyes pleading with the nurse. The nurse looked away, avoiding eye contact.

"Tell me!" Teri shouted. "Will I be able to have another?"

"You'll need to talk to the doctor about that, dear," the nurse answered. "There was already extensive damage to your organs from the rape."

Teri's eyes turned red, threatening to fill with tears. Despite her best efforts, she started to sob. The nurse rested her hand on the teen's shoulder, trying to console her.

"You don't understand," Teri sobbed. "I want a child … I need one … I need to show them…"

"Show who?" the nurse replied, confusion etched on her face. "Show them what?"

Teri sobbed one more time, sniffled, and her eyes turned hard and cold.

"Everybody," she muttered. Anger began to replace the tears in her eyes. She spoke as if she was speaking to everybody in her life who had ever let her down.

"I need to be better … better than all of them," she continued. "I'd love my baby. I'd show it how much I love it."

"Of course, you would, dear," the nurse said reassuringly.

"I'd protect it … keep it safe … nobody would ever hurt my baby …"

A SHORT figure clad entirely in black, squatted in the bushes at the edge of the forest, waiting patiently. Teri Taylor, the good girl, was nowhere to be seen. In her place, Helen breathed slowly and confidently, fondling a syringe full of ketamine in her right hand. It hadn't taken much convincing to get Allyson Grimm from her biology class to steal a syringe full of animal tranquilizer from the vet clinic where she worked part time. The poor girl was so needy and desperate for a friend that she was only too eager to please.

Helen had done her homework. She had calculated just the right dose for Jerome - enough to cause cognitive detachment and loss of motor coordination, but not enough for him to lose consciousness. Then she'd studied his routines. Jerome took the same route home after football practice every day. It was a cloudy early November evening and it was already dark, providing Helen with excellent cover. There was a distinct chill to the southern Utah air and she saw puffs of her own breath. But despite the chill, a steady flow of adrenaline helped keep her warm.

Finally, Helen saw a figure turn the corner and start walking down the street towards her. The male figure wore a black hoodie and was striding along and humming to tunes from an iPod or MP3 player, oblivious to its surroundings. Helen couldn't see the figure's face. But since little light reflected from the skin, she knew he or she was black. She waited patiently, confident that it was her target.

When the figure was only about ten feet away, a dog darted from a yard and crossed the street, heading for the forest where Helen crouched. Her target lifted his head just long enough for her to confirm that it was Jerome. The image of his face from the night of the gang rape was etched in her brain. Her muscles tensed, ready to leap, while she waited for him to walk past her hiding spot. As he passed, his hood blinded his peripheral vision while the booming of hip-hop music in his ears deafened him. He never heard the sound of rustling leaves as Helen leapt from the bushes behind him. She slammed the syringe into the side of her unsuspecting prey's neck and squeezed the plunger.

Jerome acted instinctively, wheeling around to face his attacker. He attempted to swing his arm to land a punch on Helen's jaw, but the ketamine had already made it to his brain, impairing his motor coordination. His fist flew wildly past her head. Helen kicked him behind his knees and Jerome dropped to the ground. He tried to rise to his feet, but staggered and then dropped to the ground again just before he fell face down on the pavement. Acting quickly and propelled by adrenaline, Helen grabbed Jerome's heavy body and dragged him into the forest until they were well away from the street. Once under cover, she pulled his hoody, and the t-shirt he wore underneath, up to his neck so that his chest was bare. She pulled two plastic tie-downs from her pocket and efficiently pulled them tight around his wrists and ankles. Finally, she removed one of his socks, forced his mouth open, and stuffed the sock into his mouth to gag him.

Helen felt her heart pounding and felt a euphoric sensation flooding her body. She felt powerful - almost invincible - as she straddled Jerome and sat on his midsection. She reached into her pocket and pulled out the three additional tools she'd brought with her - her father's old Swiss Army pocket knife, a small flashlight, and some alcohol swabs. She slapped Jerome in the face and waited. He was still conscious but his eyes were glazed, as if he was in another world. She slapped him in the face again to make sure he was aware of what was happening to him. He blinked and gradually managed to focus on his captor. He wore a look of confusion on his face.

Because she wore a black balaclava, Jerome couldn't make out her identity. Helen smiled beneath her mask. She flipped open the Swiss Army knife and turned on her flashlight, laying it on the ground so that it cast a dim glow. She held the knife up for Jerome to see and wiped it with an alcohol swab for dramatic effect. His eyes went wide with fear. His mind tried in vain to struggle against the plastic ties, Helen's body weight, and the ketamine, which rendered his limbs useless. Seeing the fear in his eyes, Helen was satisfied.

With the knife in her hand, she brought the freshly sharpened blade down on his dark skin and cut into it. A muffled, terrified scream came from behind the sock in his mouth. Jerome's body stiffened instinctively beneath Helen. With each cut of the knife and each scream of terror, Helen felt more powerful and invincible. After a few strokes, the pain became too much for Jerome and he passed out. She went to work quickly, carving her message deftly into his skin. When she was done, she opened another alcohol swab and started cleaning the knife. Two swabs later, she was satisfied that it was clean. She put the packaging back into her pocket and picked up the flashlight to examine her handiwork and the message she had carved into his chest:

I SUCK WHITE COCKS

Helen laughed aloud.

"Bet you can't wait to show this off to the rest of the team, eh Jerome?" she said silently to herself.

Quickly and efficiently, she used the knife to cut the tie-down from Jerome's ankles. Then she turned off the flashlight, closed the knife, and put both back into her pocket. Jerome would be able to find his way out of the forest and eventually make it back home. Her mission complete, she turned and walked quickly through the woods until she found the main walking path. Once on the path, she broke into a brisk jog. Feeling the sensations of power and elation flowing through her body, Helen pulled the balaclava from her head and jogged through the night. She felt the cool autumn air blow through her hair and across her face, and she saw her breath as she jogged. As she made her way through the woods and back to her dad's car, she made a solemn promise to herself.

Any man who ever tries to hurt me again will pay the price with his own pain ... just like Jerome did tonight!

CHAPTER 17

CHAPLAIN Soren Kristiansen sat alone at his table in the far corner of the cafeteria. Despite having been at Nellis Air Force Base for three weeks, he'd only managed to put names to a small percentage of the roughly three thousand faces on the base. All the faces looked the same to Soren, so being alone at the table didn't bother him. Except for the few people he had ever allowed to get close to him, like Sarah, Christine, or Mrs. J, he had always been more comfortable being by himself. He nibbled on his ham and cheese sandwich, glancing occasionally at the latest *TIME* magazine on the table beside him. As he watched people come and go, a timid looking young woman with short brown hair caught his attention. She had just finished loading her tray and stood by herself, scanning the tables for a place to sit. He found her strangely attractive. She was barely five feet tall, her skin was pale, and her short hair lacked style. The muscles in her face were tense and she seemed to lack emotion. While he watched, her eyes found Soren's table and met briefly with his. He looked down quickly at his magazine, not wanting her to know that he'd been watching her. When he looked up again, she was making her way towards him. Within seconds, she stood across the table in front of him.

Soren pretended to be surprised to see her. Not wanting to appear rude, he motioned to the table with his hand.

"Mind if I join you?" she asked.

"Of course not, Airman … Taylor?" he said, noticing her rank and the name tag on her chest.

"Teri Taylor," she replied. She studied the name tag on his uniform. "Pleased to meet you, Chaplain Kristiansen." She pulled out a chair and seated herself at the table across from him.

"You're new at Nellis?" the chaplain asked.

"Second day," Taylor said. "Not long enough to recognize any faces, I'm afraid. I just finished Basic at Lackland."

"Welcome to Nellis. I've only been here three weeks myself. I came straight from chaplain training at Maxwell, in Alabama," he said. It felt comforting to Soren to find somebody who was new to the base, like himself.

"How do you like it so far?" Taylor asked.

"Good," Soren replied. "They seem like a good bunch. So, where are you from, Airman? Before Lackland, I mean."

"Uhhh … I'm from Utah," Taylor answered hesitantly. Soren sensed her discomfort with his question.

"So, you're pretty close to home," he replied. "You'll be able to see your family a lot."

"Not really. I'm an only child and my parents and I aren't close," Taylor said.

Soren's eyes met the young woman's dark brown eyes. He sensed loneliness and distrust in them, feelings he knew only too well. He saw the woman's facial muscles tense. Her brown eyes were dark and untrusting.

"My father was a pastor … He was an angry, hypocritical asshole. One day I told myself: 'If he's the kind of man who does God's work, then I don't want anything to do with God or the church'," Teri continued. "Sorry if that offends you, Chaplain."

"Not at all," Soren responded. "Believe it or not, I think I understand."

Memories of his own father flashed through his mind. He felt the anger from his youth starting to simmer deep inside, threatening to surface again. He immediately became afraid of the emotion and tried to push it back behind the walls in his mind along with the memories. Instead, he tried to focus on images of Sarah, Cristina, and Mrs. J.

"How about you?" Taylor answered. "Where are you from?"

"Chicago, originally," Soren answered. "But I lived in Texas for six years for university and the seminary."

"Big family?" Taylor asked.

Soren felt himself fighting to keep the memories and his growing anxiety under wraps. He focused on the image of his mother's lawyer in Mrs. J's living room, telling him that his parents and brother were both gone. He tried to focus on Mrs. J's face. It triggered other images of her breasts and memories of her touching him, demanding that he make love to her. Then the images disappeared, replaced just as quickly by images and sensations from nights with Sarah in his bed at the reform school. He reached beneath the table with one hand and pinched his leg in a frantic effort to keep his mind in the present.

"They're all gone. They died in a car accident while I was in high school," he mumbled, unwilling to reveal the ugly truth about his own father. "I lived with another family while I finished high school. I found God while I lived with them. I wanted to go to Bible school, so I went to Texas for college. I got my bachelor's degree at Texas Christian, then my masters at Austin Presbyterian Seminary."

"I'm sorry about your family," Taylor replied. "I guess we've both been through a lot." She reached out and placed her warm hand on the one hand that Soren still had resting on the table.

He saw her eyes becoming bloodshot and red. He felt empathy in her voice that was genuine. It wasn't forced or patronizing, like it was from people who truly couldn't understand what they had both endured. He felt himself begin to relax slightly in Taylor's presence. As frightening as it was, he allowed himself to partially lower some of his defensive mental barriers.

"So, where did *you* go to school?" he asked. Another moment of silence followed while Taylor seemed to consider his question.

"I didn't go to college," she answered. "I had a breakdown in my junior year of high school, so it took a couple of extra years for me to finish school."

"Breakdown?" Soren asked. "Anything you want to share? … No pressure, if you'd rather not say."

Taylor appeared awkward and out of her comfort zone. It wasn't like Soren to ask such personal questions of somebody so soon after meeting them. He cursed himself silently for being so foolish. But there was something about the young woman that he couldn't resist. Maybe it was the fact that they'd both suffered at the hands of their fathers. Nevertheless, he felt drawn to her, like a moth being drawn to a flame.

"I was gang-raped," she answered quietly. She looked around to see if anybody nearby had heard her. Satisfied that nobody was looking, she continued. "Even worse, I got pregnant. Ironically, I had to have a therapeutic abortion. If my father had found out, he would have killed me. I guess it was all too much for me afterwards, so I fell apart … They admitted me for a while … I was told I had PTSD."

"I'm sorry to hear that. Thanks for sharing," Soren replied. "Forgive me, I shouldn't have asked such a personal question." He placed his other hand on top of hers. "But I admire your strength. It looks like you rebounded pretty well."

"That's okay. Yeah, I managed to rebound, but it took a while," Taylor continued. "I felt lost after high school, so I spent a couple of years in the Peace Corps in Senegal, helping to educate young girls. I learned to speak French while I was there, so when my two years were done, I decided to travel through Europe. I ended up falling in love with France - especially Paris. I vowed to go back there someday."

"So, how did you end up in the Air Force?" Soren asked.

"I was in Air Cadets in high school," Taylor answered. "It's the one place where I felt like I belonged. When I really stopped to think seriously about it, joining the Air Force just seemed like the natural thing to do. So here I am. What about you? What brought you to the Air Force?"

Soren paused and took a deep breath. Talking about himself was always difficult … almost painful. But he felt compelled to reciprocate this intriguing young woman's honesty.

"I did exceptionally well in the seminary," Soren began. "So, when I graduated, I was offered a prestigious job as an assistant pastor with a large, affluent congregation in Dallas. I was pumped. I thought I'd really made it as a pastor. But, to make a long story short, it was a bad experience. I was so naive. I had no idea there could be so much politics in a Christian congregation. I was disillusioned beyond belief. I guess I started second guessing myself. After that, I just wanted to find a place where I could make a difference. When I saw an ad for the Air Force, I thought: 'Why not'?

"Mind if I change the subject and pick your brain?" Taylor asked.

Soren continued to feel a bond growing between himself and the woman.

"Sure, go ahead," he answered.

"What do you know about the officers here at Nellis?" she asked. "One of them - a Lieutenant Williamson - invited me to an unofficial social this Friday night. He said it was customary for the airmen and officers to get to know each other better. But I need to be honest. I experienced a lot of harassment at Lackland. Have you heard about anything like that here at Nellis?"

"Not in the short time that I've been here," Soren answered. Then he allowed himself to smile. "As a matter of fact, I've been invited to the same gathering on Friday night."

"No kidding," Taylor said, also smiling for the first time and even laughing. Soren liked what he saw and he felt even more drawn to her.

"I guess it must be legit if they've invited the base chaplain," Taylor added.

"Yeah," Soren replied, chuckling. "But I've also heard that they know how to party hard here, so I guess we'll need to see what that means." He paused for a second, getting up his nerve one more time.

"Say, are you looking for somebody to go to the party with?" he blurted awkwardly.

He saw a brief look of panic in Taylor's eyes and cursed himself for being so bold again. He shouldn't have asked her. Anxiety started to take over his body, anticipating her rejection. But, at the same time, he knew he needed to get to know people at the base. The thought of going to the party alone was almost overwhelming. Inviting Airman Taylor felt like the lesser of two evils.

"Sure, why not?" Taylor answered, smiling and laughing again. She pulled a notepad and pen from her purse and tore out a page. She scribbled her address and phone number on the scrap of paper and handed it to Soren. "It's in North Las Vegas."

"What's a good time? Twenty-one hundred hours?" Soren asked.

"Perfect," Teri answered. "I'll be ready."

She put the notepad and pen back in her purse, and then looked at her watch.

"Shit," she muttered, then quickly put her hand over her mouth in embarrassment. "Sorry, Chaplain. Pardon my English … I've got a meeting in ten minutes and I don't need to be making any bad impressions in my first week on base. Will you excuse me?"

"Certainly," Soren answered. "I'll see you on Friday night."

Soren watched while Airman Taylor picked up her tray and cleaned it off quickly before scurrying out of the lunch room.

She's a bit timid, but I sort of like that, he thought silently.

Something about her seemed vaguely familiar … Something that reminded him a little bit of both Sarah and Mrs. J … He couldn't quite put his finger on what it was.

I like her. We seem to have some things in common and she seems like a decent person. Maybe we complement each other ... Hopefully, we'll both find a way to fit in here at the base.

144

PART NINE: DAYBREAK

CHAPTER 18

DAN GAZED out over the Thomas and Mack Center as the voice of Major Teri Taylor reverberated from the public-address system. He was impressed. The rally against military sexual abuse was an overwhelming success, with most of the basketball arena's lower seating bowl filled to capacity. He looked down his row at his friends - Angela, Ricki, and Susan - as well as Pam Holloway, Tim Jennings, and Shelley Paul, who had driven from Orange County for the event. Everybody else was listening intently to the major's message, but Dan was restless. Something about the rally was unsettling for him. And no matter how hard he tried, he couldn't put his finger on the source of his discontent.

"I speak for the Undersecretary of the Air Force when I vow to you that the United States Air Force is committed to ending the scourge of harassment and sexual abuse in our great organization. Thank you for inviting me today."

The audience erupted into applause and rose to their feet. Major Taylor forced a humble smile and nodded to the audience, acknowledging their applause. A middle-aged woman with long dark hair, one of the rally's organizers who was moderating the event, came onstage and took the podium from Major Taylor.

"Thank you everybody for coming today," the woman announced. "I know some of you have come a long way - from Utah, Arizona, and Orange County, California to be with us today. On behalf of everybody, I'd like to extend a big thank you to Major Taylor for taking the time to be with us."

The moderator turned to Major Taylor.

"We know you're an extremely busy person and we're so fortunate and thankful that you took time from your busy schedule to be here with us today."

"I'm honored to be here," Major Taylor replied. "Thank you so much for inviting me here to talk about this important topic."

The organizer turned to address the crowd again.

"Major Taylor has graciously agreed to stay and answer some questions from the audience, so if you have a question for her, please come up front to one of the microphones."

A few people, mostly women, moved into the aisles and walked to microphones that were set up near the stage.

"Let's start on Major Taylor's left," the moderator said. "You have a question for the major?"

A middle-aged woman with short, dark hair, dressed in military fatigues, stepped forward to the mic.

"Major Taylor, you say the Air Force is committed to ending sexual abuse, yet every branch of the military continues to let charges of sexual abuse be addressed within the chain of command. Don't you think this is the ultimate conflict of interest?" the woman accused.

"I'm glad you asked that question," Taylor began. "Those of us within the military who are trying to end sexual abuse believe that the chain of command is essential for maintaining discipline within any military institution. We have every confidence that our chain of command can address any behavior within our ranks that defies order and discipline, including sexual abuse. So, we don't see any conflict of interest at all, and we don't feel that any external oversight is needed."

A rumbling could be heard in the audience and some jeers drifted towards the stage. Another woman, visibly angered by what she had just heard, stepped up to the mic on Major Taylor's right.

"That's bullshit, and you know it!" the woman yelled. Shouts of encouragement and agreement rose from the seating bowl. "I was a pilot who experienced sexual harassment from the day I joined the Air Force. And when I was raped, my life turned into a living hell the day I went to my CO to report it. I've suffered from PTSD ever since, causing me to leave the career that I loved. I've listened to you as you've done your PR tour across the country, and I don't think you or the Air Force believes a single word of the bullshit that comes from your collective mouths."

Taylor seemed confused by the woman's accusations. A look of anger momentarily flashed across her face, but was soon replaced by a dazed look. A pregnant silence fell over the arena. Finally, the major looked down, gathered her thoughts, then swallowed and looked out over the audience. Her eyes were red and tears slowly filled them.

"I realize that many of you don't believe me," she began. "But I'm going to tell you something I've never told anybody before … I too am a survivor of sexual abuse."

The grumbling and jeering stopped abruptly and a hush fell over the crowd.

"So, I tell you today," she continued. "That I feel ashamed of what happened to you and every other victim of military sexual abuse. I understand some of what you've gone through. And I am every bit as committed to ridding the military of sexual abuse as you." She paused and looked down for a moment to marshal her thoughts, then she lifted her head and her eyes locked onto the eyes of her accuser at the mic.

"Where we disagree," Taylor continued, "Is that I firmly believe that victims like us can make a difference by becoming part of the chain of command, and by changing attitudes from within the military, so that sexual abuse becomes something that is abhorred by every person who wears a uniform in the name of the United States of America!"

Clearly moved, the moderator placed a hand on Major Taylor's arm and whispered something in her ear. Taylor whispered something back and stepped aside to allow the moderator to take the microphone.

"I'm sure you'll all join me in thanking Major Taylor for sharing such difficult personal information with us," she declared. "I know you understand how difficult it must have been for her to talk about this. I would like to thank you for your questions, but I think that's enough for one day. Thank you all for attending."

After a moment of silence, a smattering of isolated cheers and clapping gradually grew into steady applause, finally growing into a thundering standing ovation for the major. Awkwardly, she waved and nodded to the crowd to acknowledge them, before the moderator took her by the elbow and guided her from the stage.

Dan felt even more unsettled and confused.

"Wow, I didn't see that coming," Ricki announced. She looked down the row and noticed the look of confusion on Dan's face. "Are you alright, Dan?"

"Uh, … yeah, I'm fine," he answered. "It's funny, I feel like I know her from somewhere."

"You do," Pam interrupted. "Don't you remember? You met her at our MSA rally in Orange County a few months ago."

"Oh … that's right …," he answered. "Was that the weekend I brought Anika and introduced her to you?"

"You mean the weekend you took her to Chateau Eden and tried to turn her into a nudist?" Angela interjected, laughing. "She told me all about that!"

Dan allowed the beginning of a smile to form on his face. "Yup, that would be the weekend," he answered.

"You and Anika had just lost Soren's trail and needed some downtime in Palm Springs," Pam added.

"I wish Anika could have been here today. I miss her," Angela continued. "Anyway, that was quite a bombshell Major Taylor dropped on us. She was awfully brave to come out with that in public."

"I'll say," Dan agreed. "I wonder what kind of an effect it's going to have on the whole MSA issue. What do you think, Ricki? You're the one who's researching it."

"I'm not sure," Ricki answered. "On one hand, she's going to get a lot of empathy from many abuse victims. On the other, she's sure to upset a lot of people by defending the military's right to deal with sexual abuse internally."

"Well, if it stirs up more controversy and keeps the issue in the news, that's a good thing for us," Pam added. "Too bad Richard, Gwen, and Miriam are still in Iraq. They'll be sorry they missed this."

Dan watched with interest as a media stampede seemed to be developing at the front of the auditorium. It looked as though Major Taylor had made an appearance on the floor and was immediately engulfed by a crowd of reporters.

"That's for sure," he said, feeling distracted again. He heard his own voice in the distance. "It looks like the major's going to be all over tonight's news. And don't ask me why, but somehow I've got a weird feeling that it's a story that isn't going to go away anytime soon."

DAN FELT the lactic burn in his arms. He dug deep to push past the pain, powering himself through his sprint for the end of the pool. Each successive stroke was more of an effort. His lungs gasped for air each time he turned his head to breathe. Suddenly, his fingers contacted the pool wall and every muscle in his body uncoiled and started to relax. He fell backwards into the water, floating, while his lungs sucked in long gulps of fresh air, gradually re-oxygenating his aching tissues. The pain of his workout was a welcome diversion from dealing with Fran's abduction and his nagging suspicion that the answer to her captor's identity somehow laid just beyond his grasp.

Finally, his breathing had slowed and his mind began drifting back into the present. He rolled onto his stomach, stroked to the side of the pool, and pulled his lean, naked body up onto the pool deck. The evening air was still hot from another sizzling summer day as he walked over to the spa. The hot water provided almost immediate relief for his grateful muscles. He laid his head back, closed his eyes, and tried to relax.

Moments later, he heard the sliding glass door roll open and then close again. He opened his eyes and turned his head to see Susan and Angela moving towards the hot tub, wearing bathrobes and carrying beer.

"Mind if this old hippie skinny-dips with you?" Susan asked. "These ancient bones can always use a good soak. We thought you might like a cold beer after your workout."

"The beer sounds perfect, and I don't mind at all if you join me," Dan answered, surprised by his elderly guest's lack of modesty.

Susan handed Dan two beers, then she dropped her robe and climbed into the spa beside him. "It's been a long time since I've got naked like this. I forgot how liberating it can feel," she sighed. She took a beer from Dan and took a long gulp.

"When in Rome …," Angela said, blushing. She dropped her robe, handed Dan her beer, and climbed into the spa. Feeling self-conscious, she quickly retrieved her beer from Dan and sank down into the water until the foaming liquid covered her nakedness. She joined Dan in taking a long, refreshing swallow.

"You haven't said much over the past few days, Dan," Susan said.

"I guess not," he replied. "It's hard to keep my mind from wandering. I'm trying to imagine what Fran's going through … Worrying about whether she and the baby are still all right. My emotions are all over the map." Dan took a long gulp and let out a satisfying sigh.

"How are *you* holding up?" Dan asked.

"I think I'm still in a state of shock," Susan admitted. "It's hard to feel anything right now."

"Aren't you worried?" Dan inquired.

"Worried? Of course. I can't imagine what she's going through, especially after spending all that time behind bars in Indio," Susan replied. "But every time I find myself worrying, I remind myself of the girl I knew back in Italy."

"She went through a lot when she was young?" Angela asked.

"I didn't realize the half of it at the time," Susan answered. "But she always had that strong, independent side to her. I knew she'd find a way to survive, even when she left for Paris with that Morel fellow. I knew that was all wrong."

"Do you still believe she's that strong?" Dan asked.

"She may not have looked it after what happened in Palm Desert and while she was in jail, but you need to trust in her, Dan," she replied. "You need to believe in her strength. You can't give up."

Dan took another long gulp and then closed his eyes for a few seconds before opening them again.

"You just reminded me of some things that my wife … Chelly … told me before she died," Dan recalled. "She told me that Fran was good for me … That I had to take care of her. She also kept telling me that I had to start taking some risks in life … To 'take a walk on the wild side', as she put it … I can't get those messages out of my head. I feel like if I let anything happen to Fran, then Chelly will have died in vain. I can't let that happen."

Susan and Angela each took another sip of beer. "Did Fran ever tell you how I came to own my gallery in Manarola?" Susan asked.

"No. She never said much about you," Dan answered. "Apart from saying that you were a lot like a mother to her."

"Well, I wasn't always a person who took many risks," she replied. "But it was a matter of taking control of my own destiny. I'd fallen in love with Cinque Terre in Italy. I'd worked hard to start up my photography business and I was doing well. But there was this old guy who'd been the only photographer in town for years. He also had a big art gallery in Manarola and he had a virtual monopoly on the tourist trade. He hated the fact that I was a woman and I was cutting into his business. He did everything he could to try and run me out of town."

Dan took a sip of beer. "And you decided you weren't going to make it easy for him?"

"You know the old saying?" Susan asked. "Know your enemies?"

"A good idea if you're going to war," Angela said, chuckling. "So, you did your homework?"

"Absolutely," Susan agreed. "I found out he had an Achilles heel … two, actually … he liked his wine and he loved to gamble," she answered. "So, I challenged him to a poker game in the local pub in front of all of his buddies. I kept buying the wine and made sure he drank most of it. He was such a narcissistic prick, he thought he could beat a woman at poker without having to think."

"So how did you win the gallery?" Dan asked.

"I let him win most of my money," Susan answered. "But I begged him to give me one more chance to win it all back with one more hand. If he won, he got the rest of my money *and* I promised to leave town. But, if he lost, I got his photography business and his gallery."

"There wasn't much in it for him," Angela said, laughing. "He had virtually nothing to win and everything to lose. But something tells me you weren't as bad a poker player as he thought."

"Yup," Susan said, flashing a sly smile. "I learned poker from my dad. He was like a savant with numbers. He could figure out the odds of getting every poker hand in his head. He made it fun to learn math by teaching me how to gamble."

"So, you got the cards to beat him?" Dan asked.

"Fortunately," Susan answered. "But if I didn't know my odds, I wouldn't have known he was probably bluffing. And I wouldn't have had the confidence to hold onto my cards."

"And you won the gallery," Dan said. He saluted Susan with his bottle of beer.

"It was the first time in my life that I ever took a chance," Susan added. "More importantly, it was the night I learned to believe in myself. So, listen to what Chelly told you … Believe in yourself and believe in Fran. Take a walk on the wild side if you get the chance."

"I'll do my best," Dan replied. "But so much of this is out of my control. At this point, all I can do is help the FBI. If that still isn't enough, then I guess I'll need to see what I can do on my own … I just hate all this sitting around doing nothing."

Susan smiled. "I'm glad to hear that," she said. She took another sip of beer and paused. "I decided I need to go back to Italy. I've been away too long and I should tend to my gallery. I'm an old woman now, and I feel guilty that there's nothing more I can do to help Fran here. So, I need to trust you to find her and take care of her, Dan."

"You don't need to feel guilty," Dan answered. "You don't owe us anything. Coming from Italy to help Fran through her legal ordeal in Palm Desert was more than enough."

He paused and held up his bottle in a salute.

"Here's to finding Fran alive and well," Angela toasted. "And here's to you, Susan. I understand now why Fran is so close to you. I'm glad I met you and can call you my friend."

Dan, Susan, and Angela touched their bottles to solidify their growing friendship.

"On that note," Susan said. "I think I'm going to call it a night. I need to see if I can get on a flight back to Italy tomorrow. Can I get you folks another beer before I go upstairs?"

"Thanks for asking. I think I'll just relax here for a few more minutes," Dan said, as Susan climbed out of the hot tub. She picked up her robe and covered herself.

"I think I'll call it a night too," Angela said.

She slid over the side of the spa and quickly covered herself, still not completely comfortable with Dan and Fran's penchant for skinny-dipping.

"Thanks for the heart to heart, Dan. See you in the morning," Susan said.

"Have a good sleep," Angela echoed.

They each picked up a beer bottle, walked to the sliding door, and let themselves into the house. Angela slid the door closed behind them.

Dan finished his beer, then took a few minutes to lean back and soak his muscles … and to think … After a few moments, he climbed out of the hot tub, grabbed his towel, and began drying himself. He entered the house through the sliding patio door.

DAN SLID the door closed behind him and entered the estate's great room. He paused briefly to gaze at Fran's imposing portrait of Angela while he dried his hair. As he turned to leave the room, he noticed that he'd left his laptop open on the sofa. He picked it up and carried it into the kitchen, where he plugged it into its charger. He took a step to leave the kitchen, then stopped himself. He turned, sat down at the table, clicked the trackpad, and brought the machine back to life.

He clicked on the *Play* arrow to watch Fran's ransom video one more time before heading off to bed. He clicked on the *Fast Forward* arrows, searching to find the last sentence of Fran's message. Finally, he found what he was looking for and replayed it from that point.

'*...Dan, you probably think that the woman who abducted me is a psychopath, but I am asking you not to judge a book by its cover. She is really a good, caring person like the rest of us. Please try to overlook her anger and see that good side of her...*'

Dan stopped the video and paused to think.

"I wonder," he said to himself. He replayed the message again, just to make sure of what he'd just heard.

"Was that in the script?" he asked himself. "Or was she trying to tell me something?"

He closed the laptop and stood up slowly from his chair. Deep in thought, he walked out of the kitchen, into the front hallway, and up the stairs towards his bedroom. It could have been Fran's words, or possibly his heart-to-heart talk with Susan and Angela tonight, but Dan felt something click in his mind. For the first time since Fran disappeared, he felt a faint sense of hope.

CHAPTER 19

SOREN FINISHED making the ham and cheese sandwich and placed it on a military-style mess plate with an apple. He picked up a bottle of water and walked over to Fran, who sat on the edge of her cot.

"You dyed your hair again," she said, her voice matter-of-fact, as he approached.

Soren laughed. "You like it? We can't have people recognizing the old Pastor Soren, can we?" he asked. Sarcasm dripped from his voice. "Here, have some water and something to eat."

"I'm not hungry," she answered. Her voice was flat and devoid of emotion.

"Come on," Soren answered. "You're eating for two now. What about the baby?"

Fran sat in silence for a moment. Finally, she reluctantly took the plate and the water and laid them in her lap.

"I need to pee," she said.

Soren rolled his eyes, clearly annoyed at the inconvenience. He fished for a key in his pocket, then finally retrieved it. He stooped and disconnected the lock that linked her chain to the metal stake that was embedded deep in the desert floor.

"Thank you," Fran mumbled. She nodded her appreciation, purposely making eye contact with Soren.

"Hurry up!" he shouted. "And make sure you stay under cover of the tent."

Fran exited the tent, her chain jangling as she walked, despite her attempts to carry as much of it as possible to make walking easier. She pulled down her sweatpants and panties before settling herself on the portable toilet.

"What happens if Dan and Angela won't make a trade for me?" she shouted back towards the tent.

Soren's voice boomed from inside. "Just shut up and piss! That's none of your business."

"I'm finished," Fran announced moments later. She pulled on her clothes, picked up most of her chain and jangled her way back to her cot, sitting while Soren reconnected it to the metal stake.

"You and Helen disagree about what to do with me," she said, her comment coming out of the blue.

"I thought I told you to shut up!" Soren shouted.

"I agree with you," Fran confided. "They will never exchange Angela for me. And if they *do* agree, you know the police will be involved."

Exasperated with Fran, Soren huffed, stood up, and walked to the other end of the tent to make himself a sandwich.

"You and Helen really want to have a child … especially Helen … Why can't she have children?" Fran asked.

"I told you this is none of your fuckin' business!" Soren shouted.

"She lost a child, didn't she?" Fran continued.

With frustration and anger written across his face, Soren threw the loaf of bread down and turned to Fran.

"If I tell you, will you finally shut the fuck up?" he yelled. He stomped across the tent and stood menacingly over Fran, who was still seated on the edge of her cot. Finally, he conceded a sigh.

"She was sixteen. She was gang-banged by a bunch of guys on the high school football team and got pregnant. Her dad, the two-faced bastard of a preacher that he was, would have killed her if he found out. Turns out she had serious complications and had to have an abortion. It almost killed her and left her so she couldn't get pregnant again. Are you happy? Will you shut up and leave me alone now?"

Fran lifted her eyes to meet Soren's, truly touched by his story. She conveyed her sorrow and empathy to him through her eyes.

"How awful. I am so sorry," she said quietly. A long silence passed between them as Fran weighed her survival options and struggled to make a decision. Unable to stand her indecision and anxiety any longer, she decided to take a chance.

"I could give her my baby," Fran blurted. "I can always have another … she can't … I would do that for her … and for you. I'll help you convince her."

Another moment of silence filled the tent. Soren was distant and Fran wondered if he might actually be considering her offer. Then, abruptly, he came back into the present.

"She'll never consider it," he said solemnly. "She's too stubborn and proud."

"I can talk to her when she comes back," Fran pressed. "She'll listen to me. We're both women. I was abused as a teenager too. Trust me, I can change her mind."

"Enough!" Soren shouted impatiently. "You're just playing with me. You don't really mean what you say!"

Fran's mind scrambled to find the necessary words to convince Soren.

"I don't expect you to believe me. Why should you? What kind of woman would give up her child? But I would do it in a minute if it helps me get out of here alive. I'll still try talking to her. What harm can it do?" Fran said, shrugging her shoulders. Her eyes pleaded silently with Soren to consider her offer.

Soren shook his head in exasperation and turned away from Fran. He walked back to the table where he'd been making his sandwich and picked up the deformed loaf of bread he'd thrown down a moment ago.

Fran allowed herself a satisfied smile behind his back. She knew she was beginning to get into his head.

A CACAPHONY of restaurant sounds made it almost impossible for Dan to hear their server, a middle-aged woman with raven-black dyed hair and an anemic white complexion. She tried to smile, but the strain of her job was etched deeply in her forehead and in the strained muscles in her jaw and neck. Every booth and table in the popular Italian eatery was full of boisterous patrons, each one raising their voices to be heard over the background din. Tiffany lamps cast a yellow glow over tables and booths, while autographed black and white and faded color photographs of celebrity visitors to the restaurant covered the walls above darkly-stained pine wainscoting. Angela and Ricki sat across the table from Dan in a booth at the back of the establishment.

"If that's everything, I'll be back with your drinks in a couple of minutes," the server announced. She wheeled around and scurried back in the direction of the bar.

"Didn't Susan want to join us for dinner?" Ricki shouted over the din.

"She's flying back to Italy tonight," Angela answered. "She felt guilty about leaving, but she feels like there's nothing she can do to help right now. She's a good friend. I hope we have some good news for her soon."

"Anything new from the FBI yet?" Ricki asked.

"Still nothing," Dan answered loudly. "I've been going over and over the ransom video. I still can't decide if Fran was following a script or trying to tell us something."

"So, what do the two of you think you're going to do? You can't meet the kidnapper's demands!" She turned to Angela. "It would be suicide for you."

"We know," Angela replied, looking at Dan for confirmation. "At this point, it looks like our only option is to go along with the FBI. They want us to go along with any exchange, so they can set up a sting."

"I don't mind telling you, that makes me really nervous," Ricki said.

"We're hoping to buy time and get some leads before it comes to that," Dan answered. "How about you? How's your MSA article coming along?"

"More questions than answers at this point," Ricki replied. "But there's a common thread that keeps coming up. A number of people I've interviewed - both women and men - have mentioned that their abusers seemed to talk as though they were acting on orders from somebody higher up."

"No kidding?" Dan said, raising his eyebrows in surprise. "Someone in the chain of command?"

"Not necessarily," Ricki countered. "It could be a few rotten eggs with their own internal pecking order. He could be almost anybody in the military."

"Either way," Angela interjected, "That doesn't make Saturday's message from Major Taylor sound very good."

"No, it doesn't," Dan agreed. "So where do you go from here, Ricki?"

"AP has been pressing me for something soon, especially in the wake of Taylor's own revelations over the weekend. I'm going to write what I've got. Sometimes it's just as effective to raise questions if you don't have any concrete answers. I hope to publish it tomorrow or the next day. What about you guys?"

"Not much I can do now," Dan answered. "I'm just waiting to hear from the kidnappers. In the meantime, Angela and I thought we might do some searching for white delivery vans."

"I'll be helping Dan," Angela added. "But I'm also going to keep spreading Soren's *Wanted* posters around town. Somebody's bound to notice him eventually."

Their server appeared beside their table with a tray of drinks.

"Two pints of today's special," she said, placing two glasses of golden brew, covered in droplets of condensation, on cardboard coasters in front of Dan and Ricki. "And one glass of the house white. Do we need a few more minutes with the menus?"

"I think so," Angela answered.

"No rush," the woman replied. "I'll come back in a few minutes." She turned, pulled some customer checks from her apron, and distributed them to a few tables in their area before turning and disappearing in the direction of the kitchen.

"Speaking of plans," Angela said. "Anybody up for some entertainment tonight to help us relax a little?"

"I'm afraid not," Ricky answered. "I'll be doing an all-nighter to get that MSA article to AP tomorrow morning. But feel free to show Dan around town. Any ideas?"

Angela winked at Ricki.

"I thought Dan might appreciate a night at the San Remo with the Showgirls of Illusion," Angela said, chuckling. "What do you think, Ricki?"

Dan felt himself blush. "Thanks for thinking of me, ladies. But I think I should rest up and stay close to home in case we hear from the FBI or the kidnappers."

"Come on Dan," Angela huffed. "What did you learn from Chelly in Palm Desert?"

Dan paused, his eyes going vacant and distant for a second. Then he blinked and his eyes reconnected with Angela's again.

"Take a walk on the wild side," he mumbled, nodding his head up and down. "Okay, I get it. You're right, it will be good for me - for both of us - to get out of the house."

"Awesome!" Angela squealed. "It's only a few blocks away. If we head over there right after dinner, we can probably still get tickets for the late show. You won't be disappointed. They're the hottest, best kept secret on the Strip!"

Dan didn't hear her finish her sentence. An image of the poolside carnage from Palm Desert flashed into his mind. Chelly's face looked up at him as a pool of blood grew larger beneath her.

She's ... good ... for ... you ... Dan ... take ... good ... care ...

A buzzing sensation in his pocket jerked Dan back into reality. He blinked, paused for a moment, then pulled his mobile phone from his pocket. His eyes grew wide as he listened.

"… What? … You found it? … Where? … Yeah, absolutely! I'll be right there!"

Angela and Ricki both stared at him.

"What's going on?" Angela asked, concern etched on her face.

"That was Agent Simpson," he shouted, jumping to his feet. "They got a tip. They just found the missing van!"

A GROUP of LVPD police cars and black FBI SUV's were clustered around the garage bay in a Las Vegas industrial park when Dan drove up in Fran's Prius. He jumped from the car, followed by Angela who was only steps behind. The bay's door was rolled up, and the scene was cordoned off with yellow tape. Inside, white-clad CSI team members were combing a white delivery van.

Dan attempted to duck under the yellow tape, but was stopped by a uniformed LVPD officer.

"Sorry, sir. You can't go in there," the officer said.

"My name is Whitney and this is Angela Baranyi. Agent Simpson called us here to meet her," Dan answered.

At that moment, Lindell Simpson emerged from the garage bay and spotted Dan and Angela with the officer.

"It's okay, they're with me."

The officer lifted the tape, allowing Dan and Angela to pass. "Thanks for calling," Dan replied. "You found the van?"

"Yup," Simpson replied, smiling. "But that's not all."

She pulled out her mobile phone and showed Dan and Angela a photo of a dress with multi-colored vertical stripes. The right upper part of the garment was soaked with dried blood.

"Recognize this dress?" Simpson asked.

Both Dan's and Angela's faces registered shock as they stared at the photo.

"My God!" Angela gasped. "It's Fran's!"

"It's the one she was wearing at the party," Dan added.

"It looks like she lost a lot more blood than they let on in that ransom video," Simpson commented. "It also looks like they changed vehicles here."

Simpson looked up and noticed that her partner, Gabe Martinelli, had just concluded interviewing a man and was now walking towards them.

"Whatcha got, Gabe?" Simpson asked.

"I just finished with the guy who called this in," he replied. "He rents the bay across the road and saw our TV appeal for info on the van. Said he was working some real late nights a week or two ago. He was just locking up to go home one night, when some guy - sharp dresser - drove up in a Jeep. Somebody dressed in black rolled up the door real fast - small person, possibly female - hustled the guy into the garage, then rolled the door down. But not before our witness caught a glimpse of the van."

"Did he see Fran?" Dan asked, his eyes wide open and full of hope.

"No, but he saw something else," Martinelli continued. "The guy in the jeep was carrying something. It looked a bit like a doctor's black bag … and he also had a small box."

"A box?" Angela asked.

"Yeah, a cardboard box. Our guy didn't get a good look, cuz it was dark. But he thought it looked like it had a big cross on the side."

"Medical supplies?" Simpson asked, her eyebrows raised.

"Could be," Martinelli replied. "We know Fran was wounded."

"So, our unsub has access to somebody with medical training who drives a Jeep," Simpson mused. "We need to see if we can get our hands on any security video."

"I'll get on it," Martinelli answered. "There's got to be a few cameras around here." He hurried away, leaving Dan and Angela with Agent Simpson.

"This means you're going to find her, right?" Dan asked.

"Patience," Simpson cautioned. "I told you they'd make a mistake somewhere along the way. Things are looking up, but we'll need to see what CSI finds in the van and the garage. And we need to see if Gabe can get a plate number for that Jeep."

"Anything else we can do?" Angela asked.

"You guys have been a great help already, giving me a positive ID on that dress. Just go home now and let us do our work, okay? We'll let you know if we come up with anything else."

"Okay," Dan answered reluctantly. His face had fallen, resigned to going back to playing the waiting game after being teased by a few moments of hope. He and Angela turned and walked slowly back towards Fran's car. As they reached the car, Dan turned back towards Simpson.

"Agent Simpson?"

"Yes, Dan," she answered.

"Thanks … for everything. Sorry if I've been impatient with you lately."

Simpson nodded silently, acknowledging Dan's apology. A momentary look of empathy crossed her face. Dan turned back towards Angela. Together, they climbed into the Prius and it silently rolled away from the crime scene. As it disappeared, Lindell Simpson wheeled around and strode confidently back into the garage to continue her investigation, now fueled by a renewed sense of hope.

CHAPTER 20

EARLY MORNING sunshine streamed onto the pool deck of Dan and Fran's estate. Angela sat at a patio table, partially sheltered from sun, wearing a sunhat and sunglasses. She sipped on her morning coffee and nibbled on a piece of toast as she read the morning newspaper.

Just finished his morning swim, Dan hauled himself up on the pool deck, dried himself, and joined Angela at the patio table.

"You didn't need to wear a swim suit for me, you know," Angela said, laughing. "I'm starting to get used to you and your skinny-dipping friends."

Dan shrugged. "You're my guest. I'm trying to keep it family-rated when it's just you around. Anything new in today's paper?"

"Yeah, Ricki's article sure shook things up. Everybody from the President on down the chain of command is denying that there's any evidence of an MSA conspiracy.

"Wow, it's only been a day since she published her story, but they're already getting defensive about it. Almost makes you wonder if she struck a nerve, doesn't it?" Dan said.

"Hmmm …" Angela mumbled. She kept reading for a moment, then put the paper down. "Heard anything more from the FBI?"

"Yeah," Dan answered. "Simpson called last night to bring me up to date. Turns out the van is registered to the Air Force at Nellis, but it had just been repainted. It was going to be auctioned off along with five other identical vans. Somebody broke into the paint shop's yard and stole it."

"Nobody reported it stolen?" Angela asked. "That's odd."

"Not really," Dan replied. The paint shop owner said they were parked in a big lot, waiting for the auction house to pick them up, so nobody noticed that one of them was gone."

"Still sounds a bit fishy to me. What about fingerprints?" Angela asked.

"Nothing. Looks like the kidnappers were all careful to wear gloves," Dan answered. "Martinelli found a couple of security videos with the Jeep, but it was too dark to get a good look at the plate. All they know is that it was a dark colored, late model Renegade."

Angela shook her head in frustration. "And no follow-up call from the kidnappers about their ransom demands? Doesn't that seem odd?" she asked.

"It does to me, but not the FBI," Dan replied. "Simpson said it just shows that they're in no panic. Remember, Angela, they were trying to kill you that night. So, ending up with Fran probably caught them completely by surprise. They're likely trying to figure out what to do with her. Simpson says that's good for us, cuz it gives us time to work on the case before they contact us about a place and time for an exchange."

"Mmm hmm," Angela mumbled, as she paused to think things over. "Maybe … Or maybe our kidnappers have day jobs. Maybe they're busy doing other things?"

FRAN WAKENED to morning's bright yellow glow inside her desert prison. The sun was climbing high in the eastern sky and the temperature inside the desert hideaway was rising steadily again. Already wet with perspiration, Fran threw her blanket aside. Still fully dressed from warding off the nighttime chill, she sat up and rubbed her eyes. She looked over at Soren's cot and was surprised to see that he was nowhere to be seen. Instead, Helen had returned and was fast asleep on her cot.

Feeling the need to pee, Fran cleared her throat to make some noise. Helen's eyes fluttered open. She looked around, momentarily disoriented.

"I need to go," Fran said.

"Okay … So do I," Helen mumbled. "Just hold on a second."

"Where's Soren?" Fran asked.

"Taking care of business. Picking up supplies," Helen answered curtly. "None of your concern."

Finally, Helen threw back her blanket, sat on the edge of her cot, then stood up and stretched, wearing only her bra and panties. Fran's eyes appraised the other woman's entire physique for the first time, free from her military fatigues or the sexy bodice and high-heeled boots of her dominatrix identity. Helen was short, but her perfectly toned body radiated a natural sensuality, despite having just woken up. She shivered, then donned her military t-shirt and fatigues. She unlocked Fran's chain, allowing Fran to do her usual shuffle to the makeshift latrine outside the tent. Helen began looking for food while Fran was outside the tent.

Instead of returning to her cot, Fran walked up to Helen, her chain jangling as she walked.

"Can I help you?" Fran asked.

Surprised by Fran's offer, Helen laughed aloud.

"Are you forgetting something here? You're still a prisoner and I'm your captor, right?" Helen answered.

"I know. But I'm so bored," Fran replied.

Helen pondered the situation for a moment.

"Okay," she declared. "I'll lock up your chain and you can go as far as it allows. But no sharp utensils, understand?"

Helen dragged Fran's chain back to the metal stake and locked it again, leaving Fran with access to about half of the table where Helen and Soren prepared their food and set up their camp stove.

"Can I make some oatmeal and some coffee?" Fran asked.

Helen shrugged. "Knock yourself out. I'll be back in a minute."

Energized by her newfound partial freedom, Fran threw herself into her tasks. Helen left the tent for a few minutes to use the latrine. When she returned, she washed her hands and started peeling a banana.

Upon Helen's return, Fran rested both of her hands on her growing abdomen.

"I was talking with Soren yesterday," Fran began. "I'm so sorry to hear that you had to have an abortion when you were young. That must have been terrible."

A look of shock washed over Helen's face. Fran saw that her comment had caught Helen completely off guard, just as she had planned. She noticed a single tear escape from one eye. When Helen opened her mouth, Fran was shocked to hear a young, child-like voice emerge from her captor's mouth.

"Thanks for caring," Helen answered timidly. Then, just as quickly, her body stiffened. The muscles in her jaw tightened. A cold, distant look replaced the fleeting expression of sadness as the strong, domineering side of Helen's identity fell back into place.

"I was abused as a teenager too," Fran admitted. "My sister's husband beat me. I was also raped and I thought I was pregnant. I suppose the only small blessing is that I wasn't."

"Stop it! Why are you doing this?" Helen shouted.

Fran stared at Helen, fascinated by the mixture of emotions that were rising out of the other woman's inner turmoil.

"Because I know what it's like. There was nobody for me to talk to. I was all alone," Fran continued.

Another single tear started to trickle down Helen's face. The tightness in her jaw disappeared and her body appeared to shrink and close inward. Her eyes grew distant as she transformed back into the younger version of herself again. But this time, the strong, domineering side of Helen's personality wasn't strong enough - her consciousness was overwhelmed and helpless to stop a relentless wave of traumatic memories from her past …

TERI TAYLOR felt herself being thrown through the open door, with roars of male laughter following her, as she tumbled to the ground on the motel's second floor landing. She grunted as a heavy male body landed on top of her. The motel room's door slammed behind them. Even though the sounds coming from inside the room were now muffled, Teri bristled with anger as the sound of derisive jeers and laughter continued behind them. She tried to wriggle out from beneath Soren's body, finally using an elbow to the mid-section to get his attention.

"Get off me!" Teri shouted.

Soren grunted, then he struggled to his bare feet. He was shirtless, his trousers sagged, and his fly wasn't yet zipped up. Now free from Soren's weight, Teri lifted herself to her bare feet.

Suddenly, the door flew open again, a burst of laughter erupted behind them, and the door slammed shut. A shower of boxer shorts, panties, and a bra landed at their feet. Teri's blouse was untucked and open almost to her navel. Most of the buttons had been torn from the garment by their assailants. She bent down to pick up her undergarments. As she did, an exposed breast fell through the gaping space where buttons should have kept it hidden from view. The door opened again. This time, Soren's shirt and their shoes landed at their feet.

Soren picked up his remaining garments. He wrapped his arm around Teri's waist and they stumbled down an external staircase to ground level. They hurried away to the rear of the motel's office, away from prying eyes, before they finally stopped running. Soren helped Teri tuck in her blouse as best they could and she helped him with his shirt. Finally, they slipped on their shoes.

Teri had difficulty focusing, struggling to keep her mind from drifting someplace far away. Her entire body felt numb. Anger seethed from between Soren's clenched teeth while his arms encircled Teri and held her tight. An angry side of Pastor Soren

Kristiansen, one Teri had never seen before, started boiling inside him while rage filled his eyes.

"Who the fuck do those pricks think they are?" Soren cursed. "They think they can get away with it just because they're officers? They'll pay for it after I report them!"

Teri's eyes opened wide with fear. She grabbed onto Soren's arm and tried to reason with him.

"No, you can't!" she begged, her voice still hushed.

"What do you mean, I can't?" he answered. "They just raped you and humiliated me - an Air Force Chaplain, no less. They'll all be tossed out of the Air Force on their ears when I'm done with them!"

"You mustn't!" Teri pleaded. "It will make it worse for both of us! Don't you see? They're all in this together. They'll cover it up and make it go away!"

"Fuck em, then. We'll quit and tell the world what they're doing," Soren continued.

"No! If we do that, they win!" Teri insisted. "If we get angry or show our emotions, they win! I will never give them that satisfaction!"

"Then what do *you* propose we do? Let them keep humiliating us?" Soren demanded.

Teri gripped Soren's shoulders and locked her eyes onto his.

"Do you trust me, Soren?"

"Of course, I do. You know you're the only person in the world I trust."

"Then listen to me and calm down," Teri implored. "I have a plan. But we're both going to need to be incredibly strong for it to work." She whispered in Soren's ear. A look of surprise and shock crossed his face. Gradually, as she whispered, the tension started to drain from his face. A hint of a smile slowly replaced his anger as he began to understand her plan.

"Do you think you can do that for me? ... For us?" Teri asked, her eyes beseeching him to agree.

"For you, I'll do anything," he answered. " I love you … you know that."

"I love you too, Soren," Teri whispered. She held his head and kissed his forehead. "But we can't let them discover that we're anything more than casual acquaintances. For this to work, we need to convince them that you mean absolutely nothing to me."

Teri wrapped her arms around Soren and pulled him close. She placed her lips gently on his. They sealed their commitment with a series of deep, passionate kisses.

But while they kissed, the two lovers were blissfully unaware of a black car sitting in a dark corner of the parking lot, and a pair of eyes peering through its heavily tinted windows. The Air Force officer hidden behind the dark windows smiled to himself, pleased with what he had just discovered about the young chaplain and his girlfriend.

"Secret lovers," Lieutenant Bryce Williamson hissed sarcastically. "How sweet."

CHAPTER 21

TERI REACHED the top of the stairs and pressed the bar on the heavy steel door. She emerged into the night from the nondescript white building onto South 4th Street in downtown Las Vegas. A block to the north, she heard the booming music of the Fremont Street Experience. The bright lights from the massive illuminated canopy over Fremont Street cast an eerie yellow glow that failed to penetrate the darker recesses of the city's downtown, which existed only paces away from the tourist mecca.

Teri pulled her coat up to cover her neck and began walking south to where she'd parked her car earlier. Almost immediately, she heard footsteps behind her. She continued to walk for another five seconds, then glanced quickly over her shoulder. She thought she saw movement in an alley behind her, but she couldn't be sure. Her muscles tensed and her senses became more acute. She continued to walk southward, away from Fremont Street. Almost immediately, she heard footsteps behind her again. Instinctively, she picked up her pace and listened. The footsteps matched her pace. She looked at the streetscape around her, trying to calculate her next move, looking for shelter or ways to escape.

Just as she approached an intersection and was about to start running west to the lights of Casino Center Boulevard, a voice came out of the darkness behind her.

"What little secrets bring you downtown, Airman Taylor?" the voice asked. "Another secret prayer meeting with Chaplain Kristiansen?"

Teri froze with fear. She recognized the voice. It was one of them. She swallowed, attempting to clear her throat and muster her courage.

"You've been stalking me," she replied. Her voice was cold and matter-of-fact. She strained to recognize the voice. "What do you want with me?"

"What do you think?" the voice said. "We had such a good time that night at the motel. I thought we could get to know each other better. Just the two of us."

The voice was only a few feet behind Teri now. She wheeled around to face her stalker. When she saw his face, she had to suppress the urge to gasp.

"Lieutenant Williamson," Teri answered. "What makes you think I'd be interested in getting to know you better? And what makes you think I'm spending time with Soren Kristiansen?"

"Come on, Airman," Williamson replied. "Who do you think you're fooling. I watched the two of you comforting each other that night at the motel. What do you see in that mousy little nerd, anyway?"

Teri felt her anger starting to boil inside. She had to resist the urge to launch herself at the arrogant asshole and scratch his eyes out. Instead, she took a deep breath and shrugged.

"We're both loners. We both needed somebody to talk to," she replied. "You caught us both by surprise that night. What did you expect us to do?"

"You expect me to believe that?" Williamson answered.

"Maybe, maybe not," Teri continued. "But if I were looking for a boyfriend, he's definitely not my type."

"Really," Williamson said. He looked like the Cheshire Cat, the smirk on his face giving his intentions away. She knew what those intentions were. Like a cat, he wanted to pounce - not to kill, but just to play with her - to humiliate and abuse her instead.

"So, what is your type, Airman?" Williamson continued.

"My daddy said I always made bad choices," she began. "Seems like I always pick the bad boys. He accused me of picking the ones that I knew would piss him off. Maybe he was right. Maybe I get my thrills from forbidden fruit."

"Do you?" he answered, still smirking. "Does that include superior officers?"

This time it was Teri's turn to wear a sly smile. "Maybe. But just you and me. I'm not into sharing with the rest of your buddies," she answered. "What do you have in mind?"

"Well, we could go back to Fremont and find ourselves a craps game and have some fun," Williamson said. "Then maybe we could get a room and take the party upstairs. Just you and me. What do you say?"

"Now you're talking," Teri replied coyly, trying her best to look convincing. "You'll need to spot me some cash, though. I don't have much on me."

"Don't you worry about that," Williamson answered. "It's my treat. Let's go to the Four Queens. They still have five-dollar tables, so we can stay longer."

"What are we waiting for?" Teri answered.

Williamson put his arm out, waiting for Teri to take his arm.

So, the bastard thinks he's chivalrous, does he?

She took his arm and smiled at her former stalker as they walked back to Fremont. But beneath the façade of her smile, Teri's anger had reached a steady boil. She allowed it to simmer at that temperature - just hot enough to keep her focused on her goal, but not hot enough to let it show. As they emerged onto Fremont Street beneath the flashing canopy of lights, she felt a familiar sense of power and satisfaction starting to spread through her entire being.

BRYCE WILLIAMSON fumbled with the key lock card, finally getting a beep and a green light and pushing the hotel room's door inward. He dragged Teri into the room and proceeded to plaster his lips onto hers, even before the door closed behind them. She smelled the Jack Daniels on his breath and had to repress a shudder of revulsion. He'd already had more than a few shots of Jack while they were at the craps table. Memories of her father flashed through her consciousness.

Teri pulled the full bottle they'd just purchased at the liquor store from its brown paper bag and set it on a table. She picked up an ice bucket and thrust it into the lieutenant's hand.

"Go get us some ice while I pour us some refreshments," she said. She opened the top two buttons on her blouse, then planted a kiss on his cheek, letting him smell the subtle hint of Chanel No. 5 wafting up from between her breasts, just for some added incentive.

"I'll be right back," he answered, laughing stupidly. "Don't start without me!"

"Don't worry, I won't," Teri replied, smiling. "Hurry back!"

Williamson stumbled to the door with the ice bucket, then he opened it awkwardly and stumbled into the hallway. As soon as he was gone, Teri reached into her purse and pulled out the small envelope of pills she had carried, just for such an event. She took the paper wrappers off two glasses on the table and put two roofie tablets into the one on the right, crushing them with a lipstick tube from her purse. Then she opened the bottle of whiskey. Suddenly there was a rustling sound in the hallway, followed by a banging on the door.

"Let me in," Williamson slurred. "I forgot the key."

"Just a minute," Teri called cheerfully. She poured two generous portions of the brown liquor into the glasses, then she swirled the one with the roofies vigorously, waiting impatiently while they dissolved.

"Hurry up," Williamson shouted from the other side of the door.

"I'm in the washroom," Teri shouted. "Hang on a minute."

Once the last traces of powder disappeared into the whiskey, Teri walked into the bathroom, flushed the toilet, and then walked calmly to the door. Williamson almost fell into the room as the door swung open. Teri steadied him, smiled, and took the ice bucket from him.

"Thanks, Lieutenant. Why don't you make yourself comfortable on the bed?" she said, smiling. "Do you want ice?"

"Naw," he mumbled, as he ambled unsteadily to the bed and plopped himself down. "Real men drink it straight, right?"

"You're right about that," she answered, trying to keep up her act while her inner loathing towards her superior officer threatened to escalate from a simmer to a full boil.

Teri put two large cubes in her drink to water it down, then she picked up the glasses and handed Williamson the one with the roofies. He tipped it back and downed half the contents in a single swallow. He closed his eyes briefly as the liquor burned its way down his esophagus, and then he gave his head a shake.

"Ahhh ...," he muttered loudly. "Real men, right sweetheart?" He put his drink down on the bedside table and reached for Teri, who was still standing in front of him. He grasped her by the hips and pulled her down towards him, so that his face was at the same level as her breasts. He peered into the cleavage she had exposed and inhaled the alluring scent of her body and her perfume. She took a small sip from her drink and then set it down on the far side of the bedside table, well away from Williamson's drink. He leaned forward and planted a wet kiss at the top of one of her breasts.

Teri resisted the urge to shudder. Instead, she let out a small moan and placed her hands gently on either side of his head.

"That feels so good," she lied softly. "You *are* a real man. Let's make ourselves more comfortable, shall we?" She reached behind her, unfastened her skirt, pulled it down and stepped out of it. She stood before him clothed only in white bikini panties and a partially opened blouse that revealed a delicate white lace bra beneath.

Williamson was dressed casually. He wore blue jeans, a light cotton dress shirt tucked into the jeans, and sneakers. She loosened the buttons on his shirt, then pulled it from inside his jeans and removed it, leaving him in a white cotton t-shirt. She loosened his belt, noticing a bulge starting to form in his crotch, and pulled up on the t-shirt. She ran her hands under the shirt and over his bare skin, playing with the hair on his chest.

"You're making me real hard, darlin'," Williamson mumbled. He ripped her blouse open and tore it from her body, wanting more of the soft white mounds of flesh in front of his face.

Teri reached for Williamson's drink. "Here, honey," she said. "Have another hit. I really feel like partying tonight." Then she reached behind her and released the clasp on her bra, feeling her small, firm breasts break free.

Williamson took another giant gulp of whiskey, closed his eyes, and shook his head again. When he opened his eyes, he should have seen Teri's bare bosom. Instead, his eyes were hazy. He blinked a couple of times, then his head nodded downwards. He seemed to be searching for words.

"Yer perfec," he mumbled, almost incoherently. He leaned forward and attempted to plaster another saliva-laden kiss on one of her nipples. Teri braced herself for the assault. But Williamson's head nodded and he never made it to his goal. Teri pushed him back gently on the bed. She rubbed his chest again. He moaned softly, barely aware of what was happening. She looked at his crotch, noting that the bulge was receding.

"Just lay back and relax, lover," she said, smiling broadly. "I promise I'm going to make this a night to remember."

"… Remember …" Williamson mumbled.

No longer in command of his mental faculties, Bryce Williamson slipped into an alcohol and drug-induced fog.

Teri picked up her drink from the bedside table and took a small, satisfying sip of her diluted drink, then she set the glass back down on the table. Still bare-chested, she walked to the other side of the room and opened her purse, retrieving her mobile phone. She flipped it open and pressed speed dial.

"Soren, it's me," she said. "I've lured one of them - Lieutenant Williamson - it was easier than we thought. I'm at the Four Queens. Room 403. Get down here right away."

Not waiting for an answer, Teri ended the call and pressed another number stored on speed dial.

"It's Helen, sir. It's happened. Do you have a free room for me?"

"Tonight? This is a pleasant surprise. Do you need any help?"

"No, sir," she answered. "I think I have everything under control. We're only a couple of blocks from the dungeon. He followed me when I left there."

"Then I'll expect you shortly. You've done well, my dear."

"Thank you, sir. I'll be there soon."

Teri ended the call, closed her phone, and threw it back into her purse. She retrieved her bra from the floor and covered her breasts again. She picked up her blouse and examined it.

"Asshole," she muttered. "You ripped off a button."

She shrugged and then went to the mirror to straighten herself out. As she stared at the image in front of her, Teri's mind soared back through time. Images of her father, standing over her with his belt in one hand and an evil grin on his face, fluttered briefly through her consciousness.

"Oh well, Helen," she said to her alter ego in the mirror. "You're not a helpless victim anymore. It's payback time."

IT SEEMED like an eternity to Teri before there was a knock at the door. In reality, it had only been twenty-five minutes since she'd called Soren. The second she opened the door, he burst into the room.

"Where is he!" Soren shouted. Then he saw Williamson's body lying on the bed. He walked towards the unconscious officer, his eyes filled with rage. "I should cut the bastard's balls off while he's sleeping," he shouted.

"Shut up!" Teri said sternly. "You want the whole hotel to hear you?"

"Where are we taking him?" Soren asked.

"I'll tell you later. Just sit him up and help me get his shirt on again."

Soren grabbed Williamson's arms and pulled him to a sitting position. The man's body flopped like a rag doll, so Soren climbed onto the bed behind Williamson to prop him up. Teri tugged down Williamson's t-shirt, and then struggled to force one of his limp arms into a shirt sleeve. That task accomplished, she wrapped the shirt around his torso and managed to twist his other arm into the remaining sleeve. Finally, she fastened enough of the buttons to keep the shirt on, leaving it looking disheveled.

"There," she said. "He's the perfect passed-out drunk."

Teri donned her coat and slung her purse over her shoulder.

"Okay. You take one arm and I'll take the other. We're going to walk him out of here."

"Are you nuts?" Soren asked. "He's a good two hundred pounds of dead weight. How are you going to manage that?"

Teri glared at Soren. "Do you have a better idea? If you do, this would be the time to hear it."

"Maybe the hotel has a stretcher," Soren reasoned.

"Sure. You want the whole world to know we carried him out of here? Where's your car?" Teri demanded.

"In the parking lot behind the hotel," Soren answered.

"Good. We'll get him to the rear elevator and take him down to the parking lot. If we draw any attention, he's just a buddy who had too much to drink and we're taking him home, got it?"

"Okay, you're the boss," Soren agreed reluctantly.

"So, you take one arm, I'll take the other," Teri repeated.

Together, they managed to swing Williamson's legs around so they were resting on the floor. They each wrapped one of Williamson's arms around their own shoulders.

"Now!" Teri ordered. Together they rose to their feet. Teri struggled to shoulder the man's weight on her short five-foot frame. Even worse, because Soren was much taller, more of the Williamson's body leaned to Teri's side, making Williamson feel even heavier.

"Shit," she cursed, as Williamson almost slid off her shoulder, dislodging her purse, which fell to the floor.

"I'll get it," Soren offered. "Hang on." He stooped down quickly and retrieved the purse, then grabbed Williamson's arm again. "Don't worry about the purse. You just concentrate on hanging onto him."

Together, they managed to stumble to the door. Soren propped their captive up against a wall while Teri opened the door. Once outside the room they repeated the process, with Teri closing the door once they were in the hallway.

"You okay?" Soren asked.

"Let's do it!" Teri said, breathing heavily. She dug deep for the extra strength to shoulder the man's dead weight as they staggered down the hall towards the elevator. Once there, Soren supported Williamson while Teri pressed the button for the lift. She cursed silently when she saw that it was already on the ground floor. Finally, it began its upward journey, stopping at both the second and third floors before a bell finally signaled its arrival on their floor.

"Finally," Teri cursed. Thankfully, there were no other passengers and no explanations necessary. Together, they staggered into the conveyance with Williamson between them. Teri pressed the button for the ground level.

When the door opened on the ground floor, a young couple stood in front of them, waiting to go up to their floor. The couple looked at the unconscious, disheveled man between Soren and Teri, and the woman raised her eyebrows.

"A bit too much, eh?"

"Oh, yeah," Teri answered. "He got a big promotion today. Now we gotta take him home and explain this to his wife."

"At least he passed out before he decided to drive," the woman's partner observed.

"Amen to that," Soren replied.

"Good luck," the woman said

"Do you need some help?" the other man asked Soren.

"Thanks, but we're okay," Teri interjected. "We're almost at the car."

By now, they were getting the knack of managing Williamson's body. They maneuvered him out of the elevator and towards the hotel's rear exit, where Teri was able to bump an automatic door opener with her hip. Finally outside, they stumbled across the parking lot to Soren's battered old Chevy Cavalier. Teri opened the car door, then they managed to sit Williamson on the rear seat and swing his legs into the vehicle. Both Soren and Teri stood up and exhaled at the same time, sweat visible on both of their foreheads. Terri pulled the shoulder restraint across Williamson's chest and fastened it at his opposite hip.

"That should hold him, she declared, puffing heavily.

"Where to?" Soren asked.

"It's a surprise," Teri said with a sly smile. "One I think you're going to enjoy. And it's only a block or two away."

Soren raised his eyebrows. "Sounds intriguing," he said, as they climbed into the Cavalier.

Teri guided Soren out of the parking lot, turning left onto Carson Avenue. "Second left," Teri said as the Cavalier picked up speed, only to brake a few seconds later to turn again.

"It's the white building on the left," Teri said.

They pulled up in front of an unimposing one-story, white stucco building. There were no signs or markings whatsoever on the exterior.

"Pull into the lane on the far side," Teri said. "There's a side entrance."

Once Soren pulled into the lane and stopped the car, they opened the rear door and reversed the previous process of swinging Williamson's legs and body sideways. They pulled him to his feet, shouldered his weight between them again, and then dragged him to the side entrance, where Soren propped their victim beside the steel door.

Teri pounded on the door. When nobody answered after ten seconds, she pounded again. Finally, they heard distant footsteps ascending some stairs, growing gradually louder with each step, until the door opened in front of them.

They were greeted by a man who was clad entirely in black from head to toe. His head and face were covered by a black leather hood with cutouts for his eyes, ears, nose and mouth. He wore a sleeveless black leather vest, cut low in the chest to show off his hard pecs and powerful arms. His tight leather pants showed off legs as stout as oak trees and a well-endowed package.

Soren's eyes opened wide in surprise. He turned to Teri, his mouth hanging open. Before he could say anything, the man in black addressed Teri.

"Lady Helen," the man said. A look of pride sparkled in his eyes. "We're ready for you. Follow me."

CHAPTER 22

TWO OTHER men, also clad entirely in black, stepped out of the darkness behind their leader and took Bryce Williamson's limp body. Teri and Soren followed the three men down a flight of concrete stairs to a landing, and then down another flight until they arrived in the building's basement. They found themselves in a dimly lit corridor with doors on either side.

A door opened ahead of them and red light oozed into the darkened hallway. A shapely woman in a revealing black evening dress emerged. She tugged on a leather cord and a completely naked man, his eyes covered with a black blindfold and his hands bound in front of him, stumbled out of the room after her. His body was lathered in sweat and he looked exhausted. His penis showed the remnants of an erection.

"Follow me, slut!" the woman commanded, yanking the leather leash and almost jerking the man off his feet.

"What is this place?" Soren whispered. "Why did he call you Lady Helen?"

"Just shut up and watch," Teri answered.

"Why …"

"Silence!" Teri hissed. Even in the near darkness, Soren saw the anger flash in her eyes. "I'm in charge here. So, you'll shut up and do what I say. Understand?"

Soren swallowed and nodded. Their convoy followed the shapely woman and her submissive prisoner through the corridor until it became lighter and they emerged into a lounge with a well-stocked bar against one wall. Plushly-upholstered booths, couches, and loveseats filled the lounge, which was not busy at this relatively early hour of the night. A man and woman in formal evening attire were making out in a corner booth, the man's hands sliding inside the long slit in her evening dress and disappearing between her thighs.

Teri's escorts, still lugging Williamson between them, exited the far side of the lounge and disappeared into another dark corridor. Teri and Soren followed. As they passed a number of closed doors, men and women could be heard shouting commands against a background of moans, shouts, or screams - some in ecstasy, but others in obvious pain. When they reached a doorway at the end of the corridor, the man in black opened the door and his two helpers carried the still-unconscious Bryce Williamson into a room with dim red lighting and laid him on a waist-high table.

As Soren's eyes gradually acclimated to the dim light, his pupils opened wider. He looked around the room and realized where he was - a dungeon. The walls were covered with racks and shelves displaying every kind of sex toy and pleasure-or-pain-inflicting device imaginable.

The man in black turned to Teri. "You've learned quickly, my novice. Now it's time for you to enjoy the fruits of your labor."

"Thank you, Master," Teri answered solemnly.

The man in black stepped into the background to supervise, nodding to his two helpers to assist Teri and Soren.

"Strip him naked!" Teri shouted at the helpers, who wasted no time complying and finishing their task. When they were done, Teri nodded to a seven-foot, X-shaped pine cross in the corner of the room. The frame was simple and natural - unfinished pine with no decorative adornments, just beginning to grey with age and displaying the telltale stains of human sweat. Each branch of the cross had leather straps for immobilizing a person's limbs.

"Fasten him to the cross!" Teri barked.

The two men dragged Williamson, naked and still unconscious, to the frame and fastened both wrists and ankles to it with the leather straps

She turned to the man in black leather. "You have my things?" she asked. The man nodded to a counter at the far end of the room.

"Leave us alone," she said calmly. The hooded man nodded to the two helpers who spun on their heels and retreated from the room.

"You know how to call me if you need anything?" he asked, nodding towards a large red button on the wall beside the door.

"Yes, sir," Teri replied. "I'll be fine."

"I'm sure you will, my young novice." He bowed to her, and then without any further words, he left the room and closed the door behind him.

"Teri, what the …?" Soren asked quietly, still in a state of shock at their surroundings. She spun around to face him. Her eyes were distant and filled with fury.

"You will do exactly as I command!" she shouted. "And you will address me either as *Lady Helen* or *my lady*! Is that clear?"

Soren's mouth opened but no sounds emerged. He was completely lost for words to describe Teri's transformation. The best he could muster was to nod his head up and down slowly in a display of stunned obedience.

Teri went to a sink in the corner of the room and filled a paper cup with water. She brought it back to Soren and handed it to him.

"Throw it on his face. Wake him up while I get out of these clothes."

Soren's feet seemed to be glued to the floor as Teri turned her back to him and began stripping off her street clothes, beginning with her blouse and skirt. Still wearing her white bra and panties, she stopped and looked back over her shoulder at Soren.

"Do you have a problem with my orders, chaplain? Never seen a dungeon before?" A sarcastic grin spread slowly across her face. She was clearly enjoying the moral dilemma she had created for Soren. "Wake him up!" she screamed.

Startled by the scream, Soren jumped into action. He walked over to where Williamson's body was suspended on the wooden cross. He splashed some water in the man's face and watched as Williamson gasped and coughed instinctively, before emitting a barely audible moan.

Teri was now completely naked. Slowly and deliberately, she began dressing herself in the neatly stacked pile of garments on the counter in front of her. First, she climbed into a skin-tight black leather bodice that only zipped up as far as her navel. The garment barely contained her breasts, displaying their milky white flesh and flashes of nipple whenever she bent or twisted her torso. A hole was cut into the crotch of the bodice, clearly displaying her closely-trimmed pubic hair and genitals. Next, she stepped into knee-high, black leather stiletto boots. As she zipped up the second boot she turned around to watch Soren. She stood tall in her new attire, clearly proud of her transition into Lady Helen.

"Do it again," she ordered. She walked over to a rack containing a selection of floggers, canes, and whips. She selected a wooden cane and whipped it through the air, feeling the wood fibers snap responsively to the sharp flick of her wrist. She snapped the cane over the table where Williamson had lain initially. Soren jumped instinctively, splashing water from the paper cup onto the floor.

"Wake him up, I said!" Teri commanded.

Soren threw the remainder of the water into Williamson's face, causing him to cough and gasp again. This time, Teri's victim opened his eyelids slightly, peering out into the dungeon through the two slits. His eyes slowly opened wider. At first, a look of confusion crossed his face. Then, after he had time to digest the scene in front of him, his expression transformed into one of fear.

Teri turned to Soren. An evil smile spread across her face.

"Watch and learn!" she said. She turned to face Bryce Williamson, who was strapped naked to the wooden cross, terrified and helpless, in front of her.

LADY HELEN stared into Bryce Williamson's eyes, feeling intoxicated with a sense of power, and fueled by the stark terror engraved on her captive's face. A smile of elation and triumph radiated from her own face. She stepped close so her body invaded Williamson's personal space and pressed against his naked, vulnerable body.

"So, my friend," she whispered softly into his ear. "It seems that the tables have turned in my favor."

She kept her body pressed against his, letting him take in the delicate mixture of scents radiating from her body: leather, Chanel No. 5, and her own pheromones.

"I'm going to make this a night you'll never forget," she promised softly. "Just how you remember it is entirely up to you."

She turned her back to him and walked over to an open cabinet full of sex toys, making sure to let her hips sway seductively, and to let Williamson have a good view of her firm legs and butt, and the delicate curves of her figure. From the cabinet, she selected a black silk blindfold, a jet-black ball gag, and a giant grey-black ostrich feather. She turned and walked back towards Williamson, stopping to lay the ball gag and feather on the table in the middle of the room.

"I'm going to put this blindfold on you to heighten your senses. Trust me, this will make everything feel so much better." She saw his eyes grow wide, unwilling to trust her. She smiled, the feeling of power flowing freely through her body, as she covered his eyes and tied the blindfold tightly at the back of his head. She leaned close again, this time letting her lips brush against his and kissing them lightly.

"See. Doesn't that feel good?" Helen flicked his lips delicately with her tongue, then kissed him again as she let her hands stroke his neck and the sides of his face, and then she ran her fingers through his hair. She felt a bulge starting to grow against her crotch. She smiled again, pleased with herself. She walked back to the table, picked up the ball gag, and then walked back to

Williamson, leaning gently against his body again. She kissed him softly on the lips once more, her tongue darting and teasing him until he finally parted his lips and responded with his tongue. She responded eagerly, opening her lips and beginning to French kiss him, begging him to open his mouth to hers. As he did, Helen suddenly jammed the large rubber ball gag between his teeth and into his mouth.

Williamson responded immediately, his arms and legs jerking violently against his leather restraints, trying to mount a vocal protest of high-pitched moans against the gag.

Helen resumed stroking his head and neck gently, then she ran her fingers through his hair again.

"Shhhh," Helen whispered in his ear. "Relax. You can either go with the flow, or you can fight this. The choice is yours. Tonight, I am going to teach you all about pleasure … and pain … blurring the boundaries together until they become indistinguishable for you."

Helen turned to Soren, who stood paralyzed beside the table. She nodded towards the table.

"Bring me that object," she ordered.

Soren stood rigid and frozen, not responding. His eyes were still open wide. He looked like the stereotypical deer caught in a vehicle's headlights.

"The object on the table!" Helen repeated.

This time, Soren blinked and looked at the table beside him. He reached for the giant ostrich feather, then he walked it over to Helen and handed it to her.

"Relax Lieutenant," Helen said softly. "Open up your senses and let yourself enjoy the sensations." She began stroking one of Williamson's outstretched arms, beginning with his hand and gently stroking down his arm until she reached his chest. She ran the feather softly over his chest and up the other arm towards his fingertips. As she did, she pressed herself against his body, letting him take in the erotic mixture of scents emanating from her body, his remaining senses now heightened by his lack of vision. She felt his cock throbbing and rising against her crotch again.

"I feel you getting hard, Lieutenant. Does that feel good?"

Williamson gave a short, less panicked moan.

"That's good," Helen replied. "Because when I make you feel good, it makes me feel very good. Whatever I do, you make sure you keep yourself hard. I'll be very displeased if you let yourself go soft."

Helen handed the ostrich feather to Soren and then walked back to the cupboard full of sex toys. She selected a long, narrow strand of leather cord and then walked back to her captive. She let her fingers wander gently over the sensitive outside surface of his engorged penis, lingering briefly over the sweet spot near the frenum. She smiled as Williamson emitted a slight moan from behind the ball gag.

"I'm going to bind your balls with this cord," she said gently. "We wouldn't want those sensitive jewels to disappear or get damaged, would we?"

Helen went to work, wrapping the cord snugly underneath and behind Williamson's scrotum, finally tying the thong neatly to complete the job. As she worked, she made sure that her fingers strayed over his cock, randomly brushing different areas on the organ so that he never knew when or where she was going to touch him next. His moans grew louder and longer each time she brushed against him. She walked back to the cupboard, this time choosing a flogger with leather fronds and a pair of nipple clips. She deposited the clips on the table next to her wooden cane, and then carried the flogger back to Williamson.

She gently flicked the leather fronds of the flogger against his left ribs, before dragging them across Williamson's chest. She raised them to his nose so he could smell the scent of leather. Then she slowly dragged the fronds up the inside of his right leg, stopping at the knee to gently slap them against the inside of his thigh a few times. After that, she dragged the flogger up and over the outside of his penis, making sure to make a number of passes over the organ.

Helen lifted the flogger from Williamson and stood silently, tormenting her captive with silence and a full minute of sensory deprivation. As she did, his cock stopped throbbing and began to soften and droop. Finally, she pressed her body against his and touched her lips to his. As she did, she grasped his cock in one hand and squeezed just below the rim. He groaned loudly behind his gag and Helen grinned to herself, feeling the power she held over him. And as the feeling of power surged through her body, she began to feel a pleasant quaking sensation in her abdomen, accompanied by moisture seeping from between her labia. She slid a finger between her vaginal lips, coating it with her juices. Then she held the finger below Williamson's nose.

"Do you like how I smell, Lieutenant? Do you see what your hard cock does to me? If you're good, maybe I'll let you taste me next time."

She squeezed his rock-hard, throbbing erection again. His organ was now swollen, changing color from red to purple. After a few moments, she released his organ and resumed dragging the flogger up the inside of his left leg. She stopped again to gently slap the inside of his thigh a few times. Then she continued upwards again, dragging the fronds over his penis, causing it to twitch every time she touched it. Finally, she removed it again, forcing Williamson to endure another minute of sensory deprivation.

After the minute was over, Helen gently swung the flogger upwards between Williamson's legs, letting the fronds slap his scrotum and testicles. His body jumped defensively and he emitted a frightened squeal.

"Did that hurt?" Helen asked, her voice tainted with sarcasm. "I hardly touched you."

She swung the flogger upwards again, just a little bit harder the second time. Williamson's body jerked again. He moaned behind his gag.

Helen nodded to Soren and then pointed to the table. Puzzled, Soren pointed to the cane. Helen shook her head and pointed beside it. Soren held up a nipple clamp. Helen nodded affirmatively and motioned for him to bring the clamps to her.

"Did that really hurt?" she asked. "Because I'm not really sure you know what pain is yet."

At that moment, Helen opened up one of the nipple clamps and clamped it over Williamson's right nipple. A high-pitched, muffled squeal came from behind the gag. His nostrils flared and his breaths became sharp and quick. Helen stood back and gave her captive a moment to adjust to the searing pain in his right breast. When his breathing finally slowed, she swung the flogger upwards towards his balls with increased force. His body jerked again and he grunted. As he did, she closed the second clamp over his other nipple. He let go another squeal from behind the gag. His erection softened quickly.

Helen saw sweat beginning to form on Williamson's body. His breathing was jagged and quick. A warm smile of satisfaction covered her face. Moisture flowed freely from between her legs. The overwhelming feeling of power was concentrating in her vagina and clitoris.

Helen looked back over her shoulder at Soren, who was still frozen, his mouth gaping. The expression on his face was one of both dismay and jealousy. She locked her eyes onto his and gave him a reassuring nod, trying to tell him that she was doing this for him. He nodded unenthusiastically in return, his face still blank and confused.

Once again, Helen pressed her body against her helpless victim and whispered in his ear.

"Okay, Lieutenant. You've felt both pleasure and pain so far. How things go from here is strictly up to you, so listen up!"

Helen grasped Williamson's drooping organ and began stroking it and squeezing it gently, urging it to come back to life. After a moment, it began to grow and swell again.

"From here on, I'm making a new set of rules," Helen announced. "You and your goons will never lay another hand on me or Soren, unless we give you permission to do so. In return, your band of deplorables can continue with your hazing orgies, and I will not only turn a blind eye, I will take command of those events and you will all submit yourselves to me, Lady Helen. I will open your eyes to ways of taking everybody's pleasure to new heights that you've never imagined. Does that sound appealing?"

Williamson nodded his head vigorously to acknowledge.

"Good. If you accept my new rules, I will uphold my end of the bargain. But if you or your goons ever bother me or Soren again, I will rain shit on your life, and on the lives of every one of your men who have sexually abused or harassed anybody at Nellis. And you and I will have another little get together like this. I've given you samples of how pleasurable this can be, and how painful it can be. If you let me down, I assure you that the pain you've experienced so far today will pale in comparison to what I'll do next, and in the future. So, what's it going to be, Lieutenant? Pleasure or pain? Nod up and down for pleasure, or shake side to side for pain."

Williamson wasted no time in nodding up and down frantically.

"You are a very wise man," Helen replied, not disguising her sarcasm and her contempt. She opened one of the nipple clamps and removed it, then did the same for the other clamp. Williamson's body slumped in relief. Helen continued to stroke his cock, urging it to swell and turn red again. It's been a pleasure doing business with you."

Williamson started moaning again, partly with pleasure as Helen continued her stroking, but partly from intense pain as blood gradually returned to the pain receptors in his nipples. Then she grasped and squeezed his cock, eliciting a giant groan from the man. At the same time, she squeezed his right nipple as hard as she could, now that the nerve endings were exquisitely hypersensitive. Williamson didn't know whether to squeal or moan. Helen knew that his pain was also heightening his pleasure. She turned to Soren.

"Put a condom over his cock and make sure he has a happy ending," she ordered. "Then blindfold and drug him again, and get him back to the hotel."

"Happy ending? What do you want me to do?" Soren asked.

"Use your imagination, Soren. I don't care what you do, just relieve the man's tension. He's about ready to explode." She turned and headed towards the door.

"Where are you going dressed like that?" Soren demanded, his voice oozing jealousy.

She stopped dead in her tracks, then turned and stared at Soren, her eyes blazing with rage.

"Don't you ever question me again!" Helen screamed. "I will go where I want and do what I wish. I am Lady Helen, and you will submit to me! Is that clear?"

Soren hung his head, suddenly realizing that submission was his only way of keeping his connection with her.

"Take care of Williamson," Helen repeated. "Now, as long as I'm at the dungeon, I need to find somebody around here who can give me some decent release."

With that, she turned on her heels and strode confidently to the door. She disappeared into the dimly lit corridor, leaving Soren to carry out her orders.

CHAPTER 23

HELEN BLINKED, struggling to bring her mind back into the present. She straightened her posture, blinked again, and made eye contact with Fran. Her body gradually reassumed its former rigid, straight, and strong posture as she gradually reconnected with reality.

"That's the night I found myself and realized I had control of my own destiny," Helen recalled.

"You found your inner strength," Fran reflected.

"Men are all the same," Helen continued. "Sure, they all want sex. But what they really want is power and control. I just learned to use sex to dominate them - to give them the illusion of control. It's so easy. The trick is to give them a little reward now and then … Make them think they've won the big prize. Before long, I'm dominating them and they don't even realize what's happened. They'll do anything to get another small touch or a brief whiff of me."

"So, you stopped the abuse," Fran answered. "You changed from being a powerless victim to somebody who was strong and powerful. I must admit I admire that.

"Thank you," Helen replied. "Before long, I turned the sexual abuse and hazing of cadets like me and Soren into orgies of dominance and submission like nobody had ever witnessed before."

"And people finally treated you with respect," Fran added.

"I *earned* their respect … *We* earned it, Soren and I together … the hard way. I had to dominate and humiliate Soren to earn the respect of the others. He accepted it from me because he loved me. It made things bearable for him. It was a way for us to survive."

"I understand," Fran said, nodding. "Like you, I also managed to find a part of me that was strong. I tricked and humiliated Paolo, my brother-in-law, so he would never abuse me again."

Fran reached out and took Helen's hand, placing it over her growing baby. Her eyes searched out Helen's, making contact and not letting go.

"We are not so different, you and I," Fran said. "We both found ways to be strong and to escape."

As Fran gazed into Helen's eyes, she frowned. For a brief second, she caught another fleeting glimpse of Helen's face in a memory from her distant past. But it was gone as quickly as it came to her. A moment of silence passed between them while Fran's mind worked feverishly to recapture the tenuous missing link to a memory she knew she should remember.

Without warning, the silence was shattered by a sonic boom, followed by the roar of a jet engine thundering overhead. Any link that Fran might have been making with her distant memory, vaporized instantly. The elusive memory disappeared as fast as the roaring aircraft that was already miles away, climbing into the blue desert sky and vanishing as quickly as it had appeared.

A SLEEK F-16 aircraft roared through the clear blue sky on its training mission, soaring high above the Nevada desert and the Tonopah Mountain Range. Spotting something unusual on the ground below, the lead pilot activated his radio.

"Red Two, do you see something strange down there on our left at ten o'clock?"

"Roger, Red Leader. Is that a campsite?"

"Looks like it. I don't recall any mention of a camp in that area in our briefings," the leader replied.

"You sure it's not in that no-fly zone? Seems mighty close," Red Two asked.

"I don't think so. I'm goin' down for a look," the leader decided.

"I don't know, sir … They were pretty clear about not violating the no-fly zone," Red Two answered.

"Your concerns are noted, Red Two. I think we're okay. I'm goin' down."

Red Leader banked his F-16 and descended rapidly for a look, his aircraft racing over a large camouflage tent, part of a small campsite in the remote part of the Tonopah Test Range, before climbing back to altitude.

"I confirm that it's a campsite, Red Two," Red Leader said into his radio.

"Do you think we should mention it, sir?" Red Two asked. "I'm almost certain it's inside the no-fly zone."

"Don't worry, Red Two. I'll take any flack that comes our way. It's time to head back to base anyway. I'd like to know what's going on down there."

"FUCK! Somebody's head is going to roll!" Helen screamed, as the roar of jet engines faded rapidly into the distance. Her hand left Fran's abdomen abruptly as she jumped to her feet. She was clearly both startled and furious that the jet had flown over their camp.

Fran felt a faint sense of hope. *Maybe somebody will see us and report the campsite*, she thought to herself.

"What's wrong? Are we in danger?" she said aloud to Helen.

Helen paused, seemingly struggling to control her anger. Her eyes went distant for a few seconds. Finally, her eyes came alive again and reconnected with Fran's.

"Danger?" Helen answered, appearing to be back in control. "Of course not. This part of the bas … er, desert, has always been off limits. It's just unusual to have an aircraft fly over this area."

Fran paused, staring at Helen for a moment while she tried to get up her nerve. Finally, she felt strong enough and opened her mouth.

"I think I know you. I've seen you before," she said.

Helen stared at Fran and then broke out laughing.

"Really! It's taken you this long to get it? I'm actually shocked you haven't figured it out by now!" She walked over to the same duffel bag where she kept her leather boots and cane. She pulled out a shoulder-length platinum blonde wig and placed it over her short brown hair. Then, clearly not ashamed, she stripped down to her underwear, pulled the black leather boots from the bag and slipped into them.

Fran immediately noticed the large tattoo of a black widow spider on Helen's shoulder and neck.

"Indio Jail," Fran said meekly. "You were in my cell one day."

Helen threw her head back and laughed freely again. After a moment, she regained her composure. "You were so terrified of me that day. You were like a fish out of water in jail!"

On one hand, Fran realized she should have felt happy that she finally remembered where she'd seen Helen before. But her eyes couldn't stop staring at Helen's boots and wig. There was something else buried deep in her memory. But as hard as she tried, she simply could not find another connection.

"What is it, dear?" Helen asked. A coy smile spread across her face. "Where did you go just now? Is there something else you remember?"

Fran lied with a shake of her head. She looked away from Helen, somehow feeling afraid to make eye contact with her. She looked down and saw the containers of oatmeal and coffee on the table in front of her.

"I was going to make some oatmeal and coffee before the jet flew over," Fran said. "Do you want some?"

"Sure, knock yourself out," Helen answered. "I'll start the stove for you."

Fran busied herself by measuring out some oatmeal and then some coffee. As she worked, she racked her brain for an elusive memory that she knew was still buried deep in the dark recesses of her mind.

Indio Jail wasn't the only time, was it? There was someplace else ... why can't I remember?

TWO F-16 pilots were ushered into the office of Colonel Bryce Williamson, Commander of the Nevada Test and Training Range at Nellis Air Force Base, just north of Las Vegas. Behind and flanking Williamson's desk stood two flags, the Stars and Stripes on his right and the Air Force coat of arms on the other. The walls were adorned with photographs of classic aircraft and famous test pilots.

Still in their flight suits, the pilots stood at attention and saluted their commanding officer.

"First Lieutenant Douglas and Second Lieutenant Norman reporting, sir," the pilot on the right announced.

"Lieutenant Douglas, it's come to my attention that you intentionally defied a direct order and ventured into a no-fly zone on the Test Range. Is that correct?" Williamson asked.

"With all due respect, Colonel," Douglas answered. "I didn't think the tent was in the restricted area, sir."

Williamson shifted his gaze from the group leader to his subordinate. "Mister Norman. What do you have to say for yourself?"

The Second Lieutenant looked warily at his First Lieutenant, who nodded, signaling him to tell the Colonel what happened.

"I asked Lieutenant Douglas if he thought the tent was in the restricted area because I wasn't certain," Norman replied.

"So, you advised the Lieutenant about the no-fly zone?"

"Yes, sir," Norman answered.

Colonel Williamson glared at the two pilots, making his anger quite clear. After a moment, he lowered his eyes, then he leaned back in his chair and gazed out the window before finally looking at the pilots again.

"There must be some confusion here, gentlemen," Williamson said finally. "I'm not sure I know the first thing about any tent on the range. Is there any chance that you were mistaken, Mr. Douglas? That there was, in fact, no tent?"

The Colonel's eyes locked onto Douglas, letting him know that there was a right answer and a wrong answer to his question.

"Yes, Colonel!" Douglas answered sharply. "I think I must have been mistaken. From a distance, the vegetation fooled me. I did not see a tent when I flew over that area."

"I see," the Colonel replied. "So, there was no tent, and no flight into the restricted area?"

"That's correct, sir!" Norman confirmed.

Colonel Williamson pushed his chair back and rose to his feet. "Then I see no need to waste any more of your time, gentlemen. I trust that, since this alleged tent never existed, you will never feel the need to mention it again … to anybody. Am I correct, Mr. Douglas?"

"Yes, sir!"

"Very well, gentlemen. That will be all. I don't want to see you in here again. Dismissed!"

The two pilots saluted, turned, and walked from the Colonel's office, closing the door behind them. As it closed, Williamson sank into his chair and heaved a large sigh of relief.

"That was too fuckin' close," he muttered to himself.

CHAPTER 24

WITH NO place in the tent for privacy, Fran turned her back to Helen as she stripped herself naked for a sponge bath. She felt self-conscious and vulnerable, knowing that her captor was staring at her pregnant body. She added room-temperature water to the steaming water in the basin in front of her, then she tested its temperature. She soaked a facecloth and rubbed a bar of soap on it to create a soapy lather. The hot water felt refreshing on her face as she scrubbed first, and then rinsed the soap from her face.

"You're more beautiful now than the last time I saw you naked. Do you remember that time?" Helen asked.

Fran froze and covered her breasts instinctively with both arms. She turned sideways and looked back over her shoulder. She stared at Helen, her brain struggling once again to find the missing memory she knew she should remember.

"*Ravi de vous rencontrer*, Madame Morel," Helen said calmly.

Fran went completely numb. Helen's words sent her mind flying somewhere into her distant past, as though she had seen or heard a ghost. Her facecloth fell to the dusty desert floor. The memory finally began to crystallize in her consciousness.

FRANCESCA CAPELLINI stood beside her husband, Philippe Morel, in the salon of their Parisian apartment. She surveyed the collection of artists that Philippe managed, each of them mingling with the elite of Parisian society and doing their best to attract attention from potential buyers and patrons. Philippe pointed to an elderly gentleman in full French ceremonial military attire.

"Come, Francesca," Philippe said, pointing. "That is Général Roland Blais over there. You must meet him."

Fran's eyes followed Philippe's finger to the general, and then they panned to the older man's date, an alluring young woman who appeared to be speaking English. She was short in stature with short brown hair, but Fran noticed instantly that the woman exuded confidence and sensuality in the revealing designer evening gown and stiletto heels she wore. As Fran watched, the woman stopped talking and turned her head. Suddenly Fran realized that the woman was staring directly at her. Almost instantly, Fran felt herself being captivated by the irresistible lure of the woman's confident brown eyes.

Philippe took Fran's hand and led her over towards Général Blais and his alluring date.

"Francesca, I would like you to meet Général Blais," Philippe said.

The general snapped to attention, bowed his head, and took Fran's hand. He smiled warmly and raised her hand to his lips.

"*Enchanté, Madame*," he said.

Philippe turned his attention to the general's date, almost as if he was presenting royalty to Fran.

"And may I present, the beautiful Lady Hélène," Philippe gushed. "Lady Hélène, my wife Francesca."

"*Ravi de vous rencontrer*, Madame Morel," the woman said. "I've been looking forward to meeting you. Your husband has said so many wonderful things about you."

"RAVI DE vous recontrer, Madame Morel."

Fran's mind continued tumbling back through time. It felt as though a maze of impenetrable walls within her mind, that had held solidly in place for over twenty years, were suddenly crumbling and falling to the ground all at once. A tsunami of unwanted memories was flooding over the walls. It was all coming back to her now.

Philippe's party had degenerated into one of his famous orgies of drugs and sex. An invitation to one of Philippe's parties signaled a person's arrival at the innermost circles of Parisian society.

Fran held a martini and was clearly inebriated. Her eyes were blurry and bloodshot. She felt disengaged, almost as if she was viewing the event from the other side of a thick pane of glass. The general was flirting with her, but her attention was elsewhere. Lady Hélène - now known to Fran as Helen - was flirting with Philippe, who was also drunk. It had become obvious to Fran that he was enjoying every minute of the mysterious woman's attention. He stared longingly at the young woman's cleavage while doing his best to charm her.

Fran recalled that she had no longer felt jealous of Philippe's flirting - she had become numb to it years ago, when she had learned to push her painful emotions behind the walls, just as she was currently numb to the general's flirting and wandering hands.

Philippe smiled at Helen and nodded enthusiastically, then he turned and looked in Fran's direction. Helen turned and stared at Fran too. She locked eyes with her and flashed a knowing, devious smile.

Fran felt dizzy and the scene shifted again. She vaguely remembered Philippe trying to convince her to do something, and she had a distant memory of making a weak attempt to resist. She thought perhaps an argument ensued, but she couldn't be sure.

Finally, Fran's memory fragments began to coalesce into one distinct set of images. In the memory, she sat completely naked in the rooftop spa of their apartment building, with the general at her side. His hands had wandered eagerly over her body and she had felt completely numb to it. A woman with short brown hair, her back to Fran, was engaged in a passionate embrace and kiss with Philippe. She ended the kiss and turned towards Fran. The image was crystal clear. It was the image that had been flashing back in

Fran's mind for the past couple of weeks, ever since Helen kidnapped her from the safety of her estate in Las Vegas.

Helen reached for a small plastic container on the edge of the spa. She passed another capsule of ecstasy to everybody in the spa and they all chased it down with a glass of champagne. Helen and Philippe resumed their amorous activity, with the action becoming increasingly hot and heavy. The general made a move to kiss Fran on the lips. She responded without enthusiasm. His hands strayed downwards from her breasts to her inner thighs. Any resistance she might have felt was buried deep beneath her mental walls. As she remembered passively accepting the general's eager invasion into her most intimate spaces, Fran felt her world spinning again.

Another wave of memories flooded through her consciousness. Before she knew it, another image crystalized in her mind. Helen was dressed in a provocative black leather suit - maybe even the same leather bodice she kept in her present-day duffel bag - orchestrating another sexual orgy. The orgy seemed to have progressed to their Paris bedroom. The image that became clear was one of Helen flogging and caning the participants, including Fran herself. From her dissociated viewpoint, Fran was only vaguely aware that Philippe and the general were both in bed with her - and both men were performing sex acts on her at the same time while Helen watched and urged them on.

ANOTHER distant sonic boom over the Tonopah Test Range startled Fran back into reality. Her eyes blinked. She looked down at herself, suddenly realizing she was still completely naked. She looked over her shoulder, immediately recognizing Helen's face.

"It was *you* in Paris! Philippe was never the same again after that night," Fran said. "His appetite … His need to dominate …"

"Where do you think Philippe learned about dominance and submission?" Helen replied, laughing. "Do you really think it was just because of that one night? He'd been seeing me for months …

Just to be humiliated … Just for the chance to have a small piece of me … Like all the rest of them."

Helen walked around Fran so that the two women were now face to face. Helen locked her eyes onto Fran's. As if Helen had cast a spell on her, Fran stopped covering herself, submitted, and presented her naked body to Helen's eyes. Helen's mood seemed to soften for a moment.

"A woman I know … a woman named Teri … she was posted in Germany for a few years," Helen continued. "I spent a great deal of time with her there. I remember her being pregnant once."

Helen paused. Her mind was distant and her eyes were empty.

"I can't really say she was my friend, because we're so different. She's always been so submissive … Sometimes even whiny, like a child. I can't stand it when she gets that way!"

Fran lost eye contact with Helen. She felt her captor becoming more agitated and increasingly distant. Then, suddenly, Helen seemed to gather herself and straightened her body. Her eyes locked back onto Fran's and she regained control of herself.

"While I was in Germany, I became the most desired dominatrix in all of Europe. Men and women alike, none of them could get enough humiliation or get enough of having their sexual fantasies fulfilled by the famous Lady Helen."

Fran's eyes came alive. In that moment, she suddenly realized the full extent of the split in the Helen's personality. She was truly dealing with a female Jekyll and Hyde - a woman with dual personalities. Fran's mind started racing, trying to use her newfound information to plan her next move.

"What about Soren? Where does he fit in your life?" Fran asked.

"He and Teri fell in love," Helen answered, her voice full of contempt. "They were both so pathetic and weak when they first met. But I changed that. I made them both strong. I taught Soren how to take punishment from me, so he could take it from them. It was I who gave him the confidence to succeed. It was I who convinced him that he should go and build his church and dominate others."

"And Teri?" Fran pressed.

"She's such an ass kisser. The Air Force is perfect for her because she's so obedient. But, in the end, like all the others, she does what I command her to do," Helen replied.

"The others?" Fran asked, puzzled.

"The officers," Helen answered. "Not just those who abused Teri and Soren. But every officer I've ever taught to properly initiate and humiliate new recruits. Now they all answer to me and serve me."

Helen paused for a moment, gazing at Fran's pregnant body, and seemed confused again. Her eyes had become increasingly emotionless and cold as she told Fran her story. Without warning, she turned and walked back to Fran's cot. She picked up Fran's towel and threw it at her.

"Dry yourself and cover up. Soren will be here soon and we've got another video to make."

Helen turned and walked out of the tent, leaving Fran alone. She felt exhausted and overwhelmed from the emotional rollercoaster and the cascade of traumatic memories that had just flooded back into her consciousness. She wrapped herself with her towel, walked back to her cot, and sat down. She began trembling with fear. For the first time since she had been abducted, Fran realized just how fragile, unstable, and unpredictable Helen really was.

I must find a way to get escape! I can't wait for somebody else to save me. I need to do this by myself. If I don't, I know I'm going to die.

THE HEAT inside the tent was almost unbearable. Fran felt as if she couldn't drink enough water. Her body was drenched with perspiration and it felt as if there was a constant stream of sweat droplets dripping from her forehead. Her clothing clung to her skin, creeping into every nook and cranny of her body.

"Hurry up, Francesca," Helen barked. She made her way to Fran's cot and bent down to unfasten her chain. "We're filming the video outside."

"Why outside?" Fran asked.

"Because it's too damned hot in this fucking tent, that's why," Helen answered, mopping sweat from her forehead. "Let's get this over with so we can trade you for that Baranyi bitch and get out of this hell-hole."

As the two women rose to their feet, Helen thrust a piece of paper into Fran's hand.

"Here's your script."

Emerging from the tent, Fran squinted from the blazing desert sun. Although still incredibly hot and dry, at least the air wasn't as stifling and oppressive as in the tent. Soren had the video camera set up outside. He motioned for Fran to sit in the partial shade of some creosote brush and a large cactus.

"Sit down on that stool while I adjust the camera," Soren ordered. Bright sunshine streaked through spaces between the sparse creosote branches, shining directly in Fran's eyes.

"Can you shoot in the opposite direction? The sun is too bright. It's making me squint," she asked.

Soren huffed impatiently. "Oh, alright. Turn your body around to the left."

Soren walked around Fran, setting up the camera to shoot from the opposite direction. He was so intent on framing Fran's image, he failed to notice that he was filming the rear end of the tent, as well as a partial view of the surrounding desert and mountains.

"Hurry it up! We don't have all day," Helen shouted.

"Okay, already," Soren shouted back. He fidgeted hurriedly with his exposure and focus.

"Whenever you're ready, Francesca," he announced finally. "Start reading."

Having already read her script, Fran's mind scrambled feverishly to remember the place where she was going to embed another clue for Dan.

"Start reading!" Helen screamed. "We don't have all day!"

"Sorry," Fran answered. Her voice was meek and shaky with anxiety. "I just want to make sure I get it right for you …" She swallowed and cleared her voice - and her resolve.

"… My wound has healed, and I am in good health, as you can see. You are to follow these instructions in a uniform manner. The exchange will take place two days from now, on Wednesday morning at six am. We will phone you on your cell phone, two hours before the exchange, with directions to the location. Don't even think about getting the police involved. If we see anybody in uniform at the site, your last chance of seeing me alive will crash and burn.

"Stop!" Helen screamed. "Are you fucking with me again, Capellini? That's not what I wrote!"

"I'm sorry," Fran answered. Her throat felt dry from the combination of heat and her anxiety. "I just wanted to make sure that Dan follows the instructions. You only mentioned police, so I thought you would want me to warn him against bringing *anybody* in uniform."

"And what about that *crash and burn* shit," Helen screamed. "Why the fuck did you say that?"

"Because it's a term Dan uses all the time to describe when things go terribly wrong … like when his wife died," Fran added.

"Okay, okay. I get it! That's good enough!" Helen shouted impatiently. "It's too fucking hot to be out here much longer." She turned to Soren. "Lock her up again. Make sure she's got water, then get back here to record my voice. After that, you can alter it and make the DVD tonight."

"Right away," Soren promised. "The sooner we get Baranyi and get out of this living hell, the happier I'll be." He turned his attention to Fran again. "Back into the tent, Capellini."

With mixed emotions, Fran walked back into the stifling sauna-like atmosphere in the tent, dreading the rest of another day of oppressive heat and boredom. And yet, she had to suppress the urge to smile. She had managed to pass along another clue to Dan. Now it was up to him to put the puzzle pieces together. But she feared that her time was rapidly running out. Now it was now up to her to find a way to save herself … in case Dan didn't figure it out in time.

CHAPTER 25

DAN SAT in front of his laptop at the kitchen table with Angela, Richard, Miriam, and Gwen gathered around, watching and listening to the second ransom video.

"... *Don't even think of involving the police or FBI. You will only have two hours' notice, so make sure you and Baranyi are ready. And don't be late. Francesca's life ... and your baby's ... depend on it.*"

The video finished playing. The tense facial muscles and the deep furrows in his forehead revealed the depth of Dan's concern.

"Well, that's it," Dan concluded. "What do you think?"

"Very interestin', Richard answered. "They're only givin' y'all two hours … probably cuz they don't want th' cops t' have any time t' prepare. That ain't good fer us, neither."

"So, what can we do?" Angela asked. "Shouldn't we call the FBI?"

"Now don' gitcher shirt in a knot, l'il lady," Richard replied coolly. "I said it ain't good. I didn't say there's nothin' we kin do. Whatcha say girls?" He looked to Miriam and Gwen, who looked at each other briefly before Gwen spoke up.

"Their message says th' exchange'll happen within two hours of Las Vegas. They're probably givin' us just the right amount of time to get to the swap location. So, I'm bettin' it'll happen somewhere about two hours from here."

"I agree," Miriam added. "Have we got a map of Nevada and Arizona? And a pen or pencil?"

"Yeah, just a second," Dan answered.

He jumped up from his chair and dug around in a stack of papers on the counter. He came up with a map of Nevada and a pencil. Richard moved Dan's laptop aside to make room and spread the map open for all five of them to see. Richard studied the map's scale, then pointed to a location on Interstate 15, east of Las Vegas.

"This here's about two hours east of Vegas," he concluded. He then used the pencil to draw a rough circle on the map with the same radius around Las Vegas. "So, our exchange is gonna happen somewhere inside this circle."

The group stood in silence, staring at the map, when Miriam suddenly pointed to a spot on the map, southeast of Las Vegas. "Right there! Valley of Fire State Park. I've been there, it's perfect! Good road access, but it's up in the mountains with lots of good cover. They can get up on the high ground and see anybody coming for miles."

"Sounds like a real possibility," Richard exclaimed. "Ah'll betcher right. So, we gotta use that t'our advantage. Girls, find out everythin' y'can 'bout Valley o' Fire. Let's figger out some likely spots, then figger out what we need fer equipment."

"Anything Angela and I can do?" Dan asked.

"Nope, not fer now," Richard replied. "Jus' stay by yer phone. Try'n give us as much time as y'can. If they call in the next twenty-four hours, try'n buy us some time. Tell em that it'll take Angela a day t'get here, or somethin' like that."

Dan looked at Angela, who nodded her agreement. He turned back to Richard. "We can do that. What do I say if Martinelli or Simpson call me?"

"Ya tell em nothin'," Richard added. "We don't want those fuck-ups within a hundred miles o' that exchange." He turned to Gwen and Miriam. "Okay, gals. Let's git crackin'. We got work t'do."

DUSK FINALLY provided the occupants of the tent with some welcome relief from the relentless rays of the desert sun and its oppressive heat, as the sun finally disappeared behind the Tonopah range in the west. Fran sat on her cot trying to read, but daylight was yielding inevitably to dusk, so she put down her book. Helen, who had been sitting in a foldout camp chair, her feet resting on a makeshift ottoman, a container of supplies, did likewise. Fran's mind drifted away to the recently recovered memories and images from her previous encounters with Helen in Paris. Finally, she looked up at Helen.

"There's something I still don't understand. Why was Kelly Mulholland involved with my charges and prosecution in Palm Desert?" she asked. "Did you have some kind of control over her too?"

Helen grinned wickedly, then she cocked her head to the side, somewhat puzzled. "You really don't remember her, do you?"

"Somehow, I get the feeling I should," Fran admitted.

Helen laughed heartily from deep down inside, enjoying Fran's confusion.

"The military paid Kelly's way through law school," Helen explained. "She was posted at Ramstein, in Germany, at the same time as Teri. She was one of my new recruits back then — submissive, but I saw that she resented it. I knew she really wanted to dominate others. Nevertheless, she was in very high demand as a submissive."

"By men like the general?" Fran asked.

"Yes, of course!" Helen replied. "But also by many others. The kink scene in Germany and Paris has always been vibrant, exciting, and very much alive amongst the aristocracy."

Suddenly, Fran's brain made a connection. A look of understanding spread slowly across her face. "Of course! Philippe desired her. She came to one of our parties … I remember meeting her now."

Just as quickly, Fran's brain started to make new connections and she felt herself starting to slip into the past. Her eyes began to look glazed and distant.

Helen began laughing uncontrollably until her eyes started to water and she had difficulty breathing. Finally, she regained control of herself and grinned wickedly at Fran.

"Meeting her?" she said, still laughing. "My dear girl, you got to know her about as intimately as you could ever imagine!"

HELEN LOUNGED in the antique Louis XV armchair, with its luxurious burgundy fabric and bold silver pattern. She exuded an air of intense sexuality and total dominance. Her legs were draped casually over one of the chair's arms. Her sparkling silver bodice was slit down to her navel and cut high on the sides to reveal her shapely thighs and hips. A slit in the garment's crotch revealed her plump, smoothly shaved vaginal lips and a glimpse of her pink inner lips beneath. A wooden cane laid casually across her lap.

"You want to learn how to dominate, Kelly?" Helen asked. A sly smile glowed on her face. "Then get up and show me you can do it!"

Through an alcohol and drug-induced fog, Fran barely noticed the look of relief and excitement that spread across Kelly Mulholland's face. Fran and Kelly knelt, side by side on the bedroom's chic eighteenth-century carpet, stripped to their panties - their bodies prostrate and giving up complete control to their dominatrix. Kelly slowly turned her attention to Fran, smiling wickedly.

"Stand up! Dominate her!" Helen ordered.

Kelly rose, hesitantly at first, glaring down at Fran. She looked briefly at Helen for approval. Seeing Helen's lascivious grin, Kelly seemed to become more empowered, much like a dog that had finally been let off its leash, free to roam and do what it wanted. Through her cognitive haze, Fran sensed the difference in the blonde woman's voice. A shiver of fear washed through her body. Kelly lifted one of her bare feet from the floor and placed her sole against Fran's forehead.

"Lick it clean!" Kelly commanded. When Fran didn't respond immediately, Kelly Mulholland leaned down. She slapped Fran viciously across the side of her head. "I said lick it clean, cunt!"

Alarms went off in Fran's brain. Her fight or flight response kicked into high gear. The foggy haze began to clear and her vision and hearing became sharper. Her mouth went dry. She stuck out her tongue and forced herself to drag it across Mulholland's sole. With hardly any saliva, she had to work to satisfy the other woman's bidding. Mercifully, Mulholland pulled her foot away. Fran's relief was short-lived, as the other foot was thrust into her face.

"Do it!" Mulholland ordered. Fran heard Helen's voice in the background, laughing. The inside of Fran's mouth felt as dry as sandpaper and her tongue acquired the raspy character of a cat, as she forced herself to drag it over the sweaty, dusty surface of Mulholland's sole. Finally, the foot was withdrawn.

"Stand!" Mulholland ordered. Fran rose slowly and unsteadily to her feet. Mulholland pressed her body and face against Fran, invading her personal space. Fran shuddered as she felt the blonde's hands exploring her curves and moving slowly across her pubic area. Kelly's fingers slid inside the band of Fran's panties, sliding slowly over her closely-shaved mound towards her lips and the soft valley between them, teasing her clit. Mulholland's lips touched Fran's softly. Her tongue gently teased Fran's lips. Fran felt confused, feeling a sense of invasion and revulsion as her vagina grew moist at the same time. Her body was betraying her - wanting more of the other woman's sensuous touch. Kelly's tongue probed deeper, looking for a response from Fran. At the same time, Kelly's fingers found Fran's breasts, teasing her nipples and bringing them alive.

Kelly's tongue probed deeper into Fran's mouth. Fran couldn't bring herself to respond to the invasion. Suddenly, her nipples erupted in flames of pain as Kelly Mulholland twisted them both viciously. Fran yelped, unable to repress the pain.

"Bitch!" Kelly hissed in Fran's face. Fran instinctively covered her breasts with both arms, enraging Kelly. Kelly grabbed the waist of Fran's panties and ripped them violently away from her body. Fran used one of her hands to try to cover her womanhood, infuriating the other woman even more. Kelly turned and grabbed for Helen's cane. In one long fluid movement, it flew from Helen's lap and landed squarely on one of Fran's thighs. Fran's mind hurtled back in time to Manarola, to Giulia's and Paolo's bedroom. As the cane came slashing down on her thighs again, all Fran could see was the metal buckle on Paulo's belt, hurtling towards her. Like she did in the past, she gritted her teeth and choked down her pain.

Fran's mind was in turmoil. Part of her felt like she was a small, terrified girl, back in Manarola. But another part of her watched, without emotion, as two naked men entered the room. They walked up to Helen, knelt, bowed their heads, and kissed her hand. They were both clearly aroused by the sight of the two naked women. Helen stroked both men's erections, watching them grow. Devoid of emotion, Fran recognized one of the men as her husband, Philippe. The other blonde-haired man, she didn't recognize. As their organs continued to swell and their engorged tissues turned red, Helen rose from her chair and grabbed her cane back from Kelly Mulholland. She passed it to the blonde man.

"Kelly! Francesca! On the bed!" she commanded. "On your back, Francesca. You on top, Kelly, in sixty-nine position. Show each other some love. Taste those delicious pussies … Now!" she screamed.

Helen turned back to Philippe. She kissed him passionately, gripping his erection and squeezing until he moaned in a conflicted state of pain and ecstasy. Then she turned casually to the other man.

"Now!" Helen shouted. The man with the cane swung his body around. Fran saw the cane whipping its way towards Kelly's exposed buttocks, which were elevated in the air only inches above Fran's face. She felt the rush of air on her face. Kelly cried out. Fran couldn't tell whether it was a cry of pain or ecstasy.

"What did you say, Kelly?" Helen asked calmly. Fran sensed that the words weren't really a question. They sounded more like an order.

"More please, my lady," Kelly shouted.

"Why should I give you more?" Helen shouted.

"Because I'm a worthless piece of shit and I deserve it, ma'am," Kelly responded loudly. Helen nodded to the blonde man. The cane flashed through the air again. Once again, Fran felt the air rushing towards her face as the cane landed on Kelly's flesh, only inches from her. Mulholland's vagina pressed into Fran's face as the cane landed, almost smothering her. Fran was surprised to taste Kelly's salty juices, now flowing freely onto Fran's lips in response to the beating.

"My lady. Please hit me again!" Kelly shouted. Her hips started to grind her slick vagina harder against Fran's face. Unable to breathe, Fran started to feel herself panic. Her hands began grasping at Mulholland's body, feeling the need to push the other woman's body away from her face.

"Switch positions," Helen shouted suddenly. Fran gladly pushed Kelly Mulholland away as the other woman lifted herself away from Fran's face. Despite being free, Fran gagged and struggled to catch her breath, even as she straddled Kelly's torso. As Fran and Kelly switched positions, Helen released her grip on Philippe's throbbing cock. She picked up two silver objects from a table next to the ornate antique bed and walked around Fran until she was facing her, yet looking back towards Philippe and the other man. After a few seconds, Fran felt Helen's eyes lock onto hers and felt helpless to look away. Helen smiled a sickly sweet, sarcastic smile. Her hand reached out and cradled Fran's face, softly and gently.

"Start licking, Kelly," Helen said, in a voice that was still gentle, but definitely firm and in total command. Fran felt Kelly's tongue start exploring and teasing her vaginal area. While her mind protested, her body continued to betray her. Fran felt her own juices starting to flow onto Kelly. She felt her own hips starting to sway in rhythm with Kelly's tongue. Helen's hand moved downwards, stroking, then massaging Fran's right nipple. Fran was surprised to hear a soft moan escape from her mouth.

At that moment, her body seemed to convulse. Pain seared through her right nipple. She looked down in horror and saw a silvery metal object clamped tightly onto the firm brown tissue.

"Relax, Francesca," Helen said softly. "Breathe. Let the sensations from your nipple merge with those from your pussy. Let them become one."

Gradually, Fran felt her nipple growing numb. The pain seemed more distant. Once again, she became aware of Kelly Mulholland's tongue caressing her outer and inner vaginal lips, darting inside of her, then flicking and teasing her clit. She felt a tingling inside her belly and felt the blood flowing into her vagina. She was quickly losing mental control over her body's cravings. She heard another loud moan escape involuntarily from her own mouth.

As she did, Fran felt another explosion of pain in her other nipple. The energy from the explosion seemed to surge straight into her genitals. She moaned again as she looked down at her breasts, not at all surprised to see another clamp on her left nipple.

"Bend over and start eating Kelly's pussy," Helen commanded.

As if she was a robot, Fran did as Helen ordered. The pain in her nipples had transformed into numbness and a dull pounding sensation. Instead of killing her sexual desire, the pain seemed to fuel it instead. Nothing made sense to Fran as her tongue explored Kelly's pleasure zone more and more eagerly.

Helen walked back around behind Fran to the man with the cane. She kissed him and stroked his organ to make sure it was fully erect. As Fran's hips resumed moving eagerly against Kelly's tongue, Helen stopped kissing the man and nodded to him. He pulled the cane high into the air behind him. Fran was vaguely aware of a sensation of rushing air, just before the cane bit into the flesh of her buttocks. She yelped, her voice conveying a mixture of pain and pleasure. Then she felt the rush of air again. As she did, the image of Paolo's belt buckle came flying out of the distant past. Any pleasure she had been feeling in that moment vanished instantly. Instead, Fran's body became rigid with fear. In the distance, she felt something moist in the valley dividing the two halves of her buttocks.

"Allez, mes chers amis," Helen said to Philippe and the other man. "They're all yours. Make me proud."

Fran heard the words in the distance, but they held no meaning for her. She vaguely felt herself being pushed forward roughly. Then, without warning, she felt a tearing, burning sensation and an unfamiliar fullness in her rectum. Alarms started exploding in her brain, like a warehouse full of pyrotechnics all exploding at the same time, commanding her body to either fight or to run. But her limbs felt like concrete pillars and wouldn't respond. Instead, she felt her entire body going heavy and numb. At the same time, her pain, her fear, and her revulsion slowly receded, until they finally disappeared into a vacuum of total darkness.

FRAN'S EYES opened a slit. The morning sun streamed through translucent window coverings, flooding the room in a uniform yellow glow that overpowered her eyes. She squinted them open, but closed them again quickly. Then she tried to move her body. Her nipples, buttocks, and the back of her legs were raw. She felt a burning sensation in her anus. Her head throbbed. To help stop the pain, her body froze and gave up all attempts to move. After a few seconds, she felt a stirring next to her.

Philippe must be awake.

The body next to her stirred again. She opened her eyes. Instead of Philippe, a woman's face and her disheveled blonde hair appeared, hovering over Fran's head. The woman's naked breasts brushed against Fran's raw nipples. Fran winced in pain. The woman planted a gentle kiss on Fran's lips.

"Thank you for a fabulous night," the woman said. "Let's hope Helen lets us do this again."

Fran's body froze. She laid in bed, engulfed in fear, and watched as the woman slid from beneath the sheets. Completely naked, the woman wandered around the room, retrieving pieces of clothing. She slipped into her G-string and then picked up her bra. Fastening the rear clasp in front of her, she rotated the garment so the cups swung around beneath her breasts. She pulled up the straps and adjusted the cups, then picked up an evening gown from the floor. Within seconds, she had slipped into the gown, fastened the rear zipper, and slipped into a pair of high-heeled shoes that she retrieved from the bedroom floor. She stood still and surveyed the room. Finally spotting a small purse, she retrieved it, turned, and blew Fran a kiss. She exited the room, closing the door gently behind her.

Fran laid completely still, trying to absorb as much of the soft yellow glow that flooded into the room, as possible. As hard as she tried, she could not remember the woman's name, nor the details of what had happened the night before. But she felt an ominous sense of inner darkness threatening to overpower her. She allowed herself to lay in bed, continuing to soak up the warm morning sun. Its soothing rays helped to push the darkness into a distant recess in her mind, behind familiar, impenetrable walls. Only when the dark feeling was safely gone, did she pull back the sheets. Feeling dirty and disgusting, Fran got out of bed and walked painfully towards the bathroom. She needed a long hot shower to cleanse and soothe her, both physically and emotionally. She prayed that the stream of water would wash the feelings of filth and disgust off her body and down the drain, and hopefully leave her in peace.

CHAPTER 26

SOREN STOOD in line at the gas bar's checkout counter. The clerk, a teenage girl with piercings in her nose and both eyebrows, along with dark Goth makeup and black clothing, chatted idly with the young male customer in front of him. Soren tried to act casually, picking up a *National Enquirer* to pass the time. He chuckled to himself as he read the headline. Apparently, Angelina and Brad's relationship was on the rocks … again.

Finally, the young man ahead of him got his change, ended his chat with the clerk, and walked away. Soren stepped up to the counter.

"Hi there," he said. "Fifty dollars on pump four, and I'll take the *Enquirer* for my wife. Would you believe she thinks all this stuff is true?" He dropped sixty dollars in cash on the counter.

The girl's fingers danced on the cash register keys. "Same with my mom," she said, her eyes still focused on the cash register. She waited for it to spit out Soren's receipt.

As she waited, she lifted her eyes and began chatting idly with him. "I'm more into *People* myself," she said. Her eyes locked onto Soren's, pausing for a fraction of a second. She glanced furtively in the direction of the store entrance, then quickly back to Soren.

"Anything else I can do for you today?" she said cheerily. Soren checked the displays around the checkout counter, still trying to look casual. "Tell you what, how about a *Powerball* ticket. You can't win if you don't play, right?"

"Sorry," the girl answered. "We don't have *Powerball* in Nevada."

"Really," Soren said. "In a state where gambling is everywhere? What's with that?"

The young clerk shrugged her shoulders. "I dunno."

"Okay," Soren replied. "Just the gas and the *Enquirer*."

The girl smiled at Soren as she handed him his change.

"Have a good one," he said, returning her smile. He picked up his *Enquirer* and sauntered past a bulletin board full of missing pet posters, ads, and community event announcements. Once out the door, he climbed into the Escalade, turned the key, and drove away on the service road.

Once he was out the door, the clerk ran to the exit. She watched nervously as the Escalade drove away. When it had left, she turned to the bulletin board beside the doors, her eyes searching until she found what she was looking for. The man in the poster had glasses and longer, wavy blonde hair. Even though the customer at the checkout had short red hair, she was certain he was the same guy. She pulled a cell phone from the pocket of her black denims and dialed the number on the poster.

"Is this the FBI?" she asked. "I think I just saw that missing pastor … you know … the guy who kidnapped his son? …"

FBI AGENT Lindell Simpson burst through the door into Martinelli's office waving a sheet of paper.

"Gabe, we've had a break in the Capellini case!"

Startled by the unexpected intrusion, Gabe Martinelli's body jerked to attention as Simpson thrust a sheet of paper onto his desk in front of him. Unable to wait for him to read the report, Simpson hurriedly filled him in on the pertinent details.

"An employee at a gas bar in the north end thinks she spotted Soren Kristiansen buying gas and leaving in a black Escalade!"

"No shit!" Martinelli exclaimed. "When?"

"About half an hour ago," Simpson answered. "Dispatch called Little Rock first, because of the murder investigation.

Apparently, they weren't aware of the possible link between that case and Capellini's. It took a while before they figured it out and contacted me."

"Damn!" Martinelli cursed. "He's probably long gone now. Is our witness sure about the ID?"

"Ninety per cent," Simpson replied. "She said the guy she spotted had short red hair, but she had a decent conversation and got a really good look at him."

"Coulda cut an' dyed his hair," Martinelli thought out loud. "Any more details? Plate number, which direction he was heading?"

"She got a Nevada plate number and we've got them holding the security video for us. We can confirm the plate and hopefully get a good look at the guy. The girl says he headed north on the service road, probably to get to the northbound ramp on the other side of the I-75," Simpson explained.

"Let's hope," Martinelli retorted. He sat upright in his chair, placed both hands behind his head and stretched, giving himself a moment to think. "So, where does this fit with what we've got so far?"

"If it is him, it could just be coincidence," Simpson said. "It may not mean anything for Capellini's kidnapping."

"In that case, Whitney's theory that the good pastor is working together with our kidnapper is just that - nothing but theory," Gabe conjectured.

"Right," Simpson answered. "And we'd be jumping to conclusions. But on the other hand, we can't ignore Whitney's statements about Kristiansen having a blonde-haired accomplice, and his suspicions that they were out to kill him and the Baranyi woman."

"Which would explain him popping up in Vegas," Gabe surmised. "So, we have to take this seriously.

Martinelli removed his hands from the back of his head, sat upright in his chair and paused for a moment.

"Do we have the Little Rock reports?" he continued. "Did they have a plate number on the Escalade they think he was driving?"

Simpson passed another sheet of paper to her partner.

"I already checked," she replied. "Washington plates. But they also suspect the Escalade may have been stolen. We know the plates were reported stolen from a vehicle near the airport in Seattle."

"So, we're looking for a needle in the haystack," Martinelli huffed. "Any idea how many black Escalades there are out there within an hour of Vegas?"

"Yeah, pretty shitty odds of finding him, especially with more than a thirty-minute head start before we got the APB out to State Patrol and LVPD," Simpson answered.

"So, we're not much further ahead unless we get lucky and find the right black Escalade," Martinelli concluded.

"Not exactly," Simpson said hopefully. "If we get a good look at him on security video, we can also send out a new description to the media. We can ask the public to be on the lookout for a guy with short red hair in an Escalade. That's going to increase our odds a lot."

Martinelli looked at his watch. "We're too late to get this on the dinnertime news. Any chance we can get a security image for the late news?"

"Probably not," Simpson answered. "Realistically, we're probably looking at the morning. But I think we have another issue here."

Martinelli raised his eyebrows. "I'm all ears."

"Do we run the risk of sending him back underground if we let this go public?" Simpson asked.

"Good point," Gabe agreed. He resumed stretching in his chair, his hands behind his head in his typical thinking pose.

"This probably isn't one of those cases where we can justify keeping it from the media anyway," he answered. "So, I guess we'd better tell Whitney and Baranyi."

"I'll take care of that," Simpson replied. "Dan will likely see it on the morning news, so I'll call him before that happens. Besides, if Kristiansen is involved with Fran's kidnapper, there's a good chance they're going to get more anxious and make their demands soon. I'll tell Dan to be ready to give us a call right away when they do."

"Okay, I'm good with that," Martinelli said, nodding his agreement.

"In the meantime, want to go have a talk with our girl at the gas bar?" Simpson asked.

Martinelli pushed back his chair and stood up. He reached for his suit jacket, which was hanging on a coat stand behind his desk. "I thought you'd never ask. Any excuse to get away from this damned paperwork."

Simpson looked at her watch. "Let's grab a quick bite on the way. I think it's on me this time. How about Mexican?"

"Now you're talking," Gabe added, grinning. "Let's get outta here."

BRILLIANT morning sunshine flashed into Teri's eyes, temporarily blinding her as she turned the Escalade into the coffee shop's parking lot. She needed Wi-Fi access to answer any urgent email messages, but she also needed to appease the Director and notify him she'd be back at work soon. She grabbed her laptop from the passenger seat and exited the vehicle. Dressed casually in tight-fitting jeans and a white tank top she hurried across the parking lot and entered the shop.

Once inside, she stepped up to the counter and was greeted by a cheerful young man.

"Can I help who's next?" he asked.

Not wanting to make a lasting impression, Teri remained businesslike, keeping the conversation minimal.

"I'll have a cappuccino, please," she answered.

"One cappuccino, coming up," the clerk replied. "Would you like a breakfast sandwich with that, ma'am?"

"No thanks," Teri said brusquely. She handed him some money, including a modest tip. "Keep the change," she added.

"Thank you, ma'am. It'll be up in a moment."

Teri stepped away from the counter, surveyed the shop, and spotted an empty table. She walked over to the table and seated herself, making sure nobody was sitting behind her, before opening her laptop and connecting to the internet. After a few moments, she heard a voice calling in the background.

"One cappuccino!"

Teri closed the laptop, then got up and walked to the counter, where she picked up her drink and carried it back to the table. When she was settled, she took a relaxing sip, set down her cup, and began surfing the internet to look for developments in Fran's disappearance.

Suddenly, her eyes opened wide and her mouth dropped open. She stared at the screen in a state of shock. Her heart began pounding in her chest and her emotions raced out of control. Gradually, the look of shock on her face transformed into an angry glare. She began reading the news report that had triggered her anxiety, but found herself unable to concentrate as her anger escalated. She looked furtively around the room, suddenly paranoid that somebody might be staring at her. She took a second sip of cappuccino, then hurriedly closed the laptop and rushed from the shop, leaving her beverage virtually untouched.

Once out the door, Teri rushed to the Escalade, opened the door, and tossed the laptop into the empty passenger seat. Her heart pounded in her chest and her breaths were short and ragged as she worked to keep her mind focused. Her fear had now completely transformed into rage. Her Teri persona faded into the background as her personality transformed. She opened her purse, dug around frantically, and pulled out her cell phone. She dialed a number from memory and waited impatiently until somebody answered.

"It's me, Helen … I know … I'm in deep shit … I'm driving the Escalade right now … what if I'm stopped on the way back to camp?" she snapped.

"… Listen up. I need to speed up the timetable … Grab a pen …"

COLONEL Bryce Williamson sat at his desk, his cell phone pressed to his ear. He used his other hand to shield the phone's microphone for privacy. He whispered so his staff couldn't overhear the conversation.

"… A pair of new plates … ASAP … I can do that … A chopper? … Five days? Are you effin' kidding me? … Two armed backups again? … I can't pull that together on such short notice! … I've already stuck my neck out way too far for you."

"Listen up, asshole! If I go down, everybody else goes down too - including you! So, are you going to pull your shit together and get what I need?"

"Calm down," Williamson pleaded. "I'll see what I can do. But I can't promise anything. The plates won't be too difficult … I'll get on that right away … I'll need to get back to you on the rest of your shopping list … Where are you?"

"I'm at a coffee shop at East Craig and Losee. I can't wait in the truck in case the cops spot it. I'll be across the street, watching from the Mexican Grill."

"I'll get somebody out there right away with the new plates," Williamson answered.

"Have them call me at this number when they arrive, and I'll meet them at the truck. I'll call you same time tomorrow so we can work out the rest of the details." Helen lowered her phone, ready to disconnect, then raised it to her ear again.

"Just one more thing, Colonel. Don't fuck this up. Don't you dare disappoint me!"

"You know I wouldn't do that," Williamson replied. "Trust me, I'll figure something out."

The connection went dead. Bryce Williamson let out a long sigh of frustration. He hung his head in his hands, giving himself time to think. Finally, he dialed a number on his cell phone and waited …

"Tony, this is Bryce, I need another big favor … right away …"

FRAN LAID on her cot, trying to calculate how long she had been a prisoner. As the days dragged on and she lost track of the days, the task became more difficult. Thankfully, today was overcast so the daytime heat wasn't quite as oppressive. But despite the reprieve from the hot weather, boredom was taking its toll on her. She'd already read the few cheap novels and the magazines Soren had brought back to camp with him. It was getting harder each day to keep from retreating into the dark recesses within her mind.

The baby gave a good kick to bring her back to reality. She managed a smile. She liked to think that the child inside was stretching its limbs, readying itself for the day when it would finally be free from the confines of her womb. Then her mind drifted, replacing that fleeting happy thought with an ominous question: *Will the baby and I even live to see that day?* Another kick brought Fran back to the reality of her present dilemma. *Will I ever be free? There must be a way I can escape with my child. There must be a way to save us!*

She refocused on the present, forcing herself to survey the tent for what seemed like the millionth time. Her eyes came to rest on Soren. He slouched in a foldout camp chair, trying to read a newspaper. As she watched him, his head nodded and his eyes closed, then he jerked himself awake. Moments later, he nodded off again.

Fran's fascination with Soren was disrupted by a faint sound in the distance. She waited and concentrated. Before long, she recognized it as the sound of an approaching vehicle. The sound grew rapidly louder, signaling that the vehicle was racing towards the tent at high speed. Within moments, it reached the camp. Tires slid on the desert sand and gravel as the vehicle braked abruptly. Fran heard a door open, then the crunch of human feet on gravel, followed by the slam of a door. Determined footsteps stomped and crunched across the ground towards the tent.

"Soren!" Helen screamed. Her voice was still outside the tent, but her footsteps continued their relentless march. Her eyes blazed as she entered the tent, searching until she saw Soren dozing in his camp chair, his newspaper now lying on his chest. She stomped over to him and ripped the paper from his loose grip.

"You're an incompetent asshole!" Helen screamed. "When were you going to tell me about that gas bar?"

Soren's eyes flashed open, momentarily stunned by Helen's tirade. A blank look engulfed his face as he tried to orient himself to where he was. Then his body shrank instinctively. Fran was shocked at how easily intimidated Soren was by Helen's rage, as the other woman's diminutive shape towered menacingly over Soren's reclining body.

"What? … What are you talking about?" Soren answered, still confused by the unexpected awakening. Helen dropped a copy of today's newspaper into his lap. She pointed to the front-page headline: '*Fugitive Pastor Spotted at Gas Bar.*'

"That!" Helen screamed. "… That's what I'm talking about. The girl at that gas bar described you as 'friendly and polite'. What the fuck were you trying to do? … Hit on her?"

Soren cowered in his chair. Fran watched as he scrambled mentally for a way to defend himself against Helen's rage.

"I was … I was just trying to act normal … so she wouldn't suspect anything," he countered.

"Well, didn't you happen to notice a poster with your face on the wall?" Helen shouted, still on the attack. "Your friendly little conversation gave her plenty of time to recognize you."

"Poster?" Soren asked. His forehead creased as the bewildered look returned to his face.

"Oh, you didn't know?" Helen shouted. "Read the article. It looks like your little friend Baranyi has been handing those posters out all over town!"

Soren suddenly made sense of what had happened, and the gravity of his situation finally sank in. He sat up straight in his chair. The look of bewilderment on his face was transforming into fear and anger.

"Fuck! What are we going to do now?"

"Shut up," Helen shouted. "As usual, I've got things under control. Our friend at Nellis got us new plates for the truck. And I've moved up the timetable for the exchange. We've got to be ready by Friday morning. Get your video camera!"

Helen turned her head and her icy glare towards Fran.

Instantly, Fran felt a fresh wave of fear wash over her. Panic took control of her body as she realized she was running out of time to escape. She curled up in fetal position on the cot.

"One more message to your boyfriend," Helen snarled. "And you need to make it convincing. If he doesn't follow your instructions to the letter, he never sees you again!"

Helen turned her attention back to Soren, her eyes burning so intensely that he looked away submissively.

"You know what else this means, don't you?"

"Yes, my lady … I've been very bad," Soren muttered. "I'm yours to punish as you wish."

Helen nodded her head in the direction of the nearby duffel bag full of dominatrix gear.

"Get my bag!" Helen commanded. "Then strip!"

Helen turned back to Fran. A maniacal grin spread across her face as she glared at her captive. Fran felt another shiver of fear.

"We're going to show Francesca what happens to those who displease Lady Helen, isn't that right, Soren!"

Soren dropped the duffel bag at Helen's feet and began stripping off his clothes in full view of Fran. When he was finished, Helen stood directly in front of him. Without warning, she slapped him violently on the side of the head. He reeled, almost losing his balance.

"Help me get dressed!" she ordered.

Fran watched as Soren, naked and vulnerable, obediently helped Helen's petit, shapely body out of her jeans and tank top. Then he pulled the black leather bodice and boots from the bag, followed by the platinum blonde wig. By the time he pulled Helen's cane from the bag, Fran felt a strange feeling of déjà vu taking over her body - she felt herself going numb as she slipped into the past and a familiar darkness descended upon her again.

CHAPTER 27

RICKI MARSHALL crossed the street towards the outdoor mall's central playground and food court. The sun had sunk low in the west, causing late afternoon shadows to creep across the area. As she arrived at the food court, she spotted a Hispanic woman in an Air Force uniform sitting at a table by herself, eating an ice cream cone. Ricki approached the woman.

"Excuse me, are you Mia?"

The woman wiped ice cream from her lips with a napkin, then stood and extended her hand to Ricki.

"I'm sorry. I couldn't resist having some while I was waiting. You're Ms. Marshall?"

"Please, call me Ricki. Thanks for contacting me. What can I do for you?"

"Like I said on the phone," Mia answered. "I read your recent article about sexual abuse in the military. Thank you for doing what you're doing! It's about time somebody's willing to bring our fight out into the open."

"You're a survivor?" Ricki asked.

Mia looked away, embarrassed, then she gathered herself and forced herself to make eye contact again with Ricki.

"Damn right I am," Mia replied. "I was abused here at Nellis over a two-year period."

"I'm so sorry to hear that," Ricki replied. "Do you mind if I take notes?" When Mia nodded, Ricki took out her notepad and began writing. "You said Nellis? That's the first I've heard of it happening here."

"Yeah, but that's not why I called you." Mia added. "I was at Tailhook too … as a victim. And she was there too."

"She?" Ricki asked, puzzled by Mia's statement.

"Sorry," Mia answered. "I've gotten ahead of myself. The conspiracy you hinted at in your article … and its ringleader? You got most of it right except for one detail. It's a woman … I'm sure of it! And now I know who she is."

Ricki looked up from her notes, taken completely off guard by Mia's surprising revelation. A chill of excitement raced through her spine.

"How do you know it's a woman?"

"Because I'll never forget her voice," Mia replied stolidly. "I was watching the news after the big MSA rally at UNLV last week. That major who spoke at the rally … the one who came out and admitted she was a victim too …"

"Major Taylor?" Ricki interjected.

"Yeah, she's the one," Mia continued. "It's all bullshit. She's no victim. She was the star attraction … the famous dominatrix … they called her Lady Helen. We never saw her face, but I'd know that voice anywhere. I haven't stopped having flashbacks and nightmares since I heard her voice on the news last week."

"That can't be possible," Ricki responded, shaking her head. "She's the assistant to the Air Force Director of Public Affairs. That's one step away from the Undersecretary of the Air Force!"

"That's right," Mia answered, determination in her voice. "Don't you see? You were so right. It *is* a conspiracy. And it goes right to the very top!"

Ricki put down her notebook and pen. She paused to digest what she'd just heard and took a long hard look at the woman in front of her, as if deciding whether she could trust her as a source. Finally, she let out a long sigh.

"Damn! What else can you tell me? …"

DAN AND ANGELA sat in the great room of Dan and Francesca's estate, watching film credits roll upwards across the new fifty-inch flat screen TV. Dan was casually dressed in sweatpants and a t-shirt, but Angela was lounging in her pajamas, a bowl of popcorn in her lap. Outside, in the estate's back yard, night lights cast their soft yellow glow on the manicured gardens surrounding the pool.

"Well, I see now why *Casanova* got mixed reviews," Dan observed. "Heath Ledger was good, but the story didn't do much for me."

"You didn't like it?" Angela answered, surprised by Dan's response. "I loved the costumes, especially the scene at the ball. I'd absolutely love to be in Venice for Carnivale!"

"Maybe it was seeing all those masks … they just brought back a lot of bad memories," Dan replied. "Carnivale was one of the fantasies that Fran's ex, Philippe, used to seduce Chelly … before they both died."

"I'm so sorry," Angela replied. "I didn't know. Why didn't you say something? We could have watched something else."

"It's okay," Dan continued. "It's something I need to deal with. Besides, we need some distractions while we're waiting to hear more about Fran."

"You're sure you're alright?" Angela asked. "I can stay up with you for a while longer if you'd like."

"Thanks, but I'll be all right," Dan said, trying to reassure his friend. "I'll clean things up if you want to go to bed."

"Okay, I'll see you in the morning. Maybe we'll hear some good news," Angela answered, trying to boost their spirits. She gave Dan a friendly peck on the cheek and walked out of the great room. Dan picked up the empty popcorn bowl and two glasses, and then carried them to the kitchen where he scraped the un-popped kernels into the garbage and put the two glasses in the dishwasher. He took a step to leave the kitchen, then paused. He reached for the bottle of Scotch that sat on the counter and poured himself a shot.

He turned and walked back to the kitchen table where his laptop sat idly. He took a sip of Scotch while he woke up the sleeping computer. Once the machine was awake, Dan replayed the second ransom video. When it was over, he took another sip of the relaxing brown liquid. Then he rewound the video and replayed Fran's words over and over.

"What are you trying to tell me, Fran?" Dan said aloud.

He paused to think about Fran's words from both ransom videos. He took another sip of Scotch while his brain processed both messages.

"One. Your captor is a woman," he said, imagining himself talking to Fran. It helped him distance himself from his emotions and feel more objective. "Are you saying there's a second captor? … Soren? … Or maybe that the woman has a Jekyll and Hyde personality?"

He paused for another sip, giving himself up to the liquid's power of relaxation.

"Two. What's with the word uniform? … and crash and burn? They both seem out of place … Is it because your captor wants to make sure we don't involve the police? … You already said that later in the video … Does it have something to do with the crash in Kakadu? … What the hell, Fran … What are you trying to tell me?"

With his elbows on the table, Dan buried his head in his hands. He tried to vent his frustration by exhaling a long breath. After a few seconds, he slammed the laptop's screen closed in frustration, gulped the rest of the Scotch, then stood and headed out of the kitchen, turning off the lights as he left.

DAN WAS entranced. The mysterious woman before him wore a black cloak with a crimson lining, open in the front, revealing a seductive black leather bodice with an enticing view of cleavage that barely covered her nipples. The classic, handheld Venetian

Columbina mask that covered her face was trimmed with brilliant crimson plumage around the edges, which elegantly adorned the woman's platinum blonde hair. She teased Dan constantly, dropping the mask slightly every now and then, allowing him to catch brief glimpses of her facial features.

Feeling like he was floating outside his own body, Dan noticed that he was dressed in classic seventeenth-century black pants, white shirt, and black tie. He wore a black cloak and a black tricorn hat. His mask was a white *Volto Paggliaccio*, with red lips and black tears streaming from his eyes, giving him a tragic appearance.

"Tell me, handsome," the woman asked. "Have we met before?"

Dan wracked his memory, trying to remember any previous encounters with her.

"I don't believe so," he answered.

"Why don't we go someplace where we can get to know each other better?" she asked, seductively. "Would you like that?" She placed her free hand gently on his shoulder. Her touch was both electrifying and frightening.

"My girlfriend is here with me," Dan explained. "I'm afraid I can't."

"That's strange," the woman continued. "That's not what the bulge in your pants is telling me."

Dan looked down at himself, embarrassed at how his body was betraying his attraction to her. He looked nervously around the room for Fran, but he couldn't locate her anywhere. He turned to the woman.

"Where's Fran? Have you done something with her? Are you hiding her?"

"If you want to find out, you'll need to follow me," she said mysteriously.

The woman turned and walked away from Dan. As she did, he was shocked to see that her Carnivale costume only covered the front of her body. From the rear, Dan saw a completely different woman wearing a modern suit - a woman's USAF uniform. He also noticed that this woman had short brown hair.

Overcome with curiosity, Dan watched as the woman walked from the room and began descending a grand marble staircase. Unable to restrain himself, he followed her down the staircase. When they were only two or three steps from the bottom, the woman suddenly tripped, tumbling down the remaining steps, landing at the bottom, and losing her mask in the process. She sat up and turned her head to see if Dan had followed her.

The sight of the woman's face stunned Dan. He found himself face to face with the same woman who had boarded their plane in Darwin and sat beside Soren in the SUV in Hanoi. But most shocking of all, Dan recognized the face as one he had seen only days before - Major Teri Taylor!

Seeing the look of shock on Dan's face, she began taunting him with an evil, sarcastic laugh. Dan's heart pounded. He felt like he had an anvil sitting on his chest. He couldn't breathe and began to panic. His nightmare was so real and so frightening, that it became his mind's reality at that moment. His body's fight-or-flight response came to life, startling him out of his dream and yanking him, disoriented and gasping, back into reality …

DAN'S HEART pounded. His chest was heavy and tight. He continued to gasp for breath. His skin was wet and his sheets were soaked with perspiration. Still disoriented, it took a moment before he realized that he was still in his own bed. Slowly he looked around the room, seeing objects that told him that it was all a bad dream.

"What the hell?" Dan said to himself. He reached for a glass of water. He sat, thinking, as he took small sips of water and tried taking slower, deeper breaths. He stopped in mid-sip, suddenly realizing the significance of his dream.

"Holy shit! Teri Taylor? Is it possible? … No, she just doesn't seem to be the type."

Dan sat in silence. He took another sip of water.

"That's it! Jekyll and Hyde … split personalities. That's what Fran was trying to tell me! She's in uniform … and the hair … that's why I couldn't figure it out. It was a wig and sunglasses! That's how she fooled me!"

Dan threw the covers aside and quickly threw on a pair of sweatpants. He ran out of the room, still wiggling a t-shirt over his head. He reached Angela's room and banged on the door.

"Angela, wake up!"

"Dan? … Just a minute," she mumbled.

He waited impatiently, finally hearing Angela's bare feet shuffling towards the door. She opened it a crack, her eyes squinting and her face etched with concern.

"What is it? Is something wrong?"

"Yes … I mean, no," Dan blurted. "I think I figured out who took Fran! It's Teri Taylor … Major Taylor!"

A blank look washed over Angela's face as she digested Dan's words. Then her eyes opened wide.

"Holy shit!" she gasped. "Are you sure?"

"It makes perfect sense," Dan exclaimed excitedly. "It fits perfectly with the clues Fran embedded in the videos."

"We need to tell Ricki and the others right away!" Angela answered. "Give me a minute to get dressed."

DAN, ANGELA, and Ricki gathered around the kitchen table, cups of coffee in hand, as early morning sunshine streamed into the room. Having just shared each other's new information about Major Taylor, they were taking a moment to digest and make sense of it all. Finally, Ricki broke the silence.

"So, her fellow abusers call her *Lady Helen*," she said. "It's hard to believe, isn't it? She's so mousey and conservative in real life. Never in a million years would I have pegged her as dominatrix."

"Or the ringleader of a military sexual abuse ring," Angela added. "I agree. She just doesn't seem like the type."

"But together with Ricki's new information, Fran's clues and my dream make perfect sense," Dan concluded. "Remember, Taylor openly admitted to being a sexual abuse victim. If that's true, she could easily have a highly-dissociated identity - maybe even two distinct personalities that are as different as night and day."

"Yeah, the Air Force's own little Jekyll and Hyde," Ricki added. "Fran's clues fit perfectly with what I heard yesterday from Mia, the MSA victim at Nellis. Taylor made herself look like one of the victims at the Tailhook inquiry. She's like a chameleon. Since most of the victims were women, it was easy for her to pull that off."

"What about Soren?" Angela asked. "Where does he fit in?"

"So far, all I've discovered is that they were both stationed here at Nellis together at one time," Ricki replied. "He was a young chaplain and she'd just finished flight training. Somewhere along the way, he left the Air Force and went back to preaching, eventually landing in Victoria at the World-Wide Community of Christ."

"I can see how a small, quiet woman like Taylor could have been a natural target for abuse in the military," Dan observed. "And Anika's already told us that she doesn't know much about Soren's history."

"Maybe he's carrying around a bunch of baggage from his past too," Angela added. "He's obviously not right in the head."

Silence descended again upon the kitchen. Finally, Ricki spoke up.

"So, what do we do now? I don't have enough to go ahead with an article yet. I need at least one more source to confirm what Mia told me. She gave me some names of other women who were at Tailhook. She's going to try to convince some other victims to come forward too. I'm actually meeting with one of them this afternoon."

"That sounds hopeful," Dan observed. He turned to Angela.

"What about us? Any idea what we can do to confirm that Major Taylor is really this infamous Lady Helen?"

Angela took a sip of coffee and looked pensive. After a few seconds, she set down her coffee mug.

"Maybe … I was just thinking. I might already have a way."

Dan looked at Angela, a quizzical look on his face. Then, he realized what she was thinking.

"Soren's laptop? … But he knows you hacked him in Australia. He won't be that stupid again."

"You're partly right," Angela agreed. "I can't use the clone I created from his hard drive to see what he's been up to lately. But I still have the clone. I can go back in time and look through his files, contacts and old emails … I'll bet Helen - or Major Taylor - are in there somewhere. I could even pretend to be Soren and plant a similar Trojan to open a back door into Taylor's computer. If I get lucky, we might be able to hack into Lady Helen's contacts and appointments."

Angela looked directly at Ricki.

"Is *that* the kind of information you need to publish an exposé?"

"Are you kidding?" Ricki answered. "It would blow up the entire conspiracy!"

"So, it's decided," Angela concluded. "You look for other victims who can confirm Mia's stories about Tailhook and the abuse at Nellis. I'll try to hack Helen's computer."

"And I'll follow up with Richard today," Dan added. "Thanks to Angela's posters, we've confirmed that Soren - and probably Taylor - are hiding Fran somewhere nearby. We need a definite plan right away before Helen contacts me. Let's check in with each other tonight."

For the first time in weeks, an air of optimism crept into the room. The faces of all three members of the group displayed a new sense of determined hope. Angela left the table and headed upstairs to get her laptop. Ricki looked at her watch, mentally calculating how she was going to use her precious time today. Finally, she stood up and gulped the last of her coffee.

"I'd better get going," she said to Dan. "I'll talk to you guys this afternoon, after I've interviewed that other MSA survivor."

"Thanks for coming over and sharing your findings," Dan replied. "With your help, I think the puzzle pieces are finally starting to come together."

"I think so too," Ricki answered. "But it's been a team effort."

"See you later," Dan said.

Ricki turned and rushed from the kitchen. A moment later, Dan heard the front door close behind her, leaving him alone in the kitchen. He put their used coffee cups in the dishwasher. Suddenly, he had a craving for bacon and eggs. He went to the fridge to get his ingredients, unaware of the happy sounds of CCR's *Down on the Corner* that were whistling from his pursed lips. As he opened the fridge door, the phone rang.

Dan let out an exasperated huff. "What now?" he asked aloud. He closed the fridge door and reached for the phone.

"Hello," he said.

"Dan? This is Agent Simpson. Have you seen the morning papers or TV news yet?

Dan felt a surge of hope rush through his body.

"You've found Fran?" he asked.

"I'm sorry, not yet. But we've got some other good news. Soren Kristiansen was seen yesterday at a gas bar in North Las Vegas. He's in the area, Dan."

Dan caught his breath, allowing the new information to sink in.

"So, that means I was right. He's working with … Fran's kidnappers," Dan replied. He silently cursed himself for almost telling Simpson about Major Taylor.

"Not necessarily. It raises the probability, but we still don't know if he is, or who the kidnappers might be."

"I see," Dan answered calmly.

"But if it is true, Soren and his accomplice might be getting more anxious and they may be in contact with you shortly. I called to prepare you for that possibility."

"Thanks. I really appreciate that. You'll be the first people I'll call," Dan lied. "I'll pass along the information about Soren to Anika too. I'm sure she'll want to know."

"Thank you, Dan. That will save me a phone call. I've got lots on my plate today, so I gotta go. Keep in touch."

"Okay, bye now," Dan replied. He heard a click on the line as Simpson ended the call.

A broad smile spread across Dan's face.

"So, we were right!" he said to himself. "It *is* Taylor and Soren working together."

He turned back to the fridge and stared at it for a moment, trying to remember what he was doing before the phone rang.

"Bacon and eggs!" he said aloud to himself. He reached for the fridge handle, not realizing that the sounds of *Down on the Corner* were once again escaping from his lips.

ANGELA SAT on a cushioned chair at the patio table with her laptop computer. She was dressed for the pool deck, wearing a bikini and a cover-up, her bare feet curled up casually beneath her on a lounge chair. She was in her element, engrossed in the task of exploring her illicit clone of Soren's computer hard drive.

"Well, hello," she said to herself. "What do we have here?"

Her fingers danced on the keyboard and skated across the trackpad. She glanced at two more email messages.

"Okay, Taylor," she continued, still talking out loud to nobody in particular. "Pit Boss? … Whoa … Whoever you are, you must be a real somebody at Nellis."

Her fingers went back to work at the keyboard and trackpad. She brought up a list of recent emails. She dragged the cursor so that the arrow pointed to one recent message.

"You're getting sloppy, Taylor. You were so careful before … only using that secret government site for sending messages … why stop now?"

Angela picked up her coffee mug and took a sip. She sat back to ponder the situation for a moment.

"What if only the people in the innermost circle of the conspiracy have access to that secret government site?" she asked herself. "What if Pit Boss is a middle man - important, but not a ringleader?"

Angela went back to reading emails in the list of messages. Suddenly her eyes opened wide.

"No way! … An Escalade … and a set of Washington license plates? … Shit! … Mr. Pit Boss, you and Taylor were helping Soren while he was on the run with Jonah!"

"Angela sat back again and took another sip of coffee. She thought hard for a moment, then slowly nodded her head up and down as a plan began to form. Her fingers went back to work on the keyboard and trackpad.

"Okay, Taylor," Angela said firmly. "Let's send you a message from Pit Boss that you won't be able to ignore …"

A SLIDING DOOR opened. Dan and Ricki emerged from the house, each with a bottle of beer in hand, and walked over to where Angela still sat at the patio table. Solar garden lights started to flicker to life as dusk settled in.

"Hey, Angela," Ricki said. "Going to take a break?"

"I can't believe I didn't think to use the clone of Soren's computer before," Angela muttered. "I was sitting on a gold mine and didn't realize it."

Dan stood over Angela's shoulder, looking at her laptop's screen.

"Who's this? … Pit Boss?" Dan said, pointing at the screen.

"Seems to be someone in a pretty high position at Nellis," Angela answered. "But that isn't the best part. He, or she, has been helping Taylor and Soren since he abducted Jonah in Victoria - arranged for someone to steal an Escalade and some Washington plates for Soren after he was seen in Bremerton."

"Did you get that info from your old clone?" Ricki reasoned. "Or have you managed to hack into Taylor's computer already?"

"Both," Angela answered, smiling proudly. "I found out about Pit Boss on the clone. Then I sent an email to Taylor a couple of hours ago, pretending to be Pit Boss. I made it look like Pit Boss was in a panic because he'd learned that Ricki was going to expose their whole network. Hope you don't mind me using your name, Ricki!"

"Whatever works!" Ricki said, laughing. "You'd make a damned fine investigative reporter yourself."

"So, Taylor took your bait," Dan concluded.

"Yeah," Angela replied. "Hook, line, and sinker. It wasn't more than ten minutes before the Trojan I planted in the email activated and contacted my laptop. I had to work quickly while Taylor was online, so I downloaded the most important stuff first - her contact lists and emails."

"Lists?" Dan asked, puzzled.

"Sure, both lists," Angela confirmed. "I thought about what you said about Taylor having two identities. So, I checked for more than one user profile. Turns out she has two - one for Major Taylor and another for Helen. It's Helen's hidden profile that has all of the gold."

"We'll need to remember to thank Fran for that info," Ricki noted. "This is amazing stuff, Angela."

"So, you've got enough to start your article?" Angela asked.

"Are you kidding?" Ricki answered. "This is going to blow the whole MSA issue onto the front pages tomorrow. You found enough for a whole series of stories!"

"When will you have something to publish?" Dan asked.

"I'll have something ready for AP to publish tomorrow morning," Ricki replied. "It should be enough to whet everybody's appetite for more."

"You'll be blowing Taylor's cover in that article?" Angela asked.

"Damn right I will," Ricki confirmed.

"Then we're going to hear from her very soon," Dan predicted. "Taylor's going to panic when she finds out she's been exposed."

"How's Richard coming along?" Angela asked Dan.

"He and Gwen and Miriam have drafted a rough plan and they're putting together a shopping list of equipment tonight. They should be in Vegas by tomorrow afternoon at the latest," Dan answered.

"Great work, Angela," Ricki announced, holding her beer in the air. Dan clinked his bottle against hers.

"To Angela, the hacker queen," he added.

"I got lucky," Angela answered modestly. "Let's just hope it helps us get Fran back."

"Here's to that," Ricki confirmed. She and Dan both wrapped their arms around Angela's shoulders, giving her a hug of thanks. "Can you forward all of those emails to me, so I can use them for the story?"

"Absolutely," Angela replied. "You'll have them by the time you get home."

"Then I'd better hit the road and get to work," Ricki announced. "Looks like I have a long night ahead of me. Be sure to turn on the news tomorrow morning, you guys. It's gonna be interesting."

CHAPTER 28

DAN AND ANGELA sat beside each other on the couch in the great room, where they had watched *Casanova* just the night before. Today, however, agents Martinelli and Simpson stood before them.

"We just stopped by for a few minutes to bring you up to date on what you've undoubtedly seen on the news," Simpson announced.

"You mean the raid on Major Taylor's D.C. apartment? That you think she's Fran's kidnapper?" Dan asked, trying to look shocked. "How did you guys figure it out? And how did you manage to wrestle the investigation away from the military police?"

"It wasn't easy," Martinelli answered. "The Air Force was adamant about dealing with this internally. Even the Undersecretary of the Air Force got involved. We managed to convince a judge that we had credible evidence of Taylor being involved in Fran's kidnapping. Since that's a federal offence, she ruled we have jurisdiction. The Air Force wasn't very happy. It was the emails on her computer that told us she was Fran's kidnapper. We still can't believe it!"

"What else have you found out?" Angela asked. "Do you know where she's hiding?"

"Nothing concrete yet," Simpson interjected. "We confiscated her home computer and they're going over her hard drive as we speak."

Dan and Angela made quick, furtive eye contact with other, knowing they already had the jump on the FBI.

"Has she contacted you again?" Martinelli asked, looking at Dan.

"No, not yet," Dan replied.

"We're certain she will soon, now that her cover is blown and everybody's looking for her," Martinelli said.

"Make sure you call us as soon as she does," Simpson added. "Even though they're on standby, it still takes some time to scramble our response team."

Dan and Angela exchanged another quick glance, then Dan looked back at Simpson.

"Of course," he answered. "All I want is to get Fran back safely. I can't wait for all this to be over."

"That's everybody's goal," Martinelli added. He exchanged a look with Simpson, signaling that the short meeting was over.

"We'll call you if there are any further developments," Simpson announced.

"No need to show us out," Martinelli said. "We know the way." He and Simpson turned and walked from the great room to the front. After the door closed behind them, they walked down the porch steps toward their SUV.

"There's something they're not telling us. Did you notice?" Simpson asked.

"Yeah," Martinelli replied."

"You don't think they're stupid enough to make a deal with Taylor on their own, do you?" Simpson continued.

"I don't know. I hope they're not that dumb," Martinelli added. He shook his head as he opened the door and climbed into their vehicle.

"Yeah. Let's hope," Simpson agreed.

DAN AND ANGELA stood in the front hallway as the door closed behind Martinelli and Simpson. They paused for a moment and looked at each other until they heard the FBI agent's vehicle drive away.

"Do you think they believed us?" Angela asked.

"I don't know," Dan answered. "I don't really care, as long as they don't get in the way of Richard's plan."

Angela's cell phone rang. She ran back into the great room, looked at the caller's number, and picked it up.

"Hi Ricki, what's up?"

"I've had more than twenty calls from people - both women and men - who all claim they remember a dominatrix."

"You're kidding," Angela answered. "That's amazing!"

"Seems they were posted at bases all over the U.S. and Europe."

"That's awesome, Ricki. You're going to have a killer story by the time you've talked with them."

Angela walked to the window that overlooked the pool and gardens behind the house. She gazed out the window as she continued talking with Ricki.

"What are you up to now?"

"Me? We're just waiting for Richard and the girls to arrive. I also need to phone Anika to fill her in on the latest details. After all, Soren *is* her husband."

"Call me after they've left. You can tell me all about their plan."

"Okay, I'll call you if anything new comes up," Angela agreed.

Just as Angela finished her call, the doorbell rang.

"I'll talk to you later, Ricki. Sounds like Richard and the girls just arrived ..."

YESTERDAY'S temporary relief from the Nevada desert's relentless sun and oppressive heat was short-lived. The sky had cleared overnight and today dawned with nothing but azure skies from horizon to horizon. The temperature had been climbing steadily since sunrise.

Teri and Soren sat in their camp chairs, both trying to read, but both were restless and agitated. Soren's left leg vibrated up and down nervously as he tried to concentrate on a pulp novel. Droplets of perspiration formed on their foreheads and patches of sweat caused their t-shirts to cling to their skin. The sudden ringing of Helen's satellite phone caused them both to jump.

"Shit! Who the hell is calling?" Helen cursed. "Nobody's supposed to use that phone unless it's an emergency!"

A look of panic appeared on her face. Within seconds, she transformed from mild-mannered Teri Taylor to domineering Lady Helen. She jumped from her chair and picked up the satellite phone from a nearby table.

Fran stretched quietly on her cot on the other side of the tent. The unexpected phone call had startled her wandering mind back into reality. She listened intently to Helen's side of the conversation, trying to fill in the blanks.

"Pit Boss? What the fuck do you want? You know you're not supposed to email me or call me unless it's … What do you mean you didn't send me an email? … You didn't warn me about Marshall, the reporter? … Fuck!"

The blood drained from Helen's face. Fran saw a look of terror in her captor's eyes as she began to comprehend the danger she was in. Her eyes were wide open. Helen momentarily went silent as she digested the dangerous implications of what the mysterious Pit Boss was telling her. As she listened, the look of panic on her face gradually transformed into one of intense rage.

"Listen up, Colonel!" Helen screamed, realizing there was little need for code names now that her identity had gone public. "We need to push things forward and execute the plan tomorrow at dawn … Why the fuck not? … I don't give a shit about raising eyebrows. We're all in danger of going down! … Okay, okay, I get it … Day after tomorrow … Just make sure your men are ready … One more thing, Colonel. Don't fuck this up!"

Helen slammed the phone on the table. She turned to Soren, her eyes burning with hatred and anger.

"Fuck, fuck, fuck!" she screamed. "I'm surrounded by fucking morons! You … letting yourself get noticed at the gas bar … that idiot Williamson … and that stupid, sniveling bitch, Teri Taylor …"

Both Fran and Soren sat upright, suddenly alert and afraid as they saw Helen coming unglued in front of them. Soren turned his head for a quick glance at Fran, and she saw the fear in his eyes. Then she looked back at Helen and watched as her captor's eyes burned into Soren like superheated lasers.

"You!" she screamed at Soren. "This is all your fault! If you hadn't let that fucking Baranyi hack your computer in the first place, none of this would have happened! I'd be retired. We'd be living happily in Norway with Jonah. We'd be a happy family. But instead, you've led her straight to my computer!"

Without warning, Helen turned and unleashed her anger on Fran.

"And you! You've been a fucking thorn in my side ever since Philippe introduced me to you in Paris!"

She stomped to the duffel bag containing her dominatrix attire and the tools of her trade. She brought out her cane and brandished it in the air.

"You both deserve to feel the pain I'm feeling right now!" Once again, she focused her anger on Fran. "Unlock her chains! I want *both* of you naked … kneeling in front of me!"

"Ter … er … Helen," Soren pleaded. "Don't do this! She's five months pregnant. Think of her baby! Think of what that might do to her!"

At the mention of her baby, Fran watched Helen's face go blank. The color drained from her face and her eyes were once again glazed and distant. She was not only out of control, but she was fast losing touch with reality. Fran's fear intensified as she wondered where Helen's mind had gone … and what was going to happen next.

SIXTEEN-YEAR-OLD Teri Taylor lay back on the surgical table. Showing no emotion, she looked up at the face of the masked nurse standing beside her.

"It's for the better, dear. This is no time or place for a teenage mom to raise a mixed-race baby ... We had to take it from you ... You'd have died if we didn't ... You'll get over it in time ... You'll see ..."

"I'll be able to have another one, won't I? ... Tell me! ... Will I be able to have another?"

"You'll need to talk to the doctor about that, dear. There was already extensive damage to your organs from the rape and beating."

"You don't understand ... I want a child ... I need one ... I need to show them..."

"Show who? Show them what?"

"Everybody ... I need to be better ... better than all of them ... I'd love my baby ... I'd show it how much I love it."

"Of course, you would, dear ..."

"HELEN, GET a grip on yourself!" Soren shouted. "Listen to me!"

He shook Helen's shoulders, desperately trying to bring her back into reality.

"We need to keep Fran and the baby safe so we can trade them both for Angela! Don't you understand?"

Helen's eyes blinked. Fran watched, simultaneously afraid yet fascinated by what she was seeing. Helen was still disoriented. A flash of anger appeared on her face initially, but then she seemed to catch herself. Her face softened as she recognized Fran. Ever so slowly, Helen gradually drifted back into the present, eventually regaining control over her emotions. Moments later, Lady Helen was back.

"Of course," Helen said calmly. "We must keep them both safe." She paused to concentrate and think. Finally, she nodded to Soren.

"Get your video camera. We're going to record the message for the swap." She turned to Fran and glared at her.

"Your boyfriend needs to know you're alive," she said. "So, you're going to read the instructions. And this time, you'd better make it good … word for word … no changes … exactly like I write it … *if* you want to see him again."

Helen looked down at the cane in her hands. A look of confusion briefly crossed her face, then she seemed to realize why she was holding the object. She walked slowly over to Fran's cot and stood in front of her, looking down on her prisoner. Fran felt the other woman's eyes glaring at her. Helen raised the cane and Fran felt it pressing against the underside of her chin, forcing her to lift her head so she couldn't avoid Helen's penetrating stare.

"You know I'll never let them catch me alive. I'll never let myself be under anybody else's control again. I'd rather be dead, and I'd rather take you, Soren, and everybody else with me. So, it's up to you to make this trade work. Understand?"

With the cane still beneath her chin, Fran took a deep breath and swallowed. She pushed her fear aside and managed to replace it with a look of determination. She had already decided that she would no longer give Helen the satisfaction of seeing her fear.

"I want this to end as much as you do," Fran replied. "Tell me what you need me to say …"

CHAPTER 29

FRAN'S EYES flickered open in the darkness. Unable to stay asleep, her mind continued to be haunted by Helen's threats and her increasingly volatile temper and unpredictable actions. Fran's forehead throbbed with tension and she suddenly realized her teeth were clenched together with worry. Thunder rumbled ominously in the distance. Suddenly, a weak flash of far-off lightning lit up the tent. She saw the outlines of Soren and Helen, sleeping soundly on their cots. Apart from the threatening sounds of the approaching storm, Soren's snoring was the only noise Fran heard from them. Another flash of lightning lit up the tent. Fran caught a glint of light reflecting from a metallic object on the ground beside Soren's cot, just as a rumble of thunder reached the tent. The time between flashes of lightning and its thunder was getting shorter.

It's growing closer, Fran thought silently.

Two brighter flashes of light filled the tent in rapid succession. This time, the metallic object remained illuminated on the floor, only a few feet from her cot. Fran's eyes narrowed and she sat up to get a better look as her eyes readjusted to the darkness. Two rumbles of thunder, even louder than the last, rolled through the tent, followed by another smaller flash of lightning, illuminating the object again.

Soren's keys! ... For their vehicle ... and my chain!

Fran's mind started racing. She felt her heart pounding and her breathing growing rapid. Her stomach felt as if it was tied in knots. It took only a second for her to realize what she had to do. She flipped away the blanket that covered her and grabbed as much of the chain as possible that led from her ankle. Then, cautiously and deliberately, she swung her legs over the side of the cot and onto the sand and gravel desert floor. She began to creep, inch by inch towards the keys, trying to ignore the pebbles that bit into her knees.

Suddenly, Soren snorted and rolled on his back. Fran froze. Her breathing stopped. Another flash of lighting illuminated the tent. She waited breathlessly while an even louder rumble of thunder erupted only seconds later. Both Soren and Helen stirred briefly. Then there was silence.

Fran let herself start breathing again with slow, deliberate breaths to calm her trembling hands. She started creeping cautiously again until the keys were within reach. She picked them up, slowly and deliberately, careful not to let them rattle against each other. She felt a smaller key and reasoned that it must be the one for her padlock. She guided the tip of the key to her lock and felt it sliding on metal until it found the keyhole. She pushed gently, but the lock resisted. She ignored the pain from the pebbles that bit into her knees.

I must have the key in backwards, she said to herself.

Cautiously, she removed the key, twisted it the other way in her hand and tried again. This time, the key slid in effortlessly and seated firmly in the lock. She twisted and felt a faint click as the lock released. Fran caught herself holding her breath again. She allowed herself to exhale slowly while she deliberately opened the hasp, finally freeing her ankle.

Fran now had only one thought.

Escape!

Fortunately, she was still wearing the military issue sweatpants and a sweatshirt over the t-shirt she wore during the day. She didn't even notice the chilly desert air on her bare feet. She continued to shut out the pain in her knees, focusing only on the task at hand. More distant flashes of light filled the tent while frequent, increasingly louder rumbles of thunder rolled into the tent from the mountains to the west. She took a deep breath and waited for a break between lightning flashes.

The rumbles and flashes ceased for a few seconds and Fran made up her mind. It was now or never! She began creeping forward painfully, her speed increasing with every movement of her hands and knees towards the tent's entrance. It felt as if she would never reach it. When she finally did, Fran took one more look over her shoulder and listened carefully. At first, she heard only the reassuring sound of Soren's snoring. As she moved through the small opening in the tent's door flap, she thought she heard the sound of rustling fabric behind her. She was certain that footsteps, scrambling in the tent behind her, would follow. But there was nobody chasing her. Instead, she heard no commotion inside the tent as she emerged into the night, finally feeling safe enough to stand up.

The distinct smell of ozone and impending rain filled Fran's nostrils. It was the smell of freedom. She saw the Escalade only about twenty feet away. Her bare feet began running with short, silent strides, oblivious to the sharp stones that bit into her feet. As she ran, raindrops began to splash on the parched desert floor. She held her breath as she reached the vehicle, hoping she didn't need to unlock it. To her relief, the window was open and the driver's door unlocked.

Fran exhaled and quickly swung the door open, just as a brilliant flash lit up the night sky. A deafening explosion of thunder reverberated through the night almost immediately, causing Fran to jump. At the same time, the sky opened and began to release a torrent of rain. She realized her time was running out. She inserted the key in the ignition and the Escalade roared to life. As she looked up, she saw Soren and Helen burst from the tent, wearing expressions of terror and anger on their faces.

"Come back here, bitch!" Soren yelled.

"Stop her!" Helen screamed hysterically.

Fran slammed the vehicle into gear. Her foot hit the gas and the wheels spewed gravel and dust into the air, just as Soren reached the SUV. He lunged and managed to get one foot on the running board as Fran accelerated away from the tent. He reached through the window and grabbed Fran's hair with his free hand, yanking it viciously.

Fran screamed. Her left hand lashed out and clawed at Soren's eyes. He howled and his grip on her hair loosened.

"You'll pay for this!" Soren hollered. His face filled with rage.

Fran found the window controls with her left hand and pressed the button. As the window began moving upwards, Soren made a desperate attempt to grab the steering wheel. At the last second, when he realized his arm would be trapped inside the vehicle, he ripped his hand away from the steering wheel, escaping the window's determined jaws. He slammed his fist against the glass, making a last-ditch attempt to smash the glass and stop her.

Fran swerved the SUV from left to right and back again, almost losing control as the vehicle rocked violently from side to side, and almost causing it to roll. She gave one more desperate twist of the wheel to the right and pushed her foot to the floor, finally throwing Soren from the running board. As the Escalade righted itself, she hit the gas again and raced into the night.

The rain was now torrential. Fran found herself surrounded by brilliant flashes of lightning and deafening crashes of thunder. Her windshield wipers barely kept up with the rivers of water that swept down her windshield. She struggled to keep control on the now slippery desert road, spurring the black SUV on into the night as it fishtailed down the road towards freedom.

Without warning, a flood of water surged across the road from Fran's left as she crossed a wash in the desert floor. She felt the water grab the rear of the SUV. She hit the gas once again. The SUV didn't respond. She felt herself losing control as the rear end slid to her right. Fran screamed and threw the steering wheel to the right in a desperate attempt to counteract the spin. She put all her weight on the gas pedal and held her breath. The engine roared and she felt the tires spinning in gravel and water, searching for traction. At the last possible second, she felt her front wheels grab the far side of the wash. The vehicle strained to pull itself free from the angry flood waters and finally won its battle.

Fran's breathing was ragged. She wiped the mixture of rain and sweat from her brow, heaving a gigantic sigh of relief. She reduced her speed and hunched over the steering wheel, squinting her eyes to see glimpses of the road between futile swipes of the windshield wipers. She drove on in the rain for almost fifteen minutes, wondering how far she had to drive before she hit pavement.

Suddenly, out of nowhere, Fran heard a deafening roar and the sound of something pounding the night air above her. The Escalade rocked back and forth. Then she was blinded by an intense light. It took a few seconds for reality to sink in.

Shit! A helicopter!

Fran gasped as reality hit hard. Then she slammed on the brakes as the chopper landed in front of her, blocking the road and thwarting her escape. The SUV swerved and skidded to a stop in the mud. Exhausted and defeated, Fran rested her head on the steering wheel.

A lone figure leapt from the aircraft, its rotors still spinning as the turbine idled. The figure's head was lowered as it ran through the howling wind and slashing rain until it reached the SUV. The hooded figure yanked open the driver's door and pointed a gun at Fran's head. Another brilliant flash of white light filled the night, illuminating the face of Colonel Bryce Williamson. Seconds later, another hooded figure opened the passenger door and jumped in beside Fran, also pointing a gun at her.

"Out of the vehicle, Capellini!" Williamson screamed.

Fran remained seated, her body paralyzed with fear and her hands frozen to the steering wheel.

"Now!" Williamson bellowed.

Fran managed to force her rigid body to move. Her bare feet stepped into the stormy night and onto the rain-soaked gravel. Almost immediately, her sweatpants and sweatshirt turned into sponges, soaking her to the skin.

"You've been a very bad girl and you've pissed Helen off supremely. I would not want to be in your spot right now, believe me!"

"What are you going to do with me?" Fran asked, her voice trembling and weak.

"I'm going to fly you back to Helen, and we're all going to pray that we don't crash that chopper into the desert in this fucking rain," Williamson shouted in return. He nodded to the other man inside the vehicle.

"You'll need to follow us in the Escalade. Take your time and be careful. We'll wait for you at the camp," he said.

"Yes, sir!" the other man replied.

Williamson grabbed Fran roughly by the arm and dragged her rain-drenched body behind him to the chopper. A set of hands reached out and hauled her aboard. Another violent explosion of light and thunder shattered the night as the chopper doors closed. The rotors gradually picked up speed and the aircraft rocked back and forth with increasing frequency. Finally, the helicopter lifted off the ground and ventured tentatively into the darkness and driving rain.

Fran felt the aircraft rattling and shaking around her. At the same time, her body trembled violently inside - partly from being rain-soaked and cold, but mostly from fear of Helen's rage and thoughts of what the other woman would most certainly do to punish her for daring to escape.

"YOU CUNT!" Helen screamed as Williamson shoved Fran into the tent. Fran's hands were bound in front of her with a plastic tie-down.

Even before Fran heard the words, she felt the other woman's rage searing into her from the dark depths of her eyes.

"I'll show you what happens to anybody who dares to defy me!" She turned her head quickly to Williamson. "You did well. Get back to the base."

"What am I going to say? How am I going to explain taking a chopper out in weather like this in the middle of the night?"

"I don't give a shit, that's your problem. Tell them whatever you want. Just get out of here!" she screeched.

Helen turned her glare back to Fran, who shook so violently that her teeth chattered uncontrollably. Then Helen turned her attention to Soren, who had tried to shrink into the background.

"Cut those wet clothes off her!" Helen demanded. Soren hesitated.

"Strip her!" Helen screamed. Her face was crimson. Every muscle in her neck and face bulged. She wheeled around and marched over to the duffel bag containing the tools of her dominatrix identity.

Fran saw the anger in Soren's eyes. She had never seen him this angry before. Where she had previously seen hints of empathy in his eyes, she saw none now. He whipped a knife from a sheath on his belt and roughly grabbed the neck of her soaked sweatshirt, yanking it away from her body. The sharp blade made easy work of the tough wet cotton. When he was done, the heavy cotton garment ripped apart and slid from Fran's arms and back onto the sandy desert floor. Before she knew it, Soren slid the knife beneath her bra. She felt the cold steel resting on her chest, immediately above her pounding heart. With one swift jerk of the blade upward, he sliced the bra in half. Two quick slashes later, he had severed the shoulder straps and ripped the bra from her breasts. She stood before him, shivering, her bare skin covered in goosebumps. Her nipples were hard and erect from the cold.

Before Fran could catch her breath, Soren slipped his hands inside the waistband of her panties and yanked, pulling her undergarment and sweatpants down to her ankles in one swift motion. When he was finished, Fran stood shivering, trying to cover her breasts and her genitals with her arms and bound hands. She felt completely helpless and vulnerable.

"Hands down!" Helen commanded. Fran lowered her bound hands away from her breasts and tried to cover her genitals.

This time, Helen didn't bother with the boots or sexy bodice, but reached into her duffel bag and went straight for her cane. Standing up, she wheeled around, whipping the supple wood through the air towards Fran's exposed breasts. She caught Fran completely off guard.

Pain seared through Fran's breasts. She gasped in surprise at the sudden violence as red welts erupted in her soft flesh.

"Easy!" Soren shouted. "Don't forget the baby!"

Fran waited for Helen's eyes to go distant at Soren's mention of the baby. It was the one thing that usually had an immediate calming effect on Helen, usually transforming her back into Teri Taylor. But not tonight. Helen's eyes continued to bore into her, unflinching. Her rage had carried her mind somewhere completely different and far away. Fran felt herself shiver with fear again. Teri Taylor had lost whatever semblance of control she ever had over Helen's dangerous dark side.

"I don't fuckin' care!" Helen shrieked. The cane slashed through the air again, this time cutting into the flesh across the front of Fran's thighs. Fran sucked air into her lungs and held her breath, refusing to scream.

"Cut off that tie-down! Tie her wrists and ankles to the tent pole!" Helen bellowed.

"But ..." Soren mumbled.

"Now!" Helen screamed. The cane flashed through the air towards the unsuspecting Soren, landing across the side of his face. With fear in his eyes, he grabbed Fran's arms roughly and gave her a violent yank that she felt in both of her shoulders. He slid the blade of his knife under the tie-down and jerked the blade, snapping the plastic and temporarily freeing Fran's wrists.

Helen reached into her duffel bag and pulled a pair of black women's pumps with sharp spikes on heels from the bag. She threw them onto the gravel in front of Fran.

"Put them on, then kneel on the ground in front of the tent pole!" she demanded.

Fran did as she was told, fighting the urge to gasp again as the sharp gravel bit into her knees. As she kneeled and her buttocks came to rest on her heels, the spikes on the shoes bit into her flesh.

Helen threw a length of rough jute rope that landed on the ground beside the main tent pole. Soren went to work, yanking Fran's arms in front of her and tying them tightly to the pole. When he finished with her arms, she felt the course fibers go tight around her ankles, pulling them so close together that her ankle bones grated painfully against each other. The rope burned and dug into the flesh around her wrists and ankles. When Soren finished, Fran's naked back and her bleeding buttocks laid completely exposed and vulnerable to Helen's rage.

This time, Fran heard the air behind her being displaced by Helen's cane. She barely had time to brace herself for the onslaught before she felt the supple wood tear mercilessly into the flash on her mid-back. Before she could catch her breath, she heard the wind again. This time, it landed on her upper back and shoulders. Then her buttocks, her lower back, the sides of her legs and arms, and then again on her shoulders. Pain seared through her flesh and bright red welts erupted everywhere. Her buttocks felt as if they were on fire. A shudder of fear surged through Fran's body as she felt her baby come alive, tumbling restlessly in her womb. The thrashing was totally unlike the controlled, methodical dominance she'd seen Helen inflict on Soren when she was angry at him. She shuddered at the thought of what the beating might do to her unborn child. The cane strokes came faster as Helen raged further out of control.

Fran began to lose track of how many lashes she'd received. A dark fog descended slowly over her mind. Her body went numb and her pain gradually became more distant. Finally, mercifully, she drifted into unconsciousness - long before Helen finally displaced all her rage.

Helen stood, numb and detached from reality, over Fran's collapsed body. As she hovered over her helpless victim, she stared blankly at the bloody welts on the woman in front of her. And as she stared, her mind continued to slip away from reality, descending ever deeper into the dark recesses of her past.

CHAPTER 30

"I JUST want to thank all of you, on Fran's behalf, for being here to help her," Dan said. He wiped a tear from his eye as he stood in the great room of his and Fran's new home. Angela and Ricki sat together on part of the sectional sofa while Richard's colleagues, Gwen and Miriam, sat on the adjacent section at right angles to Angela and Ricki. Richard and Dan stood together, facing the sofa, with Fran's portrait of Angela in the background behind them.

"Now you're going to make me cry," Miriam answered, sniffling and wiping a tear from her eye. "We're glad we have the resources and the skills to help."

"It's the least we could do," Richard said. "We're glad y'all have the confidence t'rely on us, instead'a the FBI. Is this everybody that's comin'?"

"Apart from Anika in Calgary and Susan in Italy," Dan replied. "Susan's trying to get here tomorrow, but it could take a couple of days."

"Anika's going to be on a flight from Calgary tonight," Angela added.

"Okay," Richard continued. "Before we git started, I need t'know if y'all are a hundred percent on board with keepin' the FBI in the dark on this. They're gonna be real pissed when they find out we ain't invitin'em ta th' party.

"Angela, Ricki, and I have talked it over," Dan answered. "We're all with you. If Taylor's getting help from friends in the military, they'll spot an FBI operation from a mile away. We all like the idea of keeping a low profile."

Angela and Ricki nodded their agreement with Dan.

"Besides," Richard added. "From that glimps'a th' tent we saw in that last ransom video, I'd say there's a good chance Taylor may be hidin' somewhere in the Nellis test range. We don't need the feds an' Air Force fightin' with each other over jurisdiction."

Everybody in the room nodded their agreement with Richard's appraisal of the situation.

"Okay, then," Richard continued. "If Dan's right bout Fran sendin' us hidden messages in those videos, we gotta be real careful with this Major Taylor. Me an' th' girls've come up with an idea. I'll let Miriam tell y'all bout it."

Miriam stood and joined Richard while Dan took Miriam's seat beside Gwen.

"Thanks," Miriam began. "I think you'll all agree that everybody's objective is to rescue Fran without endangering either her, the baby, or Angela. The key is that we need to keep Taylor believing that we're actually going to give Angela to her for as long as possible."

"So, we need some kind of a distraction?" Ricki asked.

"Something like that," Miriam answered. She turned to Angela. "Remember the night we first met in the spa at Chateau Eden?"

"Yeah, why?" Angela asked.

"Remember what people said about us?"

Angela paused to think, then her eyes opened wide and a smile spread across her face. "Everybody said we could be twins. You're going to pretend to be me?"

"We have a winner!" Miriam replied, smiling. "If we're lucky, I'll be able to get close enough to take them by surprise. But that pretty much takes me out of the action until the actual swap, or until I'm recognized. Hopefully, it will give us the element of surprise and help us get the upper hand. So, we're going to need lots of help."

"What can we all do?" Dan asked.

"Richard, you want to fill in the rest?" Miriam said.

"Sure thing," Richard said, taking over from Miriam. "If we're right and th' swap goes down somewhere in th' Valley o' Fire, or maybe even in Red Rock Canyon, Taylor is probably goin' t'have some snipers up high in th' rocks. But they probably ain't goin' t'expect us t'do th' same. That's where Gwen an' I come in. We haveta support Miriam an' neutralize their snipers. We're goin' t'need spotters, and we're goin' t'need communications support."

"What about me and Dan?" Ricki volunteered.

"We was countin' on y'all t'be spotters for me an' Gwen," Richard replied. "Can we count on y'all?"

"Absolutely," Dan answered.

"Count me in," Ricki echoed.

"Good," Richard said. "That leaves communications. Me an' the girls thought we'd leave that t'Angela. That way we keep her outa' site an' outa' harm's way. I hear yer perty tech savvy anyway. You okay with that, Angela?"

"Sure," she answered. "Anika will be here too. Whatever we can both do to help."

"All right. So, this is the plan so far," Richard continued. "Gwen an' Miriam are gonna take our van with most of our gear out t'Valley o' Fire tomorrow to scout it out. They're gonna pretend t'be campin' so they'll already be in place when Taylor notifies Dan. I'll check out Red Rock tomorrow, just in case."

Richard turned to Dan.

"The girls'll git y'all suited up in camo, body armor, and some cold weather gear tonight. We may havta sit up in them rocks fer a few hours in th' dark, an' it's gonna be chilly. The rest we havta fill in as we go. Any questions?"

"What if the swap doesn't happen at Valley of Fire or Red Rock Canyon?" Angela asked.

"Good question," Richard replied. "I've got some buddies from Iraq who fly choppers here in Vegas. I've gotta coupl'a birds on standby, just in case. Any more questions?"

Richard looked around the room but was met with silence.

"All right then," he continued. "Gwen, Miriam, let's git these folks some gear an' show'em how t'do their jobs. From here on in, we're on two-hour standby."

SUSAN KEANER sat in the passenger seat of Fran's Prius. She fastened her seat belt while Dan loaded her baggage into the rear hatch. He walked around to the driver's door and climbed in. After getting behind the wheel and fastening his seat belt, he started the car, backed out of their parking spot, and began driving though the parking garage.

"We're all glad you're back," Dan said, smiling at Susan.

"I couldn't stay away once I heard the latest developments," Susan answered. "I want to be here when she's finally released."

Dan stopped at an exit barrier and inserted his payment ticket. The barrier raised and he exited the garage.

"Anything new since yesterday?" Susan asked.

"Richard, Gwen, and Miriam are out scouting the most possible swap sites," Dan replied. "The girls will be setting up camp out there and Angela decided to join them. Ricki and I have our instructions and we're on standby."

"Are you sure this Major Taylor is Fran's kidnapper?" Susan asked.

"We're absolutely sure of it, now that we've put together Fran's clues with everything we've discovered about Taylor," Dan answered.

"I was going to ask you about that. Your email said that you think Fran was giving you clues?"

"The more I watch the videos from her kidnappers, the more certain I am about that," Dan replied.

"I believe it. That's more like the strong Francesca I knew when she was young," Susan said proudly. "I knew she'd eventually rediscover that side of herself."

"You were right, Susan … what you said about Fran the last night you were here," Dan replied. "I should have believed you. I should have believed more in Fran's spirit and her strength - her drive to keep going. I should never have doubted it."

"It's easy to be critical in hindsight," Susan said, laying her left hand on Dan's. "It's hard to stay optimistic in the face of so much adversity. Time to quit beating yourself up."

"I know," he continued. "But I also remember the other part of our last talk - about the lesson I learned from Chelly in Palm Desert. It's time for me to step up and take some risks for Fran."

Quiet descended on the car for a few moments. Finally, Susan broke the silence.

"This plan of Richard's. Is it dangerous?" Susan asked.

"Yeah. Ricki and I are putting ourselves in the possible line of fire. I can't speak for Ricki's reasons, but I need to do it. I need to believe in me as much as Fran has shown that she believes in herself. I owe her. She saved my life in Palm Desert. I need to take some risks for her … and for the baby."

"I understand," Susan answered. "You've got to do what you've got to do. Just don't be foolish. Remember, that baby needs to have a mother *and* a father."

"I know. I'll be careful."

"So, is there anything I can do to help out?" Susan asked.

Dan smiled. "I thought you'd never ask. Anika is flying in tonight too. We need both of you to coordinate communications in the hours before the swap. Richard and the girls can't stay at the house because the FBI is watching and listening to my phones. I've had to use Fran's phone to keep them from knowing that I've been talking to Richard behind their backs."

Susan returned Dan's smile. "I get it. You need us to relay messages between everybody. Who's going to suspect that this old senior citizen is up to no good?"

"Exactly," Dan replied, chuckling. "So, you'll do it?"

"Wouldn't miss out on a chance to help Fran. Of course, I will," Susan answered.

"That's what I was hoping," Dan said, grinning. "Welcome aboard."

DAN SAT with Susan at the table as Anika walked into the kitchen with a cell phone held up to her ear. He looked up at the clock on the wall behind Susan. Two o'clock in the morning. It seemed like ages since he'd picked up Anika at McCarran Airport at nine o'clock. She'd hit the ground running and was already in contact with Angela, Gwen, and Miriam at the Valley of Fire campground.

"Okay, girlfriend," Anika said. "You girls get some sleep … Angela? … Can you still hear me? … You're breaking up a bit, that's all … Okay … Talk to you in the morning."

"What's up?" Dan asked.

"Nothing much. The cellular signal is a bit sketchy up in the Valley of Fire. I hope that's not a problem if we need to contact them. They're just going to get some sleep, since we haven't heard anything from Taylor yet," Anika replied.

"How are you doing, Susan?" Dan asked.

"Not so good," Susan replied. "It's been a long day. I think the jet lag is getting the best of me. I think I'd better get some sleep too. I want to be sharp if we hear anything from Taylor."

"Don't worry," Anika said. "I'll wake you up if we need you …"

Suddenly, all three of them were startled by the ringing of the estate's door bell. They stared at each other for a moment before Dan broke the silence.

"Who the hell could that be? It's two in the morning," Dan asked.

He walked quickly from the kitchen into the estate's main entrance and looked through the peep hole. When he didn't see anybody, he opened the front door. A padded envelope, large enough to fit a DVD, was lying in the middle of the porch. He picked up the package, looked out over the front yard of the estate and then sprinted out to the street. Once there, he looked quickly in both directions, hoping to see who delivered the package.

Dan's heart fell. "Shit," he muttered.

The street was deserted except for a ginger-colored tabby cat ambling its way across the road about fifty yards away. It stopped in the middle, looked at Dan, meowed at him, and then trotted the rest of the way across the street.

Dan turned, package in hand, and walked quickly back towards the house. As he entered, breathing quickly, Susan and Anika were waiting.

"Did you see who it was?" Anika asked.

"No. Whoever it was, they disappeared," Dan replied. "But they left this … feels like another video!" He ripped open the envelope as he rushed to the kitchen, pulling a DVD from the package as he went. He pushed the disc into the drive on his waiting laptop, his foot tapping up and down anxiously as he waited for it to load. Susan and Anika followed behind and waited eagerly.

"You think it's from Taylor?" Susan asked.

"Who else?" Dan answered. "Ricki's exposé has forced her hand. She has to make the swap so she can disappear."

A window with Fran's image opened on Dan's laptop, revealing the expected ransom message. Susan gasped.

"It's Fran!" she exclaimed, just before she burst into tears. Seeing her dear friend on the computer screen brought home the reality and gravity of Fran's situation. Dan clicked on the trackpad impatiently to start playing the video.

Fran was seated once again on her cot inside a tent.

"Hello, Dan. As you can see, I am still in good health - for now. Listen carefully to these instructions if you want to see me again …"

ANGELA, RICKI, Miriam, and Gwen all laid sleeping in their tent at the Valley of Fire State Park campground. Suddenly, the ringing of a cell phone shattered the still night. Bodies stirred and Angela sat upright, initially disoriented. The cell phone rang again. This time, Angela dived for it.

"Hi Dan, what's up?" she asked.

"Richard was right!" he shouted excitedly. "Valley of Fire at six am. Tell Richard that Anika and I will be there in about ninety minutes. It's time to rock and roll, ladies!"

"We're on it!" Angela confirmed. "We'll have things in motion by the time you get here."

Angela paused. "Dan?"

"Yeah?"

"Don't worry about me or Fran. We'll get her - *and* the baby - back unharmed."

"I know," Dan said. "We'll see you soon."

The phone went dead in Angela's hands. She looked up at Miriam, Ricki, and Gwen. Having heard Angela's side of the conversation, the other three women were already putting on their gear to face the morning chill and their impending rescue operation.

"Okay, ladies. It's show time," Gwen said calmly. "Time to show that Taylor bitch that we mean business."

CHAPTER 31

DAN AND GWEN laid in the pre-dawn darkness on frigid red rocks, blending into the landscape with their brown and tan camouflage apparel, and overlooking the picnic area in Valley of Fire Park. Dan methodically scanned the area through night-vision goggles while Gwen surveyed the terrain through the sights of her sniper's rifle. Both wore communication earpieces. Dan panned his goggles over the rocks across the road and to the north. He saw the eerie green glow of Richard's and Ricki's heads, partially concealed behind the highest rock formation in the area.

"Miriam reports a black van drivin' toward the picnic area. Any sign'a those two targets yet, Dan?" Richard's voice crackled into Dan's earpiece. *"They left th' visitor center on foot almost twenty minutes ago. Over."*

"Negative," Dan replied.

"Probably stayin' outta site an' watchin' for cops till the last minute. Stay sharp. We may only gitta small window t'spot'em. Over."

"Got that," Dan responded. "Keeping my eyes peeled. Over."

"See anythin' yet, Miriam?" Richard asked.

"Yeah. That van is definitely making its way towards the visitor center."

"Okay, people. Looks like it's show time," Richard said. *"Everybody stay sharp."*

"Confirmed," Miriam replied. *"We're following them in."*

THE BLACK van drove slowly past the Valley of Fire visitor center and continued up the windy road towards the picnic area, located across from the parking lot from the popular Mouse's Tank Trail. It stopped as it reached the parking lot, and then backed slowly into a parking spot below them. Nobody exited the vehicle.

Moments later, a white van came up the hill, moving slowly towards the parking lot and picnic areas. It stopped briefly while Miriam, the driver, surveyed the area and then parked across the road from the black van. When its engine turned off, an eerie silence descended on the valley below. Dan found himself holding his breath while he waited to see what happened next.

"See anybody else yet, Dan?" Richard's calm voice whispered into Dan's earpiece.

"Negative," Dan replied quietly. "Still looking. We're switching now from night to day-vision glasses."

"They gotta come out sooner or later to cover Soren. You seen anythin' yet, Gwen? Over," Richard asked.

"Negative," Gwen answered.

"Keep looking', y'all. We can't stall this exchange much longer," Richard answered.

At that moment, a sliding door on the black van opened, cautiously at first. After a moment, it finally opened fully. Fran, dressed in military fatigues, stepped cautiously from the van in the grasp of Soren, who stepped out behind her, holding her at gunpoint. He was also dressed in fatigues.

Soren held Fran close to his body as a shield and held the gun to her head. He stayed close to the van for partial cover. The sky had grown considerably lighter as the sun rose higher, but the picnic area was still in shade, shielded from the sun by surrounding formations of red rock.

"Whitney! Angela! Let's get this over with!" Soren called.

The sliding door of Richard's van opened slowly. Finally, Anika Kristiansen, Soren's wife, stepped from the van. Soren's eyes opened wide in shock at the sight of his wife. After his initial surprise, anger began to build on his face.

"What the fuck are you doing here? Where's Baranyi?" Soren shouted.

"It's all over Soren," Anika called. "Just set Fran free and drive away. I'm giving you that chance. If you and your new girlfriend take Angela, it's only going to make it worse for you. Do this for Jonah. He misses his dad. You're still his father. Walk away and save yourself."

"It's too late for that, Anika. I love Teri. We just want to be together and have a family … But that bitch Angela ruined everything … She owes us!"

Keeping his body pressed closely to Fran's, Soren pushed her forward a few feet. He pressed the gun closer to her head.

"Don't piss us off, Anika. Give us Angela or Whitney never sees his girlfriend - or his baby - again!"

DAN SHIVERED again in the chilly morning air. The red rock formation beneath him was doing its best to suck any remaining heat from his body as he and Gwen feverishly scanned the surrounding rock formations for the gunmen they knew were hiding somewhere in the rocks. The morning sun was both a blessing and a curse, finally providing some radiant heat for their bodies, but blinding them and turning the rock formations to the east into gigantic black silhouettes.

Soren and Anika continued to spar back and forth with words in the picnic area below. Part of Dan's mind wanted to listen, but he forced the rest of his brain to focus on the task at hand. He continued panning his binoculars to the right.

Suddenly, he caught a brief glimpse of sunlight reflecting off metal as his binoculars moved slowly over the landscape. He panned backwards slightly but saw nothing. Frustrated, he was about to resume panning again when he saw another flash of reflected light.

"I've got something," he whispered to Gwen. "About one o'clock from our white van … about a hundred yards, beside a big flat slab of rock … I think it's light reflecting off a watch or something … yeah, there he is … dressed in black, do you see him?"

Dan waited while Gwen scanned the area slowly through her telescopic sights.

"Bingo," she whispered. "I got him."

"Richard, we've got something," Dan whispered. "Single shooter dressed in black, lying under cover beside a big slab of rock, probably about a hundred yards directly south of you."

"Roger," Richard's voice crackled, then the radio went silent. Dan waited anxiously. Finally, the radio crackled to life in his ear again.

"Got'im," Richard said. *"But he's well hidden from this angle. I kin barely see'im. How's your view Gwen?"*

"Better," she answered. "I kin see his head'n shoulders."

"Then stay put," Richard responded. *"I'm gonna move an' see if I kin git a better look at'em. Anybody see a second shooter?"*

"I'll cover you," Gwen answered quietly. "No sign of the second shooter yet.

Dan looked across the road and saw Richard disappear behind a rock formation. He looked back to the south at the dark gunmen, who remained still behind the slab of rock.

"Five seconds, Anika," Soren shouted. "If I don't see Angela in five seconds, we're driving away from here and Dan never sees Francesca alive again."

Soren's words disrupted Dan's concentration. His eyes left the dark gunmen and became riveted on Soren and Fran below. Soren's body, still pressed tightly against Fran's back, blocked Dan's view of Fran. He ached to catch just a glimpse of her. He heard Miriam's voice in his earpiece.

"That's it," she said. "We can't stall any longer. Wish me luck, everybody."

Dan saw Miriam step from the white van beside Anika, wearing a cream-colored ball cap with a navy brim. Large black sunglasses covered much of her face. Blonde hair cascaded from beneath the cap to her shoulders. She was casually dressed in blue jeans and a loose-fitting cream-colored blouse. Dan was in awe. He wouldn't have been able to tell her from Angela himself. Anika shouted at Soren as Miriam emerged from the van.

"Okay, Soren. Have it your way. Here she is."

"Payback's a bitch, Angela, just like you," Soren shouted. "Cross the road and walk slowly towards me, hands where I can see them. I'll let go of Fran when you're close enough to change places with her!"

Miriam raised her hands above her head and began walking slowly and deliberately across the road towards the sandy parking area where Soren continued to hold the gun against Fran's head. When Miriam was just a few yards from Soren, Dan saw a black-clad figure leap from the back of the black van. He recognized the short brown hair instantly. It was Teri Taylor … the infamous Helen! He gasped.

Taylor grabbed Fran from Soren and quickly put another gun to her head. At the same time, Soren jumped forward, grabbed Miriam, and yanked her towards him. As he dragged her closer to the black van, Miriam's blouse was pulled away from her neck. Even from fifty yards away, Dan saw the clear image of Miriam's black scorpion tattoo on her exposed neck.

Soren froze. His eyes locked on Miriam's neck, then he stared at her face. A look of shock and confusion crossed his face. Then his eyes grew wide.

"What the …?" Soren muttered.

Anika's voice shouted into Dan's earpiece. *"Richard, he knows!"*

"Gwen, target on Soren!" Richard commanded.

Soren was only distracted for a second before he realized he wasn't holding onto Angela and loosened his grip on Miriam. Before he could react, Miriam lashed out with a violent kick to his solar plexus, dropping him to his knees. Miriam leapt backwards, giving Gwen and Dan a clear view of Soren. Dan jumped as Gwen's rifle cracked beside him. A fraction of a second later, Soren's body slumped forward and dropped to the ground as a single bullet entered his forehead and exploded in his brain. Blood pooled on the sand beneath his head.

It took only a second for Teri Taylor to realize what was happening. Dan watched in shock as Taylor grabbed Fran, threw her back into the black van, slammed the door, and jumped into the driver's seat. The van's engine roared and tires spun, spewing sand everywhere. It barely missed Miriam, who had to dive out of the way as the van spun out of the parking lot. As it hit the pavement, Taylor turned sharply onto the road. The tires squealed and the engine roared as she raced northwards, away from the picnic area.

A rush of air went past Dan's head and a bullet exploded into the rock above him. A second bullet hit him square on his body armor, just above his heart, knocking the wind out of his lungs. Gwen grabbed the shoulder of his camouflage jacket and yanked him back behind the rock. More bullets exploded on the rock, just behind them. They crawled down the backside of the rock formation for better cover.

"We're under fire, Richard," Gwen shouted into her radio. "It looks like there may be more'n one of'em!"

"Then git the hell outta there!" Richard shouted.

Gwen poked her head out from behind their rocky cover and fired a shot back in the direction of the second shooter. A burst of bullets from both shooters exploded in the rock around them. The sound of more gunfire came from Richard's direction.

"We can't! We're pinned down!" Dan answered.

"I just took out the shooter by the rock ... Fuck!" Richard muttered. *"Taylor and Fran are gone. I'll be in position to help you in a few seconds. Keep yer heads down till then!"*

"I hear you … wait a minute … what's that sound?" Dan answered. Their earpieces went silent for a few seconds.

"Shit! It's a chopper!" Gwen shouted. She looked around the edge of their cover and no more bullets exploded. "The shooters must be falling back. They're making a run for it, Richard!"

"Ah, shit," Richard cursed. *"The bitch has backup. They're gittin' away."*

ANIKA, DAN, Richard, Gwen, Miriam, and Ricki stood over Soren Kristiansen's lifeless body as Angela arrived at the scene, driving Richard's silver Land Rover. She swung the vehicle into the parking lot beside their white van and slid to a stop in the loose sand, kicking up a cloud of dust that drifted away slowly to the east. She flung open the driver's door, leapt from the vehicle and crossed the road to join the others. She went directly to Anika and embraced her before stepping back and surveying Soren's body.

"Holy shit! What happened?" she asked.

"Soren saw Miriam's tattoo an' realized it wasn't you," Gwen said. "All hell broke loose after that."

Angela looked into Anika's eyes. "How are you doing, girlfriend?" she asked. "I know you hated his guts for taking Jonah. But he *was* your husband, and he *is* Jonah's dad."

"I'll be okay," Anika answered solemnly. "It's Jonah I'm worried about. It's going to be hard telling him."

Richard looked at Dan and motioned to Soren's body. "Looks like we're gonna havta phone yer friends at the FBI now. They're gonna be real pissed."

"Don't worry about that," Dan replied. "I'm taking the heat. I just called Simpson. I told her I decided to hire a private security firm, and told her what happened. She wasn't happy, but they're on their way out here right now. Turns out they were holding out on us too."

"Really? How?" Angela asked.

"Apparently, they busted a colonel over at Nellis yesterday who was part of Taylor's ring," Dan began. "He led them to a campsite on the test range last night, but Taylor and Soren were already gone. They're certain that's where they were hiding Fran."

Angela's forehead wrinkled and her eyes narrowed as concern spread across her face.

"Speaking of Fran, do we know if she was hurt?"

"Still okay as far as I could see," Miriam answered. "Taylor took off in the van with her. They met a chopper at a rest stop over the hill and got away."

While the others talked, Gwen walked around Soren, examining his body. When she got to his feet, she knelt down to examine his shoes.

"So, we're back to square one," Angela said. "How are we going to find them?"

"It should be easier now that her ring of military cohorts has been busted," Anika replied. "Where can she run? She'll be the most wanted woman in the country."

"Hey, y'all. Have a look at this," Gwen shouted from behind the group. "This is interestin'." She pointed to Soren's right shoe.

"Looks like a shrimp," Richard said flatly, trying to make sense of what he was seeing.

"So how did he get one stuck on the bottom of his shoe?" Gwen asked.

"They couldn't have been near the ocean," Dan answered. "They were camped out in the desert."

Angela crouched down beside Gwen for a better look. She stared silently at the flattened, pale crustacean stuck to the bottom of Soren's shoe.

"I've seen one of these before," she said, finally. Ricki knelt down beside her to have a look.

"It isn't a shrimp," Ricki said. "It's a crayfish." She looked at Angela and the two women gave each other a knowing look.

Angela looked up at Dan.

"And we think we know where he might have stepped on it …"

CHAPTER 32

"SO, YOU all realize how lucky you are, right?" Agent Gabe Martinelli said. His eyes were narrow, his forehead creased and his jaw set firmly as he scolded Dan and his co-conspirators.

"Apart from almost getting yourselves killed, we should charge every one of you with obstructing justice, and all kinds of firearm offenses," Martinelli continued. "Mr. Holloway, if you didn't have friends in some very high places, you'd all be in a heap'a shit right now."

Dan, Angela, Ricki and Richard were gathered in the great room at Dan's and Fran's estate, eating humble pie and accepting their scolding from Agents Martinelli and Simpson.

"Yeah, we know," Dan answered. "We know we should have told you about our plan. But the swap was a huge risk either way, with or without the FBI. In the end, we all decided we just couldn't risk having Taylor panic if she saw your stormtroopers."

"What's done is done, Martinelli," Richard added. "Time for y'all to move on. Right now, we all need t'git on the same page so we can find Fran."

"This time I agree with you," Simpson conceded. She turned to Angela. "How do you know so much about the floodways?"

Angela blushed. "Well, it isn't something I'm proud of. When I ran from L.A. to Vegas to hide from Soren, I stumbled onto them. I spent a few weeks living down there with the street people."

"And the crayfish?" Martinelli asked, looking confused.

"They live in pools of water that never dry up in the tunnels," Ricki replied. "They're almost white because they never see the light of day."

Simpson looked at Ricki, wearing a look of surprise. "You know the floodways too?"

Angela laughed. She looked at Ricki and they smiled at each other. Angela turned to Simpson. "It was Ricki who found me. She was writing an article about all the people who were living under Las Vegas in the tunnels."

Martinelli looked at Ricki, his face still serious.

"So, you know the floodways well?" he asked. "What are we up against?"

"I'm afraid it's going to be like looking for a needle in a haystack," Ricki answered. "There's almost four hundred miles of tunnels under the city."

"Ain't that just great," Richard muttered. "Where we gonna start?"

Everybody in the group looked at each other, most wearing blank looks on their faces. Dan just shrugged his shoulders.

Agent Simpson finally broke the silence.

"If they flew into Nellis from Valley of Fire, they probably entered the floodways somewhere in the north end of the city," she said.

Her suggestion was greeted with silence as the group pondered it.

"Not necessarily," Angela spoke up. "Remember, they probably couldn't land at Nellis because you guys had busted Williamson and the MSA ring there."

"The airport," Ricki answered confidently. "McCarran's in the south end. There's a large floodway entrance on the Strip, directly across from the airport, close to the *Welcome to Las Vegas* sign. Most of the flood washes and storm drains are in the southwest. I'd put my money on that end of town."

Richard turned to Martinelli and Simpson. "Can y'all get maps from the city? An'we'll need a lotta manpower t'cover that much territory."

"We'll take care of both, even if we need to bring in the National Guard," Martinelli replied.

Dan turned to Martinelli. "How long will that take?"

"We can probably have a hundred agents and troops on the ground by tomorrow morning," he answered.

"I've called home to L.A.," Richard interjected. "Pam, Shelley, and Tim are on their way to help us, but they won't be here for another three or four hours."

Dan shook his head. "That's not soon enough. We need to get started right away."

"I agree with Dan," Simpson interjected. "Taylor's been cut off from her supports. She's probably desperate and she'll likely become erratic. We can likely supply half a dozen agents by this afternoon, but that's the best we can do for now." She turned to Ricki.

"Any suggestions for how to proceed?" Simpson continued.

The main doorway to the estate's front entrance opened. Anika and Susan Keaner entered the house and made their way into the great room, just as Simpson spoke.

"Sorry we're late," Anika said. "Don't let us interrupt you, Ricki."

"With the limited manpower we have at the moment, I'd suggest focusing on the five largest tunnels for now - two in the north and three in the south," Ricki said.

"We'll cover the two in the north," Martinelli volunteered.

"Me an' my team can take one in the south," Richard said.

"Count me in," Susan added. "I didn't fly back from Italy just to be spectator."

"Same here," Anika said. "While I'm here, I'll go wherever I'm needed."

"Alright," Dan interjected. "I can go with Susan. We'll take one of the floodways in the south."

"Anika, you can come with Angela and me," Ricki suggested.

"What about communications?" Simpson asked.

"That's going to be a problem," Ricki answered. "Once we're in the tunnels, radios and cell phones are useless. We're all on our own."

"Y'all can coordinate with my team," Richard suggested. "I've got enough radios in our van fer each team. I'll stay outside. If anybody finds Taylor, y'all get out of yer tunnel an' radio me ASAP. I'll relay th' info ta th' rest'a the teams from my van when they come outta th' tunnels."

"Okay. Sounds like we have a plan," Ricki said confidently. "Dan, if you get your Las Vegas map, I'll show everybody where the tunnel entrances are."

Dan hurried into the kitchen and reappeared a moment later. The feeling of frustration he'd had since this morning's failed plan to rescue Fran was beginning to fade. Instead, he felt a renewed sense of hope that their search would finally reunite him with Fran.

A SINGLE halo of light pierced the cold, damp darkness. Wearing the same thin military fatigues and oversized t-shirt that she'd worn throughout her captivity in the desert heat, Fran shivered as she stumbled through puddles in the darkness. Her sneakers were soaked through from stepping in unseen pools of water. Her stomach rumbled with hunger and the baby was restless. Too late, she felt the toe of one sneaker snag on a raised crack in the concrete floor. She put out her arms to break her fall and to protect the baby as she tumbled headfirst into a large puddle. Her t-shirt soaked up the cold water like a sponge. She shivered again.

"Get up! Get moving!" Taylor shouted.

Fran dragged herself to her feet and sighed.

"I'm freezing … and exhausted. I need water and something to eat. How much further do we need to go?"

"Just shut up and stop bitching," Taylor ordered. They resumed their march through the cold, damp, darkness.

"Are you sure we're not lost? What if we never find our way out? It's not too late to go back," Fran answered.

"Sure, and then what?" Taylor said sarcastically. "Turn myself in so the whole world can pass judgment on me? That'll be the day!"

"I won't let that happen," Fran pleaded. "I know you now, and I know what you've gone through. None of this is your fault. You are just a victim. You are just doing what you needed to survive. Trust me, I can help you."

Taylor was silent for a moment. Fran stopped and stared at the other woman's face in the dim light reflected back from their flashlight. Taylor's eyes looked distant for a moment. When they came back into the present, Fran almost thought she read a trace of empathy on the other woman's face.

"Who am I talking to now?" Fran asked. "Helen? … Teri?"

The floodway was silent. All Fran heard was their breathing and occasional slow drips of water. A moment of confusion moved across her captor's face. Finally, Taylor made eye contact with Fran.

"What do you mean?" Taylor asked. "Who's Helen?"

Suddenly, the silence was broken by the sound of an animal's feet scurrying through puddles in the darkness. In a flash, fear filled Taylor's eyes.

"What's that?" she asked, catching her breath.

She wheeled around and searched the darkness with her flashlight, waving her gun menacingly. Before long, a rat came into view. As soon as the light exposed it, the animal darted back into the darkness. Its tiny footsteps gradually faded into the distance. Fran watched as the other woman slowed her breathing and the fear gradually left her eyes. When she was calm enough, Taylor turned and waved Fran forward with the gun.

"Come on, let's go. It shouldn't be much further."

They walked for another few minutes. Finally, Fran saw a ghostly object materialize from the inky blackness on the right side of the tunnel. Initially, Fran couldn't make out any details. But with each footstep that drew them nearer, the object's form became clearer. Finally, Fran realized that it was a makeshift bed - a piece of plywood supported by cinder block columns that were about three feet high. A mattress laid atop the plywood, a safe distance from the floodway floor. A makeshift set of shelves, also supported by cinder blocks, stood at the head of the bed.

"Here we are. Home at last," Taylor announced.

"How long do we need to stay here?" Fran asked.

"A few days," Taylor answered. "Soren may be dead, and they may have brought down Williamson at Nellis. But I've still got lots of friends. I just need some time to sort things out."

"You're just making things worse for yourself … Can I call you Teri? Turn yourself in. I promise, I will vouch for you," Fran pleaded, appealing to a part of the other woman that Fran had seen in her over time - a part that depended on structure, duty, and honor.

Taylor shook her head.

"I can't. I've accomplished too much in my life to let things fall apart now. I won't give up. I can't … don't you see?"

AGENT Lindell Simpson and two other FBI agents, armed and wearing protective vests, finished checking their equipment outside a floodway entrance located at North Sandhill and East Washington in North Las Vegas, that drained into the Las Vegas Wash.

"Okay, listen up," Simpson said. Her voice was all business. "Our source says that going into this floodway is no picnic. Apparently, it's earned its name - the Death Drain. If a flood doesn't get you, the muggers and crackheads will."

"Sounds like fun," one of the agents mocked.

Simpson turned on her Maglite and was just about to lead her team into the floodway when she took one last look back over the city to the west. She squinted and frowned, noticing heavy clouds over the mountains. She clicked on the radio microphone attached to her vest, hoping to reach her partner on their FBI frequency.

"Martinelli? Simpson here. Can you still read me? Over."

"Gabe here. What's up Lindell?"

"Have you looked west recently? Over."

"No, why ... Ah, shit. Do you see what I see? Over," Martinelli cursed.

"Yup. Looks like it's raining out there. Who knows how much or for how long. We gotta pull the plug on this search. Are you with me? Over."

"One hundred percent," Martinelli agreed. *"That water comes through those flood drains and we could lose everybody. Over."*

"What's your team's status?" Simpson asked.

"Just checking their equipment," Martinelli answered. *"Still outside the floodway. Over."*

"Good. I'll call Holloway and tell him to abort the searches. Let's hope we're not too late. Over," Simpson replied. She reached for the radio that Richard had supplied to her team and pressed the transmitter button.

"Holloway, this is Simpson. Are you there? Over."

"Holloway," Richard responded.

"Have you looked west at the mountains recently?"

"No, why?" he asked.

"Better poke your head out the window and have a look," Simpson answered, her voice tense with concern.

"Okay, stand by," Richard replied. Simpson waited nervously while Richard did a visual check. Her radio crackled back to life.

"Rain over the mountains! Y'all gotta be effin kidding' me," Richard cursed into his mic.

"I wish I were, Richard. Make sure you stop all the other teams. Repeat. Make sure you get everybody out of the floodways!" Simpson shouted.

"Bloody hell," Richard swore. *"I just gave'em th' go ahead 'bout two minutes b'fore y'all called. I kin go after Gwen an' Miriam on foot. But it's too late fer th' others! Gotta go. Over."*

"Please confirm. You're saying all the other teams have entered the tunnels?" Simpson answered. The airwaves were quiet. She realized that Richard had just left his post, probably to warn Miriam and Gwen. She pressed the other mic button on her vest.

"Gabe? Simpson here."

"Go ahead," Martinelli replied.

"We've got a major problem!"

DAN AND SUSAN sloshed their way through the puddles, their lights cutting circular holes through the intense curtain of darkness. Dan had a headlamp on his forehead while Susan carried a Maglite torch. They both wore gumboots. Susan wore a light rain jacket while Dan wore a long-sleeved hiking shirt as a second layer to ward off the damp and cold.

They stopped as they stumbled upon some graffiti on the wall to their right: *Fuck the war! Leave Afghanistan Now!*

"My God, it's creepy down here. Home for the downtrodden and disillusioned?" Susan asked.

"No kidding. It's hard to believe that anybody would want to live down here," Dan replied. "I don't know how Angela did it, even if it was only for a couple of weeks." He saw Susan shiver beside him. "Are you alright?"

"Yeah, my old bones don't like the cold," she said. "But I guess it's one way to beat the desert heat if you're homeless.

"Or a way to avoid dealing with people if you're paranoid," Dan added. He saw Susan sniffing the air.

"It sure stinks. Smells like something died in here. Come on, let's keep moving," she said.

Dan and Susan walked on silently, their feet sloshing through puddles of water or occasionally crunching on broken glass. Their lights illuminated a myriad of unrelated objects: an abandoned shoe and a pool of water with two crayfish, just like the one on the bottom of Soren's shoe. They looked at each other, wondering if the crayfish meant they were on the right track. They marched on. After a couple more minutes, Dan heard the sound of little feet scratching against the concrete floor of the floodway, just before his headlamp illuminated the objects - a group of scurrying cockroaches.

Susan's voice broke the eerie silence. "How far does this tunnel go?"

"Ricki says it goes for a mile or two until it meets up with their tunnel," Dan said. "We could follow the second tunnel for a while, but we'll need to turn around so we can report to Richard after three hours."

They continued walking for another minute or two before Susan broke the silence again.

"Do you think Fran's still okay?"

"I sure hope so," Dan replied. "We don't think she was shot during the shooting at Valley of Fire. Let's just hope and pray that Taylor hasn't lost her senses and harmed Fran or the baby."

"I can't stop thinking about them," Susan said. "I'll bet Fran hasn't eaten since early this morning if they're still on the run. I worry that she's not getting enough to eat or drink … for her or the baby."

"Well, the sooner we find them, the sooner we won't need to worry," Dan said. "Are you okay to pick up the pace a bit?"

"Don't worry about me," Susan snickered. "I can last two or three hours. What about you? Do you think you can keep up with me?"

"That's the spirit!" Dan said, laughing. "I'm doing my best."

Susan swung her torch around so it once again sliced through the darkness, and they resumed slogging through the puddles. The sound of sloshing water and the clomping of their gumboots on concrete echoed around them again as they trudged into the darkness together.

CHAPTER 33

THE MINUTE Angela entered the *Welcome Tunnel,* through its entrance below the *Welcome to Las Vegas* sign on Las Vegas Boulevard, she felt herself shrouded in an ominous sense of déjà vu. It had only been about six months since she had descended, both physically and mentally, into the darkness of the floodway to escape her fears. But so much had happened since that time. She had met Ricki, who lured her out of the darkness and back into the real-life glitter of Las Vegas, encouraging her to rediscover herself. She had followed Soren to Australia after he abducted Jonah from Anika and fled the continent. She had joined forces with Dan and Anika in Australia, had lived with them through two attempts on their lives, and had managed to survive. In the process, she had found a love like she had never imagined in Anika. Just thinking about it felt like a dream. As she walked, she felt the warmth of Anika's hand in hers, bringing herself back to reality.

"We must be quite a sight," Anika said, laughing. "You look like a tourist on a spelunking expedition with those long pants, long sleeves, and gum boots."

"Thanks a lot," Angela replied, smiling. "You're not exactly a fashionista yourself right now. You can blame Ricki for making us dress like this."

"Quit your complaining, ladies," Ricki said, chuckling. "Another hour or two in here and you'll both thank me. By the way, Angela, I remember what you looked like when I found you down here. Not too flattering, I might add."

"Point taken," Angela said, laughing again.

"What's that ahead on the right?" Anika said. A ghostly, colorless image seemed to be suspended in the darkness. Ricki turned her head and her powerful headlamp pierced the darkness. The object immediately turned orange. As they continued walking toward it, they realized that it was a large orange tarp, suspended by rope from both a manhole cover and a drainage grate in the roof of the floodway. Partially hidden behind the tarp, a metal frame hung from the ceiling, supporting a ragged mattress. Angela gasped.

"Oh my God," Angela said. "I can't believe it's still here!"

"Just like you left it," Ricki added. "I wonder if anybody else has lived here since?"

Anika's eyes opened wide. She stared at Angela with a look of shock. "*This* is where you lived?"

Tears began to form in Anika's eyes. She let go of Angela's hand long enough to wipe the tears away, then she took Angela in her arms and embraced her for a moment before finally releasing her.

"I don't think I really understood how afraid and depressed you must have been, until I saw this," she said. She turned to Ricki. "Thank God you stumbled onto her."

"I'll say," Angela agreed. "Who knows how long I would have lived down here. If Ricki and I hadn't run into each other, I might never have met you, and we might never have found Jonah."

The three women stood in silence for a moment, letting the scene sink in.

"Okay, enough reminiscing," Angela said.

Ricki looked at her watch. "Yeah, we're wasting precious time. Let's go."

The three women pressed on, leaving the tarp behind. As they walked, their lights illuminated a pool of greenish-brown water with a few small minnows, then a sleeping bag hanging from a manhole shaft. They splashed through the puddle and emerged on relatively dry concrete. After that, the muted thumps of their rubber boots and occasional drips of water were their only companions in the floodway.

Suddenly, they heard a splashing sound coming from ahead of them.

"Shhh," Ricki commanded. "Listen."

The splashing sound stopped. Only its echo remained, bouncing repeatedly off the concrete walls until it faded completely into the distance.

"What was that?" Angela asked softly.

"Another person?" Anika whispered.

"I don't know," Ricki replied quietly. "But we'd better be careful. Let's keep the splashing to a minimum. And no more talking unless it's an emergency, okay?" Both Anika and Angela nodded their heads in agreement. The trio pressed forward, this time more slowly.

Moments later, they waded carefully through a pool of shin-high water. After that, signs of human habitation disappeared. The sound of gently swishing water was all that echoed softly through the concrete chamber, as their lights sliced through the inky darkness and they continued their desperate search for Fran and Major Taylor.

DAN AND SUSAN pressed on through the darkness. Dan's headlamp and Susan's flashlight continued to illuminate more signs of subterranean human existence, including an abandoned shopping cart and a bicycle. They pressed on, the muffled sound of their rubber boots occasionally interrupted by splashing water as they trekked through puddles. Suddenly, a ghostly grey form began to emerge from the darkness.

"What's that?" Susan asked quietly.

"I don't know," Dan answered. "Looks like a couple of cinder-block stilts."

They moved closer, with Dan in the lead. With each step, the outline of the grey shape became clearer. Suddenly, Dan realized it was a makeshift bed. Seconds later, Susan gasped.

"Is that a person?"

Together, they moved cautiously forward. Dan caught himself holding his breath, so he tried to relax and exhale. A human form, now coalescing before him out of the darkness, suddenly moved and gave him a brief glance at its face.

"Oh, my God … Is that? …" Dan muttered under his breath.

"Fran, is that you?" Susan asked, not convinced of what she saw before her.

Dan and Susan rushed forward. As the human form came into full view, they saw Fran cowering on a makeshift bed with her hands over her eyes, shielding them from her rescuer's bright searchlights. Dan surveyed the scene quickly. Six columns of cinder blocks formed the foundation for a four by eight sheet of plywood, which in turn supported a derelict mattress. One of Fran's legs was shackled to a chain, which was connected to a metal ladder that ascended to a storm grate in the tunnel's ceiling. At the sound of their voices, Fran sat up hesitantly.

"Dan? Susan? Is that really you?" she asked timidly, her voice full of disbelief.

Hearing her voice, Dan and Susan rushed to Fran and embraced her. All three had tears in their eyes. The only words they spoke were each other's names. The tears streaming from their eyes conveyed a multitude of unsaid emotions. After a few moments, Dan's eyes fell on the shackle and chain again. He took a step back and became somber as the dire reality of Fran's predicament became clear.

"Where's Taylor?" he asked.

"She's gone to find some food and water, and to try calling some friends for help," she replied.

"Good luck with that!" Susan exclaimed. "Her friends are all running in the other direction since Ricki exposed their military sexual abuse conspiracy."

"How long has she been gone?" Dan asked.

"Only about ten minutes," Fran answered.

"Good. We need to let the others know that we've found you and get somebody in here to cut off this chain," Dan said.

Suddenly, the threesome was blinded by a brilliant light, making it impossible to see who was behind it. Out of the darkness roared a female voice that was filled with venom. It was the voice of Teri Taylor's dark side - Helen.

"I don't think so!" Taylor shouted. "I'm pointing a gun at you. Drop your lights on the bed and put your hands up where I can see them!"

Stunned by her sudden unexpected appearance, Dan and Susan stood transfixed in a state of shock.

"Now!" Taylor screamed. Dan and Susan both dropped their lights on the mattress to comply, muting the intensity of light emanating from them.

Her eyes burning with anger and the muscles in her face and neck straining, Taylor stepped into the pool of light that reflected off the concrete wall from everybody's torches. She aimed the gun at Susan and Dan.

"Where … how …" Dan muttered.

"Shut up, Whitney! I almost ran into those bitches, Baranyi and Kristiansen, in the other tunnel and had to turn around. How the fuck did you find me?"

Susan started to answer. "Angela and Ricki …"

Taylor had run out of patience.

"Never mind! Shut up and listen. They're going to be here in a few minutes, so this is what we're going to do."

Taylor moved quickly to her duffel bag, which was at the foot of the mattress. She unzipped it. Still holding the gun on Dan and

Susan, she pulled out two plastic tie-downs. She tossed them onto the bed near Fran.

"You two are going to stand in front of Francesca with your hands behind your backs. Francesca, you're going to put those tie-downs around your friend's hands … nice and tight. You first, Whitney!" Taylor ordered.

Dan took a couple of steps away from Susan until he was beside Fran, He turned and put his hands behind his back.

"No funny stuff, Francesca," Taylor shouted. "I'm watching to make sure you do it right."

While Taylor had her eyes on Fran and Dan, Susan suddenly charged at Taylor. She made a desperate attempt to tackle the younger woman to the ground. As she did, Taylor's gun exploded and Susan screamed.

ANGELA, ANIKA, and Ricki continued to make their way, carefully and quietly, through the *Welcome Drain*, after passing by Angela's former living space.

"Stop!" Anika hissed. "Do you hear that?"

The trio stood motionless.

"Are those voices?" Angela whispered.

All three women stood rigid, their muscles tense and their hearts pounding in their chests.

Ricki held up her index finger, signaling for the others to be quiet. She moved her lips silently for Angela and Anika to read.

I think so.

Suddenly, out of the darkness, a single gunshot exploded and reverberated through the subterranean darkness. Close on the heels of the explosion, a blood-curdling scream caused all three women to shudder with fear.

CHAPTER 34

TERI TAYLOR scrambled to her feet. Susan laid on the ground, moaning and clutching her left shoulder, which was oozing a significant amount of blood. Taylor stood over Susan, waving the gun threateningly at her. The dark, angry Helen stood before them again, trembling with rage.

"You stupid old bitch! I should put you out of your misery right now!"

Instinctively, Dan took a step towards Susan. Taylor swung the gun back at Dan.

"Stay where you are, or you'll feel my pain too!" she shouted.

"Listen to me, Helen," Fran said, her voice steady and calm. "This is no time to inflict pain. There's still time for you to run. Leave Teri behind with us. She'll find a way out for you, like she always does."

Dan stared at Fran, amazed at her ability to stay calm with Susan moaning on the concrete floor. She locked her eyes onto Dan's momentarily, silently urging him to stay calm. He understood. She had learned how to manage her captor's mercurial dual identities. He felt proud of her resourcefulness. Susan was right - Fran *was* indeed stronger and more adaptable than he had ever realized.

Taylor went silent for a moment, seeming to be processing Fran's words. Then she blinked and stared at the scene around her.

"You," Taylor said to Dan. "Stand in front of Francesca so she can fasten your wrists."

As Dan stepped back in front of Fran, a scuffling sound came from somewhere behind Taylor. She stepped back, well away from

Dan, and swung her torch so that it lit up the entire width of the floodway. Anika, Angela, and Ricki were suddenly exposed by the torch's powerful beam. Taylor swung her gun around so that it pointed in their direction.

"Well, look who we have here!" Taylor exclaimed. A sarcastic smile spread across her face. "If it isn't the one and only Angela Baranyi and friends." She waved the gun in the direction of the mattress where Dan stood in front of Fran.

"Over there, beside Francesca and Whitney," Taylor continued.

The three women moved slowly, guided by the movement of Taylor's gun.

"So, Angela. What am I going to do with you, now that I've finally found you?"

"You've got what you wanted all along. Take me … Let Fran and the others go," Angela pleaded.

Dan, still standing beside Fran, cocked his head to one side. A puzzled look crossed his face.

"Wait … Does anybody else hear that?" he said. A worried frown slowly replaced the puzzled expression on his forehead.

Time seemed to stand still while everybody stopped to listen.

"Oh, shit!" Ricki bellowed. "There's a flood coming!"

Dan realized the danger immediately. He turned to look at Fran. Her eyes were wide with fear as she looked at her shackled ankle. She kicked her leg to rattle the chain. She stared into Taylor's eyes with a look that was terrified … pleading for compassion.

"Angela's right, Teri" Fran said. "You don't need me anymore. Throw me the key for the chain. If you don't, I'll drown … the baby will drown … you know you'd never forgive yourself …"

The sound of rushing flood waters grew clearer. It was closing in on them. Taylor stood transfixed, stuck somewhere in between the compassionate Teri and her raging Helen alter ego. Her eyes were glass-like and distant.

"The key, Teri! Before it's too late!" Dan roared.

Dan's urgent yell jolted Taylor back into the present, but back into a very young version of her adult self. She looked contrite and ashamed as she reached into her pocket for a key and threw it towards Fran on the bed.

To Dan's horror, her throw was wide. The key clinked to the dark concrete floor between Angela and Fran. Instinctively, Angela fell to her hands and knees on the cold, damp surface, feeling desperately in the shadows for the key to Fran's freedom - and her life.

The distant sound of water had now transformed into a steadily increasing crescendo. Taylor momentarily moved her torch away from her captives, anxious to see how much time they had before the flood's imminent arrival. In that split second, Ricki lunged towards her and grabbed the arm that held her gun.

"Noooooo …" Taylor screamed.

Her weapon discharged harmlessly into the air. The bullet ricocheted into the distance as Ricki wrestled Taylor to the ground. Her torch rattled to the floor and rolled. Its beam pointed uselessly back toward the floodway entrance, leaving them in virtual blackness.

Seizing the opportunity, Dan rushed to Susan, leaving it up to Angela to find the key and rescue Fran. He bent down, and took Susan into his arms.

"I found it!" Angela shouted behind him.

"Hurry!" Anika screamed.

Dan struggled to get to his feet with Susan in his arms.

Ricki rolled on top of Taylor, who fought back ferociously against the larger woman on top of her.

Angela grabbed frantically for Fran's ankle, trying to feel for the lock on her shackle … using her sense of touch to identify the keyhole. The roar of water was almost deafening now. Instinctively, Angela sucked in a lungful of air. Her hands floundered as she struggled to fit the key into the lock.

The next instant, a wall of floodwater arrived, engulfing all seven helpless people in a churning, swirling maelstrom of bubbling cold water and terrifying blackness.

AS THE WALL of water bore down on Angela and Fran, Anika grabbed Angela's belt with one hand, and the ladder that ascended to the storm grate with the other. She filled her lungs with air just before the wall of water struck. She felt as if both shoulders were being ripped from their sockets. Her hands strained to keep their grip on Angela and the ladder, but her tenuous grasp on the ladder was slowly slipping. She felt Angela squirming and thrashing below her. Terrified of losing her grip on her lover, she wondered if Angela was having any luck with the lock. Her lungs were beginning to burn. She summoned every ounce of strength to hang onto Angela and the ladder. Suddenly, a violent swirl of water ripped Angela from her grasp. Part of her brain cried out in terror and grief. But in another part of her brain, survival mode kicked in, releasing a surge of adrenalin. Anika summoned up all of her energy and rolled so that her other arm waved frantically to find the ladder. Seconds later, her fingers found the metal and grabbed on. She used the buoyancy of the water to pull herself upward, rung by rung. With her lungs burning, threatening to give up the battle and to suck a gulp of life-ending water, she forced her arms to keep climbing. When she thought both her lungs and her fingers couldn't hold on any longer, her head suddenly broke the surface of the raging torrent. Her grateful lungs gasped and sucked in a giant lungful of air, just as the fingers on her left hand slipped off the ladder, followed seconds later by her right hand. She felt herself being ripped from the ladder. Her body tumbled back into the swirling black vortex, and she completely lost her ability to discriminate between up and down.

At times, Anika felt her body bang against either the concrete floor or a wall of the tunnel. But miraculously, she sometimes bobbed to the surface like a cork and managed to gulp another life-saving breath before being dragged beneath the surface. She felt herself being drawn downwards again. She wondered if she saw a sliver of light coming from somewhere around her. It was the last thing she thought before her head hit the concrete floor of the floodway. Her world went dark and she slipped out of consciousness.

THE FEROCITY in Teri Taylor's fight caught Ricki by surprise. It was all she could do to keep the smaller woman from bucking her off and losing her struggle for control of Taylor's gun. Taylor fought like somebody fighting for her life, fueled by anger, fear, and desperation, and aided by her military training. As they struggled, the gun discharged again in the direction of the tunnel entrance. As it exploded, Ricki suddenly felt herself being picked up and ripped away from Taylor's writhing body by the full force of the flood. She managed to gulp a final breath and then used all her strength to keep her grip on Taylor's wrist as the two were engulfed in the cold, swirling current. She felt the smaller woman clawing at her grip with her other hand. Ricki latched onto Taylor's arm with her other hand and started shaking and squeezing it as hard as she possibly could. She felt her lungs starting to burn as she consumed precious oxygen in their struggle.

Suddenly, Ricki's head broke the surface and she managed to fill her lungs again. Almost instantly her muscles became stronger. With one final squeeze and shake of Taylor's wrist, she felt the other woman's grip loosen and then finally let go of the gun. She removed one hand from Taylor's wrist and grasped her gun hand, confirming that the weapon was gone. For a fleeting second, she was tempted to let go of Taylor's body, grateful to be safe. But then, Ricki realized she couldn't risk letting Taylor escape again. Instead of letting go, she wrapped her arms around the smaller woman and grabbed onto whatever body part or piece of clothing she could find. As she felt Taylor's struggle starting to subside, Ricki caught a glimpse of daylight while they continued to be buffeted in all directions by the raging flood waters. She managed to surface again for another breath of air. Her world went dark for a few more seconds before the light reappeared again, this time even brighter. After tumbling in the torrent for a few more seconds, Ricki found herself being spat out of the tunnel into the wash. She rode a wave of water for about thirty yards before being washed to the side of the flood and eventually sliding to a halt on the sandy floor. The skin on the side of her left leg and hip burned from being scraped over the rough desert floor. But as she came to a rest, she put her full weight on a nearly lifeless Teri Taylor, vowing not to let her get out of her grip or out of her sight.

DAN SUMMONED every ounce of strength in his legs to get to his feet with Susan in his arms. As he did, he sensed the raging wall of water coming at him. He inhaled deeply and tried desperately to keep his grip on Susan. Fortunately for him, the buoyant force of the water transferred much of Susan's weight from his arms to the swirling liquid around them. But trying to keep his grip on Susan was about as possible as trying to hang onto something during a tornado.

A great swirl of water threatened to rip Susan from Dan's grasp. Frantically, his hands searched for the belt that he knew she was wearing. He found it, but before he could get his fingers beneath it to get a grip, another strong vortex of water tore her away from him.

Dan continued to tumble, virtually weightless, through the cold darkness. He heard water roaring all around him. Suddenly his head broke the water's surface for a moment, allowing him to ride the wave and to fill his lungs for a brief respite from the raging torrent around him. He thought he heard someone gasping for breath at the same time, but couldn't be sure. Maybe it was

Susan, but just as likely one of the others who were swept away by the flooding waters. Then Dan felt himself being sucked back down into another vortex, tumbling and spinning again and losing all sense of direction. He felt guilty for not being able to hang onto Susan. He wondered about the injured woman's chances of surviving the forces of Mother Nature's sudden desert onslaught.

Dan's lungs started burning again. His mind flashed back to the swimming pool at Fran's and Philippe's estate in Palm Desert, just five or six months before. The vision of Philippe's huge shadow above him, and the overwhelming weight of the heavier man's body, was burned into Dan's brain forever. Finally, when he thought for sure that Philippe would drown him, Philippe released his grip and Dan saw sunlight above him. His arms clawed at the water to bring himself closer to the light and to life-giving oxygen. Dan's head broke the surface again and he gulped in more air.

It took a moment before Dan realized that he wasn't in the pool at Palm Desert any longer. He was back in the raging floodway again. But this time, there was light at the end of the tunnel. He was riding the crest of the flood now, his head staying above water. Daylight raced towards him. Finally, he emerged from the floodway, riding the wave into the wash until he felt his feet scrape the sandy bottom of the wash. He managed to slow himself by dragging his boots along the sandy ground. The flooding waters raced past him as he slowed himself, until he finally managed to plant his feet in the sand and stand upright. Miraculously, Dan walked himself out of the flood and onto the bank of the wash. He should have felt thankful. But instead, all he could think about were Fran, Susan, and the others. He looked out over the wash, his eyes frantically searching the aftermath for any other signs of life.

ANGELA RODE the gigantic wave out of the darkness into brilliant afternoon sunshine. She'd felt Anika's hold on her belt disappear within seconds after the giant tidal wave of water had struck. She had barely managed to open the lock on Fran's shackle as the wave washed over them, only partially opening it. Swept along into the wash by the wave, Angela's eyes roamed frantically, looking for any signs of life around her as the water gradually dispersed and the wave slowed. Moments later, she landed on solid ground on one side of the wash. She realized that she ached everywhere. Her body was scraped and bruised after being bashed repeatedly against concrete walls by merciless whirlpools during the ordeal. Her legs still shook with fear. She thanked her lucky stars that she was still alive, but feared for the others.

Angela finally found the strength to force her trembling legs to stand. She looked around and was relieved to see Ricki, battered and scraped, rolling on the ground and struggling with Teri Taylor only yards away. Angela rushed to Ricki's aid, wincing in pain as she started to run.

"I'm coming, Ricki!" she shouted.

Taylor screamed and clawed at Ricki, trying to move the larger woman off her body. Her eyes were filled with fear and hatred.

"You'll pay … bitch …" Taylor grunted.

"Help me roll her!" Ricki managed to shout. She panted heavily as she struggled with Taylor. "She's small … but she's like … a fucking banshee! … Bitch tried her best to drown me …"

Angela threw herself into the fray, trying to grab one of Taylor's flying fists. With her added weight, and with Ricki on top of the pile, they finally managed to gain the advantage. Before long, they had Taylor face down on the ground. Breathing heavily, Ricki surveyed the area around them.

"We need to tie her hands," she shouted to Angela. Her eyes scoured the area. She spotted a plastic grocery bag that had washed out of the tunnel with the flood. "See that plastic bag over there? … Get it for me!"

Angela lifted herself off Taylor, ran to retrieve the bag, and rushed back to Ricki.

"Hold her wrists together!" Angela shouted to Ricki. "I'll tie them."

Taylor continued to struggle and thrash, making Angela's job difficult. She finally succeeded in tying the bag tightly around Helen's wrists.

"There! That should do it. The more she struggles, the tighter that knot's going to get."

"What about the others?" Ricki answered. "Do you see anybody else?"

Angela surveyed the wash. About thirty yards away, she spotted Anika and Fran, both on their knees. Fran gagged and retched violently while Anika vomited. Angela's eyes continued to roam over the wash. She gasped when she saw Susan lying on her back with Dan kneeling on the ground beside her.

"Hold on, Dan, I'm coming!" she shouted. She rushed to Dan's side and knelt beside him. Like her, he was covered in scrapes and bruises. She saw blood oozing from Susan's shoulder. Dan had rolled Susan onto her non-injured side and pounded on her back, managing to drain water from the older woman's lungs.

"How can I help?" Angela asked.

"Find somebody with a phone. Call 911. Tell them we've got potential drowning victims, one of them with a gunshot wound. Now!"

Dan rolled Susan onto her back and started CPR. Angela surveyed the scene to get her bearings. She realized they were in the wash beside the southbound lanes of Las Vegas Boulevard. Then she looked up and saw the top of a familiar sign poking its head over the bank of the wash.

Welcome to Las Vegas.

She rushed across the wash and scrambled up the embankment to the street. Cars were parked in the median next to the famous sign. Tourists laughed and smiled for snapshots of each other to send to friends or the folks back home. Angela bolted across the southbound lane of traffic. Tires screeched to a stop and horns blared. Angry drivers flipped her the bird and shouted insults from their vehicles, but Angela was oblivious to both the danger and the commotion. She rushed up to a startled couple who were in the middle of having their picture taken by another tourist.

"Help me!" Angela shouted. "I need a cell phone to call 911!"

"Uh … Sure … Here," mumbled one of the startled tourists. The man pulled a cell phone from his pocket, dialed 911, and handed the phone to Angela.

"… 911? … We've got two possible drowning victims, one with a gunshot wound … Las Vegas Boulevard, in the wash beside the *Welcome to Las Vegas* sign? … And we need the FBI. We've captured Major Teri Taylor … Hurry!"

Angela thrust the phone back into the hands of the stunned tourist and started running back across southbound traffic towards the wash. As she ran away, she shouted back over her shoulder at the bewildered couple.

"Thanks!"

She ran back across the street, down the bank and into the wash. She saw Susan sputtering and coughing. Dan rolled her over on her side again as she continued to cough and gasp for air. Before long, she vomited and continued retching, gasping, and coughing. Angela nodded to Dan, letting him know that she'd made the 911 call.

"Everything's going to be okay, Susan," she heard Dan say. He rested his hand reassuringly on Susan's back while she continued to retch and gasp. "Help is on the way. You're going to be all right."

Satisfied that Dan had Susan's situation under control, Angela turned her attention to Anika and Fran. Anika knelt beside Fran, who was still lying on her side in the wash, exhausted and coughing. Both women were scraped, bruised, and exhausted like all the others. Angela marveled that they had all managed to survive the deluge. She ran to Anika and wrapped her arms around her.

"Thank God you're all right!" she cried. A mixture of relief and joy flooded through her body.

The two women fell into each other's arms and embraced, clinging to each other and kissing passionately. When they finally ended their kiss, Angela looked over at Fran.

"How's she doing?"

"She's okay, thanks to you," Anika answered. "She took on some water and she's still shaky, but I think she'll be okay."

Angela hurried over to Fran and knelt beside her, sweeping some hair away from Fran's eyes and running her fingers through her hair to soothe her. She heard sirens in the distance.

"You're safe, Fran," she reassured. "Everything's going to be okay. Ricki has Taylor on the ground and the police are on their way."

Fran coughed again. "What about Dan? … Susan?"

"They're going to be okay too," Angela replied.

Fran managed to sit upright. She took Angela's hand in hers in a silent gesture of thanks. Then, instinctively, she rested her other hand on the baby growing inside her, waiting for it to move. She didn't need to wait long. Her baby was restless. Fran gazed into Angela's eyes. Her eyes were red and tears were forming. At the sight of her tears, Angela and Anika burst into tears as well. All at once, all three women realized how close they had come to dying and how lucky they were to have survived. They were overwhelmed with relief.

"Thank you," Fran said simply.

The approaching sirens grew to painful decibel levels as emergency responders squealed around the corner from Tropicana and rumbled to a stop on the street above them. The sirens stopped suddenly, leaving only the sound of an idling diesel engine from a fire truck in the background. The sound from another smaller engine joined the fire truck seconds later.

Angela saw two firefighters rush down the embankment into the wash. Each one carried a first aid kit and an oxygen tank. One rushed towards them to attend to Fran while the other rushed over to where Dan knelt beside Susan. Police and ambulance sirens continued to wail in the distance, growing louder with each passing second.

CHAPTER 35

DAN HEARD pounding footsteps and the swishing of fabric behind him. As he looked up, a firefighter jogged up to him. He heard more sirens in the distance, but they were growing closer by the second.

"What do we have here?" asked a short muscular female firefighter, carrying a small tank of oxygen and a first aid kit.

"She took on a lot of water in the floodway" Dan shouted. "And she's been shot in the shoulder!" He still felt the adrenalin pumping through his arteries. "I tried to drain her lungs and I've been doing CPR. She's breathing now!"

"Okay, sir. I'll take over," the woman said.

Dan stood up and gave the firefighter room to work. She took Susan's pulse and checked her breathing. When she was assured that Susan was breathing on her own, she placed a mask over Susan's nose and mouth and turned on the flow of oxygen. Then she examined Susan's shoulder, which was still oozing blood. She reached into the first aid kit, pulled out some packaged bandages, ripped one open, and began applying pressure. With her other hand, she pressed a microphone clipped to her uniform.

"I'm with one of the victims. I've got her on oxygen and she's breathing on her own. She has a gunshot wound to her left shoulder and she's still losing some blood, over."

Dan watched impatiently as the firefighter listened to a response in her earpiece. Finally, she looked up at Dan.

"Is she going to make it?" Dan asked anxiously.

"I think so," the woman replied. "Her pulse is weak because she's lost some blood, but an ambulance is going to be here any second."

"Thank God," Dan muttered. The firefighter was right. He heard an ambulance siren on the street above. The siren went mute as the vehicle arrived on the scene, but another one grew louder and closer in the background.

With Susan in good hands, Dan's thoughts went immediately to Fran. He looked over to where he had seen Angela tending to her a few moments before. Seeing a firefighter kneeling beside her, he felt overwhelmed by fear for her, his heart pounding in his chest. He sprinted towards Fran, who was now sitting up beside the firefighter.

"How is she?" Dan shouted as he pulled up beside them. Fran's head snapped to attention and her eyes met Dan's. Tears filled his eyes as he saw her look of relief, then a look of joy and tears streaking down her cheek. Dan dropped to his knees. Without waiting to hear from the firefighter, he took Fran in his arms and pressed her close to his body. He felt Fran doing the same. In the background, Dan vaguely heard the firefighter answering his question.

"She seems to be okay," the man replied. "She seems to be in a bit of shock, but her pulse and breathing are acceptable."

"I was afraid I'd never see you again," Fran said, still weeping into Dan's shoulder. She coughed again, her lungs still trying to expel the last remnants of water from her terrifying ordeal. He placed his hand gently on each side of her head and lifted it from his shoulder so he could see her face.

"Me too," he sniffled. "Until I made sense of the clues you left us in the ransom videos. Then I realized how strong you are. I knew I needed to believe in you and had to be just as strong myself."

"Thinking of the three of us together was the only thing that kept me going," Fran said, sniffling.

Dan's eyes moved from Fran's face and he gazed at the growing bulge in her midsection. He placed his hand over their baby.

"How's our baby doing?" Dan asked. Just then, he felt a sharp kick and his face lit up in a broad smile.

"Just fine," Fran answered, wiping away a tear and smiling too. She coughed again. "For the most part, Soren and Helen … or Teri … treated us well … at least until the end when she started to come apart. She couldn't bring herself to hurt the baby. I think that's what saved me."

"Well, thank God for that," Dan replied. He saw four paramedics hustling down the embankment. Two of them rushed towards them, while the other two headed in Susan's direction. Seconds later, two paramedics, a middle-aged man and a younger woman, arrived to relieve the firefighter.

"How are we doing here?" the woman asked.

"Good," the firefighter responded. "She took on some water, but nothing too serious. She's also got a lot of scrapes and bruises."

The male paramedic clipped a sensor to Fran's finger and wrapped a blood pressure cuff around her upper arm.

"Are you Francesca, the kidnapping victim?" he asked.

Fran nodded in silent agreement.

"How did they treat you?" the man asked, his eyes scanning her body for signs of injury. "Any significant injuries?"

"No," Fran answered, shaking her head. She looked at Dan. "Can I just go home now?"

The female paramedic laughed. "That's the spirit, but I'm afraid we can't do that," she answered. "The FBI wants you admitted to hospital for evaluation, just to document your present condition. Don't worry, from what I've seen, I don't think they'll keep you for long."

"Ready to load her onto the stretcher?" the male paramedic asked.

"I think I can walk," Fran interjected.

"Just relax and enjoy the ride, dear," the female partner answered. "It's just a precaution."

"Can I ride in the ambulance with her?" Dan asked.

The two paramedics looked at each other and exchanged glances.

"I don't see why not," the man replied. "It's not like she needs a lot of medical attention on the ride in." He turned to Fran. "Can you slide onto our stretcher?"

Fran lifted herself up, slid onto the stretcher, and lay down. Dan reached out and took one of her hands. She squeezed gently and smiled up at him as the paramedics lifted the stretcher, began trekking across the wash towards Las Vegas Boulevard, and climbed up the embankment to the waiting ambulance.

"I love you," Fran said.

Dan squeezed her hand lovingly and gazed down at her, realizing how much he had missed her and how much she meant to him.

"I love you too."

MOMENTS LATER, FBI agents Simpson and Martinelli hurried down the embankment into the wash, followed closely by two other agents. They made their way over to Ricki, who still sat on top of Teri Taylor. Simpson looked down at Ricki and chuckled.

"Looks like we're too late for the party. You seem to have everything under control. Whose idea was the garbage bag to tie her hands?" she asked.

Exhausted from her ordeal in the rampaging floodwater and the struggle with Taylor, Ricki finally lifted her body off Taylor and got to her feet slowly. She rubbed the bruises on her hips and a shoulder.

"Yeah, we finally got the little banshee subdued! But not before Taylor put up quite a fight," Ricki answered. "The bag was my idea but Angela did the dirty work".

Ricki's eyes scanned the two FBI agents.

"You two look like you survived without a scratch," she observed.

Simpson looked at Martinelli, letting him answer.

"We saw the rain in the mountains," he explained. "We radioed Richard Holloway to abort the search, but we were too late. You'd already gone in."

With Fran and Susan now safely in the care of paramedics, Angela and Anika joined Ricki, Simpson, and Martinelli.

"So, Richard and the girls are alright?" Angela asked.

"They should be here any minute," Simpson answered.

Martinelli turned his attention to Teri Taylor, who had rolled over on her side and managed to get to her knees.

"Teri Taylor, you have the right to remain silent. Anything you say may be used against you in a court of law. You have the right to consult an attorney before speaking, and to have an attorney present. If you cannot afford an attorney, one will be appointed for. Do you understand?"

Taylor slumped, sitting back on her heels. She said nothing, but her deflated posture telegraphed her sense of defeat. She was timid and afraid. When she finally answered, there was nothing of the confident, domineering Lady Helen in her voice. Instead, she sounded more like a sullen young child. She nodded her understanding.

"I understand," she mumbled.

Martinelli turned to the other two agents.

"Cuff her and take her away," he said.

The two agents led Teri Taylor up the embankment towards Las Vegas Boulevard and their waiting vehicle.

"You guys are so lucky nobody was killed," Simpson said.

"No kidding," Anika remarked. She turned to Angela.

"I didn't think you were ever going to get Fran's shackle unlocked. I thought I was going to lose you both," she said.

Angela's eyes met Anika's and were full of love. She took Anika's hand in her own and smiled.

"You're the only reason I managed. You hung onto me just long enough to give me a couple extra seconds. That's all I needed. Then the water ripped me away from both of you," Angela replied.

"I'm glad everything worked out in the end," Simpson said. "Even if all you guys *should* have your knuckles rapped for trying to do this all on your own. What do you say, Gabe?"

"Ditto on that," he answered. "You were lucky you had friends like Richard and the girls. But next time, please trust the experts, will ya?"

Martinelli glanced toward the embankment where Richard, Gwen, and Miriam were making their way into the wash to join them."

"Speak of the devil, here they come now" he said to Simpson. "What do you say? Time we get back to the office to deal with Taylor?"

"Yeah," Simpson replied. She turned to Ricki. "Hopefully she'll spill it all without a fight. With any luck, you'll have lots more material for your MSA story by the time we're finished questioning her."

"I'm counting on it," Ricki answered, grinning.

"Catch you all later," Martinelli said. "Let's hope we don't meet again too soon."

"That's for sure," Angela agreed, laughing. She looked at Ricki and Anika.

"I met some amazing people and had the biggest adventure of my life over the past few months. But it's time for me … and Anika … to get back to our lives and our kids. I think we've had enough adventure for a while!"

"You've got that right," Anika agreed.

The three women watched as the two FBI agents turned and walked towards the embankment, stopping to talk with Richard, Gwen, and Miriam. Up on Las Vegas Boulevard, they saw two paramedics loading Fran into an ambulance, accompanied by Dan. Moments later, Richard and his crew finished their conversation with Martinelli and Simpson and headed towards the threesome.

"Sounds like y'all did some surfin'," Richard joked. A broad smile flashed across his face before he became serious again. "We were damn scared when we heard about the rain an' realized y'all were in the tunnels already. Glad to see y'all made it out alive."

"Thanks, Richard," Ricki answered. "We're glad you, Gwen, and Miriam didn't get caught." She turned to Angela and Anika.

"Let's follow Fran and Susan to the hospital. I won't be able to sleep tonight until I know they're both going to be alright."

"Absolutely," Anika answered.

"Damn right," Richard echoed. He turned to Gwen and Miriam. "Whatcha say ladies?"

"What are we waitin' for?" Gwen added. "Let's go. Richard's van is parked up on the boulevard by the sign."

Ricki, Angela, and Anika turned and walked briskly as a group towards the *Welcome to Las Vegas* sign while Richard, Gwen, and Miriam followed close behind.

CHAPTER 36

A WAVE of happiness and relief overwhelmed Fran as she and Dan emerged from the Southern Hills Hospital emergency room, with Dan pushing her in a wheelchair. The first thing she saw was a waiting room filled with many of her closest friends.

Angela and Anika saw the couple first and rushed towards Fran's wheelchair. Ricki, Richard, Gwen, and Miriam followed closely behind. Angela's face wrinkled with concern when she saw the wheelchair.

"Are you alright?" she asked. "What's with the wheels?"

"It's just a precaution," Fran replied. "They say there is still danger from water in the lungs. They want to keep me in overnight to make absolutely sure everything's alright with me and the baby."

"Better safe than sorry," Anika added. She stepped forward and hugged Fran. Angela waited for her turn and did the same. Dan then pushed her wheelchair closer to Richard, Gwen, Miriam, and Ricki, who each greeted Fran with warm embraces.

"Y'all don't know how happy we all are to see ya safe an' sound!" Richard remarked.

Fran smiled, feeling the genuine warmth in her friend's voice. "I hear I owe that to you and your team," she replied, glancing at Gwen and Miriam. "The three of you didn't need to risk your lives. You could have left it to the FBI."

"Like hell we could," Gwen scoffed. "No tellin' what would have happened if we'd left it to that ship o' fools."

Fran turned to Miriam. "I especially want to thank you, Miriam. You took the biggest risk by pretending to be Angela."

"You're welcome," Miriam replied. "Too bad it all went south when he saw my tattoo."

"Yes, but everything turned out okay in the end," Fran continued. "Thank you for trying."

Fran turned to say something to Richard, but stopped in her tracks when she saw Richard's wife, Pam, walk into the waiting room with Shelley Paul and Tim Jennings. Tears welled in her eyes at the sight of more of her close friends.

"Fran!" they shouted in unison.

"Thank God you're safe," Shelley added. The trio rushed to Fran's wheelchair and embraced her in a joyous group hug.

"I am so glad to see you guys!" Fran gushed. "Thanks for driving in from L.A."

"Nonsense," Pam answered. "We dropped everything when Richard called us to help with the search. I'm so glad they didn't need us, and that you're all safe!"

"How's the baby?" Shelley asked, concern etched on her forehead.

"It's fine," Fran replied. "The doctors did some initial tests and everything looks completely normal. They just want to keep me for the night to make sure."

"We're all just relieved that you're both alright," Tim added.

Fran watched Pam turn to Dan and wrap him in her arms, giving him a bear hug and a kiss on the cheek. She recalled the night at Chateau Eden, only five months before, when Philippe told her about spying on Pam and Richard's advances on Dan and Chelly in the spa. She shivered. Memories of Palm Desert flashed through her mind. She couldn't help but wonder how different things might have been if Dan and Chelly had hooked up with the Holloways instead of with herself and Philippe. She felt Dan squeeze her hand. Her mind came back into the present.

I might not have fallen in love with Dan if things had turned out any differently.

She squeezed Dan's hand and smiled. He leaned down and she gave him a grateful kiss.

"Congratulations on getting Fran and the baby back," Tim said, as Fran and Dan ended their kiss. He took his turn at giving Fran a hug and shaking Dan's hand.

"How's Susan doing?" Pam asked.

"We're waiting for her to get out of surgery so we can visit with her," Dan replied. "The nurses say she'll be out of recovery any time … wait a second … looks like somebody's coming now."

"Are you Susan Keaner's family?" the nurse asked.

"I am," Fran replied, knowing that she and Susan were closer with each other than with either of their respective families.

"They're just taking her up to her room now," the nurse said. "She should be settled in ten or fifteen minutes. You can visit, but please make your visit short. She's been through a lot."

"Thank you," Fran answered. "We just want to let her know that we're here with her."

SUSAN'S EYELIDS flickered. She struggled to keep them open, but failed in her first attempt. A second later, they flickered open again, this time staying open. She initially registered a look of confusion, but a smile gradually spread across her face as she began to recognize the faces circled around her bed.

Susan took a deeper breath while she gathered her senses. Finally, she found the energy to speak.

"If being shot is what it takes to get this kind of attention … I should have done it years ago," she whispered through dry lips. She coughed while her visitors laughed, easing the previously solemn mood within the hospital room.

"Would you like some water?" Fran asked.

"I'd love some," Susan whispered again. "Help me sit up?"

Dan helped her sit up and placed two pillows behind her back. Fran handed her a cup of water. While she sipped, the rest of Dan's and Fran's friends waited patiently. Angela and Anika stood with their arms wrapped around each other's waists. Richard and Pam Holloway stood to Susan's left while Shelley and Tim stood on the right. Ricki, Miriam, and Gwen were gathered around the foot of Susan's bed.

Susan handed the cup back to Fran. She smiled as her eyes rested on Fran's abdomen. Tears came to her eyes as the reality of their mutual brush with death set in.

"Thank God you and the baby are both safe!" Susan sniffled through her tears.

Fran offered her a tissue and rested her hand on her mentor's shoulder. She turned to address their friends.

"Susan, Dan, and I need to thank everybody in this room," she said. She smiled at the group, conveying her gratitude with eyes full of love. "You've all been here for me and Dan since Philippe and Chelly died. Pam and Richard ... Shelley and Tim ... you've been close friends ever since you started visiting Chateau Eden. I don't know what we would have done without you."

Fran's eyes went to Richard. "Especially you, Gwen, and Miriam," she continued. "We never asked you to risk your lives for us."

"It ain't nothin'," Richard replied. "We would've done it fer any friend. Ain't that right, girls?" Gwen and Miriam smiled at Fran and nodded their agreement.

"I think this happy ending calls for a celebration!" Pam interjected.

Fran smiled at Pam. "The nurses told us we need to keep our visit with Susan short." She turned to Susan. "We should let you rest now. Dan and I will be back first thing in the morning, okay?"

"Thank you ... everybody ... for coming," Susan said. Her voice was still raspy and weak.

Shelley stepped forward and silently kissed Susan on her forehead as Fran had done.

"Thank you so much for coming all the way from Italy to be with Fran," she said.

One by one, the rest of Dan and Fran's friends came forward and did the same. When they were finished, Dan broke the silence.

"Pam's right about having a celebration. If I remember correctly, we never got to finish our housewarming party because we were so rudely interrupted." He smiled at Fran. "If Fran is up to it, I'm sure we'd both love to have you back to the house for a while after she's discharged tomorrow."

"There is nothing I would love more," Fran answered, smiling. "Maybe we could order in some pizza. For some strange reason, I craved it the entire time I was in that tent in the desert!"

Everybody in the group laughed. "Pregnancy cravings," Angela added.

Susan smiled warmly at Fran and her friends.

"I'll be there, come hell or high water," she rasped. She took a long breath to summon some more strength. "We should all be proud of what we did together. We showed Taylor and her deluded mob … our collective spirit … love, cooperation, and positive energy … it will always win … over hatred, anger, and the need to dominate others."

"Amen to that," Ricki added.

"Amen," the others echoed.

One by one, the group turned and began filing out of the room, led by Ricki, Angela, and Anika.

Fran and Dan were the last to leave. Dan leaned over and kissed Susan on her cheek.

"Thanks for everything," he said. "If it wasn't for you, I don't know if I could have found the strength to keep going. Have a good sleep. We'll see you in the morning."

"Thank *you*," Susan said. "Thank you for finding and loving Fran. Take good care of her."

"You know I will," Dan reassured her. He stepped back so Fran could say goodbye.

Tears welled up in her eyes as she leaned over Susan.

"I love you," Fran whispered in Susan's ear.

"I know," Susan replied as tears began filling her eyes.

"We'll be here right after breakfast to pick you up, okay?"

Susan smiled and nodded. Fran turned to Dan and saw the love in his eyes. She took his hand and gave Susan one last smile and a small wave before she went to her wheelchair and sat down. Dan released the brake and pushed Fran from the room to say goodbye to their friends. When they were finished, he wheeled Fran to an elevator to take her down one floor, so she could settle into her room for the night.

ANGELA FELT a click as she turned the key in the lock. She twisted the key, pushed the door open, and her senses were assaulted instantly by a wall of musty, hot, stagnant air.

"Eew, that's gross," she muttered as she swung the door wide. "I turned off the AC when I left to find Soren in Australia."

Angela walked to the window and opened the blinds. Bright daylight flooded into the dingy office space. The skyline of the Las Vegas strip glimmered and sparkled in the mid-day sunshine. In the distance, behind the MGM Grand and the Luxor's dark glass pyramid, the Spring and Nopah mountain ranges shimmered against a brilliant blue sky.

"This is it?" Anika asked, obviously shocked by what she saw. "*This* is where you lived? You actually brought Ricki up here to see this dump?"

Angela laughed. "C'mon. It was a big step up from living in the floodway. At least I could come up here at night, wash up, and heat some food in the microwave."

She walked over to a thermostat on one wall and turned on the AC. The ancient unit growled and vibrated as its old bones reluctantly came back to life. She looked around the room at the dirty, neutral grey walls, the flattened, worn carpet, and the yellow-stained ceiling tiles. Memories of that time came flooding back. To her left, a small wooden table still stood with a microwave sitting on top. Beside the table, her small bar fridge sat silently. To her right, her shiny new grey safe was still fastened firmly to the wall. Beside the entrance, she poked her head into the tiny bathroom where she had settled for sponge baths to wash away the odor and grime of the floodway, where she had spent the bulk of her time after arriving in Las Vegas. On the other side of the entrance in a tiny closet, an assortment of dresses, skirts, blouses and camisoles still hung on plastic hangers. The clothing was all that remained of her excursions into the business world under her assumed identities, Grace Wagner and Anna Benz.

Finally, sitting forlornly in front of the window, stood Angela's IKEA office table and her rolling office chair - the one she'd bought during her time in Las Angeles - where she had sat for so many hours at night with her laptop, stalking Soren. She had taken her laptop with her when she left for Australia, but Angela's ancient portable TV still sat atop two red plastic milk crates. The shocking memory of seeing the NBC news report from Palm Springs, with her own image captured in Fran's huge black-and-white portrait for the whole world to see, flashed through her mind.

Angela felt Anika take her hand and squeeze it gently. It brought her back into the present.

"I can't imagine what you must have been going through at the time," Anika said quietly. Angela saw her lover's eyes becoming red and watery.

"It served its purpose," Angela answered. "It helped me track down Soren. It helped me find a reason to keep on living my life. If I hadn't done that, I never would have met you and we might never have been able to get our children back." She gazed into Anika's eyes and smiled.

"Thanks for bringing me here," Anika replied, wiping away a remnant of a tear. "It helps me know you better."

As Anika smiled back, Angela saw the love in her new partner's eyes. She felt tears of happiness welling up in her own eyes. Choking back her tears, she put on a more business-like face. "I guess we'd better get started," she said.

Angela stepped outside the apartment to the landing, where she and Anika had left a vacuum, bucket and mop, and a box of green trash bags. She handed the bucket and mop through the doorway to Anika, and then picked up the vacuum and garbage bags and carried them into the musty apartment. She propped the door open with an old doorstop she found in the closet.

"I don't care if it's going to be over a hundred degrees out there," she declared. "At least the outside air is dry and we can air this place out while we clean."

"Things worked out really well," Anika replied. "We got back to Vegas and found Fran just before your deal with your landlord expired."

"Yeah," Angela agreed. "I could have lived with walking away from most of the stuff in this room. But I really needed to clean out the safe."

She pulled a green trash bag from its box, walked over to the safe, and knelt down. She twirled the combination dial on the safe's door back and forth three times. When she was done, she pulled down on the handle and the steel door swung open. The safe was mostly empty, apart from a small bundle containing her Grace Wagner passport and identification. There was also a few thousand dollars' worth of U.S. currency, the remainder of her emergency cash that she hadn't taken with her when she left for Australia. She paused and looked through the stack of ID documents.

"Are you throwing those away?" Anika asked.

Angela paused to think. "I don't know. Realistically, they're illegal and I know I won't need them again," she answered. She paused again as she stared at her photo in the passport.

"But on the other hand, I don't think I can throw them away," she continued.

"Then don't," Anika answered. "They were important. They helped you survive. It's something you always want to remember."

Angela paused once again. After a few seconds, she placed the money and documents in the trash bag and carefully rolled it into a bundle. She left the safe open and went to the IKEA table, looking for a pen and paper. When she found what she was looking for, she scribbled a note and three numbers on a notepad and tore off the top sheet. She went back to the safe and left the note on top.

"No sense taking the safe," Angela said. She let out a deep breath, as if she was allowing herself to let go of part of her past. "Might as well leave it behind, along with the combination, for Mr. Lau or his next lucky tenant."

Anika laughed. "I can see the ad now. *Office space for lease. Out of the way location. Comes equipped with brand new safe. Perfect for hiding money and hiding from the police.*"

Both women laughed aloud.

At that moment, Angela realized how good she felt. She had accomplished her mission to free herself from Soren and to reunite herself with her children, Nicholas and Julia, and with her momma and papa. In the process, she had rediscovered herself and found Anika, her first real love. Life was good. She gave Anika a quick kiss on the cheek.

"C'mon, love. Let's get busy. We've got a plane to catch this afternoon. I don't know about you, but I can't wait to get back to Calgary to be with the kids."

As she turned away to reach for the vacuum, Anika grabbed her hand and pulled Angela back towards her. She pressed her lips against Angela's and pulled their bodies close together.

"I don't know about you, but there's something about this little hideaway that is really sexy. Is that just me?" Anika whispered.

"No, it's not just you," Angela answered. She kissed Anika lightly and tenderly. "I think we have some time to spare before we need to leave. What do you say?"

Angela felt Anika's lips answer her question. She felt her warm body pressing against her own and felt Anika's hands starting to roam over her body. She pulled her lips from Anika's, just enough to speak.

"That's what I thought," she whispered. With her foot, she kicked the doorstop away from the entrance door. It swung shut and she and Anika were alone.

325

PART TEN: BACK TO EDEN

CHAPTER 37

THE GREAT ROOM in Dan and Fran's Las Vegas estate buzzed with anxious anticipation. The front doorbell rang and the guests looked at each other anxiously, remembering the last time their celebration was interrupted by the ringing of that same doorbell.

Angela looked at Anika, ready to answer the door.

"Don't you dare," Anika said, laughing nervously.

"I'll get it," boomed a voice from the back of the room. Richard Holloway, with Miriam and Gwen following behind, worked their way towards the front entrance. Miriam and Gwen went to the front windows and peered cautiously through cracks in the blinds. They glanced at Richard and both gave him the thumbs up. He reached for the shiny brass doorknob and opened the door. Two middle-aged women stood in front of Richard. One of them flashed a badge at him.

"Detective Beverly Dixon, Palm Springs Police," she said. "This is Detective Julie Jameson from Palm Desert. When we heard from Dan that Ms. Capellini - Francesca - had been found yesterday, we wanted to come in person to congratulate her."

"Welcome, detectives," Richard answered. "Come on in. The more the merrier." He extended his hand to greet each detective as they stepped through the doorway, and then closed the door behind them. He ushered the detectives into the great room to introduce them. Detective Dixon immediately recognized Fran's portrait of Angela on the wall. Seconds later, she was surprised to have the real-life Angela standing in front of her, hand extended.

"Hi, I'm Angela," she said. "Welcome to Dan and Fran's home. They should be here shortly."

"We're glad to be here for the occasion," Detective Jameson replied. "We're both relieved to know that Francesca is safe. It's gratifying to see the loose ends of this case being tied up, even if we weren't involved anymore."

"And it's nice to finally meet the subject of that stunning portrait," Dixon added. "Care to tell us the story behind it?"

Angela blushed. "It's not very flattering, I can assure you."

"Don't be so modest," Jameson continued. "From what I hear, you've had quite a journey."

Still blushing, Angela diverted the subject away from herself.

"I should introduce you to everybody," she said. "You've met Richard Holloway, I see."

Beverly Dixon smiled at Richard without missing a beat. "Actually, I think we might have seen each other once before at Chateau Eden. But I didn't recognize him with his clothes on."

People around them erupted into laughter.

"The two ladies with him are his colleagues, Miriam Fox and Gwen Perkins," Angela continued, still chuckling. She motioned to Anika, who had just joined her. "This is my friend, Anika Kristiansen."

Dixon and Jameson glanced at each other in surprise. Anika and Angela both laughed.

"Yes, I'm *that* Anika Kristiansen," Anika replied.

Angela continued ushering the two detectives through the room.

"This is our friend Ricki Marshall, who broke the story on Major Taylor's link to the MSA conspiracy."

"Pleased to meet you," Dixon answered, as she shook Ricki's hand.

"That was a great piece of investigative journalism," Jameson added.

"Thank you. It's a pleasure to meet both of you."

"And last, but not least," Angela continued. "This is Pam Holloway, Richard's wife, along with their friends Shelley Paul and Tim Jennings. They're all from L.A."

Dixon and Jameson shook hands with the rest of the group, just as the front door opened. The room erupted in cheers and applause as Dan stepped into the entrance, followed by Fran and Susan. All the guests flocked to the front door, where they embraced Fran and Susan one by one.

When the greetings were done, Richard popped the cork on a bottle of champagne and proceeded to fill glasses with the golden, bubbly liquid. Pam passed the glasses around the room until everybody had one. When they were finished, Angela stepped forward.

"I'd like to propose a toast to two incredibly strong and brave women, my friends Fran and Susan!"

"To Fran and Susan," the guests cheered in unison. They all raised their drinks in the air, doing their best to touch glasses with every other guest. As they did, Pam stepped forward and raised her glass high in the air.

"We have some unfinished business from the last time we were gathered here," she said. "If I remember correctly, we were here to celebrate Dan and Fran, their new home, and their new lives together."

The guests all raised their glassed. "Dan and Fran!" they cheered. This time, Susan took a step forward so that she stood beside Fran and Dan.

"I'd like to say a few words about Dan and Francesca if I may," she said, her voice much stronger than it had been the previous day. "Over the past few months, these two people have been through a living hell. They lost their spouses at Palm Desert. Fran had to endure being a prisoner - not just once, but twice. And Dan, along with Angela and Anika, put his life on the line to help save their children. Then he did it again to help save Fran. I am in awe of the strength of their determination and optimism - and their spirit of love - that has helped them to rise above everything that has happened to them. I couldn't be prouder to be their friend."

Once again, glasses clinked in the air and the friends cheered and applauded in unison. Dan and Fran looked at each other through watery eyes, trying to decide who would respond. Dan nodded to Fran and nudged her forward. She wiped tears from her cheeks and took a moment to compose herself.

"It means so much to me and Dan that you are all here tonight," she began. "We could not have survived the past few months together without the spirit of love, cooperation, and optimism from every one of you in this room. Dan and I may have found each other by accident, but with your help, we have both managed to find ourselves again. And because of your help, I think we have both truly discovered how to love each other."

Fran reached out one hand to Susan and pulled her closer, so that Susan now stood between Fran and Dan.

"Dan and I especially want to thank Susan. Most of you know that she was my mentor when I was young. I probably should have listened more to her advice back then," she said. She laughed and smiled at Susan. "But I want her to know that I learned my strength and my determination from her."

Dan nodded to Fran, letting her know that he wanted to say a few words. She took a step back, allowing him to step forward.

"I agree with Fran completely," he began. "I was at my lowest when Fran was in the Indio Jail, and again after she was abducted by Major Taylor. But it was Susan who helped me believe in Fran's strength. In doing so, she helped me realize my own inner strength and potential. I'd like you all to join me and Fran in a toast to our dear friend, Susan."

The champagne glasses raised again, with the guests chanting Susan's name. As they cheered, Fran turned to face Dan. She took his hands in hers, looked him in the eye, and cleared her voice.

"I had a lot of time to think while I was in that tent with Taylor and Soren. And it helped me see one thing very clearly, Dan. More than anything, I want to live my life with you and to raise our child together. And I think I would like to take you to my home in Manarola to meet my family … to help me reconnect with them. Will you do that with me?"

Dan broke into a smile that spread from ear to ear. He took Fran into his arms, embraced her, and gave her another long kiss that was met by the loudest cheer yet from their guests.

"Francesca Capellini. There is nothing in this world that I would rather do."

DARKNESS had descended on Las Vegas, providing some welcome relief from the oppressive late August daytime heat. The party eventually spread onto the pool deck of Fran and Dan's estate, allowing the guests to enjoy the evening outside, where they had gathered in a large circle to talk about the recent events.

"Who would have believed that Teri Taylor was such a wolf in sheep's clothing," Shelly Paul said, shaking her head. "I still can't believe she fooled us and everybody who was trying to expose the whole military sexual abuse scandal."

"It seems like such a huge coincidence that she was the one who kidnapped Francesca," Detective Dixon added, shaking her head in disbelief. "How did you ever manage to put the pieces together, Ricki?"

"It was partly coincidence," Ricki answered. "It was also partly due to Taylor's arrogance. In her position as a spokesperson for the Air Force, it was only a matter of time before somebody recognized her. But mostly, it was Dan who figured it out."

All heads turned towards Dan.

"So, how'd you do it, Dan?" Detective Jameson asked.

"Like Ricki said, it was only a matter of time before somebody recognized her. The answer was right in front of my eyes all the time, but it was the wig that threw me off."

"The wig?" Dixon asked.

"Yeah, the blonde wig," Dan replied. "The woman who boarded our plane and sabotaged it in Darwin, and the woman involved in the bombing in Hanoi, was wearing a blonde wig and sunglasses. Turns out it was the same wig she wore to fool everybody at the Atlanta airport when she helped Soren flee the country with Jonah."

"So, how did you get past that?" Tim Jennings interjected.

"Actually, it finally came to me in a dream," Dan admitted, shrugging his shoulders. "The answer was right there all the time. Part of my brain knew it, but couldn't figure it out. That's the best part of dreams. They're our brain's way of trying to make sense of stuff that's happening in our world. Sometimes they're so absurd that we miss the message. But in my case, Taylor showed up in my dream as a two-faced person - she was wearing a blonde wig and a mask for a masquerade ball on her front, but she had brown hair and was wearing a military uniform from behind. I only realized something was wrong in the dream when her mask fell off."

"Bizarre," Pam Holloway exclaimed.

"No foolin'," Richard Holloway echoed.

"But it was coincidence that I figured it out just as one of Ricki's sources recognized Taylor from the Las Vegas MSA rally. It was perfect timing. The information was much more compelling coming from three completely different places," Dan added.

"Three places?" Detective Dixon asked. "You've just mentioned two."

"We can't forget about the clues Fran dropped in the ransom videos," Dan added. "That's probably what triggered my dreams in the first place. She managed to give us clues about Taylor having a Jekyll and Hyde personality, as well as being in uniform."

"I see," Dixon replied. "But there's one part of this that Julie and I still don't understand. We know that former Riverside District Attorney Mulholland was involved in prosecuting Francesca's murder case. And we know that something caused her to commit suicide. But, for the life of us, we can't link it to Taylor."

"I can explain that," Fran said suddenly. She had been listening intently to Dan and Ricki as they related the events that unfolded while she was in captivity.

"I managed to get Taylor to trust me. Like Dan, she also managed to fool me with the blonde wig at first, when she pretended to be an inmate that day at the Indio jail."

"You're kidding!" Dan blurted. "She really did that?"

"Yes," Fran continued. "But I finally realized I'd met her many years before that, when I lived in Paris with Philippe."

"Paris?" Ricki asked. "Where does that fit into the big picture?"

"Europe is where Taylor - or Lady Helen to be exact - came into her own. She was posted with the Air Force in Germany. She managed to work her way inside the military establishment by becoming the most desirable dominatrix in Europe. Eventually, Philippe couldn't resist her and invited her to one of his grand parties, where I became one of her victims."

Dan's eyes went wide as the pieces of the puzzle began falling into place.

"That's where Philippe got his interest in BDSM and domination!" he exclaimed. "But where does Mulholland figure into that?"

"She was one of Helen's students. She wanted to be a dominatrix, just like Helen … er, Taylor. But Helen was always the 'alpha' dominatrix. Mulholland did her best to become part of Helen's scene, so she got more and more involved in the debauchery while she was in the military. Eventually, she developed gambling and cocaine problems … and she was involved in something called … Tailhook?"

"The Tailhook scandal," Pam blurted. "It was a convention of the Tailhook Association symposium here in Vegas back in ninety-one. At least eighty women and men were alleged to have been sexually assaulted at that event. It's infamous in the history of MSA."

Fran nodded as another piece of the puzzle fell into place for her. "Taylor laughed when she told me the story about how she portrayed herself and Mulholland as victims of the abuse, instead of the perpetrators they really were. She and Soren bailed Mulholland out of her gambling and drug debts, got her clean, and cut all ties with her when she left the military. But she always owed them for helping her get her life and her law career back on track."

"I get it now," Dixon continued. "Taylor and Soren finally called in their debt with Mulholland." She stared at Fran's portrait of Angela in the great room. "Somehow they linked Fran to Angela through that portrait! They needed Mulholland to get to Fran, so they called in her debt."

"The news reports!" Jameson shouted. "That portrait was front and center in the news reports that came from the murder scene at your estate in Pam Desert!"

"Exactly," Dixon answered. "But Mulholland couldn't deliver. Taylor must have threatened to expose her past and she couldn't find a way out."

"Except by blowing her brains out," Dixon added quietly.

"Wow," Ricki said solemnly. "Another huge coincidence. Just look at all of the chance events that had to take place for all of this to happen." She looked up at all the guests who were gathered around the pool. She smiled and nodded her head in approval. Her eyes met Richard Holloway's.

"Ricki's right," Richard added. "Y'all did a great job, given the odds against us. Ah'm proud'a every one o' y'all, especially Fran." He turned so that he was facing her.

"I know y'all aren't runnin' Chateau Eden any more, Fran," Richard continued. "But ah think we need a name fer this fine place that you an' Dan call home. How bout Chateau Freedom!"

Dan, Fran, and all their guests looked at each other silently for a moment. Then, they spontaneously broke into smiles and nodded their agreement with Richard's suggestion. One by one, they raised their glasses in a salute to Fran and Dan's new home.

"Chateau Freedom," the guests chanted.

"Now," Richard continued. "Ah'm in the mood fer celebratin'. Anybody else up fer some skinny-dippin'?"

Everybody burst into laughter.

A voice from behind Dan and Fran emerged out of the commotion.

"Sure, why not! What better way to celebrate freedom. You only live once!"

The voice belonged to Susan Keaner, the self-proclaimed "old hippie". She started shedding her clothes and then began walking unashamedly to the spa, followed by Richard and Pam, Tim and Shelley, and Gwen and Miriam. Within minutes, even Detectives Dixon and Jameson, who both looked startled and hesitant initially, had shed their clothes and plunged into the pool to join Dan and Fran, Ricki, and Angela and Anika.

Dan watched as Fran's head came up from beneath the water's surface. Her face was covered in a broad smile.

"Feel good?" Dan asked.

"You have no idea how much I craved this while I was cooped up in that hot, dusty tent!" she replied.

Beverly Dixon and Julie Jameson looked at each other and couldn't stop giggling.

"What do you say, Julie?" Dixon asked.

"If you'd told me I'd be skinny-dipping by the end of the night, I would have said you were crazy," Jameson said, still giggling.

"I know, me too," Dixon answered. "But with Francesca finally enjoying her freedom, and seeing everybody else so carefree, it seems like the natural way to share the evening with them."

"So, does that mean that I'll see you at Chateau Eden next weekend?" Jameson asked, winking at her colleague.

"Don't push it, Julie," Dixon answered, smiling. "Baby steps. Let's just enjoy the moment."

CHAPTER 38

DAN LED FRAN into their sumptuous, newly redecorated bedroom. He slid the dimmer switch upward until the room was bathed in a soft, warm, romantic glow. The renovations had been completed just in time for their housewarming party. The night Fran disappeared was to be their first night together in their new conjugal hideaway, but their romantic tryst never materialized, thanks to Teri Taylor and Fran's abduction. But nothing was going to come between Dan and Fran tonight.

The room had a vaulted ceiling and was painted a deep navy blue. It was accessorized with a modern white Italian bedroom suite, including matching armoires, with classic European details. A fluffy duvet, the lower half navy and the upper half white, covered a king-size mattress, which was mounted on a simple white platform with thin legs. The white and navy duvet was accented with navy-colored pillow covers.

Not readily visible to the casual eye, leather wrist and ankle straps were attached to bed's legs.

The floor was finished in a herringbone pattern of multi-tone reclaimed wood, painstakingly installed by a local craftsman. The extra time required to install the floor was the primary reason why the room had barely been ready on time for their housewarming.

Directly in front of them was a luxurious bathroom of white Italian marble, complete with a large Jacuzzi and a walk-in shower with three-sixty-degree shower and steam heads. To their right was a set of French doors with frosted glass.

Dan pulled Fran close to him, embraced her, and gazed into her brown eyes.

"Welcome home, beautiful," he whispered softly.

"It's wonderful to be home," Fran whispered in return.

"Your wish is my desire," Dan said, grinning. "What would you like first? A relaxing bath? A shower? There's plenty of room for both of us."

Fran motioned towards the French doors with a nod. "Is it finished?" she asked.

Dan nodded and flashed a rather lascivious smile. "Indeed, it is," he replied. "Would you like to see it?"

"I would," she answered. Dan walked to the French doors and swung them open. Soft recessed lighting turned on automatically as the doors opened, revealing a small, but well-equipped room of essential BDSM toys. This room was painted a dark burgundy with another white armoire and shelving units in the same style as the master bedroom. A large X-shaped cross with leather wrist and ankle straps stood against one wall. A white bondage swing was suspended from the high ceiling. Dan opened the armoire for Fran, revealing an ample assortment of silk scarves and ties, floggers, riding crops, and bamboo canes. He opened two drawers in a cabinet beside the armoire, displaying an assortment of blindfolds, gags, nipple clamps and butt plugs.

"I'm impressed," Fran said quietly. She became silent as she paused to survey the room. Her smile gradually vanished and her eyes became distant.

"Something wrong?" Dan asked.

"No," Fran sighed, unconvincingly.

"What is it?" Dan repeated. "Was it something that happened with Taylor in the desert?" Fran only nodded.

"We don't have to do any of this," Dan answered. Fran paused, taking slow breaths to calm herself. Finally, she stepped forward and selected a black blindfold, before turning to Dan.

"Go and turn on the shower while I choose some things. I'll be the dominant tonight," she declared.

Dan's face took on a more somber expression. He nodded his understanding.

"I love you, Fran."

DAN LAID spread-eagled on their bed. His wrists and ankles were fastened tightly by the leather cuffs attached to the bed's legs, his hands extended above his head. His world was black due to the blindfold, but the rest of his senses were heightened because of his inability to see. He smelled Fran's freshly bathed body, wearing just a hint of perfume, and he felt her warm breath near his ear. He felt himself becoming aroused almost instantly.

Without warning, he felt something soft on his chest … a silk tie or scarf … or was it an ostrich feather? The object moved slowly and methodically, gradually circling and teasing his right nipple, and then moving on to the other.

A feather. An ostrich feather, he decided, talking to himself.

The feather began travelling downward toward his navel. It paused briefly as it passed over a large bruise near his sternum, then continued its journey to his navel. It lingered there, teasing that it might go even lower. But instead, it headed sideways across his belly towards his right hip, where it travelled slowly down the outside of his leg and over the top of his foot. Then, suddenly, Fran lifted the feather from his foot. She didn't move, causing the room to go completely silent. The only thing he sensed was the room's air-conditioned circulation flowing gently over the nerve endings of his skin, causing his body hair to stand on end. He still smelled the erotic fragrance of Fran's perfume. Every nerve ending in his body was on high alert, while his erection stood at full attention.

Without warning he felt the feather on the sole of his left foot. At first, it tickled and Dan felt his leg try to jerk away from the stimulation, only to be restrained by a leather strap. But as he slowed his breath, the gentle strokes of the object became more erotic and relaxing. After a moment, he felt the feather start moving slowing up the inside of his left leg, teasing him as it made its way towards his genitals. When it got to his scrotum, Fran teased his testicles for what seemed like an eternity. Dan felt his penis longing for the object to touch and caress it. Then Fran pulled the feather away and his nerve endings went back on full alert. He felt and heard Fran moving around the bed, going to a bedside table. Then he sensed her body moving back around the bed until she was beside him again.

This time, the feather started at his right ankle and worked its way slowly up to his testicles. Once again it lingered, teasing Dan's penis. He felt it throbbing, longing for more stimulation. Then, once again the teasing stopped. Again, he felt every hair on his body standing at attention. Then, out of nowhere, he felt pain searing through his chest as Fran attached a clamp to his right nipple. He moaned in agony. Fran waited patiently until his body started to habituate to the pain. And then another searing pain in his other nipple. Dan moaned again, this time louder.

"Silence!" Fran hissed in his ear. "You want everybody in the house to hear what we're doing? Do you want more pain?"

"No, not right now," Dan whispered, nodding his head in understanding.

He felt the pain in his chest transforming from a searing sensation into a numb kind of pain. Then, out of the background pain, he felt Fran's feather teasing his testicles again. But this time, when his penis started craving more, she finally obliged him. She moved the feather methodically up and down his shaft, teasing the sweet spot at his frenum, making it crave even more stimulation. Once again, she stopped the teasing. He wanted to scream, his senses demanding more. He felt her moving beside the bed. Then, suddenly, she grasped his organ and squeezed.

Dan's first instinct was to moan, but he caught himself. Instead, he exhaled long and slow. The combination of numbness and pain in his chest, combined with the overwhelming pleasure in his rock-hard cock, was exquisite.

Before he knew it, Fran was on the bed. She straddled his chest, with her backside facing him, and she took him in her mouth. He felt her tongue, first teasing his ultra-sensitive rim, and then licking down his shaft and back up again. Then her lips were on his rim again, sucking and nibbling until he thought he couldn't stand it. He felt himself wanting to let out a moan, but managed to keep it to a low growl in the back of his throat. All the while, Fran's womanhood hovered over him. He smelled her musky essence and reached out with his tongue, hoping for a taste, but his efforts were in vain.

Fran's tongue paused again on top of his frenum and remained motionless, giving him a short reprieve from her relentless stimulation and the growing sense of urgency in his cock. He slowed his breathing. Then he sensed Fran lowering herself over his face. Her musky fragrance grew stronger and he felt the warmth of her body growing closer. He reached out with his tongue and was finally rewarded. His tongue started exploring and teasing her exposed vulva, reveling in the sweet, salty taste of her fluids. She began swaying her pelvis, moving herself back and forth, side to side, and around in circles, guiding Dan's tongue where she wanted it to go. He flicked his tongue over her swollen, hard clitoris and heard her gasp. Her breathing grew faster and heavier.

Then, he felt her lean forward again, enabling her to press her tongue against his frenum. At the same time, he felt her fingernails dig into the skin on the inside of his right leg, slowly clawing their way upwards toward his genitals. As they drew closer, all the energy from those sensations seemed to flood towards his cock, focusing on his frenum like rays of sunshine being focused through a lens. He felt the urgency in his organ starting to build. His breathing started coming harder and faster.

Suddenly, Fran shifted her weight and lifted herself off his body, only to land back on top of him, facing his head. He felt her take his throbbing cock in her hand and position it against her vulva. When she had it in position, she lowered herself onto him. He felt himself being surrounded by exquisite pressure from her vaginal muscles. At the same time, she leaned forward so that he felt their baby pressing against his abdomen, while her breasts pressed against his chest. She was releasing his wrists from their leather restraints. Then she removed his blindfold so he could finally see the beauty of her eyes and face, her beautiful round belly, and her breasts. He reached out and fondled her breasts, before letting his hand roam over their baby. She leaned over and kissed him, her lips and tongue flaming with desire. He wrapped his arms around her, pressed her close, and his lips and tongue responded. After a moment, Fran disengaged her lips and gazed down at him.

"I love you and missed you more than you can imagine," she whispered.

"I don't know what I'd do without you now," Dan whispered back.

Fran started moving her pelvis, alternating vertical thrusts with gyrating her hips and grinding her pelvis against Dan's. He felt her movements become more desperate and urgent, gripping him tightly inside while she ground her clit against his pelvis. As her urgency grew, he felt his own starting to build inside again. He felt a familiar ache starting to move slowly upward from the base of his shaft, making its way slowly towards the head of his cock. Their pelvises moved faster and harder. Then Dan felt Fran's vaginal muscles tighten around him. Her body went tense, her back arched backwards, and her breathing stopped. He felt her muscles contracting rhythmically around his cock. At the same time, the aching sensation reached the tip of his organ. His body tensed, and he felt himself explode repeatedly inside Fran. Unable to remain silent, Fran emitted a subdued cry of joy while Dan emitted a muffled moan of ecstasy. When their rhythmic contractions finally ebbed. Fran collapsed, exhausted, onto Dan's chest. He wrapped his arms around her and pulled her tightly against him.

He heard Fran sniffle and felt teardrops on his chest.

"Everything's alright," he said. "You're safe now."

Fran's tears began to flow freely, as though she finally felt safe enough to let go of all the emotions she'd been holding inside.

"I never thought … I'd ever … see you, again," she sobbed. "I thought she was going to kill me … after I tried to escape."

"She hurt you terribly, didn't she," Dan said. Fran nodded while she continued to sob.

"She turned into Helen. She bound me, gagged me, and gave me everything she had with her cane," she whimpered. "She forced me to squat on high-heeled shoes with spikes that punctured my butt. I was totally helpless … terrified. It was so different … than doing any of these things with you," she said, still sobbing.

"What she did wasn't BDSM," Dan whispered. "Like the things Philippe did with Chelly, it was sadistic torture. She did it out of anger and hatred. Anything we do together is done with love and trust."

"I know," Fran said. Her sobbing had ebbed, but she was still sniffling.

"It's going to take a while … before I can be the sub," she whispered. "I'm so sorry. I get flashbacks even thinking about it."

"I understand," Dan said. "We don't ever have to do that again, if you don't want to."

He pulled Fran close to him. He let his hands roam over her body, enjoying the smooth curves of her waist, her shoulders, and her breasts. He felt scabs and welts on her back and buttocks, and he felt an instant sadness for what she'd endured.

"But I want to … be the sub … eventually," she said. She gazed into his eyes with a look of determination. "I can't let her get to me. If I do, she wins. Can you be patient with me?"

Dan returned her gaze, feeling so full of love for her that he didn't think he could contain it.

"I'll wait as long as you need, and I'll do whatever it takes to help you," he said.

Fran lifted herself off Dan and he felt himself slip out of her. She laid down next to him so they were facing each other. She entwined her legs with his so their bodies were pressed as closely together as possible.

They rested in near silence, listening as each other's exhausted panting slowly transformed into a state of peaceful bliss.

"I'm completely spent," Fran said. "I want to fall asleep this way. I just want to feel your breath … so I know I'm safe," she said.

"You *are* safe," Dan said.

Fran reached out and gently touched the large bruise on Dan's chest.

"Where did you get this?" she asked.

Dan gazed into her eyes and paused.

"Oh, that. It's nothing really. It doesn't hurt," he answered.

"That's not what I asked. Where did you get it?"

Dan paused and swallowed while he chose his words. "It happened during the shootout after Taylor threw you in the van and escaped," he said.

Fran frowned and Dan saw fear in her eyes. "What happened?" she asked again.

Dan sighed. "I took a bullet in my body armor after Gwen took down Soren. I'm okay … really."

Tears filled Fran's eyes. "A bullet? … You mean you would have died without the body armor?"

"It's okay, Fran. That's why Richard made us wear it. It did its job."

"You risked your life to save me?" Fran asked.

Dan nodded his head. "Of course. I'd have done anything to get you and our baby back. I love you so much."

Fran pressed herself against Dan, wrapping her arms around him. "Hold me tight," she whispered. "I want to feel your heartbeat and your breathing, so I know you're alive."

"Don't worry, Fran. Nothing bad is going to happen. I'm not ever going to leave you, if I have any say in the matter." He kissed her forehead.

"Sweet dreams, my love," he whispered.

Fran didn't answer. Her eyes were already closed and her face was relaxed and contented. Dan realized she had already drifted off to sleep. Satisfied, he let his eyes close and allowed himself to do the same.

CHAPTER 39

DAN FELT the gentle rhythmic sway of the train, along with the rhythm of its wheels against steel rails, beginning to slow. The train emerged from the darkness of a tunnel into bright mid-day September sunshine, displaying signs that their arrival was imminent. A platform came into view. Seconds later a large sign with black and white lettering appeared through the windows on the far side of the rail car… *MANAROLA*.

The air in their car was stifling. The weather was unseasonably hot for late September. He felt perspiration dripping from his forehead and soaking through his shirt. He saw beads of sweat on Fran's forehead and knew that travel fatigue and the heat must be taking its toll on her. Now over six months pregnant, she had insisted that she make this journey before their baby was born.

"How do you feel?" Dan asked.

"Nervous," Fran answered. "But this is something I must do. I want to show you where I came from, and I need to put the past behind me."

The train finally came to a stop. Passengers began scrambling for the exits, many of them carrying huge pieces of baggage. Dan waited patiently with Fran until the bulk of the passengers had exited onto the platform. He helped her from her seat and followed her to the exit with her suitcase. He helped her down and then left her with her luggage while he went to retrieve his own bag. Finally, he stepped onto the platform beside her and paused to look at the swarm of humanity around them. The platform was a virtual island, with tracks on either side. The only way across to the station was to descend into a tunnel beneath the tracks, and then to ascend back to the station. The other passengers streamed down the stairs.

"There's a lift off to the side," Fran said, diverting Dan's attention from the rest of the passengers.

"That's a relief!" he replied. "You don't need to be doing stairs and I would have needed to make two trips with the bags."

"I'm not totally helpless, you know," Fran answered. "I can pull my bag to the elevator."

Together, they pulled up the handles on their suitcases and began walking to the lift, rolling their bags along behind them. They waited patiently for the lift doors to open, finally loading themselves and their baggage into the cramped space for the ride to the tunnel below. Once in the tunnel, they proceeded to the other side of the tracks and reversed the process in a second lift. Finally, they emerged from the second lift at Manarola's station. Dan looked around. Most of the other passengers were long gone. The stragglers disappeared into a tunnel that led from the station.

"Through the tunnel," Fran said, pointing down the dimly illuminated passage.

As they rolled their baggage along behind them through the tunnel, Dan saw that the walls were decorated with posters and photographs of various sights in Cinque Terre, the five local Italian villages that occupied this eight-mile stretch of steep Italian coastline.

"I know how difficult it was for you to make this trip. You've done great," Dan said, proud of what Fran was doing and how well she had tolerated their journey so far. As they reached the end of the tunnel, he saw a sign just outside the tunnel on their left, advertising an art gallery.

"Is that Susan's gallery?" he asked.

"Yes," Fran answered. "That's where I worked as a young girl … Where Philippe found me."

"So, a lot of mixed emotions?"

"That would be an understatement," Fran replied.

They arrived at the front door of Susan's gallery, Arte Dell'Aquila. Dan opened the door and they entered, dragging their luggage behind them. As the door opened, a bell rang to announce their entry. Susan, just finishing up with a couple of customers at the front desk, handed the customers their wrapped artwork and a receipt, and then looked up just in time to see Fran and Dan enter.

"Francesca! Dan! You're finally here!" she shouted.

She rushed around the end of the counter to embrace Fran. Even though it had only been two weeks since they were last together in Las Vegas, both women had tears in their eyes as they embraced tightly. Dan realized it was more than just seeing each other. It was a much overdue homecoming. Finally, Susan released Fran and her eyes found Dan.

"Come here, young man. Give this old lady a hug," Susan said.

Dan and Susan embraced like the close friends they had become. Afterwards, Susan took each of her visitors by one hand. She looked lovingly at Fran's pregnancy bump.

"How was the trip for you?"

"Not bad, considering," Fran replied. "I think it's a good thing that I'm still less than seven months along. I would not want to be doing this next month."

"What are your plans right now?" Susan said to Dan.

"First, we'll get settled into our room so Fran can rest for a while," Dan answered. "Then we've decided we're going to go to her mamma's restaurant for dinner."

Susan turned back to Fran and smiled. Tears began to form in her eyes as she took both of Fran's hands in hers.

"I'm so glad you're doing this," she said, sniffling. "You'll never be able to move forward until you let go of the past."

Dan, Fran, and Susan took each other's hands and stood together in a tight circle.

"And I'm so thankful to have Dan here with me," Fran answered, looking at him as she spoke. "I need my past to be part of our future together. I need that so we can be whole as a couple."

Susan let go of Dan's hand and wiped away a tear.

"Now you've got me crying again." She noticed Dan and Fran's luggage, wiped away her tears, and regained her composure.

"I'll call for a taxi to drive you up the hill to your room," Susan said. "I'll also make a reservation for you at your mamma's place. If they're full, I can pull some strings." She smiled at Dan. "I'll book it in your name, Dan, so it will be a surprise."

"Thanks for everything, Susan," Dan replied. "Not just for the taxi and the reservation … I don't know what we would have done if you hadn't come to the States to help Fran."

"Enough, enough. You're going to make me cry again," Susan said, choking back her tears. "Fran, why don't you show Dan around the gallery while I call the taxi. Things haven't really changed that much since you were here."

Susan scurried around the end of the counter and disappeared into a dark alcove. As Fran took Dan by the hand to give him a tour, Susan began dialing the number for Mamma's restaurant.

DAN AND FRAN entered the restaurant on Via di Corniglia. It was bustling and packed with people. Fran was glad that Dan was holding her hand, which was clammy with nervous perspiration. They were greeted by a polite young man. As Dan talked with the young man, Fran stared. He was definitely familiar. She wondered if she knew him, but she couldn't tell for sure.

"You have a reservation, Signore?" the young man asked.

"Yes, Dan Whitney … for two."

The young man looked through his reservation book for the booking. He glanced up at Fran quickly, aware that she was staring at him. A puzzled expression crossed his face, then he looked back at the bookings.

"Ahhh, here it is. This way Signore e Signora." He led them to a table, where he pulled Fran's chair back to allow her to sit. Then he glided around to the other side of the table and seated Dan.

"May I bring you something to drink?" the young man asked Fran.

"Sì, due l'acqua con gas, per favore," she answered.

A surprised look crossed the man's face when he realized that Fran spoke fluent Italian. After hearing her voice, a puzzled look settled on his face, replacing his initial surprise.

"Si, Signora," he replied.

The young man hurried away from the table towards the kitchen, taking another look over his shoulder along the way. Fran leaned across the table to Dan. She now wore a look of excitement.

"I think he might be one of the twins, Dan! I'm almost certain!" she whispered.

"Do you think he recognized you?" Dan asked.

"I don't know. How could he? He was only a young boy when I left."

At that moment, the young man emerged from the kitchen, accompanied by a middle-aged Italian woman. Because Fran's back faced the kitchen, she didn't see them coming. Dan's eyes caught her attention.

"I think you have your answer," he said, nodding in the direction of the kitchen.

When Fran turned around, she saw her sister Giulia standing behind her. At that moment, she knew with certainty that the young man was one of her twin nephews. Her eyes met with Giulia. Tears began to spill from Giulia's eyes. She moved towards Fran's table, hesitant at first, but picking up speed as she neared her long-lost sister.

"Francesca? Is it really you?" Giulia asked, her voice timid and unsure.

Fran nodded. She found herself unable to talk. Instead, she only swallowed. Like Giulia, her eyes began to fill with tears. Giulia embraced Fran, even though her sister was still sitting.

"Yes, it's really me," Fran answered, finally. "How are you?"

"I'm fine," Giulia replied. "How are you?"

"I'm good," Fran said. She paused for a moment. "How is Mamma?"

Giulia sniffled and gathered her composure, wiping away any remaining tears.

"You know Mamma," she answered. "Just as gruff as ever!"

Suddenly, Giulia noticed Fran's sizeable pregnancy bump.

"Oh, my God! You're pregnant?" she gasped. "Is this your first?"

Fran nodded and a broad smile spread across her face. She turned to Dan, and then back to Giulia.

"I would like you to meet my boyfriend, Dan … Dan, this is Giulia."

Giulia hurried around the table as Dan stood to greet her. She embraced him and gave him the traditional kiss on each cheek.

"I am so happy to meet you, Dan. This is so exciting!" she squealed. "Maurizio, go get Mamma and Guido!"

Maurizio hurried back to the kitchen. The commotion from the reunion had begun to attract the attention of other patrons, who smiled and nodded approvingly as they watched. After a moment, the kitchen door opened and Maurizio returned with Mamma and his identical twin brother, Guido, by his side. Mamma's face was white with shock, while Guido's face beamed with happiness. He rushed to greet Fran.

"You remember your Aunt Francesca, Guido?" Giulia asked.

Guido smiled. "A little. We both remember how kind you were."

All eyes turned to Mamma. Her look of shock was gradually being replaced by tears. Her face conveyed a conflicting mixture of sadness and joy. Fran pushed her chair back from the table and stood. She walked to Mamma and took her in her arms.

No longer able to hold them back, Fran allowed the tears to flow freely from her eyes.

"It's me, Mamma. It's Francesca. I'm home."

The room filled with silence while the restaurant's patrons listened and processed what was going on. Then suddenly, they erupted into cheers and applause in response to the emotional reunion, as Fran and Mamma continued to embrace. Finally, Fran escaped from Mamma's bear-hug and turned to Dan.

"Mamma. I want you to meet my boyfriend, Dan Whitney."

Mamma's face became serious. Her eyes scrutinized Dan, and then Fran's pregnant figure. After a moment, she turned to Fran.

"You love him, Francesca?"

"I love him very much, Mamma."

Mamma turned to Dan and stared, expressionless for what seemed like an eternity to Fran. Finally, she nodded with approval. A smile appeared on her face and she opened her arms to Dan in a gesture of acceptance.

The patrons responded again with more cheering and applause.

Dan got to his feet and walked around the table, where he embraced Fran's Mamma and kissed her on both cheeks.

Fran felt herself exhale long and slow. She realized that she'd been holding her breath - for how long, she couldn't be sure. The only other thing she noticed was an enormous sense of relief washing over her body. She felt like the weight of the world had finally been removed from her shoulders.

CHAPTER 40

A FULL autumn moon seemed to be laying down a golden carpet of light that extended all the way from its surface, and then across the Mediterranean to Fran and Dan. They walked hand in hand along the pathway between Riomaggiore and Manarola, the two southernmost towns in Cinque Terre. The path was normally dimly lit, but the light from the full moon guided their way back to Manarola. The late September night was still comfortably warm. Suddenly, Fran stopped to lean on a fence beside the pathway and to look out over the Mediterranean. The fence along the seaward side of the path was covered with padlocks. Dan came up beside her and put his arm around her waist. The moonlight seemed to follow them whichever direction they leaned.

"This is the place you told me about, isn't it?" Dan asked.

"It is," Fran replied. She turned to him and gazed into his eyes. "What do you think?"

"Words don't do it justice. It's more beautiful than you could ever have described," Dan answered, smiling. He gazed at Fran's face and saw the carpet of reflected moonlight sparkling in her eyes. He leaned towards her and his lips touched hers tenderly.

"I'm glad we came back to Manarola together," Dan continued. "It means a lot for me to meet your family and to see where you came from."

The only sound they heard was the rhythmic undulation of small waves, gently washing up against the rocks below them. The rhythm was almost hypnotic. Dan pulled Fran towards him and took her in his arms, feeling their baby pushing against his stomach. He felt the baby kick and was overwhelmed with a feeling of love. He kissed Fran passionately on the lips. She responded, gently but enthusiastically. After a few moments, he lifted his lips from hers and gazed into her eyes.

"I love you, Fran," he whispered. "It's been a strange journey, but I'm so glad we found each other." He saw tears of joy forming in her eyes and felt his own vision growing blurred from his own tears.

"And I love you, Dan. More than you can ever imagine."

After holding each other tight for a long, peaceful moment, Fran broke their embrace and slid her purse from her shoulder. She opened it and rummaged around, finally removing an object wrapped in white tissue paper. She handed the bundle to Dan.

"A gift for you, from me," she said softly.

Dan kissed her on the lips and then started unwrapping the gift. As the object gradually came into view, a smile spread across Dan's face.

"It's a lock for us. What a perfect idea!"

"That's what I thought," Fran replied, a loving smile enveloping her face. "Look on the back."

Dan held the back of the lock up to the moonlight to study it.

"You had it engraved," he replied. "Let's see … Dan and Francesca … September 2006 … Two spirits joined into one."

Dan lowered the lock and turned to Fran, his eyes filled with a love unlike anything he'd ever experienced for anybody - not Anika in his youth nor Chelly when they were married.

"It's perfect," he whispered, his voice trembling with emotion. "Do you want to help me do the honors?"

Dan kissed her tenderly on the lips, and then he twisted the key that Fran had left in the lock. The hasp popped open. He handed the lock to Fran, who hung it on a link on the fence beside hundreds of other locks. She took Dan's hand, and together they snapped the hasp closed. They wrapped their arms around each other's waists and stared out over the moonlit Mediterranean.

"We found some amazing friends on this journey of ours, didn't we," Dan said, finally breaking the silence.

"We are incredibly lucky," Fran answered. She and Dan continued to silently take in the breathtaking beauty before them. After a moment, Fran broke the silence.

"Have you heard from Angela and Anika since they flew back to Calgary?"

"As a matter of fact," Dan replied. "I just got an email from Angela while you were resting this afternoon. Anika decided to sell her practice in Victoria. She wants to start a practice in Calgary so she and Jonah can be closer to her family. Angela and her parents decided to move there too, so they can all be together."

"I'm so happy that Anika and Angela found each other. They are such a beautiful couple, and they are fortunate to have such supportive families."

"Speaking of Anika's family," Dan continued. "Her dad's chemotherapy is over. He's starting to gain some weight and he's looking much healthier."

"We're all very lucky," Fran reflected.

"I'm not sure it's just luck," Dan answered. "I prefer to believe what Susan says - that the spirit of love eventually wins out in the end over hatred and the lust for power and domination."

"She's right. Maybe we wouldn't have survived Philippe, Soren, and Teri Taylor if Susan and all of our friends hadn't been there to pass that spirit along to us."

They fell silent and watched the golden trail of light from the full moon, the gentle ripples of the Mediterranean causing the light to shimmer and twinkle hypnotically.

"Shall we make our way back to Manarola?" Dan asked, finally. "It's been a long day for you."

"Good idea," Fran replied, moonlight still twinkling in her eyes. "I think I'm in the mood to show that spirit of love to somebody special tonight."

"Anybody I know?" Dan asked. He smiled and brought her body close to his, wrapping his arms around her.

"Maybe. And tomorrow morning, I have one more surprise for that somebody special," she said softly.

"Francesca Capellini, you're just full of pleasant surprises, aren't you. What are you up to now?"

Fran pressed her lips softly against Dan's and lingered there for a long, breathless moment.

"I guess you will just need to wait and see," she whispered. "Come on, take me home."

FRAN'S EYES popped open. Dawn's first light was creeping through cracks in the hotel room's curtains. She pulled back the covers and swung her legs over the side of the bed. She hopped off the bed onto her feet and found the old pair of sweatpants, a pair of socks, and a t-shirt she'd left out the night before. When she was dressed, she pulled on an old sweater to keep away the morning chill, then she leaned over the bed and gave Dan a gentle shake.

"Time to wake up, Dan," she said softly. "Time for your surprise!"

"Hmmm?" Dan mumbled, his brain still half asleep and momentarily disoriented.

"Come on, sleepyhead," Fran urged. She tossed some clothes at him. "We don't want to waste the best part of the day."

"Where are we going?" Dan asked, still confused.

"I told you, it's a surprise," Fran answered impatiently. "Hurry!" She grabbed his arm and began dragging Dan out of bed.

"Okay, okay," he groaned, grabbing his clothes and crawling to the side of the bed where Fran stood. He swung his legs over the edge, pulled on a shirt, and then stood to put on the jeans that Fran had left for him. Finally, he walked over to find a pair of shoes.

"Wear your running shoes," Fran advised. "You'll be doing a bit of hiking."

Dan smiled. "Hiking, eh? Aren't we going to eat something first?"

"Not enough time," Fran said sternly. "Come on, we want to be there to see the sunrise."

Once his shoes were tied, Fran took Dan by the hand and led him out of their room, down a hallway, and out the front door of their hotel. They followed a narrow alley to a stone staircase that descended to a small piazza below. An elderly Italian couple sat quietly, holding hands, looking out over the eastern sky, where a gentle pink hue was starting to push back the deep azure night sky in the west.

She led Dan down sets of steep stone stairs and through narrow alleys until they emerged onto Via di Corniglia, just across the street from Mamma's restaurant. They walked swiftly and quietly down the street towards the Manarola marina. When they reached the marina, they came upon a handful of fishermen who were readying their skiffs and nets for another day's work. The fishermen were too busy to pay any attention to the two strangers who scurried past them down the boat ramp, and then clambered up over the dark rocks that separated the tiny harbor from the open Mediterranean.

Once on the other side of the rocks and out of sight of the fishermen, Francesca quickly peeled off her sweater and t-shirt, then gingerly lowered her sweatpants until she was wearing only her panties. Her bare skin responded with goosebumps, and the tiny hairs on her body all stood at attention in a futile attempt to keep her skin warm. She folded her arms over her breasts in a vain attempt to keep herself from shivering from the morning chill.

"Your turn," she said, smiling slyly. "Take it all off. We're going skinny-dipping."

"What? Out here? The whole town can see us."

"Don't worry," she replied. "Everybody in town has done this at some time in their lives. They won't mind. This is what I want to share with you. It's the one thing that gave me a sense of peace when I was young. Come on, let's go! Take it all off!"

While Dan stripped, Fran peeled off the last of her clothing and stared out over the calm, glassy water. Finally, they both stood naked on the rocks. Fran saw Dan's eyes gazing at her pregnant body. He placed his hands over their baby and she felt their warmth. Fran kissed him and then turned and lowered herself down a metal ladder into the early morning calm of the Mediterranean. Dan followed behind her.

The seawater was only slightly more frigid than the cool morning air. She took a deep breath and dived. Just as it had in her youth, Fran felt the salt water flowing gently over every square centimeter of her body, caressing and soothing it as it washed over her skin. She surfaced from her dive, feeling exhilarated and energized. When she surfaced, she saw two dolphins about a hundred meters to the northwest.

Dan surfaced beside her after his own dive. She touched his shoulder and pointed to the dolphins.

"Look! The dolphins have joined us!" she exclaimed, a broad smile beaming on her face. "Just like they did when I was young."

"This is amazing!" Dan replied. "Swimming with the dolphins. So, this is your surprise."

"See. I told you this was going to be special," Fran answered.

Dan dived beneath the surface again. As he did, the dolphins slid beneath the surface. Fran dived behind Dan and opened her eyes underwater. Before she knew it, she saw the two streamlined cetaceans streaking gracefully towards them with effortless thrusts of their tails. Feeling the need for air, Fran surfaced. Seconds later, Dan broke the surface beside her.

"This is so perfect!" Dan said, his voice full of wonder. "For the first time in my life, I feel like this is where I'm meant to be, and you're who I'm meant to be with. Thank you for being here with me."

The dolphins surfaced only meters away and started chattering, as if they were urging Dan and Fran to play with them. Fran leaned backwards and floated on her back, gazing up at Manarola in the distance, perched high on its rocky perch. The sun was just peeking over the eastern horizon to the right of the village.

"I never noticed how beautiful the terraced homes and their colorful walls were when I was young," Fran remarked. Her hands and feet moved slowly to keep her afloat. "I think there were too many walls in my mind that got in the way. But now, for the first time in my life, my mind feels open. I finally see the village's beauty."

"I know what you mean," Dan agreed. "For the first time in a long time, I feel like my mind is truly open, so I can finally let my guard down and share everything with you."

Fran rolled onto her stomach and swam the two meters between her and Dan. She wrapped her arms around his body. Their legs continued to kick slowly in rhythm, allowing them to keep their heads above water. She placed her lips on Dan's and kissed him with all her passion.

"I love you, Dan," she whispered. Tears of joy began to form in her eyes.

"And I love you," Dan sighed. "I want to spend the rest of my life with you. Will you marry me?"

Fran's tears overflowed and started trickling down both cheeks. She gazed into his eyes.

"Of course, I will!" she exclaimed, squeezing Dan tightly and pressing her lips passionately against his again. When she finally released him, her eyes looked up at the multicolored walls of Manarola, rising high above them in the east.

"What do you think about getting married here in Manarola and inviting all of our friends?"

"I can't think of a more beautiful place to do it," Dan answered. "I love you. And when we get back to our room, I can't wait to show you how much."

"I thought you were hungry," Fran teased.

"Oh, I am," Dan answered, a lascivious grin spreading across his face. "But breakfast is going to have to wait."

EPILOGUE

"THERE'S the head, Francesca! You're doing great … keep breathing!" Dr. Wendy MacMillan urged.

"Whoo, whoo, whoo, whoo …"

Fran continued huffing and puffing as the end of her ordeal drew nearer. Dan felt perspiration dripping down his forehead. His entire body trembled with anxious anticipation as he held Fran's hand and watched helplessly.

"You're almost there! You can do it, Fran!" he urged.

"Okay, dear, bear down," the delivery nurse coached. Her voice was calm and reassuring "Another big push … you're almost there."

Dan saw their child's entire head emerge. Its eyes were closed and its face was red, wrinkled, and covered with a waxy liquid. It was the most exciting and beautiful thing he had ever seen.

"I see the whole head!" Dan exclaimed. "I see the shoulders. You're doing awesome, Fran … you're almost there!"

"Whoo, whoo, whoo, whoo …"

Fran gazed up at Dan as she continued huffing and puffing. He saw the pain in her eyes. He smiled, filled with love and admiration for her, and he lifted her hand to his lips and kissed it.

"I love you!"

"One more push and that should do it, dear," the nurse urged.

Fran bore down one more time. The baby's shoulders and torso squeezed through Fran's vagina, gathering momentum as the widest part of its fragile little body slipped past its final barrier and into Dr. MacMillan's waiting hands.

"You have a beautiful baby girl, Francesca! Just in time for Christmas," Dr. MacMillan exclaimed. She looked up at the delivery nurse. "Let's clamp the cord." She looked down at the infant. "Come on, little girl. Let's hear you cry."

Dan felt a wave of emotions sweep through his body as he gazed down at his new daughter, emotions unlike anything he'd ever felt before - a flood of love and admiration for Fran, combined with a euphoric rush of dopamine. At the same time, he felt his anxiety beginning to climb as he waited to hear signs of life from the tiny body.

This must be what they mean when they talk about a 'natural high.'

Dan's thoughts were interrupted by a tentative wail from the tiny infant's mouth. Her eyes opened and then squinted, seeming sensitive to the bright overhead lights. She opened her mouth again, this time wailing her displeasure at the bright lights and her strange, cold, new world. Dan felt a wave of relief wash over him. The delivery nurse handed him a pair of surgical scissors.

"Would you like to do the honors, Dan?" she asked, nodding towards the waiting umbilical cord. Needing no encouragement, Dan took the scissors from her and made a clean cut through the rubbery tissue. Dr. MacMillan handed the little girl to the delivery nurse, who placed the tiny infant on Fran's warm chest.

"Here you go, dear. Here's your beautiful new daughter!"

Dan leaned down and kissed Fran on the forehead.

"You were awesome," he said to Fran. He felt his eyes filling with tears of joy. "She's got dark hair, just like you. Isn't she beautiful?"

Fran kissed her new daughter's head gently, then she reached up and pulled Dan's head down towards her lips. Dan had never felt so much love in a kiss before.

"Sorry to interrupt," Dr. MacMillan said, as the delivery nurse wheeled a cart with a plastic tub, a scale, and some medical instruments up to Fran's bed. "We just need to weigh her and do a few tests to make sure everything's alright."

The nurse held a measuring tape out for Dan.

"Would you like to hold the tape while I measure her?"

"I'd love to," Dan said, beaming with fatherly pride. He held the tape beside his daughter's tiny foot while the nurse stretched the tape up to her head.

"Twenty and one-half inches," the nurse said. She picked the infant up and laid her on the scale. The little girl started to wail when her bare skin touched the scale's cold plastic surface.

"It's okay, sweetheart," Dan said calmly. "We'll only be a minute." The tiny girl's cries gained in volume and her little face turned a deeper red.

"Eight pounds, five ounces," the nurse declared. "Just a good healthy size."

"Looks like she might be tall, like her mother," Dan said, smiling and looking back to Fran, who was still catching her breath on the delivery bed.

The nurse completed a series of quick reflex tests while the infant continued to wail.

"Perfect. Now let's get you wrapped up and back to your mom."

The nurse expertly wrapped the tiny newborn, who began to calm almost instantly. She carried the baby back to Fran, who was now sitting up straight in bed, and placed the infant gently in Fran's arms. Dan went to the bed and sat on the edge beside Fran. Their new daughter went quiet as she settled into her mother's arms.

"She is beautiful," Fran said. "I think she has your eyes."

"I don't know," Dan replied. "They look a bit hazel to me. I think she's got some of both of us."

"I suppose we should give her a name," Fran said. "Do you still like Angela?"

"I do," Dan answered. "Do you still like it?"

"I do," Fran replied. "But I have been thinking a lot lately. What do think about Michelle?"

Dan raised his eyebrows in surprise.

"You don't like it?" Fran asked.

"It's not that," Dan answered. "You just caught me off guard. Aren't you uncomfortable naming our daughter after my ex-wife?"

Fran reached out with her free hand and took Dan's in hers. "If it wasn't for Chelly, we probably would have remained casual acquaintances at best - you, one of our customers at Chateau Eden, and me, the owner of a quiet naturist resort. Chelly gave up her life so we could be together, Dan."

Dan felt tears forming in his eyes again. He felt overcome by a mixture of sadness for Chelly's loss, and love and admiration for the new love of his life.

"As long as you're okay with it," he answered. "I think it's a wonderful idea. What do think about Angela for a middle name?"

Fran smiled and squeezed Dan's hand. "After all she has done for us, as well as for Anika, I'm proud to name our little girl after her too."

Dan gazed down with awe and wonder upon little Michelle Angela, who now slept soundly in Fran's arms. Then he put his arm around Fran and embraced her.

"Every time I look at our little girl, I know I'll be reminded of Chelly and all of the tragedy we endured. But more importantly, she's our future. I hope she'll always remind us to believe in ourselves as a family, to stay optimistic, and to love each other no matter what life throws at us."

Fran smiled and pulled Dan close.

"Do you remember that first, surreal night we ever made love at Palm Desert?"

"How can I ever forget that," Dan replied, smiling. "It's the night we conceived this beautiful little girl."

"Do you remember asking me what I really wanted?" Fran asked.

"I do."

"This," Fran answered. "This is all I ever really wanted. To have you. To have a family. To love and be loved. What more could a person really want?"

"Absolutely nothing," Dan answered. "It's all I've ever wanted too. It's what I wanted with Chelly, but I realize now that it probably never would have worked. There were too many walls standing between us. But I'm so thankful that she brought us together that night. I love you so much, Francesca."

"I love you too, Dan."

Dan rested his head against Fran's. Together, they sat silently, allowing themselves to feel and embrace the moment … just listening together to the soft, gentle breaths of life from the precious little girl they had created and brought into the world together.

THE END

ACKNOWLEDGEMENTS

Once again, I would like to thank my loving wife and best friend, Peggy, for her continued love and infinite patience with my exploration into the world of writing as I wrote *The Survivor Trilogy* over a period of six years.

A huge thank you goes to Lianne Viau for her vision and collaboration in creating the truly unique cover photography for *Walls, Faces, and Spirits.*

I would like to extend a special thanks to Julia Gibbs for proofreading this manuscript and for spotting and correcting all of the little irregularities and typos that an author inevitably fails to see. For more information about Julia, go to https://juliaproofreader.wordpress.com/.

I am grateful to Jennifer Norris, USAF Retired, for talking with me when the story line for *Spirits* was germinating in my mind. She was gracious enough to take my phone call and to talk about her ongoing struggle for Military Justice for the victims of military sexual abuse.

Finally, thanks once again to all my friends, family, coworkers, and the other writers I've met through the social media. I thank you all for your support and positive feedback about *Walls, Faces,* and *Angela's* Eyes, and also for your encouragement while waiting so patiently for the conclusion of the trilogy, *Spirits.* I truly hope that it was worth the long wait, and that you enjoy this novel and the rest of the trilogy as much as I enjoyed writing it.

David Alex Jones
December 2022

OTHER BOOKS BY DAVID ALEX JONES

THE NIGHT CLASS
An Alternative Tale of Reconciliation

***

Originally written as Alex Jones:

WALLS:
The Survivor Trilogy, Book One

ANGELA'S EYES:
The Survivor Trilogy, Prequel

FACES:
The Survivor Trilogy, Book Two

Find out where to purchase David Alex Jones' books
by visiting his website:
http://www.davidalexjones.com

ABOUT THE AUTHOR

David Alex Jones is a retired Clinical Psychologist who lives in Ontario, Canada. In his writing, he combines his understanding of human identity and personality, his passion for helping victims of trauma, abuse, and Post-traumatic Stress Disorder, and his love of reading fiction, to create a unique brand of psychological suspense and political commentary. His writing is rich with complex characters and controversial social issues, resulting in an abundance of internal and interpersonal conflict, dysfunction, and tension. Dave also enjoys spending time with his grandchildren, travelling with his wife, photography, and home brewing craft beer.

EXCERPT: THE NIGHT CLASS

I OFTEN wondered why I continued going to therapy sessions every week back then. Don't get me wrong, Dr. Way was a really good psychologist. She was calm, understanding, and empathic. Sometimes she even let me call her by her first name, Barbara. But most importantly, she never judged me, even when I dyed my hair purple and showed up with a nose ring one week. She helped me curb my cutting habit and eating disorder, and she helped me through my first stressful year of grad school. But after a year of therapy, I still had a strange, lingering feeling that I couldn't explain … something Barbara never managed to help me find during those sessions. I had always had a feeling that something important was missing from my life.

Sure, my birth mother, Diane, physically and verbally abused me from a young age, and my sperm-donor dad ran out the door when I was three. But my uncle and aunt rescued me and gave me a loving home, and they provided anything I needed or desired. So things couldn't have been too bad, right? I couldn't have been the only teenager who rebelled and pushed back against their parents. And I can't be the only twenty-six-year-old grad student who still has flashbacks and a history of anorexia and cutting—who still feels like there's something missing from her life, or who is constantly in danger of flunking out.

Looking back, who would have predicted that it wasn't therapy that would finally give me the answer and save me from a lifetime of searching. Instead, it was a ragtag group of undergraduate students and a kindly, long-lost aunt, who would converge in my life and turn my world upside down over a period of only thirteen weeks. Together, they would school me and send me in a direction on my life's journey that I never could have imagined.

"I'M PROUD of how much you've improved over the summer," Dr. Way says. "You did some difficult work identifying some important inner voices … the angry and judgmental ones, the masochistic one, the fearful and abandoned three-year-old one, the intellectual and creative ones …"

"Don't forget my non-conformist and survivor voices," I add. "I rely on them a lot."

My eyes roam around Barbara Way's office. The room in the old sandstone building can only be described as neutral … institutional, at best. The light grey paint job is old and tired, and the blue-grey carpet shows signs of becoming threadbare. Barbara's attempts to warm up the room won't win any design awards. While the pillows on her grey couch have some orange and blue accents, they do little to brighten the space. The framed prints on the wall wouldn't be out of place in a hotel room. I chuckle to myself.

Did she decorate this way on purpose? With all the grey and neutral colours, did she turn the room into a three-dimensional Rorschach card experiment? Is she expecting me to project all of my conflicted inner voices onto the walls of this room?

"Yes, you do," Dr. Way answers, her voice waking me from my brief daydream. "Many of those EMDR sessions this summer were extremely intense and emotional. But you did well to keep yourself stable while you processed some very difficult memories. I guess I'm curious to see where you want to go next in therapy."

"Hmmh … I don't know," I answer honestly. "It took a few days to recover from some of those sessions. I don't think I can afford to have that happen, now that classes are starting up again. Things are going to be pretty stressful."

"I agree," Dr. Way says. "I think you need some time to consolidate your recent gains."

Uh, oh! Is she going to end my therapy? I feel my abandoned, fearful, inner three-year-old self coming alive and starting to panic.

"Does that mean you don't want to see me anymore?" I ask, almost on the verge of tears.

"Oh, no! Not at all," Dr. Way exclaims. "I was thinking we should still meet every week, just so I can stay up to date on how you're managing your stress. What do you think?"

My inner three-year-old heaves a huge sigh of relief.

"That would be great," I say. "I don't want to let things overwhelm me, like they did last year."

"I just want to make sure that you're still able to keep yourself stable … using your slow breathing, going to your safe place, and using lots of positive self-talk. If you keep using those skills, I'm confident you'll do fine this term," she says.

"I'll use them. I promise!"

"Speaking of big stressors," Barbara asks. "Have you heard back from your mother yet?"

"You mean about finding my biological father?" I answer. "No, and I'm not going to hold my breath waiting for her. I doubt if she'll ever follow up on that."

Dependability isn't one of Diane's strong points. In fact, I'm pretty sure my birth mother doesn't have any strong points. What can you say about a mother who still smokes, swears, and drinks like a sailor, who screamed and beat me anytime I cried as a child, and who left me home alone for hours on end, with little else other than goldfish crackers to eat?

"I'll probably have to stop in and see her this weekend," I continue. "She's been phoning and laying the usual guilt trip on me about not visiting enough."

"Is there anybody else you could contact for information about your dad? Any family members?" Dr. Way asks. "Or what about contacting Family and Children's Services?"

"I don't know. I don't have much for family. And now that classes are starting, I really don't need the added stress of dealing with Children's Services. I won't have the time …"

Time … Classes … Oh shit!

A quick glance at my watch tells me that my first class starts in five minutes, and I'm going to have to run all the way across campus. I jump to my feet, grab my bag, head towards the door, and shout over my shoulder to Dr. Way.

"I'm so sorry! Tonight's the first class of the term, and I'm going to be late! I'll see you next week! Gotta run!"

I bolt from Dr. Way's office, run down the hallway, and then I fly down a set of stairs. At the bottom of the stairs, I push the bar on an exit door and sprint into the September dusk.

MOMENTS LATER, I burst through a set of doors into a small lecture theatre, breathing heavily. I stop to catch my breath, stuffing a sheaf of papers and a book back into my bag, just before they fall to the floor.

All eyes in the room are immediately drawn to me—the woman with the purple hair and a nose ring who is causing the ruckus. Below, at the base of the theatre, sixty-five-year-old Dr. Eric Sanderson stands ready to begin his lecture. With his white hair tied back into a ponytail and his white beard, he comes across more as a grandfather than a professor. He is amongst the most popular professors on campus every year. He looks up to see what's causing the commotion and gives me the evil eye. I catch his glare, run down the stairs, and slump into a tiny desk in the first row, still breathing heavily.

As I catch my breath, I gaze up at the perfect domed ceiling in the old lecture theatre, admiring the architecture. We're in one of the oldest buildings on campus, and most students have no idea that the parabolic shape of the ceiling is acoustically perfect.

Students in the back of the room can hear the lecturer perfectly without the need of a microphone. They can also hear whispers about last night's sexual encounters from students in the front row. But it works both ways. People in the front row, where I'm sitting, can also hear whispers from the upper rows. And right now, I hear them whispering about me.

"Who's that scatterbrain?"

"I wonder what group she's in? I hope she's not in mine!"

"Seriously? That babe can't keep her own shit together, let alone help us!"

My eavesdropping is interrupted by the sound of Dr. Sanderson clearing his throat.

"Welcome to *Team Building 201*," he begins. "This course is offered jointly by the School of Business and the Department of Psychology. We designed it as an option for students in *all* faculties, because we feel that learning to work as part of a team is an essential skill for anybody, whether you graduate from Business School, the arts, science, or any of the professional schools."

He clicks a remote control to bring up another slide, then walks across the front of the room, taking up position behind a lectern.

"In the past, before COVID, this course had a bit of a reputation for being an easy 'A'. Unfortunately for you, I took time during the pandemic to rethink and redesign the course to incorporate a team project, so you could all have an opportunity to apply what you learn in the course."

Moans and grumbles fill the room as Dr. Sanderson continues his introduction, raising his voice over the background noise.

I chuckle to myself. Little do the students know that Dr. Sanderson and I can hear every little derogatory comment they make.

"You'll see on your course outline that I've randomly assigned the thirty-two students in this class to four teams that will each complete a different group project, worth fifty percent of your final grade. The topic for each team is intentionally controversial and challenging."

Dr. Sanderson pauses and moves purposely across to the other side of the room.

"Each team will be responsible for doing research on your topic, writing a final report, and presenting your findings during the last lecture, during Week 13 of the term."

The background grumbling continues unabated while Dr. Sanderson brings up a new slide.

"Here are your topics. Team number one, your project is *What Did Humanity Learn from the COVID-19 Pandemic, and What Could We Do Differently Next Time?"*

The background grumbling gets louder and the students start shifting restlessly in their seats.

"Team number two: Systemic Racism in Policing: Would your team defund police forces to deal with the problem?"

Tough crowd! ... They're like a school of piraña ... They could tear me apart if I'm not careful!

"Okay, settle down!" Dr. Sanderson shouts. "You can save your comments and questions until I'm finished."

He pauses and waits for the noise to gradually subside.

"Team number three, your topic is *Climate Change: What Would You Do to Help Canada Meet Glasgow Agreement Targets?* And finally, team number four: *What is Indigenous Truth and Reconciliation? (And How Can Indigenous and Non-Indigenous People Work Together to Achieve It?)* Okay, now. Any questions?"

The students resume talking to each other and the background noise rises in a steady crescendo. A middle-aged woman with curly, strawberry-blonde hair raises her hand and Dr. Sanderson nods to her.

"Your name and your question?" he asks.

"My name is Katya. How much information do you expect us to cover?" she asks, with a noticeable German accent. "It seems like a lot, especially when most of us haven't studied any of these topics. For instance, I've got the reconciliation question, and I wouldn't know where to start on such a big topic. How long will our presentations be?"

"Good questions. You're only going to have forty-five minutes per group for your presentation, so you will only have time to cover the major points in that amount of time. But I expect much more detail in your reports."

Dr. Sanderson pauses and moves back toward the middle of his platform.

"As for the second part of your question, remember that this is a team building project. I don't expect that you'll all become experts on your topic. I'm more interested in how you organize your team, your report, and your presentation, and in how well your team is applying the course material along the way. We want to see how well you listen to each other, whether you can learn to trust your teammates, whether you can reach a consensus, and whether you can all commit to the same goals."

The grumbling and discontent grow louder again.

"Oh, that reminds me … I forgot to introduce your TA, Samantha Bower, one of my grad students. She'll be running the tutorial session and will be grading your participation in your team's project. Would you stand up, Sam?"

He motions to me. But as I rise from my seat, I bump my overstuffed bag that's balanced precariously on the tiny desk. It hits the floor with a thud and spreads its contents … books, pens, phone, tampons, and sheaves of paper over the floor.

Nice work, Sam! Way to make a good first impression!

I hear the whispers and laughter from the upper rows, most of it expressing dismay that they're going to have to put up with me as their TA for the term. The heat in my face tells me I'm already crimson with embarrassment. I turn to face the class and give a timid wave, while I try to think of a way to salvage the situation.

"Just call me Sam," I say meekly. "I guess I'll be meeting you all next week in the first tutorial session … does anybody have any questions about the tutorial?"

Really? … That was so lame! … Is that the best you could do for a first impression?

I see a middle-aged, African-American woman with her hand raised. Eager to shift attention away from the mess I've just made, I point to her.

"Let's start with you, up there," I say.

"My name is Shanise. I work during the day, so I'm wondering if you have later office hours, in case any of us need some individual help?

"Good question," I reply. "I'll be available in my office for the hour just before the lecture each week. However, if you can't make it then, I'll hang around for a few minutes after each week's tutorial."

Feeling like the flush is slowly leaving my face, I feel a semblance of confidence returning. A young, darker-skinned man with curly black hair, raises his hand and I acknowledge him.

"I'm Uri," he says, with a noticeable Middle-Eastern accent. "Are we expected to stay for the entire two hours of the tutorial?"

"Another good question," I reply. "And the short answer is yes. Each team will get thirty minutes to meet with me every week, so I can answer questions and give you some guidance. The schedule will rotate, so some weeks you'll meet with me first, but other weeks I'm afraid you'll have to stay later. And when you're not meeting with me, we expect your team to use the time to work together on your project."

Groaning and grumbling starts to fill the room again.

"We're sorry for that," I add, raising my voice to be heard over the din. "But we understand that this is a night class, and many of you, like Shanise, work and have different course schedules. So we thought the easiest time to meet with your teammates would be after the lecture, during the tutorial session, when you're not meeting with me."

I see Dr. Sanderson pointing to his watch.

"If you have more questions, you can ask them when we meet next week," I say, then I nod at Eric to take over.

"Thanks, Sam. The first lecture and tutorial will be next Tuesday. Be ready to get down to work then, since you'll only have twelve more weeks until your presentations. If you don't have the handout showing which team you're on, I still have a few on the table down here. See you all next week!"

As students rise from their seats and start talking, I kneel down to gather my belongings, grateful that my first shaky appearance as a teaching assistant is now behind me.

STUDENTS CONTINUE to file out of the lecture hall while I'm still crawling around the floor, gathering my belongings and stuffing them back into my bag. As the room thins out, the noise levels gradually lessen.

Behind me in the second row, I see a young Indigenous man with twin braids of long black hair, and a middle-aged, blonde caucasian woman seated beside him, looking at each other and rolling their eyes. Unaware of the room's perfect acoustics, they start whispering about me.

"Are you kidding," the young man whispers. "That klutz is supposed to help *us*?"

"Hard to believe!" the woman whispers. "By the way, my name's Terri. What team are you on?"

"I'm Hunter. I'm on the reconciliation team. I wonder if Sanderson knew I was Indigenous when he picked the teams?"

Terri smiles and chuckles quietly. "That *is* funny! I'm on the reconciliation team too. Looks like we're going to be teammates."

I'm finally finished filling my bag, so I sling it over my shoulder and start making my way up the stairs towards the top of the lecture theatre.

You don't think I can hear you, do you? Something tells me that you two aren't going to make things easy for me this term!

Hunter gives me a furtive glance as I climb the stairs.

"How much do you suppose Sam knows about reconciliation?" he asks Terri.

She shrugs her shoulders and shakes her head as she looks in my direction.

"I don't know. How much do any of us really know about it?"

* * *